MORE THAN YOU KNOW

As they approached the last crosswalk, passing a corner convenience store, slowing their pace to wait for the light to change, a car suddenly made a turn against the light and angled in their direction, its headlights pointing directly at them, blinding Maddy.

Nick was looking up at the stoplight. Maddy grabbed his arm and yanked him sideways, causing both of them to fall over the low rock wall that edged the convenience store's parking lot.

The car zoomed past, two wheels on the sidewalk, almost clipping the wall.

"What the hell!" Nick exclaimed. "I didn't even see the stupid idiot."

Maddy put her hand on his arm. "The driver wasn't stupid, Nick. It was deliberate. The light was still red. He aimed the car right at us."

MORE THAN
YOU
KNOW

Meg Chittenden

BERKLEY SENSATION, NEW YORK

MORE THAN YOU KNOW

A Berkley Sensation Book / published by arrangement with the author

PRINTING HISTORY
Berkley Sensation edition / September 2003

ISBN: 0-425-19210-5

A BERKLEY SENSATION™ BOOK
Berkley Sensation Books are published by The Berkley Publishing Group, a division of Penguin Group (USA) Inc.,
375 Hudson Street, New York, New York 10014.
BERKLEY SENSATION and the "B" design
are trademarks belonging to Penguin Group (USA) Inc.

PRINTED IN THE UNITED STATES OF AMERICA

10 9 8 7 6 5 4 3 2 1

For my husband, Jim, with my gratitude:
For driving me around on research trips.
For dropping me off and picking me up at airports.
For knowing esoteric stuff like upstream and downstream, and north, south, east, and west, a boon to his direction-challenged wife.
For taking photos of everything I ask him to take photos of.
For making drawings of things so I can understand how they work.
For always making lunch.
For having the patience to stay married to a writer!

Acknowledgments

I wish to thank the following people for answering the many questions that came up in relation to various aspects of this novel:

Jeff Thurman, special agent, FBI, San Diego, California
Rich McEachin, chief of police, Ocean Shores, Washington
Jayne Ann Krentz, *New York Times* bestselling author
Sharon Ilstrup, recruiter for Yahoo! (and also my wonderful daughter)
Robin Burcell, Sacramento County criminal investigator and author of *Fatal Truth* and *Deadly Legacy*
Teresa Loftin, for her careful and sharp-eyed reading of the manuscript
Camille Minichino, author of the Gloria Lamerino mystery series, for the Italian lesson

Any factual errors are not theirs; they are mine, or else I unblushingly altered the facts to suit the demands of the story.

Prologue

NICK THOUGHT THE image would probably burn itself into his memory forever. There he was, Nick Ciacia (pronounced Cha-cha—he had to sound it out for everyone who didn't live in the neighborhood), thirteen years old, tall for his age, wearing his Sunday suit on a Monday, coal black hair slicked down, looking out through a stained glass window in the church basement.

Watching the snowflakes melt and flatten on the colorful glass, he felt separated from the sounds and sights of the people around him, as if he were trapped inside the millefiori paperweight that his mother used to hold bills in place until the end of the month.

During the fine and formal funeral the Chicago Police Department had put on, he'd managed to keep his shoulders stiff with pride as officers and friends spoke of his father's character and heroism. But now he was fighting hard to keep tears of grief and pain and murderous anger from pushing forward from the backs of his eyes.

"Sorry for your loss, Nicky," a slight man in a shabby-looking sport coat said to him. "No reason for that punk to go breaking into Figlioli's grocery—everybody knew Figlioli never left a cent in the cash register. Best little store in the neighborhood, Figlioli's. Missus never minded waiting till payday."

Nick nodded dumbly, picturing his father driving home from a meeting of the Italian-American Police Association, seeing a light where no light should be, going in to investigate, doing his duty, getting shot for it.

"A fine man, Alfeo Ciacia," the man added.

Nick nodded again, afraid to trust his voice, the muscles in his jaw rigid. Looking around the church basement, he hoped the man would move on.

Next to the buffet table bountifully spread with the food that friends and church members had supplied, a sea of blue uniforms surrounded his mother, his dad's colleagues paying their respects, offering comfort as best they could.

Instead of leaving, the man leaned in closer. He had a large head for the size of his body. Nick could smell garlic on his breath, not an unusual thing in this predominantly Italian neighborhood.

"I heard a rumor."

The man's voice had dropped to a harsh whisper.

Heat surged through Nick's body. There had been no eyewitnesses to his father's slaying. None who would admit to it at least.

He focused all his attention on the seedy little man, his stomach clenching.

The man glanced shiftily over each shoulder, making it fairly obvious he was sharing a secret. That was dumb, Nick thought. If you wanted to be secretive you had to try to appear perfectly innocent, relaxed, straightforward, normal. Body language was always an important clue. His dad had told him that.

"I'm not a rich man."

Nick felt in his jacket pocket. One of his dad's friends had given him a twenty "to help with lunch money," he'd said. Nick gave it to the man, who pocketed it in the neatest sleight of hand Nick had ever seen.

"They call him the Snowman," the man murmured. "He's young, they say. Twenty-one maybe. Came from Germany three years ago. Left town now, they say. Gone way out west to Seattle."

Nick tried to keep his face expressionless. "Who says?"

The man didn't answer.

"You *are* talking about the man who shot my father?"

The man's mouth twitched in a way that signified agreement, and Nick's stomach clenched again, but with hope this time.

"What's the Snowman's real name?"

The man blinked, his mouth a tight line. Either he didn't know or he was afraid to tell.

"What kind of name is that, anyway?" Nick demanded. "The Snowman. What does it mean?"

The man shrugged. "They say he's got white hair, even though he's real young. Maybe that's it. And it's said he's got a block of ice for a heart."

Someone coughed nearby, and the man jerked around, then headed rapidly for the door.

"Who was that, Nicky?" Nick's mother asked.

Her green eyes were still red-rimmed, but she'd made a brave attempt to cover up with makeup. Even crushed with grief, she was a beautiful woman, his mother—large and soft and dark-haired, with those Irish eyes that used to smile so much, especially when she looked at her husband or her only son.

His mouth open to tell her what the man had said, Nick closed it again. This was no place to discuss secrets. He'd tell her later, after he'd had a chance to think about it. "I've never seen him before," he said instead. "Have you?"

She shook her head, frowning, and Nick pushed his new knowledge down into a ball that sat cold and hard inside him throughout the evening and the night.

He told her a limited version of the story the next morning. Just the nickname and that the man had supposedly emigrated from Germany, nothing about Seattle. He was already formulating a plan.

She'd never heard of the Snowman either. "Someone your father arrested, maybe," she suggested. "Someone who held a grudge."

She advised him to take the story to Alfeo's boss.

"Dad didn't like his boss," Nick reminded her.

"No more do I," she agreed, "but he's the one who would know if it was someone your father had trouble with."

"And who might this strange little man have been?" Captain Riley asked when Nick caught him about to enter his office. "A leprechaun perhaps?"

Angered by the put-down, Nick hated having to admit he didn't know who the man was, had been too stunned to ask him his name.

"Well, at a guess I'd say he must've been playing a joke on you, Nicky. A cruel thing to do. I've never heard of any Snowman." He smiled suddenly. "Unless you count Frosty. We've had some major snowstorms this year, desperate cold too. But I didn't hear that Frosty came to life and went around shooting people. According to the story I used to read to my boys, he just took the children sledding and skating and then he melted. I trust you didn't give the little man any money for this wild tale?"

Nick swallowed. "He said the Snowman came from Germany."

"Well, 'tis true there are Germans in Chicago but I think I'd have known straightaway if a German criminal showed up in this neighborhood. I'm well acquainted with all of the malefactors around here."

He looked at Nick with kindly blue eyes that had a coldness in their depths. "Don't you worry, my boy, we'll find the man, whoever he is. I've never yet let a good man's death go unpunished. You just leave it to me."

With that, he disappeared into his office. Nick stood there feeling helpless, humiliated, dismissed as if he were a little kid, the cold hard ball inside him swelling until he could hardly breathe, resolution growing with it.

Someday, he vowed, some way, he'd find the cowardly

rat who'd killed his dad, and he'd make him pay. He'd kill him with his own bare hands, or a gun. It wouldn't matter how the Snowman died, just as long as he died. Nick would feel better then.

Chapter 1

RUNNING LATE FOR a lunch date on Seattle's 1st Avenue, Nick Ciacia flagged down a cab outside his apartment building and jumped in. "Cutter's," he said.

The black driver nodded, then turned sideways to grin at him. "Hey, G-man. How's it goin'?"

Nick did a double take. "Arnie Arnold. It's been a while."

It had been several years. Nick's old informant hadn't changed much—he'd always looked older than God. Last Nick had heard, Arnie had been peripherally connected to a couple of badly bungled armed robberies. Story of Arnie's life.

"How're *you* doing, Arnie?" Nick asked, warily.

Arnie pulled away from the curb. "Doin' okay now I'm out. Goin' to AA again."

"Good for you."

"Yeah, well, the doc scared the shit out of me—said my old ticker was gonna give up if I drank one more drop. Got a good job drivin' this cab." He sighed. "Same old drunken woman at home, though—only one I can get. So

I guess the best you could say is things lookin' fair to middlin'."

"Well, I'm glad you're out," Nick said. Tactfully, he refrained from asking for details. There were other ways to find out, if he really wanted to know.

"It's gettin' so I don't have to worry about spendin' too much time inside," Arnie went on. "Got so many crooks, they don't have space for a small-time fool like me."

He sped through a traffic light as it changed from yellow to red, didn't speak again for several blocks, but kept flicking glances in the mirror at Nick. "Wasn't it you used to ask around about a fella called the Snowman?" he asked as he stopped at the light on the corner of Seneca and 1st Avenue. "You ever track him down?"

For a couple of seconds Nick was too stunned to respond. He'd been searching for the Snowman for twenty-three years. Not continuously—he wasn't some single-minded psycho—but he had never attempted to keep his interest in the Snowman to himself. Ever since he and his mother had relocated after his father's death, he'd formed a habit of asking anyone remotely connected to crime or crime solving if they'd heard of a man nicknamed the Snowman. Nobody ever had. He'd decided many years ago that the Snowman was probably dead. Or had never really existed. He'd put his need for revenge behind him. He'd thought.

Arnie had evidently caught his electrified glance, the half turn of his body. As the light changed and Arnie turned right, the old man was grimacing as if he wished he'd kept his big mouth shut.

Nick straightened in his seat and set about deliberately relaxing his body. Feeling calmer, he glanced out the window. They were about to pass the forty-eight-foot-high steel *Hammering Man* outside SAM, the Seattle Art Museum. He took one more calming breath, let it out as the hammer started down.

"Yeah, that was me," he said evenly. "I'm still interested."

"How *much* you interested?" Arnie asked.

Nick pulled his cell phone out of his belt holster and called his lunch date to warn her he was irrevocably delayed. After attempting and failing to soothe her justifiable irritation, he accepted her cancellation stoically. Then he directed Arnie to an ATM machine. Five minutes later Nick sat him down in a Starbucks. Arnie was grinning happily; becoming a hundred dollars richer had miraculously restored his courage.

"Sometime back," Arnie said, "in the prison gym—me drivin' iron—two peckerwoods close by were talkin' about the Snowman."

Nick silently translated the prison slang. *Working out with weights—two white convicts.*

"Me, I guess I was invisible. Not the first time. One of 'em said somethin' about a dude called the Snowman, still operating in Seattle after somethin' like twenty years. West Coast rep, they said, then laughed like it was a joke."

Still operating in Seattle? This was the first time Nick had heard any suggestion that the Snowman was still active, that he was still in the U.S., or even that there really was a man nicknamed the Snowman. "West Coast rep of what?"

Arnie shrugged.

"What kind of operating?"

"They didn't say. I didn't ask. Far as they concerned, I didn't hear. Doesn't pay to hear shit like that."

"Did either of them mention the Snowman's real name?"

"Not sure I can remember it."

He looked hopefully at Nick. Nick shook his head.

Casting his gaze at the ceiling, Arnie took a long slurping swig of his tall caffé latte, and Nick suppressed the urge to reach out and throttle him.

"Bart L. Fritz," Arnie said, surfacing with a milk mustache. "They said he started out someplace in Germany."

A disgusted expression further wrinkled the man's wizened face. "Said this Fritz claimed he was a pure Aryan, like the old Nazis used to say was the superior race. Whitey with no Jewish blood in him."

Nick's brain was racing, reaching. . . . "Any talk about him maybe being a neo-Nazi?"

"One a them dudes hangs out in Idaho? Not that I heard."

"Anything about Chicago?"

"Nope. Seattle and Germany the only places they mention."

"That's all you've got for my hundred dollars?"

"That's it, G-man. The Snowman. Germany. Bart L. Fritz. Operatin' out of Seattle. Hell of a lot, you ask me."

"When did you hear all this?"

"Two, maybe three years back."

Nick exploded. "Why the hell didn't you let me know?"

Arnie shrugged. "Don't remember you visitin' me none."

Now that he had a name to go on, Nick spent a considerable amount of time checking databases such as ChoicePoint, which the Bureau subscribed to, and ACS— Automated Case Support—to see if Bart L. Fritz had popped up in an FBI case. He went on to look for a criminal record or fingerprints in NCIC—National Crime Information Center. He even checked Yahoo! People Search. He found nothing.

Through Grady Logan, a contact at INS, Nick tracked immigrants for the year his father was killed—both Arnie and the little man at the funeral had said the Snowman was fresh out of Germany.

Grady drew a blank. No Bart L. Fritz. Grady then checked the prior year. Nothing. Persuaded by Nick to look again, Grady exclaimed, "Got a Bartel Franz here— Bartel Wilhelm Franz—entered the U.S. from Stuttgart, Germany, twenty-three years ago."

Barely remembering to thank Grady, Nick got off the phone, excitement filling him.

Arnie had overheard the name two, three years ago.

He'd been eavesdropping in a prison gym. Probably
noisy. Easy enough to misunderstand. And Arnie never
had been that reliable when it came to names.

Bart L.—Bartel. Fritz—Franz. It wasn't too much of
a long shot. Wanting to at least check out the possibility
of error, he drove to the taxi company Arnie was working
for. Arnie had quit—moved on. Nick got his home address, checked with the "same old drunken woman" who
lived there. She was drunk. "He gone" was all she could
manage to say.

Either Arnie regretted passing on the information, or
he'd gone on a binge with Nick's hundred dollars, or he'd
been recruited for another job that would take him back
to prison. Recidivism "R" Us.

Returning to his various contacts and online sources,
Nick came across more information on Bartel Wilhelm
Franz. It was a fragile lead, but it was a lead.

After arriving in the U.S., Franz had shown up in Chicago. Okay, that was more like it. A link to Chicago was
a possible link to the Snowman.

Nick called a special agent friend in Chicago and had
him check to see if Bartel Wilhelm Franz had registered
as an alien. He had. Three years running. Did that make
him an upright honorable citizen? Not necessarily.

The SA friend discovered that one Bartel Franz had
been employed by a Chicago pharmacy.

Nick's phone call to the pharmacy elicited the information that Bartel Wilhelm Franz had been a good worker
but not given to socializing. Kept to himself. He was
young when he had come to work there. Very young.
Eighteen. He'd stayed until he was twenty-one.

The Snowman was supposedly around twenty-one when
he shot Alfeo Ciacia.

After the required three years, the pharmacist said, Bartel Franz had become an American citizen. The pharmacist had agreed to be one of his witnesses. He had been
surprised to be asked. "Not as if we were ever friends,"
he added.

He couldn't remember who the other witness was—

two were necessary. Right after becoming a citizen, Bartel Wilhelm Franz had gone to court and changed his name to Bart Williams. A week after that, he'd stopped coming to work and the pharmacist had discovered he'd left town. He'd never seen him again. "Good-looking kid, but kind of an oddball," he confided over the phone. "Knew him three years, but never knew him."

With this information to go on, Nick was able to track Franz/Williams to Seattle. That's when things began to get really intense. He was quite sure it was no coincidence that the man he'd been tracking had come to the same town as the little man at his dad's funeral had named as the Snowman's destination.

It was Nick's knowledge of that destination that had brought Nick and his mother and grandmother to Seattle. His mother had been happy enough to leave Chicago, and she hadn't cared where they went. Nick had managed to make the two women in his life think the move west was their idea.

Within a few hours, Nick had linked Bart Williams to Mawsom Pharmaceuticals in Seattle, gone to the Mawsom website, and checked out Bart's bio and photograph—he had blond hair that was almost snowy white. Just as the Snowman's hair was reputed to be. "West Coast rep," Arnie's voice repeated in his memory.

Subsequently, Nick traced Bart Williams from Mawsom headquarters to Oak River and the house Bart shared with his wife, Madison Sloane.

His next step was to apply for the annual leave that was due him. It was near enough to the end of the year that there was no opposition to his request.

He was still far from proving that Bart Williams was the Snowman, but facts were piling up that seemed to support the possibility. Now all he had to do was prove that Bart Williams had killed Alfeo Ciacia.

Over the years, Nick had banked his hatred of the Snowman down to smoldering embers, but now he could feel the hot lick of a flame that could turn into an inferno if he tended it. As he meant to tend it.

Of course, he reminded himself, it was possible that Arnie had made up the whole story in order to get money out of Nick. Or that Nick's gut instinct that Fritz was really Franz was totally without justification.

In which case, Bartel Wilhelm Franz, aka Bart Williams, could be a perfectly innocent immigrant who'd tired of pharmacy work and Chicago and had moved to Seattle to find work as a company rep and eventually married Madison Sloane, while Bart L. Fritz was still out there somewhere "operating in Seattle."

Chapter 2

SEATTLE'S 6TH AVENUE. Noon on a bright Thursday in October. Cars and people all over the place.

Nick Ciacia was discreetly following Bart Williams's Ford Taurus from a few cars behind when Williams unexpectedly turned on to Pine, dropped his wife off outside Nordstrom, gunned the engine, and shot down Pine to 1st Avenue, where he turned left, all without signaling.

Nick kept up, earning a couple of horn blasts. Had Bart Williams realized he was being followed? It seemed unlikely. Nick had stayed well back all the way from Oak River, and traffic had been heavy.

Just as he was about to turn on to 1st Avenue himself, a truck cut in front of him. Craning his neck, he thought he saw the Taurus do a sharp right into Pike Place Market. But by the time the truck got out of his way and he could follow, the Taurus was out of sight. He beat the steering wheel with his open hand. "Shit!"

Driving slowly along the redbrick road that fronted the market, he checked every parked car without any luck, then made a snap decision to *cherchez la femme* instead of wasting any more time trying to find Bart. Thinking that a change in strategy just might kickstart some information, he hung a right on to the steep slope of Virginia and returned to Nordstrom.

He'd been tailing Bart Williams for three days without getting any closer to determining if he was the man Nick had been looking for for more than a couple of decades.

Two days back, he'd managed to get himself introduced to *Mrs.* Bart Williams, aka Madison (Maddy) Sloane. Maybe he'd get luckier with her. He often did get lucky with the ladies.

After a couple of mistaken guesses, he tracked Maddy down in Nordstrom's women's activewear department.

She was probably not much past thirty, he thought, watching her from a safe distance—a tall, slender, but in no way twiggy woman. Not particularly beautiful, but definitely easy on the eyes, with thick golden blond hair cut in one of those trendy choppy Meg Ryan cuts he usually didn't care for but had to admit looked good on her. Casually dressed in blue jeans, a white T-shirt, and a brown suede jacket, she somehow managed to look elegant. Classy. He'd always been drawn to classy women, though they weren't always drawn to him.

A large brown leather bag hung from her right shoulder, a padded camera bag under it. Interesting. What was she going to take pictures of?

He watched as she selected sweatpants, a sports bra, and bicycle shorts. Add those purchases to the confident way she balanced herself, shoulders straight, head up, and all indications were that, like him, she worked out regularly. He liked athletic women as much as he liked classy women. Too bad she was probably married to the man he'd sworn to kill.

She looked tired, he thought. Not just shopping tired, or didn't get much sleep last night tired, but weary to the bone. She'd looked fairly drawn when he met her at the wine fair, but when she'd smiled he'd thought, *Yeah—that's the way her face is supposed to look.*

She wasn't smiling now.

When she finished shopping, her purchases stored in a Nordstrom bag with handles, she headed to a crowded Chinese restaurant, where she met with a petite, pretty, and fast-talking black woman with large dark eyes and close-cropped curly hair. There was obvious affection between them—this woman was a close friend. And according to what he could overhear of their animated conversation from the next booth, this woman was also a real estate agent working on finding a suitable apartment for Maddy to buy.

Were Bart Williams and his wife preparing to move out of their house in Oak River? Or just acquiring a pied-à-terre?

So that he'd finish when the two women did, he ordered the same meal: vegetables sautéed in a soy-based sauce, with steamed rice on the side. Tasty enough, but hardly filling for a big guy with a healthy appetite.

After the women laughingly discussed the promises in their fortune cookies—he didn't open his—he followed them on foot down the hill to a ritzy doorman-protected condo building overlooking Elliott Bay. They stayed in there for well over an hour before parting on the sidewalk, perilously close to the store doorway where he'd concealed himself. Their good-bye hug was slightly awkward owing to Maddy's collection of bags. He noticed that the camera bag was unzipped.

The pretty real estate agent hailed a taxi and sped away, and Maddy Sloane continued on downhill to Seattle's bustling Pike Place Market, Nick trailing behind.

A lot of people in the market, vendors as well as customers, were in costume. This surprised him until he remembered it was Halloween. Not having kids or a wife, he tended to lose track of such celebrations.

Maddy pulled her camera out of its bag but didn't photograph any of the people manning the craft booths. She was interested only in the bright displays of vegetables and the tubs of flowers. As she walked along, she also managed to fill a string bag with veggies.

Exciting stuff, this, Nick thought. Good thing he was

on leave and didn't have to write a report of his afternoon's work.

Four and three-quarter hours after exiting her husband's car, Maddy Sloane ended up beside Rachel, the oversized bronze piggy bank that guarded the entrance to the market, a sack of vegetables and the sturdy Nordstrom bag at her feet.

Obviously, husband Bart must have arranged to pick her up there. Nick's car was still up the hill, and he debated going to get it, but chances were he'd miss Bart's arrival. Scratch one more wasted afternoon. No point following the pair home to Oak River anyway. He could pick up the car and drive there later.

Establishing himself next to a pillar beneath the PLACE PIGALLE sign, he waited, not expecting much, but still attentively watching Maddy Sloane. He had to admit he didn't exactly mind watching Maddy Sloane. He even came up with a mini-fantasy in which he approached her and touched that flyaway golden hair, she smiled at him, and they walked off together. . . .

Jeez, Ciacia, where are you going to walk? Into the sunset? This is not some sappy movie. This woman is not a prospective date. This woman is to be used if possible to get you closer to her spouse.

Deliberately, he allowed himself to be partially distracted by the antics at nearby Pike Place Fish, which advertised itself as the "home of the loud-mouthed fishmongers."

As usual, the performance had drawn a crowd. As soon as a customer selected a whole salmon, tuna, or whatever from the rows of fish laid out on ice, a trio of fishmongers at the back would set up a chatter, and their bearded colleague at the front would toss the fish to one of them, yelling, "Steak it!" The fishmongers would sometimes fling the large and slippery fish back and forth several times along with repartee that became even more boisterous when one of the tourists was spotted wielding a camcorder.

Maddy Sloane aimed her camera at the fish laid out in

neat rows at the front of the stall. Not at the people. Why would a woman take photos of veggies, flowers, and fish?

She continued to stand waiting patiently, casually looking around. When another fifteen minutes had passed, she began fidgeting, glancing at her watch, closely watching cars approaching from 1st Avenue, and looking north along the redbrick road.

Nick was taken by surprise when she unexpectedly stepped forward and turned to look up at the big market clock, then took a picture of it. He eased back into the shelter of the pillar just as she took another shot in his direction.

AT FIRST MADDY had enjoyed browsing the market, admiring the various craft items for sale, taking photographs of the elaborate displays of polished fruits and fresh vegetables, picking up carrots, kale, broccoli, and the beets her Scottish-born mother still called beetroots even after all her years of living in the United States and Canada.

The fall blooms and dried flowers were beautiful enough to photograph too but she hadn't wanted to buy any. She remembered when Bart used to send her flowers before their marriage. Never since.

When she moved into the Seattle condo, she'd fill it with flowers. Here their perfume was overwhelmed by the odors of Don & Joe's Meats and the decidedly fishy smell emanating from Pike Place Fish.

The market was crowded with people in costume either going to or coming from Halloween parties, or just entering into the spirit of the day. There were several traditional witches, ghosts, and skeletons; one little boy in a Barney the Dinosaur outfit; a couple of Harry Potters; a cowboy; a slim black woman with fiery orange hair dressed as the Cowardly Lion from *The Wizard of Oz*, accompanied by a very attentive Scarecrow; and two almost identical middle-aged men dressed as Tweedledum and Tweedledee. Did today's children still read *Alice*? Maddy wondered.

A pretty little Asian girl wearing a flowered kimono

climbed up on Rachel the piggy bank while her mother
paid for flowers at a nearby stall. Rachel was a Seattle
institution. *Meet me at the pig*, people often said. Bart had
said. Where *was* he?

Maddy watched the child nervously, tensing to catch
her if she showed any sign of slipping.

The child's mother, also bound tightly into a kimono,
reached the pig a moment later, scolding the girl but with
a loving note in her voice. The girl laughed and slid to
the ground without assistance. With a sudden burning in
her throat, Maddy watched mother and daughter as they
walked gracefully hand in hand across the redbrick road
that fronted the market.

She'd caught herself gazing yearningly at little children
lately. A habit to be stamped out as long as she was married to Bart. Which, now that her friend Sally had found
a condo for her, was not going to be much longer. Ap-
prehension shivered down her spine—or was it a chill?

A threatening darkness hovered at the edges of the
clouds. After a lukewarm but sunny day, a breeze had
kicked up. Sometimes western Washington became bored
with fall and delivered December weather just to break
the monotony.

Still holding her camera, Maddy mentally checked off
possible reasons for Bart's tardiness. He'd been caught in
heavy traffic. His meeting had run late. He'd parked in
some odd place and gotten blocked and couldn't get out.
Bart objected to what he considered Seattle's exorbitant
parking fees and would go to any lengths to avoid paying
them even though he could easily afford them.

Maybe he'd had a heart attack. He'd surely been
stressed when he dropped her off at Nordy's—coldly angry with her for questioning him about his last business
trip, when she was just trying to express an interest, make
conversation. Foolish of her. She knew by now that he
didn't like talking about his work—as if it were classified
information.

Perhaps he'd just *forgotten* he was supposed to pick
her up. He might not even notice she was missing until a

couple of days had passed. For a few minutes she enter-
tained herself by composing a children's story in which
the stalwart heroine stood on a corner, watching people
go about their business, all of them happy and loving and
loved, while she waited and waited and waited—getting
colder and colder as day turned to night, until at last she
turned into a purple Popsicle.

Sounded like a cross between Hans Christian Ander-
sen's "Steadfast Tin Soldier" and "Little Match Girl,"
with a bit of *Charlie and the Chocolate Factory* thrown
in—the girl who turned into a giant blueberry. She'd better stick to her day job and avoid charges of plagiarism.

She'd give Bart fifteen more minutes, then go looking
for a bus.

The people at the flower stall were packing their colorful bouquets in boxes. There were fewer cars going by
on the redbrick road. She ejected the floppy disk from her
Sony Mavica, put in a new one, and looked through the
viewfinder at the shops and buildings opposite. The light
wasn't great, but the shadows were interesting.

Suddenly, just as her shot stopped recording, she
caught a glimpse of her husband's white-blond hair and
looked up to see him waiting to cross the street. He was
behind a herd of kids dressed as Disney dwarfs. They
were accompanied by two women—twins?—both dressed
as Snow White. A couple of Asian tourists sauntered
along behind, cameras at the ready.

As always, Maddy was momentarily startled by how
good-looking Bart was; it was an effect he had on everyone. One of the Snow Whites was giving him the eye as
he and the group started across the street. He wasn't paying any attention. He was looking all around—for her,
she supposed. She picked up her shopping bags in one
hand and waved at him. He focused in her direction, his
handsome face clouding into a frown. He was probably
figuring out how to make this delay her fault. But to her
amazement, he didn't stop. She hadn't quite finished asking, "Where have you—" when he muttered, "Rest room,"
and brushed past her before she could react.

At the same moment, the kids closed around their leaders, the pig and Maddy, and the Snow Whites began doing inventory, calling each one by name to deposit coins in Rachel's slot.

Unwilling to bowl the tots over by rushing after her husband, Maddy watched Bart disappear down the steps to a lower area of the market, her lips parted in disbelief. He could at least have paused long enough to tell her where the car was parked and give her the keys.

As soon as the kids moved over to watch the flying fish, she eased herself past the two Asian tourists, who had also stopped, and stormed off in the direction Bart had disappeared until she came to a FOR MEN ONLY sign. She was so furious she didn't even hesitate. In she marched, past the row of urinals to the stalls, all of which were empty.

A tall, tough-looking man entered as she started back out. He looked vaguely familiar, probably because he was dressed in clothing remarkably similar to her own—blue jeans, a white tee, and a worn brown leather bomber jacket. "I didn't know this was a coed rest room," he said.

"I was looking for someone," she explained, mildly but not terminally embarrassed.

A glint appeared in his dark eyes. "You're *that* lonesome?"

She wasn't in the mood for off-color humor. She was in the mood to kick butt. Preferably Bart's butt, but a stranger's would do. Her irritation must have shown on her face—he hastily stepped aside, gesturing her forward in knightly fashion.

She hesitated outside the door. Bart could have exited the area by any one of the concrete walkways and ramps that formed the labyrinth beneath the market—he might even have gone all the way down the Hillclimb to the waterfront. But why would he? Why hadn't he gone back up to the pig after going to the rest room?

Why was she asking why? It was always a waste of time where Bart was concerned.

Sighing with exasperation, she headed back up the

steps, preparing a few choice comments for Bart if he was waiting by the pig.

He wasn't.

A few minutes later the tall man in the bomber jacket started to go past her, then did a comic double take. "The lady in the john! We meet again." He stared at her for a moment, then snapped his fingers. "Maddy Sloane. I *thought* you looked familiar. I'm Nick Chacha. We met Tuesday at the International Wine Fair. Lara and Todd Wakefield were pouring some kind of expensive stuff. Todd got in trouble for giving the customers too much. Lara introduced me to you. Lara's some kind of woman, isn't she? She'd make a great Brunnhilde in Wagner's *Ring of the Nibelungs*."

He broke off, but started in again before she could find her voice. "My family's from Sicily, so along with an ingrained tendency to flirt with pretty ladies like Lara, I have opera stamped on my DNA. Even when it's in German. Do you like German opera?"

He held out his hand, and she was so bemused by his torrent of words she automatically gave him hers.

She and Lara Donatelli Wakefield had been friends since they met at the University of Washington. Lara and Todd owned Buon Gusto Ristorante in Seattle's University district. They often invited Maddy to join them on outings, knowing Bart wasn't interested in social events that weren't connected with his work. While she was hanging around their table the night of the wine fair, they had introduced her to at least two dozen people—they always seemed to know everyone in Seattle, maybe in the entire state of Washington. She'd have thought she would surely remember a name like Chacha, but then she'd been so stressed out lately it was surprising she could remember her own name.

The man was at least six-foot-four. There was a muscular look about him, and his face was mostly planes and angles, with a take-no-prisoners expression. His black hair was cut short enough to be spiky. Mid-thirties maybe, she thought.

"Chacha?" she echoed, retrieving her hand.

"It's spelled C-I-A-C-I-A, but it's nothing to do with Central Intelligence. It's not a Latin American dance either." He twitched his slanting dark eyebrows, as though inviting her to smile even though he wasn't doing so.

"I don't know if your knowing who I am makes it better or worse that you caught me snooping in the men's room," she said.

"Maddy, it will be our secret forever."

She eyed him balefully.

"You're thinking I might be a pervert," he said. "But I just may be the nicest guy you ever met. Kind to puppies and babies. Stopped beating my mother years ago. She kept beating me back." He looked around. "Are you waiting for someone?"

About to tell him that was none of his damn business, she bit the words back. If he was a friend of Lara's, she should at least try to be pleasant. "My husband was supposed to pick me up here," she explained.

"Ah, that's who you were looking for in the john?"

He obviously wasn't going to let her forget their earlier encounter. "He had a business meeting this morning. He dropped me off at Nordy's, my car's at Dooley's, getting a new water pump, and I had an important appointment with a friend. He said he'd meet me at the pig at four forty-five. He showed up briefly a few minutes ago, said he had to go to the rest room, and promptly disappeared. I've no idea what happened to him. Did you ever hear anything so ridiculous?"

"Where would he park?"

"Who knows? The market has around eight hundred parking places if you count nearby lots as well as the garage. Wherever he could get in, I suppose."

"What does he look like? Was he with you at the wine fair?"

Maddy looked around distractedly, still clutching her shopping bags, her camera and leather purse beginning to drag at her shoulder. She always packed her purse too full. Her chiropractor lectured her about it.

Hitching the purse up, she sighed. "Bart doesn't like gatherings unless they're work-related. And he doesn't drink any kind of alcohol, not even wine."

She realized she hadn't answered his first question. "He's my height, five-ten, forty-four, and extraordinarily good-looking—people think he's a movie star. Buff too— he works out a lot. He has blond hair that is so white it glows in the dark. Blue eyes, much paler than mine. Very fair complexion. Did you see anyone like that down below?"

He shook his head. "Not the sort to fade into the woodwork, is he? Odd that he'd disappear so suddenly. Do you have a cell phone?"

"Bart's is either with him or in the car. I leave mine at the house whenever I can get away with it. Sometimes it's a relief not to have to reach out and touch anyone."

"Isn't that the truth." He produced *his* cell phone from a belt holster. "Maybe you could make an exception in this case?"

Why on earth hadn't she thought of calling Bart's cell from a public telephone!

Her call was immediately sent to voice mail. "I'm still waiting at the pig," she said into the phone. "I'm not going to hang around much longer. I'll look for the car. If I don't find it, I'll take a bus." She hung up.

"Apparently he's turned his cell off," she said. She tried calling the house. The phone rang four times, then her own voice delivered the brief answering machine message she'd dictated to replace the generic one the manufacturer had installed and Bart had been content to leave on.

She shook her head. "This is not like Bart at all. He always keeps the cell phone on, and his plan covers a large area—because of his job."

Nick's right eyebrow posed a question.

"He's a sales rep for Mawsom. The pharmaceutical division. He deals with experimental drugs used for cancer treatments."

"And you?"

"I work for TheHub—an Internet portal company based here in Seattle."

The eyebrow went up again.

"You click on TheHub's URL when you want to find anything, buy anything, sell anything, communicate with anyone. It can also be used as an intranet for small businesses. I don't have anything to do with that end of it, though. I'm a recruiter."

"You recruit in public markets? Men's rooms?"

She shot him a look. His expression was bland. So far he hadn't smiled once. Okay, she'd answer him seriously. Best way to treat a smart aleck. "Mostly I lurk in cyberspace. Checking out résumé databases. Headhunting agencies. Our internal business managers need someone, I look for quality candidates to fill their needs."

"You're a matchmaker? Like Barbra Streisand in *Hello, Dolly*? Do you sing?"

"Are you ever serious?" she asked.

"All the time. The problem is that people don't take me seriously." He glanced at her shopping bags. "You aren't working today?"

"I work at the office Monday through Wednesday, from the house Thursday and Friday. I make my own hours those two days." She had no idea why she felt she needed to explain having the time to wander around Seattle on a Thursday.

"I thought perhaps you were a photographer," he said, indicating her camera.

"It's a hobby. I make notecards on my computer. Strictly for my own use." She hesitated. "What do *you* do?"

"At the moment, I'm self-employed."

That was a nonanswer if ever she'd heard one.

She squinted, picturing the glimpse she'd had of Bart when he appeared among the day-care children, then pointed left. "I think Bart came from that direction. I guess I'll go look for the car." She held out her hand. "Nice to meet you, Mr. Ciacia."

"Nick." He took her hand and held on to it. "Why don't I walk along with you?"

This was getting to seem too much like a pickup. Pulling her hand free, she made eye contact and was momentarily distracted by the glint in his very dark brown eyes. Catching herself on the verge of smiling, she tried to think of a polite way to refuse. *Get lost, buster* was hardly the way to address a friend of her best friend.

The sky was still clear to the east, but directly above, darker cauliflower-shaped clouds were rolling in from Puget Sound. "Looks a lot like rain. You go ahead with whatever you were going to do. I can take it from here. There's no need for you to get wet."

"Lara would have my head if I left you in the lurch."

That was true. She guessed she was stuck with him for a while longer.

As she hesitated, he took her shopping bags from her and they started along the sidewalk opposite the market, dodging a couple of in-line skaters, a fiddle-playing itinerant entertainer who was doing a fair job of the Intermezzo from *Cavalleria Rusticana*, and a tall, thin man dressed as a clown, who was ricocheting a radio-controlled toy car off the various storefronts. The smell of freshly baked bread wafted out at them from a café, making Maddy realize she was getting hungry. Her Chinese lunch hadn't stayed with her.

"What kind of car are we looking for?" Nick asked.

"A gray Ford Taurus. Company car." She laughed shortly. "Given a choice, Bart would prefer a Mercedes because of the German engineering. He believes anything connected to Germany is better than anything made in America." One of the many things he hadn't revealed until after their wedding. One of the many things that had disenchanted her.

Nick seemed very interested. "He's *from* Germany?"

"Immigrated to the U.S. twenty-six years ago—when he was eighteen. But he's not completely Americanized yet, still has a fairly strong German accent."

Nick was looking even more interested.

The Taurus wasn't parked in the street. Nor was it in the lot down the hill.

They came back up on the Hillclimb to the lower floor of the market, then walked past a leather shop, a sports store, a coin dealer, and a store that sold crafts from around the world. All the stores were closing. A children's consignment store at the far end was already dark. The young woman locking the door was dressed appropriately, though rather too cutely, in a red-and-white polka-dotted shirt and white bib overalls, with a raggedy straw hat tipped saucily on the back of her long black hair. She smiled at Nick, ignoring Maddy.

They returned to the pig. "Not much point searching any farther," Maddy said. "Exercise in futility. Bart could be anywhere."

"You want to call the police?"

"Bart would kill me if I called the police just because he's gone off somewhere without telling me." She laughed shortly. "I may need the police later, though. I'm going to kill *him* for forgetting to come back for me."

"Where's home?"

"Oak River."

"I've heard that's a nice little town. You commute to Seattle every day?"

"Three days a week."

"Oh, yeah, you said." Nick hesitated, studying Maddy's face, wondering if the suggestion he was about to make would make her nervous. "My car's up the hill. How about I drive you home?"

"That's okay. I can take a bus."

"I'm sure you can, but you'd be much more comfortable my way."

Her eyebrows pulled together as she frowned. He liked her eyes. They were a particularly vivid blue, with a darker blue rim around the iris, the whites clear, her gaze straight on.

"I can't believe you're hesitating," he said. "My famous charm must be having an out-of-body experience."

The comment forced a laugh out of her. She had a great laugh. The word *melodic* came to mind, surprising the hell out of him. *Melodic* was not a word that belonged in his vocabulary. What was this not quite beautiful but definitely luscious if occasionally snippy woman doing married to the Snowman? It seemed suddenly possible that in spite of the German connection, Bart Williams might not be who Nick thought he was, hoped he was, dreaded he was. Face it: Arnie wasn't the most reliable or truthful of informants.

"How well do you know Lara?" Maddy asked abruptly.

Was that suspicion rearing its ugly head? He had the feeling those expressive blue eyes were inspecting the dark corners of his soul, seeing through him, literally and metaphorically, right through to the creds in his pocket that identified him as an employee of the Federal Bureau of Investigation.

Which he'd better forget about while on this personal quest, especially when in her company. He'd already made a conscious decision to deceive her. He had no choice. If Bart Williams *was* the Snowman, not only his father's killer but someone known by convicts to be running some kind of "operations," any hint of FBI interest, unauthorized though it might be, was liable to send Bart—possibly had already sent him—running for cover faster than you could say Energizer bunny.

It was also entirely possible that Maddy Sloane would close off any information if she suspected for one moment that he was not an innocent bystander here. He'd started off with friendly flirtation and so far it had worked. He might as well keep it up—it was his usual approach to the female gender anyway. Second nature. Maybe even first.

"Lara really did introduce us, Maddy," he said, injecting a miffed note into his voice. "I can even tell you what you were wearing. A long open coat with a long black dress with glittery stuff on it. You said you'd just come from a gallery opening. Somebody's woodblock prints, you said."

"Hiroshige," she said.

"Sounds about right. Here's the clincher. We were all standing around and I proposed a toast to Lara—'Here's looking at you, kid,'—and Lara said, 'You have to meet Maddy. She's always quoting *Casablanca* too.' "

"I remember Lara saying that," she said. "I mentioned that I have my computer set so that Humphrey Bogart says that same quote when Windows logs off."

He nodded. "Some young thing asked, 'What's *Casablanca*?' and you said, 'Only the best Hollywood movie of all time,' and I immediately fell in like."

"In *like*?"

"I think of that as the good L word. The bad L word seldom crosses my lips."

"What's so bad about it?"

"Every time I've said it to a woman, she's started re-organizing my life, and me, from the cellar to the attic."

They both laughed. "I'm sorry," Maddy said. "I don't usually forget that I've met someone—there was such a lot going on, so many people."

He appraised her thoughtfully. "Your hair was longer. At the wine fair you wore it up with some ends sticking out like a feather duster." He twirled a finger over his own head to demonstrate.

He was right; she'd had her hair cut since the wine fair, already regretted it. She held up both hands in surrender. "Okay, I'm convinced," she said.

Nick Ciacia, pronounced Chacha, might not smile much, but he was quite a charmer, she thought. Unfortunately, she totally distrusted charm, especially in men. Bart could still be charming on occasion, though nowhere near as charming as he had been when she met him. Con men were often charming—and Nick Ciacia was just slick enough to be one.

She considered her options. She wasn't sure she had enough cash left in her purse to pay for a cab all the way to Oak River, and it would take a cab to Seattle's bus depot and two buses to get her there the only other way. She could find an ATM machine. Or she could get a cab to Lara's restaurant and have an early dinner, then call the house . . . No, she was tired and cold. If Bart didn't show up, Lara and Todd would be far too busy to offer transportation.

"What kind of business did you say you were in?" she asked.

"I'm a licensed CPA. That's the kind of guy who does taxes, estates, gives financial advice whether people want it or not. Eminently trustworthy. Terminally dull."

She frowned. "You don't look like an accountant."

"I don't?" He had very mobile eyebrows. "What *do* I look like?"

She thought for a minute. "A stevedore."

"You hang with stevedores a lot?"

"I'm not even sure exactly what a stevedore does. But you look like I'd expect one to look. Tough. Strong. Capable of anything."

"I bet there are a hell of a lot of CPAs who are tough, strong, and capable of anything."

She inclined her head. "I always thought people in your line of work wore suits."

Startled, for one moment he thought she was referring to his real job. But he made a fast recovery. "On a Thursday? You don't think an accountant can take Thursdays off, just like doctors do? Or dot-com recruiters?"

She laughed again and let her guard down. "Okay," she said. "If you *are* an accountant and you're not in prison, and you know Lara and Todd, and you even remember hairstyles, I guess you must be an okay guy. The clincher, of course, is that you can quote from *Casablanca*. I first saw it on late night TV, bought the video. I'm such a fan I chose the auto repair shop I take my car to because its owner's name is Dooley." She hesitated, smiling. "Maybe you know only one *Casablanca* quote."

"Humphrey Bogart said, 'You played it for her and you can play it for me,'" he said promptly. "Ingrid Bergman said, 'Play it, Sam. Play "As Time Goes By."'' Almost everyone misquotes it as 'Play it again, Sam.' Dooley

Wilson was Sam. he played the piano and sang, 'As Time Goes By.' "

Maddy beamed at him. "I guess I'll accept your kind offer."

They hiked up the steep street to the parking garage where he'd left his car, close to Nordstrom. He was in good shape, she noticed. He was no more out of breath than she was.

He drove a Chevy sedan. That surprised her. "I'd have expected you to own a muscle car of some kind," she said as she climbed in and pulled the door closed.

"In my dreams, I own a '57 Corvette Super Sport, Venetian red, but it just doesn't fit the boring accountant image."

He'd been parked for some time, evidently. It cost him a considerable amount to ransom his car. As they drove out of the garage, she realized the sky had suddenly gone even darker. No sooner had the thought entered her mind than the clouds burst and Nick hit the brakes.

Seattle rain was normally user-friendly, a steady but gentle mizzle, the kind you could turn up your coat collar for and not worry about, especially if you had hair like hers that just became curlier when damp. Most veteran Seattleites didn't even bother with umbrellas.

This rain obviously had some hail in it. It hammered down ever more loudly, as if a mad builder was battering hundreds of sixpenny nails into the car roof.

Dumbfounded, deafened, they stared at each other. And something arced between them—a feeling, an urgency, some kind of connection. Maddy wasn't sure if she was embarrassed or exhilarated. The air felt—smelled—electric, pheromones and testosterone and estrogen mixing it up all over the place. Nick was the first to look away. Maddy felt relieved when he did.

"My mother's a Scot," she said over the racket. "She'd say it's mekkin' a lot of wet ootside."

It was almost impossible to talk over the noise, and certainly nobody could drive in such a torrent. All they could do was wait it out. There was hardly any light penetrating the interior of the car now; the downpour had closed them off from the rest of the world, intensifying that awkward intimacy that had developed between them.

The storm ended as suddenly as it had begun. Within seconds, it was as though a director had called for "Lights, camera, action!" The sun shone on glistening streets and automobiles. Men and women emerged smiling from shop doorways where they had taken shelter. A couple of small boys, one in a fireman outfit, one cloaked vampire style, ran to splash in the water racing down the gutter before their father could stop them. The vampire grinned at her and Nick showing fake fangs, as Nick started the car and the windshield wipers.

They talked little during the drive. The strange intimacy had not completely dissipated. Traffic was as heavy as usual, in both directions. Rush hour always lasted several hours on I-5. At one point there was a fabulous view of Mount Rainier to the east, its ice-cream-sundae summit stained pink by the sun setting in the west. Maddy got out her camera and leaned forward to get beyond Nick, who obligingly opened his window. Deciding they were going too fast for her to get a good shot, she packed the camera away in its padded case.

She still couldn't imagine why Bart had appeared and disappeared so quickly. She wasn't exactly worried. Bart was not the kind of man who required worrying about. He was self-sufficient—too much so. To be fair, he was usually also courteous, though often distant. Cold, even. One of the main problems she had with Bart, one she hadn't been able to figure out in the six months they'd been married, was that he'd turned into a different man from the romantic, caring, charming man of their whirlwind courtship. The man she'd fallen for had put a lot of effort into courting her, but the man he'd turned into put none at all into keeping her.

"Your husband works in Seattle?" Nick asked after a long silence. "Was his meeting there?"

"Well, his head office is in Seattle. I suppose that's where the meeting was. But mostly he's on the road. His territory covers Oregon and California as well as Washington."

West Coast rep. Arnie's words kept coming back to Nick.

"You're both headquartered in Seattle? Why live in Oak River?"

"My question too." She sighed. "Bart likes it there. It's quiet. Secluded. He's had a house there since long before we were married. Doesn't want to move."

Remembering her lunch with the real estate agent, he couldn't resist asking, "You wouldn't rather move to the city? Closer to work?"

She opened her mouth slightly, but closed it again without comment.

Nick tried a different tack. "Your husband's often on the road? Doesn't he get tired of that?"

"He says not. He's been offered promotions but turns them down. He likes his job a lot, has no ambition to move up at the company. And, of course, it's an important job. These are potentially life-saving, innovative drugs, the kind that target individual cancers, the kind that attack cancer at the genetic level. Bart mostly visits oncology people, people who treat cancer patients. It's part of Mawsom's mission statement that their purpose is to extend life and to enhance its quality."

Nick gave her a narrow-eyed glance and decided she was sincere. "That's a lofty goal." He paused. "Your husband travels around to doctors' offices?"

"Hospitals mostly. Spreading information about experimental drugs is not the same as with established drugs. He deals primarily with specialists and surgeons, though he gives presentations to nurses and other people too. He works very hard at his presentations. He doesn't just take in samples and hand them out. Before he leaves on a business trip, he shuts himself up in the office in the house and figures out exactly what he's going to say, works out ways to convince doctors that Mawsom products can serve their particular needs, improve life, and prolong life for their patients."

It sounded as if she were repeating a speech her husband had given or an article someone had written.

"He doesn't make a habit of disappearing?"

She shook her head, her mouth tightening.

Nick lapsed into a thoughtful silence that lasted until they reached their destination.

Once a suburb of Tacoma, the now incorporated city of Oak River had built up in an era when lots were large, leaving room for considerable space between houses. Old-growth Douglas firs, Sitka spruce, and the stout, craggy, and ubiquitous Oregon white oaks that had given the town the first half of its name had been left intact, built around. Strewn right now with red, yellow, and russet vine maple leaves, most yards were landscaped like mini-parks, with manicured golf-club-green lawns, a boulder or two to lend interest, small rivers of flat stones, and flower beds that were mainly dormant at this time of year.

There were sidewalks, streetlights—and trick-or-treaters. Dozens of them. Maddy hoped none of them had soaped the windows of Bart's house. He'd be furious. She wondered sometimes if he'd ever been a kid; he had no patience with them. But then neither had her father.

In urban areas of Washington, trick-or-treating had died down in recent years, mostly due to parents' fears of psychos who inserted razor blades or needles into apples, or poison into candy. In Oak River, people felt safe. There were teenagers dressed as pop stars—Maddy counted several Britneys—and a few kids in *Star Wars* costumes. As in the market, there was a large number of ghosts and skeletons, and on Maddy's street a whole gang of grade school kids were dressed in *Toy Story* outfits.

Maddy had watched the popular movie several times while baby-sitting Sally Carstairs's twin boys. Three years old, they never wanted to watch any other video.

The tall dad accompanying the group was dressed as Woody and wore a large backpack with the Nike swoosh on it, presumably to stash the candy in.

Bart's large two-story house was backed by the ram-

bling stream that had given Oak River the second half of
its name.

Nick got out of the car when Maddy did and asked if
he could make a pit stop. She could hardly refuse. He
carried her shopping bags and watched as she unlocked
the front door, eyeing the canister her key ring was attached to. "Is that pepper spray?" he asked.

"I bought it from a guy who came to TheHub to teach
a self-defense class for women a couple of years ago.
TheHub offices are in an area of Seattle that hasn't been
gentrified yet. It has one of those multifloor parking complexes. Sometimes I work late. I'm not anxious to become
a victim." She operated the light switches on the inside
wall, dumped her camera bag and purse, then entered the
living room.

And stopped, sniffing.

"That's odd!" she muttered.

Nick was beside her immediately. "What?" he asked.

Chapter 3

"CIGARETTE SMOKE," MADDY said. "Someone's been smoking in here. Neither Bart nor I smoke. And Bart is militant about not letting anyone smoke in his house. He's very—well, he's something of an ascetic, I guess. He doesn't smoke or drink, and he's a health food nut. Likes everything clean, including the air."

She sniffed a couple more times. "There's something else too. Old Spice. My father used to wear Old Spice. I didn't think it was all that popular now."

"Could your father have visited? Does he smoke?"

"No. And he and my mother live in Victoria. They don't . . . visit."

Hesitation there. Interesting. Nick could smell smoke too, and some kind of cologne. Though he sure wouldn't have known how to identify it.

"When I was working my way through college, I took a job as a perfume model at Nordy's," Maddy explained, as if she'd read his mind. "I have a good nose."

"Doesn't look as if anyone disturbed anything," Nick

said. "Looks perfect, you ask me. You're a great house-keeper."

"We have a maid—Kazuko," Maddy said absently. "She's worked for Bart since long before we were married. As I said, he's very particular about cleanliness."

Nick had nothing against cleanliness, but Bart was sounding more and more like a hell of a prig. Or a prick. "Kazuko doesn't smoke either?"

"No way. Nor does she use Old Spice."

They were both still standing on the threshold of the living room. Maddy glanced around at the bright and lively Impressionist prints she'd bought to replace the surreal, and to her eyes unattractive, prints Bart owned. Nothing out of the ordinary there. The cups, saucers, and plates in the china cabinets that divided the living room from the dining room were intact; none of the furniture had been moved. Why did she feel it might have been?

Previously, the furniture had been dark, massive. Bart had hired a designer with his own old-fashioned tastes to do the whole house right after he'd bought it. Before they were married, Maddy had suggested some redecorating, which in her mind translated to donating all the furniture to the Salvation Army and starting over at IKEA, Crate & Barrel, and Pottery Barn, with light woods and pale linen fabrics. Bart had given her a free hand, not seeming to care what she got rid of, except for the paintings, which he'd transferred to his office and bedroom.

She listened as if the room would tell her something, but could hear nothing except the ticking of the grandfather clock in the hall. All the same . . .

"Someone's been in here," she said firmly. "Someone who doesn't belong."

Nick immediately set both shopping bags down. Motioning her to stay where she was, he drifted silently through the living room to the dining room then turned toward the kitchen. Coming out again, he checked the bathroom and her office. A few seconds later, he went up the stairs, treading carefully as a cat. He could sure move quietly. After what seemed a long time, he came back down, muttered that there was nobody in sight and everything looked okay. Then off he went to finally use the bathroom.

Maybe he'd disappear in there the way Bart had at the rest room in the market. She could imagine the tabloid headlines: "Careless woman loses two men in rest rooms in one day."

She went through the dining room to the kitchen and then on to her small office. Her desktop computer, printer, scanner, fax machine, and copier were intact, she was relieved to see. Her laptop was still in its case, leaning against the wall.

"I guess you like to read," Nick said, making her jump as she reentered the living room. He was looking at the wide, glass-fronted, floor-to-ceiling cabinet that covered one wall.

"Bart would have a fit if anything happened to those books. He won't let me read them. He won't even let Kazuko dust the shelves. I'm not sure he's even read them himself. Keeps the cabinet locked. The books are all first editions—collectibles. Each one wrapped in a Brodart cover, made of Mylar. Some are already valuable, some Bart says will become valuable in a few years."

"Does the maid live in?"

"She comes in on weekdays. She'll have been here today, but she leaves at four."

She shook her head. "If someone did break in, they'd probably be looking for drugs. Every once in a while someone asks me about Bart and drugs. Some people can't distinguish between a sales rep for a pharmaceutical company and a drug dealer or trafficker. They'd be out of luck. Bart doesn't keep any samples here and I'm pretty sure the drugs he works with wouldn't give anyone a high."

"Jewelry? Money? Do you have a safe anywhere?"

She spun around and ran into the hall and then up the stairs. As Nick had said, none of the three bedrooms had been disturbed. Her jewelry box in her nightstand cabinet still held her few good pieces of jewelry—earrings, a gold bracelet watch she seldom wore, some gold chains, her pearls, a sapphire and diamond pin her mother had brought from Victoria for the blue in her wedding outfit.

She went on into Bart's office. He didn't own a computer—he had some kind of Big Brother complex, called himself a Luddite, was convinced the Internet was not a safe place to do business or preserve privacy. Bart was very big on privacy. Pulling out his large leather office chair, she sat down and swiveled slowly. One of his large framed prints—Hieronymus Bosch's *Garden of Delights*— was a little askew. She lifted it down and set it carefully against the desk. The safe behind it opened easily when she pulled on the recessed handle. There was absolutely nothing inside.

Nick had followed her up. "Whatever they were hunting for, they found it," she told him, gesturing for him to take a look.

"What was in there?" Nick asked.

"Bart told me he kept his work records in there." Avoiding Nick's sharp gaze, she felt called upon to explain further. "My husband is a secretive guy. I know he has a safe underneath that painting only because I came once to tell him lunch was ready and he had the painting down just like this. I guess I'd better call the police," she added.

Nick couldn't argue with that, even though the last thing he wanted was to have the Oak River police find him on the premises. He searched his mind for a way to free himself from the trap he'd gotten into.

"You sound reluctant," he said, seizing on the flat note in her voice.

Her mouth tightened.

"You *are* reluctant."

She sighed. "I'm on the proverbial horns of a dilemma here. I want to call the police, but my husband values his privacy above all else. If I found him bleeding on the carpet and called a doctor, he'd probably tell me I should have let him tie the tourniquet himself. Besides which, what I'm afraid of, what has occurred to me is that . . ."

She broke off, started over. "My husband was . . . upset when he dropped me off in Seattle this morning. I was talking about his last trip—he was gone even longer than usual—and I was just trying to show some interest, but he got very . . . perturbed."

Afraid of spooking her, he waited.

"Recently, he's been extra . . . jittery, nervous, jumping when the phone rang or the UPS man came to the door. It seemed almost as if he was afraid of something. Or someone."

"For how long?"

"Since he came back from his last business trip. A few days ago."

Shit. Had Bart Williams made him? He'd been careful, but there had been one or two close calls when the man had turned suddenly, forcing Nick to be more obvious than he liked or risk losing him. Bart might even have made him today at the market. Nick might very well be the reason Bart had darted away from Maddy and disappeared. And if that was so, it didn't say much for Bart, ditching his wife like that, especially if he thought Nick spelled danger.

On the other hand, if Nick was the reason for Bart's disappearance, then it would seem more possible that Bart Williams *was* his man. Innocent citizens didn't worry too much about the cars that happened to be behind them or a man standing next to a pillar.

"So what exactly do you suspect?" he asked.

"I'm wondering if Bart came back here himself. While we were looking through the market for him."

"You think he was angry enough with you to walk past you, disappear, come here and remove whatever he had stashed in the safe, and take off?"

Her eyebrows drew together in a frown, and she let out a long breath. "It sounds unlikely, doesn't it? And Bart's not really the type to lose his temper anyway. As a rule, he suppresses everything, zips his lips, and walks away without saying a word. That's what he was doing in the car this morning—not the walks away apart, the

zipped lips part. Besides, if he was the one who opened
the safe, that doesn't explain the smell of smoke and Old
Spice."

"He brought along a friend, maybe?"

"Bart doesn't have any—" She broke off. "I guess it's
possible he brought someone else along."

She sighed.

"You're thinking that if he did disappear voluntarily,
then came back to empty the safe himself, he probably
wouldn't take kindly to you calling in the cops?" Nick
queried.

"Exactly."

"This bears some thinking about." He started down the
stairs, and she followed him.

In the kitchen he lifted a bottle from one of the wine
racks, held it toward her, label uppermost, and waited until she nodded approval, then rooted around in the drawer
beneath the wine racks until he found a cork remover.
Carrying the bottle into the living room, he sat on the
linen-covered sofa, set the bottle down on the coffee table,
and opened the wine. One good thing about undercover
work, especially when it wasn't officially authorized, was
that you could have a glass of wine just to fit in.

Nick Ciacia probably thought she was overreacting,
Maddy decided as she followed him into the living room
with a couple of glasses and some napkins. "I really don't
know what's the best thing to do," she said. "Given Bart's
recent behavior, it's *possible* he's responsible for his own
disappearance. He might *possibly* have come here and
opened up the safe."

"Can you think of anyone else who might be responsible?" Nick asked.

"No. Kazuko certainly wouldn't suddenly come in and
burglarize us. She's alone here a lot of the time. Bart hired
her long before I came along. We're very lucky to have
her—she's an amazing woman. She's been a good friend
to me."

She decided the cabernet had breathed long enough,
poured them each a glass, and took a sip of hers, appre-

ciating its rich blackberry and currant flavors even while she was trying to think through the situation. "Kazuko's a kick. She came here from Japan. Even though she speaks fluent English and became an American citizen before I was born, she insists on calling Bart '*dannasan*' and me '*okusan*,' which means something like 'master of the house' and 'the missus.' She came here as an army bride in the early sixties, had two children, now grown and married, and lost her husband to diabetes-related problems a few years ago. She gets half her husband's army pension plus social security and there was generous insurance. Her kids adore her and would be happy to support her if she needed it, but she prefers to work. Fortunately for me."

"She lives around here?"

"Yes. She has a small house on the street behind the library." She shook her head. "I've really never heard of anyone breaking into a house around here—" She broke off. "I had to use my key. Whoever came in must have had a key."

Nick picked up a napkin, got up, and headed for the front door. Maddy followed him. Opening the door carefully with the napkin over two fingers, he crouched down to examine the lock. "Got a few scratches," he told her. "Could be general use, could be someone picked the lock." He closed the door. "Which way's the back door?"

She showed him. He repeated the procedure on the back door. "It's been jimmied," he told her, and showed her the scars in the wood.

They returned to the living room. "I guess it wasn't Bart who broke in," she said tightly.

"Unless he forgot his key."

She shook her head. "He wouldn't break in, he'd get a locksmith."

"Maybe he was in a hurry." He hesitated. "Could you stay with Kazuko tonight?"

She set her glass down and looked at him. "Why would I do that? I'm worried about Bart, yes, but I'm not some helpless chick who needs a hand to hold. I can stay in an

empty house by myself. I do it all the time when Bart's
on the road. I don't know why you would—"

Nick held up a hand to stop her. "I didn't mean to
insult you, Maddy. I meant, if you still don't want to call
the police, at least right away, then maybe for your own
protection . . ."

"You think I'm in danger?" She frowned. "I suppose
it's possible Bart could have gotten himself in some kind
of trouble. That would also explain the way he's been
behaving. I didn't think of that. I thought he was neglect-
ing me, or mad at me. But whatever is going on, his disappearance has to be connected with the break-in and that
empty safe. . . ."

She stood up. "I guess I'll call the police after all."

He picked up his wineglass and swigged a mouthful.
Nice going, Ciacia, he moaned to himself. "Okay," he said
reluctantly.

Her eyebrows drew together in a quick frown. "It's
probably not a good idea for the police to find you here.
They might misinterpret . . ."

"Our relationship?"

"Don't you think?"

"You could be right. You tell them your husband disappeared and there's an empty safe in the house, they'll
take a hard look at you and me."

She nodded. "You'd better go."

Which of course was what he wanted to do. And yet
didn't want to. What he really wanted was for her to decide not to call the police and instead go off to this Kazuko's house for the night so he could find his way back
in and snoop. He'd looked around a little in the office and
the bedrooms upstairs without touching anything, but
hadn't been able to do the thorough search he was itching
to do.

On the other hand, no way did he want to become the
number one suspect in the disappearance of Bart Williams. So far his supervisor had been supportive—well,
at least he'd let Nick take annual leave to track down the
Snowman even though his boss wasn't sure he believed

there was such a character. If Nick got himself in trouble with the local law, that support would be withdrawn.

He stood up. "Are you sure you'll be okay?"

She gave him the withering look she'd given him earlier when he made a joke about meeting her in the men's room, then extended her hand. "Thank you so much, Nick. I appreciate everything you've done."

He was being dismissed, lady of the manor style. He ought to feel snubbed, but what he felt was disappointment. Like a kid who'd had a promised treat taken away from him. What? He wanted her to *like* him?

Yes, he did.

"Not so fast," he said, making it sound as breezy as possible. "I'm not leaving here until I'm sure you're in good hands. I really do think you should have someone with you when the police get here."

What he meant was he wanted to be sure someone really did call the police.

Her mouth tightened up. He held her gaze. She blinked first, ending the standoff, then sighed and went into the kitchen to call the housekeeper. A couple of minutes later he heard her go into the bathroom.

He cocked an eye at the glassed-in bookcases again. The fact that Bart Williams didn't want even his wife to touch them had awakened his curiosity and tweaked a memory of a story he'd read in college. Something about a stolen letter. A *purloined* letter. As he recalled the story, the stolen letter had been hidden in the most obvious place there was, and so had not been noticed.

Walking over to the wall of books, he craned his neck to look upward. Maddy had said the cabinet was kept locked. The locks had been well hidden under the cornice that was otherwise purely decorative, but they weren't invisible.

He heard the toilet flush, then the bathroom door opened. At about the same time, a car drew up outside. While Maddy went to the door, he went into the kitchen, where he wiped his fingerprints off the bottle, the opener, and his wineglass, and put them back in their proper places.

When he reentered the living room, Maddy introduced him to a petite Japanese woman who appeared to be in her sixties, judging by the lines on her face and the gray mixed in her black hair. Those expressive lines had all been turned upward, but they took a severe downward turn when she saw Nick.

After Maddy explained the situation but not Nick's presence, the woman muttered something in Japanese, then said in English, "Yes, I smelled cigarette smoke when I came in here, but I thought it was . . ." She hesitated, turning to flick some imaginary dust from the end table. "Your friend," she finally added, with a sideways glance at Nick.

Nick tried to remember if Maddy had mentioned Bart's last name. He didn't think so. So he wouldn't be expected to know it. "Probably best not to touch anything," he said. "Even if Mr. Sloane is okay, this could be a crime scene. The police will want to check it for prints."

"My fingerprints are all over this house," Kazuko said in a tone that meant he should have known that if he had any sense.

"You might obliterate somebody else's," he explained.

"Bart's last name is Williams," Maddy said as Kazuko looked at him narrow-eyed. "I kept my own name because of my job, everyone knew me as Maddy Sloane."

He nodded acceptance of that and made a mental note that it was now okay for him to "know" Bart's last name. "Williams doesn't sound German," he commented.

"He changed it when he came to this country."

"Yeah? What was it before?"

"Wilhelm. Bartel Wilhelm."

That didn't quite jell with his information. He'd understood Williams's original name was Bartel Wilhelm *Franz*.

"You think maybe something bad happened to *dannasan*?" Kazuko asked.

"I wouldn't rule it out," Nick said.

Maddy sighed. "I don't know what to think. You've known him much longer than I have, Kazuko. You have any ideas?"

"Nobody knows *dannasan*," Kazuko stated. "*Dannasan* doesn't wish to be known." There was a harsh note in her voice suddenly.

Maddy blinked. Nick paid attention.

"I always thought you liked Bart," Maddy said.

Kazuko hesitated, then nodded as if to give herself permission to speak. "It is not always necessary to like your boss. All that is necessary is to do good work and make good pay."

"Is that how you feel about me too?" Maddy demanded.

Kazuko smiled. She was pretty when she smiled. "*Okusan*, there is no comparison here. You and I are friends, *tomodach ine*?" Her smile disappeared. "You know what *dannasan* is like. Very private person. Very particular person. Many rules. More rules than anyone I ever worked for. Before you marry *dannasan*, anybody came by, he wanted me to leave always, leave them alone, get out of here, no matter what work I was doing."

"Nobody's come by since we were married," Maddy said.

Kazuko nodded. "I noticed."

"You never mentioned any of this before."

"*Dannasan* never disappeared before."

"What kind of people came to the house before Bart and Maddy were married?" Nick asked.

Kazuko frowned at him, her dark eyes clouded with suspicion. "I think maybe I've seen you before," she said.

"Mr. Ciacia has been very kind, Kazuko," Maddy said.

Kazuko nodded. "That's good, *okusan*. I'm just curious where I might have seen him."

Probably sometime in the four days when I was shadowing your employer, Nick thought. "I haven't visited Oak River before," he lied. "Do you get into Seattle much? That's mostly where I hang out."

She shook her head. "I don't like big cities."

He realized she hadn't answered his question about the people who had visited before Maddy married Bart. He was very interested in that, but he didn't want to draw attention or Kazuko's ire by repeating the question.

Both women were looking at him expectantly. Time to beat a graceful retreat.

He held out his hand to Maddy and put on his best manners. "It was nice to see you again. May I call you tomorrow to see if your husband has shown up?"

She hesitated.

"I'm offering you friendship, Maddy. We have friends in common, so why not? Besides, if I didn't follow up, Lara would—"

"Have your head. Yes, so you said before. You sure are afraid of Lara."

"She's a scary lady. But lovable."

"Okay," she said finally. She found her shoulder bag where she'd dropped it, rooted through what seemed like an incredible amount of stuff, and took out a card to give him. "This one has all my numbers."

He handed her the genuine fake business card that identified him as a CPA and gave only his Seattle apartment phone. "Take care," he said as she opened the front door for him.

He realized as he walked to his car that though he was now sure that Bart Williams was the man he'd been looking for, he was no closer to knowing if Maddy Sloane was aware of anything her husband might have done in his past. She'd been critical of the man. And they hadn't been married long. But he didn't know how well or how long she had known him before their marriage. Twenty-six years ago, when Bart had come to the United States, she was barely potty-trained. She probably *didn't* know everything there was to know about Bart Williams. *Probably* wasn't *absolutely*, though.

Chapter 4

THE SLIGHTLY PUDGY detective who came to the house in response to Maddy's phone call did not possess a happy spirit. His nose was pink tinged, his eyes were bleary. When he spoke, Maddy realized he had a cold.

"You shoulda called 911 right away," he said, after she'd explained the situation and he'd noted everything on his clipboard. "Trail's cold now. You'd called right away, Seattle police coulda been looking for your man— we coulda had a dog out, checked the neighborhood."

"I doubt my neighbors entered my house—they never did before."

He glowered at her.

She glowered back, then said she'd been in shock for a while. She also pointed out that she'd heard the police wouldn't search for a missing spouse until he or she had been gone forty-eight hours.

"That's correct," he conceded.

"Well, then," she said.

"That's if there's no other evidence of a crime," he

said, looking around. "You've got a break-in through the back door; you've got a safe opened."

"I didn't know any of that until a few minutes ago."

She clamped her mouth closed as he shook his head sorrowfully. The best way to deal with someone who treated you as if you were missing a few chunks of brain was to agree with him. "You're right, of course. I should have called right away. I kept thinking Bart would show up."

Although she didn't think much of the detective so far, she was impressed by the efficiency of the two men who'd come along with him. They photographed the safe, then checked it, Bart's office and its door, the front door, the back door, and the kitchen for fingerprints.

The detective wouldn't answer her "What do you think?" questions, but finally unbent enough to explain to her that the fingerprints would be helpful only if they could match them up with someone.

Which she thought she might have been able to figure out for herself.

Hoping she might get more out of him, she invited him to have a snack with her after the lab people had left. She was going to starve to death if she didn't have something soon.

Beyond the kitchen window, the outside lights illuminated the fog that hung low over the river. The branches of the Sitka spruce that dominated the backyard were invisible; she could see only the lower part of the huge scaly trunk. The deck looked wet and slick.

"Tell me again about what happened today," Detective Bradford said, clipboard in hand.

"I've already told you."

"Humor me."

She sighed. "My husband drove me to Seattle, dropped me off at Nordstrom around noon, said he'd meet me at the pig at Pike Place Market at four forty-five, then went to his business meeting. He's always very precise about time, so I was at the pig right at four forty-five, but he didn't come and didn't come. I waited. At around five-fifteen he showed up in a hurry, said he had to go to the rest room, and went down the steps at the back. I followed him a couple of minutes later, but there was nobody in the men's room. After a while, I went looking for him along the street in front of the market and down the hill, came back up the Hillclimb, looked around some more, then gave up and came here."

She waited for him to ask how she got home, knowing she'd have to tell him about Nick Ciacia and that the detective would probably read something into that, but he didn't ask.

"You and your husband get along okay, ma'am?"

She supposed it was inevitable he'd suspect her of being responsible for Bart's disappearance.

Kazuko had refused her invitation to eat with them. She always refused, evidently feeling, in spite of Maddy's arguments, that it wasn't her place. But she had made coffee for Maddy, tea for the detective—with honey to soothe his throat—and put out sliced roast beef, lettuce, onions, cheese, mayonnaise, mustard, wheat bread, and a wooden bowl full of tossed salad with a wonderfully fragrant vinaigrette.

Maddy and the detective were seated on high stools at the island counter. Kazuko had started cleaning and bagging the vegetables Maddy had bought at the market.

The coffee was black and strong, just the way Maddy liked it. Kazuko always wanted her to drink green tea, which tasted okay, and, according to Kazuko, was full of antioxidants, but Maddy did love her Kona coffee.

"We've only been married six months," she said to the detective.

"Uh-huh."

He was obviously going to wait for her to answer.

"We never fight," she said. "We do argue sometimes."

"Did you argue today?"

He had an unusually expressionless face, she thought. She imagined detectives probably trained themselves to not show what they were thinking.

"We did."

"Where and about what?"

"In the car on the way to Seattle. I asked my husband a couple of questions about his last business trip, and he seemed to think I was prying. I wasn't. I was just curious. He'd been gone longer than usual."

"Uh-huh."

He made a few notes.

She couldn't read them, but she could read his mind. There'd been a fight. The husband had come home, grabbed some cash, and taken off for a few days. "A stranger was in this house," she said for what seemed the umpteenth time. "Someone who broke in through the back door, wore Old Spice and smoked cigarettes."

"Not much of a description to go on, ma'am."

"I don't know what happened to my husband, Detective. It's a total mystery to me. But isn't it possible, given the circumstances, that he might have had an accident or been the victim of a crime—kidnapping, assault, something? Shouldn't you be checking hospitals?"

"Already being done, ma'am." He raised his eyebrows. "Tell me again about the drugs."

She explained once more that Bart's job involved calling on hospitals in Washington, Oregon, and California and providing them with information about Mawsom Pharmaceuticals, especially promising experimental drugs for the treatment of cancer.

He nodded as he wrote, then said, "So did either of you . . . Well, let me put it this way: Are there any boyfriends or girlfriends involved?"

She wanted to hit him over the head with the coffeepot for his smarmy tone, but decided that probably wouldn't help the situation. "None that Bart ever told me about."

He was still squinting at her. She looked at him directly. "And no, I didn't—*don't*—have a boyfriend." She was glad she hadn't mentioned meeting Nick in the market.

"Do you suppose we'll find other prints here besides yours and Mr. Williams's and your housekeeper's?"

"Of course you will. Unless . . . Would the burglars or whatever they were wear gloves?"

"Possibly."

"What do you mean, *possibly*? You don't believe someone was here? You think I emptied the safe myself? Waved a magic wand and made my husband disappear in the middle of Pike Place Market?"

He drank some tea, then nodded at Kazuko in appreciation as she refilled his cup and stirred in another dollop of honey. "Did you?" he asked.

Kazuko rolled her eyes in sympathy.

Maddy took a deep breath, let it out. "I do not know anything about my husband's disappearance or the contents of that safe," she said flatly. "Look, Detective Bradford, I'm as much in the dark about this as you are. I've no idea who was in here or why. I've no idea why my husband disappeared or where he went. I can only hope he'll show up soon and answer your questions himself."

"That would help."

"Aren't you supposed to canvass the neighborhood? See if anyone heard or saw anything?"

He frowned. "Halloween," he said. "Don't usually have real problems here. Few windows soaped, few garbage cans overturned. But there were a lot of strangers about, kids still on the streets, when I drove here. Don't know what gets into some parents, letting their kids roam around in the dark. Wouldn't let mine . . ."

He paused and looked down at his notes. "This meeting of your husband's, what was it about?"

"I don't know. I imagine it had something to do with his job."

"At Mawsom Pharmaceuticals."

"Yes."

"We'll check on that." He looked at her directly. "He didn't tell you anything *about* the meeting?"

"As you have kids, I take it you are married?"

"Yes, ma'am."

"Do you tell your wife everything you do?"

"This isn't about me," he said shortly, but he didn't

pursue that particular question any further and, after a few seconds, set his clipboard down. "We'll put this on the agenda for our daily patrol turnout session and we'll work with Seattle police, see what they can find out—probably put out an 'attempt to locate' on your husband's Ford Taurus. It's easier to trace a car than to stop every"—he turned back a few pages on the clipboard—"every five-foot-ten, blond-haired, blue-eyed guy wearing a gray suit and a blue-and-white-striped dress shirt." He looked up. "You have any questions, Mrs. Williams? Anything you wish to add?"

She shook her head. She had seen no reason to tell him she didn't use her husband's name as her own. This wasn't a good time to point out any differences.

"If you want to give me a photo, we'll get that out, but mostly we'll follow up on the information you've given me." He hesitated and gave her a grimace that was evidently supposed to be a smile. "And yeah, we'll check with the neighbors—see if they saw anyone or anything unusual. Though on Halloween . . ."

She went into her office, booted up her computer and printer, searched out their wedding photo, and opened it in Photoshop. She'd scanned it soon after their wedding. Bart had been too busy for a honeymoon. She didn't have any other photos that included him, though there were plenty taken of her and their guests: Sally Carstairs, who had been her matron of honor; the best man—a friend of Bart's she hadn't met before or since; her friends from work and from the gym where she worked out; her parents; and a large delegation from Bart's company, including Bart's boss, Simon Hatfield, who had been accompanied by his wife.

Bart's obsession with privacy extended to photo taking. She'd wondered once or twice if he shared the belief of some primitive tribes that a camera could steal your soul.

After carefully separating his image from hers—symbolic, she thought—she printed it out.

The detective glanced at the photo and clipped it onto his board. "He'll turn up none the worse for wear, I'm sure, ma'am," he said with apparent sympathy, but his gaze was watchful. "Maybe he just had a need to get away for a day or two. Guys do that."

She was tempted to ask if he didn't think women ever felt such a need. But she bit her lip instead.

"Be sure to let us know when you hear from him," he went on as he stood up. "And let me know if you figure out what might have been in that safe and if anything else is missing."

"You want me to stay here tonight, *okusan*?" Kazuko said, picking up the dishes, after the detective left.

Maddy summoned a smile. "Nick thought it would be a good idea for me to spend the night elsewhere. I think he was doing the protective male thing, watching out for the frightened little woman. I'm not really fearful, but on the other hand, if I stay here I'll be watching and listening all night. Would you—"

Kazuko didn't hesitate. "You come home with me, *okusan*. I think this Nick guy is right about that if for nothing else."

Maddy saw the concern and curiosity in Kazuko's glance. For a moment she resisted it, but then realized that's what Bart would have done. God help her if she started to become as noncommunicative as him. "Nick's a friend of Lara and Todd Wakefield's," she explained. "I've told you about them, the restaurant people. Lara introduced me to Nick briefly at the wine fair I went to on Tuesday. I ran into him at Pike Place Market after Bart went missing and he offered to drive me back here. My car's in the shop, remember? It should be ready for me around one tomorrow. Dooley promised." She hesitated. "I didn't mention Nick to the detective—I was afraid he might make something of it."

"Mr. Chacha seem okay to you?" Kazuko asked. "He looks like a tough guy—maybe not so much gentleman as you might think. When I drove up tonight I saw him through the window, looking at *dannasan*'s books on the wall."

"People often do that in a strange house, Kazuko. You

can tell a lot about the occupants by the books they have around."

Kazuko nodded reluctantly. Her forehead was still creased. "Isn't the chacha some kind of dance? In Japan we had samba clubs, and I think maybe—"

Maddy spelled Nick's last name for her.

"English is a very strange language," Kazuko said.

"His name's Italian," Maddy pointed out.

"Same-o, same-o," Kazuko said. "What you say—all Greek to me."

Maddy laughed and felt a bit better. She loved this woman. "Don't worry about Nick Ciacia. We'll probably never see him again. Anyway, if Bart doesn't come back by tomorrow, I'm going to take a look through the whole house. I've got to find out if there are any clues around. I need to know if he's just walked out on me, and if not, see if I can figure out what the hell has happened to him. Then I think I'll give Simon Hatfield a call. Bart's district manager. Maybe Saturday. That'll give Bart another day to come back. I don't want to alarm Mr. Hatfield before I have to." She thought for a minute. "If Bart's not back by Saturday morning, something must be wrong, wouldn't you think?"

"I think so now, *okusan*."

Maddy nodded. "Me too, but all the same . . ."

She took a calming breath that came out as a long sigh. "God knows what Bart's reaction is going to be to me calling the police."

"You worry too much, *okusan*," Kazuko said blithely, as if she hadn't just been worrying herself. "You need to just let things roll off your back, like oil."

Maddy laughed. Kazuko frequently mixed up such references. "I think you mean like water off a duck's back. Oil's the stuff you spread on troubled waters." She patted Kazuko's sweater-clad arm. "You're much better at handling Bart than I am. You've lasted a long time. Has he always been . . ."

"Strange? Yes, *okusan*, always. My number one son says to me all the time, 'Chill, Mom.' I think maybe *dan-*

nasan chill too much. Sometimes nice. But sometimes very cold." She tilted her head to one side. "I think you are not so happy with *dannasan.*"

"You think right," Maddy said. "I'm about to leave him. Don't tell the police that, though, or they'll be sure I've bumped him off."

"It's too bad we didn't talk before you married," Kazuko said, her forehead furrowed. "I could have warned you."

Maddy looked at her fondly. "It probably wouldn't have done any good. I thought the sun rose and set on Bart Williams." She sighed and slid off the high stool. "Can we go now? I'm fading fast."

Kazuko enfolded her in a warming hug, then finished putting away the dishes while Maddy sorted out a backpack and some nightwear. She also packed a few toilet articles and picked up the Nordstrom bag to take along.

At the last minute, she wrote a note for Bart, explaining where she'd gone and suggesting he call her the minute he arrived. But he didn't call.

Chapter 5

To Maddy's surprise she slept exceptionally well, and late. Maybe because, despite all her concern about the man she was still married to, this was the first time in six months she had not slept in Bart's house.

She'd heard people who had been burglarized say that they felt violated. She didn't feel that way, she realized. Probably because she had no emotional attachment to Bart's house. What she felt was anger—with Bart, with whomever had entered the house with or without him, with the house itself for being so . . . sterile.

Kazuko insisted on fixing brunch and it was after noon before the two women came back to the house. Looking through the kitchen window at the river, Maddy saw that the sun had burned last night's fog away. The deck was no longer wet.

"I hardly know where to start," she said.

Kazuko pulled the teakettle from the back of the counter and put it on the stove. "I do," she said with a smile as she retrieved a packet of Tazo Zen teabags and the beautiful iron teapot etched with a dragon that she'd given Maddy as a wedding gift.

Maddy smiled back at her, wishing tea was the answer to all her problems. What she really, selfishly, wanted to do was to just walk out of this sterile house forever and get on with her life. She wasn't afraid to stay there, in spite of Nick's warning, but Bart's strange disappearance, added to all his other strange ways, had provided her with the impetus to speed things up in regard to getting out of her marriage. She wanted to pack up all her clothes and personal belongings, call her friend Sally at her real estate office and see if she could get an earlier moving-in date, then get out of here before Bart returned. But that would look more than a little suspicious to the police, and it would be a cowardly thing to do anyway.

She no longer believed Bart might have come with whomever the Old Spice wearer was. Apart from not letting that person smoke, he would have locked the safe back up even when it was empty and he would never have left a painting at anything but the correct, squared-off angle. And he wouldn't have let anyone jimmy the back door.

She was still reasonably sure he'd walk in at any moment as if it were perfectly normal for him to take off and leave her stranded in Pike Place Market. She could almost hear him saying in that cold, clipped voice he'd adopted since shortly after their wedding, "You surely do not expect me to report my every movement, do you, Madison?"

He had commented when he was wooing her that he thought her name "interesting," but lately he had managed to pronounce it more like "medicine." Foul-tasting medicine.

She shook her head. There was no sense in dwelling on Bart's failings as a husband. The Bart she'd married had changed beyond recognition into some kind of hollow excuse for a man. Yes, a hollow man. An empty man.

She was leaving him—that was all that counted. And as soon as he came back from wherever he had gone, she would tell him so.

After she had carefully examined everything in her office, Bart's office, the bedrooms, the bathrooms, the kitchen, and the dining room, she wandered back into the living room and found herself staring at the bookcases that contained Bart's first edition collection. Neither Detective Bradford nor the men who'd come with him had given the neat rows of classics more than a glance. Why would they? But Nick had. Why? Was his interest just as she'd told Kazuko, a mild curiosity about Bart's taste in books? But she'd told him she didn't think Bart had read them, hadn't she? Was that before Kazuko drove up or after? She wasn't sure.

She'd always wondered why Bart would hold on to so many books without ever reading anything other than the two daily newspapers he subscribed to and company literature.

Following a sudden urge, she returned upstairs to Bart's office and went through every single item again. The big mahogany desk held in and out trays and a typewriter. Both trays were empty, but Bart never did let work pile up. Right at the back of one of the little interior drawers in the secretary Bart used when he was figuring out his travel itinerary, she came across a tissue-wrapped bundle. Inside were two bunches of small keys, each on a wire key ring.

Going to the kitchen, she picked up the step stool, which she placed at the base of the bookcase. She could barely reach the lock at the top of the bookcase, and the step stool wobbled as she stood on tiptoe, but the fourth key she tried unlocked the cabinet, and she was able to slide one door aside.

"*Dannasan* isn't going to like you getting in those books," Kazuko said behind her, startling her so she almost fell off the stool. "Those books are like Blackbeard's forbidden room. The one he kept his dead wives in."

"It was Bluebeard who had the forbidden room," Maddy corrected. "Blackbeard was a pirate. Edward Blackbeard Teach."

"Same-o, same-o," Kazuko said. "Not people to be messed with."

Maddy opened a book at random. "Oh my God!" she exclaimed.

"You didn't tear the dustcover, did you?" Kazuko asked, sounding alarmed. "*Dannasan* told me collectible books are worth much more money with good dustcovers."

"There's *money* in here," Maddy said faintly. She passed the book down to Kazuko, who shook it over the carpet. Hundred-dollar bills fluttered down. The housekeeper counted them. "Looks like fifty times a hundred, *okusan*," she said, her voice soft with awe.

Maddy opened another book. Tucked between the front and back covers and the first and last pages she found more hundred-dollar bills. In the next book too, and then another. All stuffed with hundred-dollar bills.

Kazuko started checking books on the lower shelf, muttering something that sounded like "You cash."

"What?" Maddy asked.

"*Yukashita*," Kazuko said. "Means under the floor. Like maybe someplace to hide something. This is like *yukashita*." She frowned, looking up at Maddy. "Maybe better leave the money in here," she suggested. "*Dannasan*'s not going to be happy when he comes home and finds we disturbed his money."

"I don't *care* how unhappy he is," Maddy said, passing down yet another book filled with bills. "This I want an explanation for. I won't do anything with it until I find out where it came from and why it's in the books, but I'm for damn sure not going to leave it in here. Keep going, get it all out."

It took a long time, but eventually they decided they hadn't missed any of the hidden bills. They made a huge pile on the carpet. While Maddy replaced the keys in the drawer where she'd found them, Kazuko went in search of a container and returned with a large wine box; Bart preferred a certain wine, which he had shipped in. A German wine, of course.

They layered the bills in the box, then squatted on the floor beside it and stared at it.

"There must be thousands of dollars here, *okusan*," Kazuko said.

Maddy nodded. "I'd estimate close to two million."

Kazuko sucked in air between her teeth in a hissing sound. "Some kind petty cash!"

They couldn't seem to stop staring at the money. "I've no idea what to do with it," Maddy said finally. "Do you suppose this is what whoever came in the house was looking for?"

"Maybe so. But we don't know what was in that safe. Maybe more money, *okusan*."

"I suppose." Maddy bit her lower lip, again remembering Nick's curiosity about Bart's books. Idle curiosity, or something more? Was it really just a coincidence that he'd bumped into her at the market?

She stored the question in the back of her mind for some deeper thought later and looked at Kazuko. "Could you keep this money at your place?"

Kazuko nodded. "There's that metal footlocker Robert kept after he retired from the army. It's in the bottom of a clothes closet with a quilted cover over it. It has a few of his army papers in it and our birth certificates and other papers, but there's room for the money, I think. Nothing in the bottom part at all."

"Thanks, Kazuko."

They still kept staring at the money. How many more mysteries surrounded Bart Williams? Maddy wondered. How could she have been married to the man for six months without learning any more about him than she knew at the start? Come to think of it, how could she have stayed married to the man for six months?

When the phone rang they both jumped guiltily. Maddy waved Kazuko down as she started to rise, and hurried into the kitchen herself.

"Nick Ciacia here," the voice said.

So. Here he was again. Why? There really was no reason why she should be feeling suspicious of him. He was an attractive man, a nice man. Friendly. He'd been very helpful to her. But all the same, there was something in his attitude that told her he was not being entirely straight with her. After six months of Bart's evasiveness and secretiveness, she was probably overreacting, but if Nick Ciacia had an agenda of his own here, she wished he'd spit it out so she'd know if she could trust him or not.

"Maddy?" he queried. "Are you just going to stand there and breathe?"

"Sorry!" she said. "I was . . . distracted."

"Your husband hasn't shown up?"

"Nope. The Oak River police have put out something called an 'attempt to find,' no, that's not quite—"

"An 'attempt to locate'?"

"Yes, that's it—on the car."

"You did call the police then?"

"Of course. A detective was here for a good chunk of time, along with a couple of lab people who checked for fingerprints and whatever. The detective said he'd be in touch with the Seattle police. When I called him he said they hadn't found any clues to Bart's disappearance. I've been looking for some clues myself, without any luck so far."

She certainly wasn't going to tell him about the money.

"Did the police check hospitals and so forth?"

"So the detective said. They evidently didn't find out anything there either. I doubt they are all that concerned. From the detective's questions, I suspect he's convinced Bart just skipped out on me. Which doesn't seem very probable to me. It would be more likely to be the other way around."

As soon as the words were out of her mouth, she wished she could take them back. There was a moment's silence that persuaded her that Nick had not missed their import.

"I think it would be a good idea for us to talk," he said. "Is it okay for me to come over?"

She was curious to know why he kept bothering—what his personal stake was. But she wasn't quite ready to agree with his every suggestion either. Apart from anything else, she suspected Nick Ciacia could complicate her life in ways she could not yet imagine. It was probably best to keep him at arm's length, at least until she knew which way was up.

"I don't think that's a good idea," she said crisply. "It's entirely possible Bart could walk in right behind you. I don't want to have any more complications in my life than I have already."

"Will you be at your office on Monday?"

"I'm not sure. I have some things I want to do."

"Isn't there anything I can do to help?"

"That's not necessary. But thank you. Why don't I call you whenever everything gets resolved around here? I have your card."

"Okay." He sounded disappointed.

Which, she was forced to admit to her dismay, did not entirely displease her.

After she hung up the telephone, she went up to her bedroom, picked up the phone in there, and punched in the number for Buon Gusto. Yes, Lara was in, working in the office, the receptionist told her.

It took a while to fill Lara in on what had happened with Bart—Lara was not one to listen without questions or dramatic exclamations, usually in Italian. "But what can Todd and I do, *cara*?" she said when Maddy finally got through the story.

"Not a thing," Maddy said. "There's nothing I can do myself except wait and see if Bart shows up."

"Did you tell him you're leaving him?"

Lara was one of three people privy to Maddy's plans. The second was Kazuko—the third was her other close friend, Sally Carstairs, the real estate agent who'd found the condo for her. "Not yet. I was waiting until I had a place to live. I did make an offer on the place I told you about, by the way. Sally was pretty sure it would be accepted, though you can't ever be sure until everything goes through."

"*Bene*. It will be good to have you close again. But

you know, you could have come to stay with Todd and me and—"

"We already discussed that, Lara."

"You are so independent. And stubborn."

Maddy laughed. "So are you."

"This is so true."

"I did want to ask you about something," Maddy added. "I met a man yesterday, name of Nick Ciacia. He says you introduced me to him."

"I did?"

There was a silence, during which Maddy's stomach lurched, then Lara said, "Oh, I remember. The wine fair. So many people. So much fuss. Did you know there was a line marked on the wineglasses and we weren't supposed to pour the Chateau Lafite-Rothschild beyond that? People were supposed to take just a swallow, then spit it out in a bowl. Such deplorable manners. Imagine, almost a hundred dollars a bottle, and they wanted people to spit it out like it was an ordinary wine. Told me not to give them the dregs. Dregs! I held every bottle to the light and there were no dregs. So Todd and I drank the bottom inch. It was very good wine, very mellow. I think we both ended up a little looped." She paused for breath, then went on, "I introduced him to you. Yes, Nick Ciacia, I remember now. Isn't he adorable? So big! Sicilian father, Irish mother. The mixture produced a magnificent package, don't you think? You met him again? You're interested?"

"Not like that, Lara. I've no desire to get involved with any man for some time to come."

"Oh my poor darling, I can for sure understand that." She took a breath. "Todd and I don't really *know* Nick, Maddy. He comes into the restaurant. Knows his ciabatta from his bruschetta. Loves antipasti, especially my insalata caprese."

She hesitated, then said, "Now you must tell me about your meeting with Mr. Ciacia. Are you going to see him again?"

"Have I ever had caprese?" Maddy asked to distract

her. Lara could always be distracted with anything to do with food.

"Surely! One of the simplest and most delicious of starters. Sliced tomatoes—local tomatoes, fresh from the vine—sprinkled with chopped fresh garden-grown basil, and topped with creamy ricotta cheese. Some people prefer mozzarella. And drizzled with the very best extra-virgin olive oil at the last minute. Drizzled, I repeat. Not soaked. And no vinegar—no, never! Best in summertime."

She paused, and Maddy imagined her arching her well-groomed eyebrows. "He's a hunk, that Nick Ciacia. You sure you're not interested? Maybe I'll divorce Todd and take a closer look at Mr. Ciacia myself."

"I was hoping you might know something about him."

"You have heard it all, *cara*. But I can talk to him next time he comes in."

"No, please, don't do that." Tact was not Lara's forte.

Nick Ciacia hadn't exactly lied about knowing Lara and Todd, Maddy conceded after she hung up the phone. But he had *implied* that he knew them more than as a customer in the restaurant. It would seem to be wisest to stay away from Nick Ciacia altogether.

Chapter 6

FRIDAY NIGHT DINNER at Bridget Ciacia's condo, in a Seattle complex not far from Nick's own, was a tradition. Nick loved his mother, so he looked forward to the weekly visit. He enjoyed watching her prepare dinner in her colorful kitchen, which she'd decorated in blue and yellow to match the ceramic dishes her mother-in-law, Nick's grandmother, had bequeathed to her.

Orphaned young, Bridget had grown very close to her mother-in-law, especially after their beloved Alfeo's death. She'd also inherited all of Nonna's recipes.

Not only could Bridget Ciacia serve up great-tasting traditional Irish food like colcannon, soda bread, and various stews—including one made with Guinness—but in order to please Nick's father and widowed grandmother, she'd reinvented herself as a Sicilian cook and had perfected the art.

Nick also admired his mother's attitude toward life. When she wasn't working at the county hospital admissions desk, from which she showed no inclination to retire despite her sixty-four years, she had at least a dozen hobbies, mostly to do with art or music. When at home, she most often dressed, as now, in jeans and a cotton T-shirt. She liked slogans on her T-shirts: "I have an attitude and I know what to do with it." "Girl power!" "Let me do the talking—I'm good at it."

Her long curls of gray-brown hair were tied up in a ponytail. She was a big-boned, good-natured woman—the Irish washerwoman type, she called herself. Earth mother, Nick called her. She had been larger and taller than Nick's slender Sicilian father—"big bosoms, big butt, big heart," Alfeo had teased—and she was still larger than life.

She'd spent a large part of the afternoon hiking along Seattle's waterfront with four of her friends. All five were widows and called themselves "The Loose Women," and were all concerned with keeping their bones strong. They had come in for an espresso with "Bridey"—as everyone called her—and hadn't left until Nick arrived. He'd heard a lot of laughter coming from the apartment when he got off the elevator. "Bridey's a hoot," one of the women had told him—as she always told him.

Bridget, who doted on him, having suffered three miscarriages before successfully birthing Nick, tried every once in a while to get him to call her Bridey, but he couldn't think of her as anyone but Ma.

"Featured on the menu today," she informed him with a fake Italian accent and a kiss to her bunched fingers, "is Coho salmon thrown around at the market, steamed to perfection, and chilled; and Nonna's famous Mediterranean garden bake, which includes artichoke hearts, fresh Roma tomatoes, capers, black olives, and green onions mixed with bread crumbs and chopped parsley and topped with mozzarella. All of this accompanied by home-baked crusty Italian bread. To be followed by cannolis for dessert. Antipasti for starters, of course."

"Sounds great, but you should let me do dinner sometimes, Ma," Nick said, as he always said.

Bridget rolled her green eyes at him and blew her jaggedly cut bangs off her forehead. "When you get married, I'll come to your place for dinner. You can cook then.

Unless your wife prefers to do it, of course. And provided she's as good a cook as you and me."

"That's blackmail!"

"Nagging hasn't worked. Time for a change."

She put a glass of white wine in front of him and poured one for herself. He glanced at the label on the bottle. Bianca. Italia. His mother definitely had a dual persona.

He thought about Maddy Sloane at the wine fair in her glamorous black dress and coat. Their conversation on the phone a couple of hours earlier, if it could be called a conversation, had frustrated him. No word from Bart, Maddy had said. No accident reports involving him. Nick had checked several hospitals himself and discovered nobody knew anything about the man, but he hadn't told her that. She'd want to know why he'd taken it upon himself, and he wasn't about to tell her.

She didn't need his help, she'd said, but he sure wasn't going to wait until "everything was resolved" to see her again. It had taken him more than two decades to come up with anyone who even came close to being the Snowman.

He wondered suddenly if Maddy Sloane could cook, then laughed shortly. That was about the last thing he usually wondered about a woman. He must be getting old.

"What's so funny?" Bridget asked.

"You and your blackmail. Trying to marry me off."

"I don't want you turning into a *mammoni*."

In Italy, he recalled, a *mammoni* was a grown man who lived with his mother.

"I don't remember you inviting me to move in."

She gave a mock shudder. "God forbid. You'd interfere with my love life."

He decided not to go there.

"Speaking of which, how's *your* love life?" she asked.

"That's none of your business, Ma."

She squinted at him. "Uh-huh, just as I thought. You don't *have* a love life, do you? Not a real love life with serious dating, sincere dating, thinking of settling down dating—not just calling the morning after."

"I'm too busy for a love life," he said, as he always said.

"You've been too busy since puberty."

Usually such talk from his mother amused him, but lately he'd been thinking that something *was* seriously missing from his life. Sometimes, by himself in his condo at night, while relishing the peace and quiet, he felt . . . lonely.

"I've dated regularly since puberty, Ma," he protested. "It's just that recently I haven't even had time for a drink with my buddies. I'm keeping up at the gym, swimming, volleyball, taking my vitamins. All the other stuff you worry about. And I haven't met anyone I want to spend forever with. But I do keep looking, Ma, honest." He gave her a sly sideways glance. "I guess you're forgetting you haven't liked any woman I ever brought around to meet you."

"I liked Olivia."

"Olivia liked you. Unfortunately, she didn't like my job. Kept telling me I shouldn't let it interfere with our arrangements. I could just imagine Toss's reaction if I told him I couldn't work a case because I had a date with Olivia."

Bridget sighed. "I guess she wouldn't have worked out. But there must be a woman somewhere who would understand the demands of your work and be supportive." Her green eyes lit up. "Maybe we could hire a matchmaker."

The word reminded him forcibly of Maddy Sloane. Now there was a woman . . .

He broke off that useless line of thought.

"Maybe I *should* become a *mammoni*," he said, to get Bridget off the subject. "I'm sure you'd enjoy giving me the royal treatment. Waiting on me hand and foot. Treating me like a prince. Isn't that the Italian tradition?"

She made a face at him. "Sometimes I revert to the Irish ways. Go wash your hands, okay? Now that you're grown, all I'm required to do is feed you fish on Fridays."

He did as bid, stopping on the way back down the hall, as usual, to look at the photos of his father that his mother had mounted in beautiful pale wood frames many years ago. The light from the clear-faceted globes in the hall fixtures cast fractured shadows across the photographs of Alfeo Ciacia, making it seem as if he really was playing baseball or, in the next frame, mowing the lawn that had surrounded their old house in Chicago, laughing, his head thrown back.

There was a picture of him fishing with Nick on a lake in Ontario, the vibrantly colorful trees in the background dating the occasion to late September or early October.

In the last photo, his father's mouth seemed almost ready to twitch in a smile. It was a formal photograph of Alfeo in uniform when he had become a sergeant in the Chicago Police Department.

Alfeo Ciacia had been forty-five when he died. He'd hoped to get beyond sergeant, to lieutenant at least, and maybe captain or even commander. But as long as Captain Riley was in charge, he'd confided to Nick, there was no chance an Italian was going to get far. Captain Riley, Alfeo had added gloomily, was convinced all Italians, no matter how honest and honorable and hardworking, were mafiosi.

Nick had recognized long ago that the captain's attitude toward and about his father was probably the number one motive for his becoming an FBI agent.

This was probably the last photo that had been taken of Alfeo Ciacia. Nick had outgrown his father by several inches here and there. His Irish grandfather had been very tall, his mother had told him. But Nick and his father had the same black hair, the same Italian nose and craggy face, even a similar pugnacious expression, leavened around the edges with humor.

"Such a long, long time ago," Bridget said from behind him. "A former life." She tucked a hand into his arm. "I was so relieved when you stopped wanting to hunt down the man who killed your father. What was his nickname— the Snowman? He's probably dead himself by now. Or in prison somewhere. Those kind of sneaky, cowardly crooks usually don't change." Her solemn gaze searched his face. "A desire for revenge can destroy a body's soul."

From somewhere deep down he pulled up enough strength of purpose to produce a smile he hoped was believable. "Like you said, Ma, a former life."

Relief brightened her green eyes. "What are you working on now?" she asked. "Anything I might have heard of on the news?"

"Nothing I can tell you about."

She sighed. "As usual. Other mothers can discuss their sons' work with them—me, I had to give birth to 007!"

"Dinner ready?" he asked.

"Just about."

He lingered a moment longer, flexing his shoulders to shake off the shadows of the past, then joined his mother in the kitchen.

She'd set a brightly colored ceramic dish of antipasti on the small table in the dining alcove. Green and black olives, sun-dried tomatoes, the large capers Nonna had preferred, two wedges of cheese, salami, eggplant.

The whole meal was terrific, as always. While they ate, Bridget watched him closely. She'd always been psychic where he was concerned, always known when he was coming down with something, contemplating some mischief, feeling guilty over mischief he'd already committed. He half expected her to feel his forehead.

He was glad he hadn't told her about the information Arnie Arnold had given to him out of the blue a week ago. At the time, he'd been torn, knowing it was her right to know. But he'd decided it would be better to wait until he had something more concrete to tell her. Then he'd tell her everything—how he'd come up with a possible name and identity for the Snowman. How that had led him to Bart Williams and his wife, Madison Sloane.

Bart Williams had disappeared. That had to mean something. . . .

"I'd offer you a penny for your thoughts, but they look desperate dark," Bridget said.

Startled, he discovered she'd served him dessert and he hadn't even noticed. "Sorry, Ma, I've a lot on my mind."

"Care to share?"

He shook his head, forcing a smile. "Not worth the price of admission."

His mother's expression showed disbelief, but to his relief, she let it go and didn't connect his distraction with her former comments about revenge.

Was it really revenge he was looking for, after all these years? he wondered as she enveloped him in a good-bye hug.

Possibly.

But he'd prefer to think his motivation was the nobler one of seeking justice.

Chapter 7

HER HUSBAND, SIMON, was at his office, Irene Hatfield said. He often went in on Saturday mornings, so he could catch up on things without being interrupted every few minutes. "He's sooo dedicated," she gushed.

She was a gushy sort of woman, Maddy remembered. She'd gushed all over Bart on the three occasions Maddy had attended Mawsom events. Bart had responded with the kind of charm he'd used on Maddy before they were married, but had made some very sarcastic comments afterward.

Maddy drove to Mawsom right away.

Simon Hatfield was obviously surprised to see her, but not at all reluctant to take a break from the work he was catching up on. Swiveling his office chair away from his computer, he turned to face her, assuming his familiar benign expression, which she had never quite trusted.

He had a graying mustache that was as bristly as a nail brush and gray hair carefully combed over his scalp from a very low part. He wore a gray shirt, gray slacks. A gray man. He even had gray eyes. Resting his elbows on his desk, he steepled his fingers as she talked, index fingers tapping against his lower lip.

"This is all very shocking," he said after Maddy filled him in on Bart's disappearance. He tapped some more as he mulled over the situation. "According to my predecessor, Bart had always been a very reliable employee. He has certainly proven himself so since I came on board a year ago. I cannot imagine him disappearing in such an untidy manner. You haven't heard anything from him at all?"

Maddy shook her head. "I hoped you might be able to shed some light."

He adopted a rueful expression. Maddy had noted at previous meetings that all of his expressions seemed adopted to fit the occasion.

She leaned forward. "On Thursday, when Bart dropped me off at Nordstrom, he was on his way to a business meeting somewhere in Seattle. Were you there?"

His forehead creased mightily. "I know of no such meeting."

"Could there have been a meeting you didn't know about?"

Shock widened his pale eyes. "I know everything that happens in this company, Madison. I'm a hands-on kind of person."

The suddenly meaningful tone of his voice made that last sentence sound suggestive, she thought, but perhaps her imagination was working overtime.

His district manager had old-fashioned values, Bart had told her, with an edge to his voice. Fancied himself a father to his staff and didn't hesitate to advise them on personal matters that were none of his business.

"Bart told me his meeting was work related," Maddy insisted.

Hatfield shook his head. "Not so." He seemed very sure.

"You're telling me my husband lied to me?"

"It would seem so. There is absolutely no possibility of a business meeting going forward without my knowledge. I'm sorry." For a second or so he didn't look at all sorry, then he evidently remembered his face should fit his words, and the proper mournful expression appeared.

There didn't seem much for Maddy to say to that. Hatfield drummed his fingers on his desk for a couple of minutes, then said, "Your husband had an appointment with a surgeon in Eugene, Oregon, on Friday. Yesterday."

She remembered for the first time that Bart had said something about that.

"Perhaps he simply drove down to Oregon a day early," Hatfield said.

He seemed about to stand up, perhaps concluding that the interview was over, but Maddy shook her head. "He'd hardly tell me he was going to the men's room and then take off for Oregon, wouldn't you think? When he was supposed to drive me to Oak River and I had no other way to get there?"

Red streaks edged his cheekbones. Possibly she'd sounded sarcastic. Or maybe he was shocked that she'd mentioned the men's room.

"Do you know the name of the surgeon in Eugene?" she asked.

"Of course. Dr. Powell. Henry Powell." Before she could ask for a number, he consulted his PDA, then picked up his telephone. Within a couple of minutes he was talking to Dr. Powell, who wasn't giving any useful information—the sound of his irritated voice came through clearly to Maddy.

"Mr. Williams seems to have disappeared," Hatfield said to Dr. Powell.

The sounds on the other end became less irritated and more questioning.

"We have no idea," Hatfield said. "Yes, of course we'll get the information to you at once. I'll see to it personally."

When Hatfield hung up, he paused to assume a properly regretful expression, then said, "I'm afraid your husband did not keep his Friday three o'clock appointment with Dr. Powell. Dr. Powell had an emergency surgery yesterday morning, but he was through well before noon and waited until four o'clock to see Bart. He was quite aggravated that Bart did not appear."

He clucked his tongue against the roof of his mouth. "This is not good for Mawsom Pharmaceuticals's reputation. Missing appointments. Not good at all."

Maddy bit back the rude response that had sprung to her tongue. Standing, she picked up her shoulder bag from the floor.

"I'd like to look in my husband's office—see if there are any clues to his whereabouts on his desk calendar—"

He was already shaking his head. "I couldn't possibly allow that without Bart's permission."

"But we don't know where he is—"

"I'm sure he'll turn up. He's a reliable man. However, if I can assist you in any other way, Madison, please don't hesitate to call."

He shook her proffered hand and held on to it, covering it with his other hand. For a second, she was afraid he was going to pull her in for a hug—and he wasn't at all a person she wanted to hug.

"I was very pleased when I heard Bart had found himself a suitable wife at last," he said, pasting a simpering smile on his face. "I have to admit that after I'd been around these parts for a couple of months, settling in, you might say, I joshed him about being single at his age. I look upon Mawsom as a family company, you see, and I prefer to work with people who have families and embrace family values. That's the fast track to success, in my humble opinion."

Maddy didn't think he was at all humble. She thought he might have been very successful as a televangelist. She was relieved when he released her hand—she'd been considering a knee to the groin maneuver she'd learned in that self-defense course.

Chapter 8

MADDY SAT IN her car in Mawsom's parking lot, pondering the depressing possibility that Bart had married her to please his boss and solidify his position. Was that why he had refused to consider a long engagement? Had he been disappointed as he got to know her better? When he got through doing whatever he'd gone off to do, was he going to be as happy as she would be to cut the tie that hadn't quite bound?

When he did show up, and before she told him she was leaving, she was going to find out from him exactly why he'd married her and why he'd become a totally different man almost as soon as he'd put a ring on her finger. Otherwise she'd spend the rest of her life wondering.

Her cell phone rang while she was deciding what to do next. She thought it might be Detective Bradford.

"Hey, you don't have your cell phone turned off. Does that mean you're ready to reach out?"

Nick Ciacia. Mr. Persistent.

It worried her that she'd felt a lift of her spirits at the sound of his voice. "I thought Bart might call," she said.

"Did he?"

"Not so far."

"Any news at all?" he asked.

"Nothing."

"Ah. I'm sorry. Where are you?"

"I'm in Mawsom Pharmaceuticals's parking lot. I've been talking to Bart's boss."

"Great. I'm not far from there. I'm glad I caught you. I wanted to invite you to lunch, but I was afraid you might not want to drive into the city. I was going to suggest a halfway point, but as you're already here and it's such a beautiful day, how about the Space Needle?"

"I don't have time for lunch," she said. "I have things to do. I'm going to question the people who work in the market. The Space Needle would be a bit out of the way." She was hedging, knowing the idea of lunch with Nick was appealing, but still not sure if she trusted the man. She definitely wasn't indifferent to him.

"The body needs protein," he said in a firm voice. "My mother tells me that all the time. She says if I don't have protein, I'll lose my hair. You don't want to lose *your* hair, do you?"

She laughed. It felt good to laugh. "Not particularly."

Maybe she *should* lunch with him—she might find out why he was sticking around, why he'd shown up in the first place, and if there was any significance in his coming into her life at that particular moment.

He evidently sensed she was weakening. "You've been up there in Sky City, the rotating restaurant, surely? Great views. You get in that glass-fronted elevator and shoot right up there—makes you feel like you've left all your troubles down below. How about I meet you in the restaurant? We could talk about what you've found out so far, maybe come up with a plan of action."

Okay, so he definitely had some special interest in her search for Bart. And evidently he wasn't going to just go away.

She glanced at her watch. Twelve forty-five. She

should probably eat anyway. Having company would take her mind off Hatfield's revelation.

She was making excuses to accept Nick's invitation, she realized. She might as well face facts—the man attracted her.

What the hell was she thinking? Hadn't she learned anything in the last six months? Before that, even. Where men were concerned, she was a walking disaster.

In which case, it would probably be best not to . . . Oh, the hell with all this dithering. "Okay," she said. "I guess I could spare an hour or so."

"Great," he said, sounding really pleased.

Leaving her troubles down below might feel good, she thought. And it wasn't as if he was asking her to dinner. Lunch was casual. Lunch was innocuous.

NICK WAITED UNTIL Maddy's Pontiac Grand Prix pulled out of the Mawsom lot and disappeared in traffic, not wanting her to suspect he'd been following her, especially not wanting her to know he'd followed her all the way from Oak River. This morning he'd watched her walk into Mawsom's plant and then out again, admiring how shapely she looked in her navy pantsuit and crisp white blouse. He had called her from a street near Mawsom's parking lot.

He hated pushing her like this, concerned it might make her suspicious of his interest, but his window of opportunity was limited.

Twenty minutes later, he and Maddy were sitting opposite each other at a window table in Sky City, the restaurant just below the observation deck of the Space Needle, Seattle's famous landmark.

Until Nick mentioned the weather, Maddy hadn't realized the early morning clouds had dissipated. In the distance, Mount Rainier was as majestic as always, a study in black and white, sharply etched against a clear blue sky.

Both rows of the tables that stretched all the way around the circular restaurant were full, but people were keeping their voices down. Seattle was a polite city.

Maddy could smell garlic and rosemary wafting from a nearby table, beckoning her. She realized she was hungry.

"I'd forgotten it's brunch-only on Saturday," Nick apologized. "We do have some choice though."

Nick was dressed as casually as before. She had the idea that his jeans and brown leather jacket were his regular uniform. Once they'd ordered their starters, entrées, and drinks, she told him about her conversation with Simon Hatfield, more to see what Nick would have to say than with any desire to impart information.

"Odd that Hatfield would deny Bart had a business meeting," he said after the waiter served their salads.

She thought about the implications of that. "You think he was lying? He's a weird old duck, fancies himself a fatherly type, talks about family values, but there's something about him that's— Well, I may be a poor judge of character, but he strikes me as a bit on the sleazy side."

"He made a pass at you?"

"No way. I'd have decked him at the first hint. But I had the impression he wanted to. I've sensed that every time I've been around him. Fatherly types often turn out to be old leeches."

Nick made a mental note never to act in a fatherly manner toward Maddy, or any other woman, for that matter. "You don't think Hatfield was lying about the meeting?"

She put her fork down. "I took it for granted that Bart had lied."

"He lied often?"

The waiter arrived with their entrées before she could answer. Shrimp omelette for her, prime rib and roast potatoes for him.

She wasn't sure she wanted to answer Nick's question. "I might have guessed you'd be a meat and potatoes man," she said.

He shook his head. "I eat a lot of Italian food, but the prime rib here is as unbeatable as the view."

Maddy looked out the window. The restaurant had re-volved enough to show them all of Elliott Bay, the sun-light dazzling on the blue water and on the white superstructure of the ferry crossing to Bainbridge Island. Several sailboats and power boats were taking advantage of the good weather.

Evidently sensing his question had made her uncom-fortable, Nick changed the subject. "I don't really know too much about you and your husband. Have you been married long? How did you meet? Had Bart been married before?"

She squinted at him. "Is there a prize if I give the right answers?"

"I'm sorry," he said at once. "I was born with an in-quiring mind. When I was a kid, my mother called me Snoopy. Confused hell out of me. Until I was six I thought I was a dog."

"*My* mother would call you a Nosey Parker," Maddy said, but she couldn't help laughing.

"I just want to help, Maddy," he said. "Having been there at the start, so to speak, I feel as if I'm part of the action, but I don't really know what the action is. I don't mean to intrude where I'm not welcome, but I do want to help. I can't help if I don't know the background."

He looked very earnest, very sincere.

It was entirely possible that he was telling the truth. And she couldn't imagine what harm could come from filling him in on the past. She didn't have to tell him everything. She surely wasn't going to mention the money she'd found in Bart's books.

And she hadn't yet decided how to proceed in her search for information about Bart. Maybe just talking about him would encourage her subconscious to provide some advice.

She sighed. "I usually avoid talking about my marriage to anyone, even Lara. It makes me feel stupid. I'm good at my job, I make a lot of money, I can balance my check-book, stay out of debt, make sensible decisions every day. I don't cry in sad movies, and I can bench-press twenty pounds over my own weight. I'm even a good cook. . . . Why are you smiling?"

"Just a stray thought, sorry. Go on."

"I read a book by Michael Connelly, the mystery writer, where his detective character said everyone has a fatal flaw. So my point is—I have this one fatal flaw. I'm inevitably dumb when it comes to men. I'm some kind of magnet for men who lie. Send me a man who tells lies, and I'm guaranteed to fall for him."

Remember that lesson, she instructed herself as Nick's mouth twitched. But then the twitch became a sympathetic expression. He really did have a good face, even though he didn't smile much—there was a warmth that started in his eyes and moved to his mouth. Good strong mouth too. Firm.

"Six months," she said abruptly. "Bart and I have been married six months. Bart's forty-four, fourteen years older than me, but he said—" She broke off. Bart had said he'd never met anyone he wanted to spend his life with until he met her. He'd been quick with pretty speeches when they met. "It's his first marriage; mine too. I came close a couple of times before Bart, but . . ."

She took a breath. Just answer his questions, she reminded herself. "Mawsom Pharmaceuticals tried to recruit me early this year. At the time, things were looking shaky for dot-com companies, thousands of jobs cut. My own company seemed to be surviving, but it never hurts to have another bird in the bush, so I agreed to talk to Mawsom's staffing director. As I walked into Mawsom's lobby, this amazingly good-looking man with platinum blond hair came toward me, smiling, his hand outstretched."

She smiled wryly, ate a little more of her delicious omelette, then went on. "One of the very young women at Mawsom told me at the annual summer picnic that Bart was the 'rise up on your toes and yell *take me, I'm yours!* kind of gorgeous.' And she wasn't far off. 'You must be Dr. Jamieson,' he said to me. 'I'm Bart Williams.' I was so—what my mother would call gobsmacked—by his looks, I was almost ready to pass myself off as Dr. Jamieson."

Instead she'd told Bart her name and he'd apologized, saying he was expecting to meet a new Mawsom customer at that same time. He'd heard, he said, that Dr. Jamieson was extremely beautiful, so it was a natural mistake.

A week later Maddy went to Lara and Todd Wakefield's restaurant, where she had arranged to meet with Mawsom's senior recruiter and a couple of the hiring managers whom she would be recruiting for if she accepted their job offer. She arrived early, and while she was waiting and chatting with Lara, in walked Bart again, alone. They talked briefly, and he asked for her business card. She thought he might be one of the people she was there to meet, but he wasn't. He was a pharmaceutical sales rep, and he was *personally* interested in Maddy Sloane. He'd made that fairly obvious. Lara's mouth had formed a silent "Wow!" as he walked away.

"He called me a couple of days later, after I decided Mawsom wasn't for me."

"You turned the job down?"

"Yes."

"Why?"

She shrugged. "Mawsom's senior recruiter didn't offer as much base as I have at TheHub."

Bart had invited her to a Mawsom social event, after which they dated awhile. "He was considerate and generous. Flowers, dinners, thoughtful little gifts. And he had these wonderfully courteous European manners. I was smitten senseless. My friends said he was a great catch. I took him up to Victoria and introduced him to my parents. They raved about him—they'd never thought much of previous guys I'd known. I thought it was Someday and he was my Prince, come at last."

Nick was frowning. She wasn't sure why.

"I was totally wrong," she said, and watched his face clear. She kept watching. "I think part of the problem was that I was coming out of my second failed relationship. Richard had admired me only for my brains, which became tiresome, while Buzz had been interested only in my body. Bart seemed to like everything about me. *Seemed* being the operative word. I was all wrong about Bart, but I didn't know that until I was dumb enough to marry him."

"What happened?" he asked, suddenly leaning forward, his dark eyes intense.

"He became a different person," she said. "One who was very critical, unfriendly, cold. It was a dramatic change. Shocking, even. I had no idea what I'd done to turn him off. Moving from the city to Oak River, I felt isolated. I had my work and my friends at work, but Bart didn't want my friends to visit and apparently had none of his own he wanted to invite over."

"But that's typical of abusive behavior, Maddy. First you isolate the spouse, cut her off from everyone and everything, cut her down, make her feel worthless. Did he ever—"

"Never." She hesitated again. "He didn't abuse me, and I never felt worthless—I've a healthy dose of self-esteem. I was mostly bewildered, puzzled, confused. Whatever happened, happened right after we left the altar. I married sweet, fascinating Prince Charming, and he morphed into a disinterested and uninteresting person with the personality of a flowerpot. A cold, unfeeling flowerpot. If our wedding had been a TV soap opera, I'd have believed he'd been replaced right after the reception by his evil twin. At first, I thought he was just having difficulty adjusting to married life after being on his own for so long. The only times he was even halfway pleasant toward me was when we attended Mawsom's company events. I think he didn't want to embarrass himself in front of his colleagues."

She was revealing far too much to this man. Next she'd be telling him how disappointed she'd been the few times she and Bart had had sex. Wham, bam, and not even a thank you, ma'am. She'd hoped he'd get better at it. Had thought at first she could teach him. But before long she hadn't wanted to have sex with him anymore and had moved to a separate bedroom.

Cut to the chase, she told herself. "Long before Thursday, I was ready to leave Bart. It sounds stupid to say it, but I was busy and I kept putting off the upheaval. But I finally decided the time had come. All I had to do was pack my stuff and move out, move on, get on with my life. And then he vanished. I feel like an escaped convict who's hacked her way through a tunnel only to find out she's still inside the electrified perimeter fence. How can I walk out on someone who isn't there!"

She sighed. "I looked at a condo the day Bart disappeared. I even made an offer on it. What do you suppose the police would make of that?"

He didn't answer. "Could Bart be gay?" he asked after a minute or two.

She'd wondered that herself from time to time. "If he is, he's hiding way back in the closet." She shook her head. "He never seems to be interested in men—that way or any other. He doesn't even have male friends. Or at least none he's ever introduced me to. Even the best man at our wedding didn't seem all that close to him. Nice guy, but I haven't seen him since. I can't even remember his name."

She paused, then decided, *What the hell.* "I thought it was possible Bart might be having an affair with some other woman. He's always buying new underwear, new shirts. That's supposed to be a clue, I understand. At least that's what Lara told me."

"You confided in Lara?"

"In both Lara and Sally. They're my closest friends. Sally's a real estate agent. I don't tell Lara everything, though. She has a tendency to advise me."

"You don't want advice?"

"I don't need it. I know what needs to be done. The marriage isn't working, hasn't worked from day one, and there are no children. I gave it six months to be fair. Now it's time to opt out."

She thought about, but decided not to mention, Simon

Hatfield's suggestion to Bart that he should get a wife. There was something demeaning about that whole possibility, and she didn't want to bring it up or even think about it.

"As well as saying Bart didn't have a Mawsom meeting on Thursday, Hatfield told me Bart was supposed to have a meeting with a surgeon in Eugene yesterday. A Dr. Powell. Bart didn't show up. Hatfield called the surgeon while I was there. He sounded very irritated. Powell, I mean. At least until Hatfield told him Bart had gone missing."

She sighed. "Hatfield said Bart's always been very conscientious. I don't know what to think."

"What kind of routine does Bart have?"

"He's on the road a lot, of course. It's the nature of his job, with three states to cover."

"You haven't noticed anything out of the ordinary lately? Any change in habits?"

She glanced at him sharply. He was asking a lot of questions. But he was a good listener. He looked totally relaxed. He'd finished his prime rib and his second cup of coffee. Her omelette was half gone. And that was enough, she decided. It had looked as if it were made with at least a half dozen eggs, not to mention the hundred or so cocktail shrimp.

Talking to Nick was helping her clarify her picture of the situation. And apparently Nick really did want to help. Trouble was, she still didn't know why.

"I'm weighing a suggestion or two," he said. "That's why I'm asking about his routine. Is it always the same? Can you think of anything unusual—anything at all?"

"Mmm." She thought about it. "There's nothing I can put my finger on. Except—"

The waiter showed up to take their plates and ask if they were ready for dessert. They were. They both chose the chocolate brownie with vanilla bean ice cream and chocolate sauce.

"Except?" Nick prompted when their desserts arrived.

Maddy took a bite of the brownie and sauce and took

a moment more to appreciate the taste. "As I told you, Bart seemed nervous lately. That's strange, because as long as I've known him, which admittedly isn't very long, he's never shown any emotion about anything, except a couple of times when he was starting out on trips, when he acted a little nervous. He never wants to talk about his business trips. He'll come back to the house and I'll ask how it went and he'll say okay. That's about it. Before we were married, when he acted as if he cared about me, I questioned him about his job, and he said it was a perfect job for him and he was happy to have it. But he is not a man who seems happy—at least not since our marriage, not since he changed. On those occasions when he seemed nervous and I asked him why, he got very tight-lipped and said there were aspects of his work I had no need to know." She looked at Nick directly. "What suggestions do you have?"

"Have you considered that he might have made enemies? Maybe he wasn't all that charming outside the home either."

He stopped speaking abruptly and concentrated on his dessert for a few minutes. "You don't call it home, do you?" he said at last. "You say, 'Bart came back,' 'Bart drove me to Oak River,' and 'Back to the house,' but you don't say 'home.' "

"I don't think of it as home," Maddy said.

Nick looked at her levelly and she felt the connection again that she'd felt during the storm, the day they met. She didn't look away.

After a minute, he went on, his gaze still holding hers. "Perhaps his enemies were following him and he saw them at the same time he saw you, so he told you he was going to the rest room. Maybe he didn't want them to know he was meeting you, didn't want to put you in harm's way, and knew they wouldn't recognize you. So then he tried to get away. Either he did get away and then drove to your house and emptied the safe and went into hiding, or else whoever was following caught up with him and is holding him—maybe for information, maybe for ransom."

"I guess you must watch a lot of television."

He looked surprised, then laughed shortly. "Only the cops and robbers shows."

"That's what I thought. For an accountant you have one hell of an imagination."

"You're not impressed by my attempts at detection?"

"Well, okay, not all of it is too far out. Someone did get into our house and found the safe and maybe took off with a stash of money or something they considered valuable." She thought for a while. "I hadn't thought of Bart catching sight of someone at the market. He did kind of look around and scowl when I first saw him, but I just thought he was scowling at *me*. I guess you could be right. It would go a long way toward explaining his behavior. I've no idea who would be his enemy though." She laughed shortly. "Unless it was a former wife."

"Did he have one?"

"Not that he told me about."

She paused to pour some coffee from the carafe the waiter had left. The dessert was wonderful, but very sweet. "I'd actually *thought* of kidnapping. I even suggested it to Detective Bradford. But nobody's called me with threats or demands. You'd think they would have by now. As for information Bart might have, what would it be?"

"I keep coming back to drugs." He hesitated. "Look, don't get me wrong, this is just a thought—is it possible Bart *could* be dealing drugs?"

"He didn't carry the kind of street drugs people want."

"OxyContin is a legitimate medication, a painkiller used by some terminal cancer patients, I believe, yet it's number one on the hit parade drug list right now," Nick said. "People crush it into a powder and snort it or inject it."

"How do you know that?"

"TV news. Newspaper reports."

"You're saying it's possible Bart *is* trafficking in drugs.

I'd hate to think you were right. That would be a dreadful thing, to think I'm married to a man involved in that kind of activity. We're not going to see any real lessening of crime as long as people are getting hooked on drugs. It's so damn destructive."

She shivered. "I can't swear Bart wouldn't do such a thing. He's so secretive about everything, I wouldn't be surprised to learn he's been leading a whole other life while he's on his trips."

"Some kind of criminal activity, you think?"

She looked at him helplessly, her expression so suddenly weary that Nick wanted to . . .

Wanted to what? Yeah, okay, he knew what he wanted to do, but he sure as hell wasn't going to do it even if Maddy Sloane was willing, which she had given no signs of.

"I guess it doesn't do much good to wonder why or how Bart vanished, anyway," she said slowly. "It would probably be better to concentrate on the *where to* and hope to find out the why later." She reached around to where she'd hung her shoulder bag on her chair. "I've brought along a photo of him. I thought I'd show it to the vendors in the market, see if they saw him the day he disappeared, or maybe saw him *with* someone."

"Good thinking. May I see the photo?"

She fumbled around in the bag for what seemed a long time, then started unpacking it. Nick watched. He was always amazed at the amount of stuff women could get into their handbags. Maddy pulled out a makeup bag, a key ring with multiple keys attached to a hefty-looking object—a blackjack? No, that was her pepper spray, he remembered. Out came a notebook, a pocket calculator, a fat wallet, a small hairbrush, a toothbrush, toothpaste, floss, sunglasses, and an envelope.

He eyed the formidable pile on the table. "You forgot your hand weights?" he asked as she handed the envelope to him.

She made a face at him.

His amusement faded as he studied the picture he'd removed from the envelope.

"It's half of our wedding photo," she explained. "I used Photoshop to cut myself out of it. Seemed very symbolic. It's actually the only photo I have of Bart. He doesn't like having his photo taken."

"Why not? He's not exactly homely."

"It seems strange to me too. He could be a photographic model and make a fortune. But he even balked at having this photo taken, but I insisted, and he said he supposed he could frame it and keep it on his desk at work. I don't know if he ever did."

Nick could think of several reasons why a man would not want to have his photograph taken: something in his past, something he didn't want anyone to know, something that caused him to keep a low profile. This would go along with his own suspicions about Bart Williams. But he had to be careful here to follow the evidence and not jump to conclusions based on speculation. "If the meeting he was supposed to go to on Thursday wasn't a business meeting, what kind of meeting could it have been?" he asked.

Maddy was suddenly gazing at him with wary eyes. She had put down her spoon some minutes ago, evidently losing interest in her dessert. "I've no idea who he was meeting. Or why."

"Is he a member of anything? Kiwanis? Rotary? How about hobbies? Anything that would involve meetings?"

"He really doesn't do anything except work—at least he hasn't in the six months that we've been married."

"How about people he knows, old friends? You said he emigrated from Germany. Did he come directly to Seattle? Or did he live anywhere else in the United States? Somewhere he might have gone back to?"

She frowned. "You know what? I've no idea. He's never said. And I hadn't even realized that he hadn't said." She paused. "When we applied for a marriage license, he gave his birthplace as Stuttgart. I don't think any other place came up."

"Did he become an American citizen?"

"He must have, because I know he votes."

"So he must have naturalization papers. Might they have been in the safe that was emptied?"

"It's possible, but I don't know."

"Did he have a passport? I'm wondering if he might have left the country. You might take a look around at home, see if you can find his papers or a passport."

She nodded. "I'll do that."

She glanced around distractedly and saw that they had come full circle and were looking out on Elliott Bay again. She'd completely missed seeing Lake Union and a repeat of the downtown buildings. "Do you see our waiter? I should really get going. I don't know what time the market closes on Saturdays."

"Six o'clock. With some variation among the vendors." He hesitated, trying to decide how best to lead into his next suggestion. "Why are you going to question the vendors? I mean, you've already admitted you don't like your husband a whole hell of a lot. You're ready to leave him. So why go to all this bother?"

"Don't think I haven't considered just letting the police handle everything." She sighed. "As I told you before, I expected to be free by now. I was going to tell Bart Thursday night that I'd found a condo. I was excited. Happy. I was planning to move out right away. That night. Rent a place in Seattle until the condo deal went through. Now I'm stuck."

She chewed on her lower lip for a few seconds, then looked down at the gold ring on the third finger of her left hand. "Bart's still my husband. I feel a certain responsibility toward him. I can't just go gaily off to a new life when I don't have any idea what's happened to him. If something *has* happened to him, I'd feel guilty. If nothing's happened to him and he just shows up in his own sweet time, then I can feel okay about moving out and starting divorce proceedings. Does that make sense?"

"You're telling me you are an honorable woman?"

"If you want to put it that way. You don't think much of that?"

"I think it's admirable." And he wanted very much to believe it. He did believe it, but maybe just because he wanted to. He still wasn't quite ready to count on it.

"I think I should come with you," he said.

He liked the way her eyebrows twitched together when she was puzzled. "To the market—asking questions," he explained.

She leaned forward and met his gaze directly, her eyes narrowed. "Why would you *do* that, Ciacia?"

Uh-oh, He'd have to make a case for himself now or risk an outright brush-off.

"Fess up," she said bluntly before his brain had a chance to kick in. "You've either fallen madly in love with me and can't bear to have me out of your sight, which I doubt very much considering our brief acquaintance, and I certainly wouldn't want to encourage you if you're some kind of mad stalker. Or you have an agenda of your own, which I suspect involves my missing husband."

Normally he adored intelligent women, but he could have wished this one was just a tad dumber. He turned over several excuses in rapid suggestion, discarded each in turn, including the one where he tried to convince her he just enjoyed her company and wanted to be her friend, even though there was a lot of truth in that one and truth always played better than an outright lie. But she'd just told him she'd been stupid to fall in love with the guy she'd married and had been stupid about men all along. He decided he was going to have to offer her a modified version of the truth. "Maybe we should have another cup of coffee," he said.

She nodded and settled back with an air of satisfaction.

"I do like you, Maddy, and I do want to help you," he began after pouring more coffee from the carafe and passing her the cream.

"But?"

"But I haven't been exactly straight with you."

"I figured that much out for myself."

"I'm not a stevedore, which was your first guess, if you remember! I do have a CPA license. That part's true. I supported myself doing people's taxes while I was going through college."

"U Dub? University of Washington?"

"WSU." He wasn't about to mention his later education.

"You're a Washington native?"

"I grew up in Chicago." He watched her face closely. Nothing in her expression changed.

He went on. "My father was a police officer there. He died when I was thirteen. Twenty-three years ago."

Again he waited.

No reaction.

"As a matter of fact, I became a police cadet when I was in high school, but I was also a math whiz, which is why I got into accounting."

"And?" she prompted.

"I've had some experience with investigation."

"You're a PI? I knew you had some kind of ulterior motive!"

When you were lying and wished you didn't have to lie, it was best to either ignore questions or find a way around them. "When I was a kid, I ODed on tales of King Arthur. I wanted to be a knight, a defender and zealous upholder of a cause, the devoted champion of a lady, tie her ribbons on my lance. Later on I amended the ambition a tad. 'Down these mean streets a man must go who is not himself mean.' "

Her eyebrows rose.

"Raymond Chandler—the mystery author. He said that. The last part. I'm mixing my literary references, Maddy."

She regarded him with great suspicion. Possibly she sensed that he was throwing out a crock full of persiflage designed to keep him from having to answer too specifically.

"What do you do?" she asked after a moment's pause.

"Investigate insurance fraud? Check people's backgrounds, their credit ratings? Find missing persons?"

"I've been known to spend time tracking people down, sure."

"Why didn't you tell me that in the beginning?"

"I didn't want to worry you. You had enough on your mind." He rushed on. "Right now I'm looking for someone."

He paused to reflect. He certainly couldn't tell her about the Snowman. Given her intelligence and Bart Williams's semi-albino appearance, she was likely to put two and two together.

"I'm looking for a man named . . . Quentin." He had no idea where that name had come from, but he was stuck with it now. "It seems possible that your husband might have been acquainted with Quentin at one time—might be able to tell me where Quentin is now."

He was quite proud—justifiably so, he thought—of this story. It was at least close to the truth.

"What makes you think Bart would know this guy?"

He brought up his most innocent expression. "You remember I told you my mother called me Snoopy when I was a little kid? I guess that turned me on to the *Peanuts* strip. So this one time Charlie Brown was in bed, looking up at the ceiling, and he said something like 'Every once in a while I ask, Why me, Lord?' and the answer comes back: 'Oh, your name just happened to come up.' "

"Bart's name happened to come up in connection with Quentin?"

"You catch on quick."

"What did Quentin do? Why are you looking for him?"

"Let's just say Quentin doesn't have a sterling character."

He was beginning to dread the narrowing of her eyes. Here it was again. "You were *following* Bart on Thursday, weren't you? That's why you showed up right after he disappeared?"

She was no dummy, this woman, he thought again.

She leaned forward. "You were *following* him—so you know where he went, where he is."

He shook his head. "I lost him soon after he dropped you off at Nordstrom. I think he turned into Pike Place Market, but I can't be sure."

Tight-lipped, she stared at him. "So then you followed me instead?"

He nodded. "At a respectful distance."

"When I was shopping in Nordstrom?"

"Yes."

"When I had lunch with Sally?"

He nodded.

"You were *spying* on me. Why?"

"I thought you'd lead me back to Bart."

"Then why didn't you keep on following him after he showed up? How did you know I was his wife? Did you *arrange* to meet me at the wine fair?"

"Could we do this one question at a time?" he asked, at the same moment the waiter showed up to take their dessert plates. "Wouldn't you like to finish your dessert?" he added as the waiter hovered.

"I-do-not-want-the-rest-of-my-dessert," she said with great emphasis.

The waiter rolled his eyes at Nick, which didn't appear to help Maddy's mood.

"I lost him again just as you did," Nick said after the waiter discreetly withdrew, taking Maddy's dessert with him. "The munchkins got in the way."

The truth was, of course, that he'd been enjoying watching Maddy and hadn't seen Bart approach until the man had already spoken to her. *Then* the children got in his way.

"I heard your name in the course of my investigation," he went on. "Only that you were Bart Williams's wife, nothing else. I recognized your name when Lara introduced us." That was a slight twisting of the truth. He'd known damn well who she was when he angled for an intro.

Her forehead was still furrowed, her eyes narrowed.

"You talked about him seeing an enemy. Are you the enemy? He saw *you*? Is that what happened? He saw you watching me and that's why he went past me in such a hurry? He was getting away from *you*?"

She'd make a pretty good agent, he thought admiringly, even as he scrambled to come up with a denial.

"He wouldn't have known me, Maddy," he said simply. "There was no reason for him to try to avoid me."

He could see she wasn't convinced. "I'm not your husband's enemy, Maddy. I'm Quentin's enemy." Just a little more twisting of the truth—substituting Quentin for the Snowman.

"How come you haven't asked if *I* know Quentin?" she asked.

"I'd have thought you'd tell me that when I mentioned him. *Do* you know him? Do you know where he is?" He leaned forward, gazing at her intently, wishing he'd come up with some other story. He was already tired of the nonexistent Quentin.

"No, I don't know Quentin. I've never known anyone named Quentin. And I've never heard Bart mention anyone named Quentin. Is that his first name or his last?"

"I don't know." That was at least an honest answer.

Maddy's eyes glazed, unseeing, then focused again. On him.

Uh-oh.

"You're an accountant *and* an investigator? Did Quentin rob a bank? You think Bart helped him?"

"Whoa! I don't think anything of the kind." He played her own method back at her. "Why would *you* think it?"

Her facial expression went through several minor contortions, then she sat back in her chair, took a couple of breaths, shrugged, and reached for her coffee. There was a slight tremor in her hand, he noticed. It worried him. Just when he'd begun to believe she was totally innocent—a deceived woman, more to be pitied than suspected of knowing anything about her husband's past or present—he was starting to get suspicious again. What was she afraid of? And where had that bank robber scenario come from?

"Why are you looking for Quentin?" she demanded. "Has someone hired you to find him?"

He screwed his mouth sideways in what he hoped looked like a regretful grimace. "Sorry, that's privileged information."

"You're a lawyer as well as a CPA?"

"No."

"Well, I won't believe you're a priest. So what's privilege got to do with anything?"

"Let's just say I operate on a need-to-know basis."

"In other words, you aren't going to tell me anything about Quentin or Bart's relationship to him. But you want to help me find Bart."

"That pretty well sums it up."

"What you really want is to find Bart yourself."

"I think he could aid in my investigation, yes."

She studied his face for a long moment, then asked, "How much?"

"Say what?"

"How much do you charge for your investigations?"

"For you, nothing. We're friends, aren't we? We've had a date." He smiled as ingratiatingly as he knew how and gestured at their bright surroundings.

Didn't fool her, not for a second.

"This is not a date, it's a business meeting. And the only relationship we have is a business relationship. Let's talk plain talk, okay? We may have different motives, but we both want to find Bart. If you have expertise in finding people, I'd be a fool not to accept your assistance. But if you won't let me pay you, then I won't allow you to accompany me."

The underlying message being, Nick recognized, that she wanted to be in control. He signaled the waiter to bring their check, grabbed it before she could, and put his credit card in the folder.

The price was steep, but worth it, he thought, not only for the meal but for the progress he was making with

Maddy Sloane. "Okay," he said. "I'll accept payment if I get results."

"No, that won't be—"

"I *always* get results," he assured her. And assured himself at the same time that the end quite often justified the means. "Trust is a beautiful thing, Maddy," he added, making solid eye contact, his brown eyes to her blue.

She let him hold her gaze, her expression stubborn, unyielding, and then she let go—he saw the softening happen in her eyes. "Okay," she said.

Gotcha, he thought, and spared a glance for Lake Union, just coming around for the second time.

Chapter 9

SHE'D HANDLED THAT rather well, Maddy thought as Nick followed her into the glass-fronted elevator. She'd let him think he'd persuaded her to trust him, when she was actually planning on using his offer of help while keeping a close watch on him until she found out exactly what he was up to. She was pretty sure she'd managed not to show her shock when he'd mentioned accounting and investigating together. At that moment, a vivid image of Bart's wall of collectible books stuffed with hundred-dollar bills had appeared in her mind like a pop-up advertisement on a computer. An advertisement of Bart's guilt.

Nick stayed close beside her as she questioned owners of the various stalls in Pike Place Market's main arcade, starting at the other end from Rachel the pig. The perennially popular market was even more crowded than it had been on Thursday.

"I've heard that around nine million people visit the market every year," Nick said. "I think they're all here today."

"At least nobody's in costume this time," Maddy said.

She showed Bart's photograph to all the craftspeople with negative results until they reached a somewhat shriveled elderly man in a battered and stained Stetson that was too big for him. He made whimsical copper earrings and pins in the shapes of horses and cows, cowboys with lassos, cowgirls in skirts, Santa Claus in a cowboy hat.

"I might have seen this here hombre," he said, tapping the photo with a gnarled, tobacco-stained finger. "Couldn't tell you when, though. Hombre I'm thinkin' of had a gal with him, right buxom gal. Said they was on their honeymoon. He bought a whole heap of gear for his bride."

He smiled at Nick. "A woman's heart is like a campfire. If'n you don't tend to it regular, you'll likely lose it. Your little lady has pierced ears, I see. You want to look at them earrings there? Copper's good for her—helps with the aches and pains."

"She doesn't have any aches and pains," Nick said, as he handed the man his CPA card. He'd passed out cards to each vendor, asking them to call if Bart happened to show up but without telling him that anyone had been asking about him. "She's so particular she won't wear anything but pure gold," he added as they moved away.

"You're incorrigible," Maddy said.

"My middle name," Nick said. "But you *are* wearing gold earrings."

"They're only fourteen karat, though," Maddy pointed out. "Pure gold is twenty-four karat, I believe."

"Picky," he said.

A landscape artist and a husband and wife at the next stall who made sheepskin slippers also thought they might have run into Bart somewhere. They discussed the possibility back and forth among the three of them for some time, but couldn't reach a decision.

The man who sold handmade ocarinas and the elderly twins with the huge display of refrigerator magnets dominated by variations on Old Glory said they'd never seen him or anyone who looked like him before. "Never," the twins added in one voice, "Never in our entire lives."

"They were pretty adamant," Maddy commented, as she and Nick walked away.

Nick nodded. "You think they protested too much? Maybe they were afraid they were going to be subpoenaed."

Their luck was not much better when they moved on to the tall produce stalls and flower stands. A middle-aged woman in a very bad brown wig came out from behind a stand featuring beautifully arranged colorful vegetables and fruits. She stared at the photograph in complete silence for a long time before shaking her head and handing the photo back, still without speaking.

On the lower level of the market, a blazer-clad gentleman in an art gallery that featured Northwest artists gave his opinion that Bart might have bought several paintings of Mount Rainier. "People of discernment can't resist them," he informed them.

There were a lot of paintings of Mount Rainier in his gallery, some in unusual colors. " 'Purple mountain majesties' sounds pretty good in the song, but doesn't look all that great on canvas," Nick murmured close to Maddy's ear, his breath fanning her hair, sending a shiver of awareness down her spine.

The man wanted to tell them the provenance of each painting, but after listening politely for a while, they begged off until another time.

Seattle had a well-deserved reputation for friendliness. With the exception of the woman in the wig and the twins with the magnets, everyone was inclined to be helpful. Unfortunately, the people who thought Bart looked familiar didn't remember when or where they might have seen him, and the others had no memory of seeing him around the market at any time.

Three hours went by in this fashion, with a coffee break in the middle. A half hour before the market shut down, they reached the children's clothing store that had been closing when they looked for Bart on Thursday. It was open now. A white sign with red polka-dotted letters identified it as "Second Chance Togs." A consignment store, apparently.

"Hardly seems a place Bart would set foot in," Maddy said.

"He could have passed by," Nick pointed out. "He might have had a cup of coffee across the way."

The place was stocked with good-looking clothing and equipment for babies and toddlers. All very colorful— none of that boring old pink and blue stuff. It made a lot of sense to recycle little kids' clothes, Maddy thought— babies grew so fast. Some of the clothing still had the original price tags on them. Everything looked very clean. She'd have to remember this place, if ever . . .

The dark-haired young woman in charge was the one they had seen closing the store on Thursday. She was dressed as before in white bib overalls, a red-and-white polka-dotted shirt, and a straw hat with a ragged fringe around the brim. A name tag on her overalls identified her as Ellie.

"That's one fine-looking dude," Ellie enthused when Maddy handed over Bart's photograph. She flashed wide dark eyes at Nick, then batted her eyelashes in an exaggerated manner. "I like older men. They've a lot more class than jerks my own age. They know how to treat a girl—you know what I'm saying?"

"Did this particular man come into or go by the store on Thursday?" Maddy asked.

Ellie went into deep-thought mode, squinting her eyes, furrowing her forehead, then looked with apparent directness and curiosity at Nick. "He's a customer here? You mean he's married? Has kids? Darn!"

Her manner seemed forced, deliberately ingenuous.

"Was he looking to buy something?" she asked Nick, going with the eyelashes again.

Nick looked at Maddy. "I don't know," she said. "I don't know that he would buy anything in here."

Ellie pouted. Again, a reaction that seemed uncalled for. "Then why are you asking for him here? What are you looking for him for, anyway? He skip out on the rent?"

"Something like that," Nick said.

Ellie bent her head to Bart's photo again and came up looking animated. "He's a singer or something? All dressed up like he's at a wedding."

"Something like that," Nick said again.

"Well, that's a shame. Nice-looking dude like that, cheating his landlord. Guess I'll have to change my mind about him." She rolled her eyes. "I don't need any more deadbeats, that's the truth, though I can't say I'd mind paying *his* rent."

She surrendered the photo. "Seems like I remember him from somewhere, but I don't know if I saw him here or someplace else. Sorry about that, guys."

Nick eyed her suspiciously, mirroring Maddy's reaction, then gave Ellie his CPA card and asked her to call if the man happened to show up or if she happened to remember anything about him later.

"Messed up on his taxes, did he?" Ellie suggested airily. Neither Nick nor Maddy answered her.

"I got the impression she knew something," Maddy said when they were standing beside their parked cars. "Isn't there some way we could get it out of her?"

"Pulling out toenails is against the law," Nick said.

"I guess all we can do now is wait," Maddy said. "I guess you're out of luck on Quentin too."

"Maybe Bart will have shown up by the time you get home."

She gave him that narrow-eyed look she was so good at. "Should I have him call you? Or ask him if he knows anything about Quentin?"

Again Nick tried not to wince. Absolute trust, he gathered, was not yet established. But at least he had her tacit permission to represent her, which meant he could now use *her* name as that of the interested party, rather than his own.

"I'd rather ask him myself, Maddy, if you don't mind."

"You don't think Bart would tell me the truth? Or you don't think I would tell you the truth?"

The phrase "between a rock and a hard place" came to mind. "I could maybe help trigger his memory if I asked him personally," he managed.

Her eyes were still narrowed, but she seemed prepared to accept his evasion as an answer.

Chapter 10

NICK SPENT THE next day telephoning various contacts, pursuing every possible path he could think of to find out where Bart Williams might have disappeared to.

One of the calls was to the home of his supervisor, Thomas McCormack, known to his friends as Toss. Having gone through Quantico with him, Toss counted Nick as a friend and handed him slack when necessary. With Nick, it was often necessary.

Nick gave him an extremely informal verbal report on his progress, hoping Toss might be ready to put this case on the books.

"In other words, you've got zilch," Toss said, when he was done.

"It's coming together. I've a strong feeling I'm on the right track. I was told years ago the Snowman had moved to Seattle, but Arnie said he'd switched *operations* to Seattle. That he was a West Coast rep. That could mean almost anything. It could mean he's part of something organized, something ongoing."

"Or it could be nothing."

"Bart Williams is a pharmaceutical sales rep, Toss. A West Coast rep. And he's disappeared. Possibly because he saw me."

"He was obviously a wise man. Disappearing is what I should do when you come to me with stuff that can't even rightly be called circumstantial."

Nick sighed. "So I'm still officially on annual leave? Still flying solo without a parachute?"

"Step out of the plane, you're in free fall." Toss paused. "I can't decide if you're insanely single-minded about this thing or just bullheaded!" He relented slightly. "But I'm still okay with it. If it were my father, I'd be the same way."

"Thanks," Nick said, then hung up before Toss could change his mind.

He returned to Pike Place Market one more time, drawn back to the children's clothing consignment store, where he interviewed good-natured Ellie with the devious attitude—okay, he *flirted* with good-natured Ellie, who flirted right back so enthusiastically and skillfully he had difficulty extricating himself.

But he hadn't found out much more than she'd already told him and Maddy. Nobody else worked in the store, she'd assured him. The owner hardly ever showed up. Gus was an absentee landlord. He trusted her totally to take care of business, though he didn't pay her nearly enough. Got so she could hardly afford to eat out unless someone invited her to do it.

She was really good at batting those eyelashes, but Nick managed to avoid being taken in. Or taken. She was good, he conceded. So good, he could almost convince himself she was genuine.

On Monday he interviewed Simon Hatfield on Maddy's behalf, keeping his personal interest concealed. Hatfield had no idea where Bart might have disappeared to. He insisted there was nothing in the drugs Bart carried that would interest traffickers. According to Hatfield, Bart was an ideal employee, reliable, popular with his customers, a nondrinker, a nonsmoker, and now that he'd married

Madison, a total asset to Mawsom Pharmaceuticals. *Especially* since he'd married Madison.

Maddy was right, Nick decided—there was some prurient interest there.

With Hatfield's permission, grudgingly given, Nick also interviewed several of Bart's colleagues, none of whom admitted knowing anything personal about Bart or where he might have gone. Every one of them offered some variation on the opinion that the man was a loner, hard to know, a cold fish altogether, though apparently good at the job. None wanted to claim Bart as a friend.

Acting on the information given him by Maddy and Simon Hatfield, Nick drove down to Eugene to see Dr. Powell, Bart's last known appointment—the one he'd missed.

Dr. Powell, an oncologist, was a tall, slender man with an English accent, a shock of white hair, and good, possibly false, teeth. He had recovered from his irritation over what he termed "Mr. Williams's no-show," and welcomed Nick into his hospital office, without even asking for any ID. Powell provided Nick with tea strong enough to take the tarnish off the silver pot he served it in, and he sympathized over the storm Nick had driven through.

"I didn't even know Mr. Williams had a wife," he said when Nick told him he was representing Maddy.

He went on to offer, like Simon Hatfield had, an excess of praise for Bart Williams. "Very efficient. In and out. No fuss. Unlike some reps, he is never one to bore me with a rehearsed sales routine. He provides consistently good information plus published evidence from respected journals. He is also invariably straightforward about possible side effects and tolerability. One has to be most careful dealing with some reps," he added. "There are unfortunately a few pharmaceutical companies that are more concerned with the bottom line than with the improvement of patients' lives. Why, I read in a newspaper recently that one clinic had become so tired of drug reps with high-powered sales pitches disrupting their doctors' days, it has suggested charging them for the doctors' time.

One has to also be alert for the occasional company that is *too* generous to physicians and surgeons, flying them off on tropical vacations and such. Not that they are all like that. Mawsom is one of several reliable and trustworthy companies."

Nick was glad to hear it. He'd wondered about a company that would employ Simon Hatfield and Bart Williams.

The doctor was amazed and concerned when Nick told him Bart was still missing. "You think he's done a runner?" he asked.

It took a minute for Nick to figure that out, then he said, "It's *possible* he just took off, but the circumstances were strange. It's also entirely possible that he got involved in something he couldn't get out of, or ran up against some kind of trouble, maybe connected with his work, maybe his private life."

"Well, I know nothing of his private life, I'm afraid. Mr. Williams is not the type to chat about himself. I don't even know his country of origin, though I've noticed his accent of course."

"He came here from Germany."

Dr. Powell nodded. "He has always seemed a steady sort, keen on his work, but not pushy. I do hope nothing unfortunate has befallen him. I thought him—still think him—quite a splendid chap."

"Splendid" didn't match the Bart Williams Nick had heard about from Maddy or from Bart's colleagues. He remembered Maddy saying that Bart had become another person altogether after their wedding.

"When was Mr. Williams last here?" he asked.

The doctor thought for a minute, then consulted a calendar on his desk. A calendar provided by Mawsom Pharmaceuticals, Nick noted. "March," the doctor reported.

So he'd last seen Bart before Maddy had married him. That same charming Bart Maddy had first met. Maddy had said something had changed Bart Williams six months ago. And yet Maddy's description of Bart's post-wedding character—"the personality of a flowerpot, a cold, un-

feeling flowerpot"—and his colleague's summation—"a
cold fish"—could easily fit the man Nick had started out
looking for. "A block of ice for a heart," the little man at
his father's funeral had said.

Was Bart Williams a chameleon? Or did he have another identity that behaved in some circumstances in a
completely different way from the man himself? Who was
the real Bart Williams? The charmer Maddy had met and
married? Dr. Powell's splendid chap? Simon Hatfield's
ideal employee? Or the cold character Bart's colleagues
had never quite known and Maddy had not been able to
go on living with?

"Did he ever seem nervous to you? Irritable?"

Dr. Powell gave the question some thought, then shook
his head. "Nervous, no. Quite calm. Very even-tempered
sort of chap, actually. Not terribly outgoing. But efficient.
Definitely efficient."

"Did he usually call on you at the start of his trips, or
on the way back?"

The doctor frowned, then laughed shortly. "Actually,
that's something I do know. I'd have thought he'd start
with a hospital in Washington State and work his way
down I-5, but apparently he hopscotched down and back,
according to fancy, and usually caught me on the way
back. I asked him about it once, and he said he liked
variety."

Nick sighed as he returned to his car. That last bit had
been interesting, but he had no idea how to apply it to
this riddle he was trying to solve, the riddle of Bart Williams.

He wasn't getting very far very fast in his quest for the
Snowman. He still had nothing solid to go on. And time
was running short. He'd had only five weeks to find out
for sure if Bart Williams was really the Snowman—the
man who'd shot and killed his father. He'd already used
up eight days.

Chapter 11

CRESCENT BEACH WAS a very pleasant resort town on the Pacific coast of Washington. There were several large hotels, a few time-share complexes, vacation houses that were occupied only on weekends or national holidays and during the summer, and about four thousand permanent residents. The houses varied in size and style between two-room cabins with shake roofs to four-story mini-mansions sprawling over two or three lots.

Sometimes people tired of paying a second mortgage and keeping up a summer house that was used only occasionally, so they put it up for sale, often including all the furnishings. Who wanted the headache of disposing of the extra beds and tables and chairs separately?

On the first Wednesday in November, her fiftieth birthday, Pam Dyson, an excellent and experienced real estate agent who had sold millions of dollars' worth of Crescent Beach properties, some of them several times over, struggled with cold fingers to unlock the door of one such house, trying at the same time to smile reassuringly at the prospective buyers, who were showing signs of fatigue.

"I'm all fingers and thumbs today," she said, forcing a cheery note into her voice.

Finally the stubborn lock gave and she pushed open the door. "Hello?" she called as a precaution. She hadn't shown this house for a month or more. The owners had flown to Carmel around Labor Day to spend the winter there. Unfortunately, the male half of the couple had died a couple of weeks later. None of the family had any interest in coming out to the house. She'd just been instructed to sell it "as is."

She'd expected houses to be empty before, however, only to walk in on someone's son and girlfriend making whoopee in the master bedroom or bath.

"Anyone home?" she called, as she pushed the door wider. "Smells a bit off," she added, sniffing as she moved over to the deck doors. "We do get some mildew here, natural enough with all that ocean at our front door. A little soap and water and Clorox should take care of it."

"Smells a lot like our neighbor's chicken house back home, don't it, Mother?" Mr. Rossiter said. "We've complained about it fifty million times. Never did any good."

Mrs. Rossiter made a clucking sound with her tongue.

Pam sighed. She'd already shown the Rossiters four houses. Mr. Rossiter had found something wrong with each one immediately. Each time, Mrs. Rossiter had clucked. Possibly she'd caught the habit from the neighbor's chickens.

She should have stuck to her vow to take the day off, Pam thought, and let someone else handle the Rossiters or anyone else who came along.

She pulled on cords to draw back the vertical blinds, then pushed the sliding glass door open. The pure fresh air straight off the Pacific filled her lungs.

She was pretty sure the Rossiters were looky-loos, retired, bored, visiting the beach for a few days, fed up with the cold weather, needing something to do that would get them out of the wind without costing them anything extra. She wished they'd just give it up and go soak their feet and protruding bellies in their hotel's hot tub.

"Isn't that the most incredible view of the ocean?" she said, working to infuse her voice with vitality. She gestured like a magician's assistant at the glorious expanse of the Pacific, incoming waves foaming high, white as the clouds billowing above.

Both Rossiters spared the Pacific a brief glance. "Very nice," Mrs. Rossiter said flatly.

"Furniture looks worn in spots, Mother," Mr. Rossiter said, as though to dampen his wife's enthusiasm. "Floor's dirty. Carpet has holes in it."

Pam walked through the dining area to the kitchen, opened the door to the garage, and poked her head in. There was a car parked in there—a Ford Taurus. She wondered if the owner of the house had left it there or if someone was visiting.

"How many bedrooms?" Mrs. Rossiter asked.

Pam mentally awarded her four stars for effort. "Three," she said, closing the garage door. "The one at the back is the master bedroom. Come and take a look. It's really a self-contained suite, has its own master bath, walk-in closets and—"

She broke off as she opened the suite door. The sickening pungent odor almost knocked her backwards.

"What in tarnation *is* that smell?" Mr. Rossiter demanded.

Pam coughed. Her eyes watered. She blinked hard, then blinked again in case she was seeing things. She wasn't. On the bed, underneath a white comforter patterned with sprays of pink roses and green leaves, was a body-size mound. The words from the Goldilocks story, with which she'd become reacquainted since her grandson was born, rang in her memory. *Someone's been sleeping in my bed. And they're still there!*

"Whatever that is, it surely smells dead," Mr. Rossiter said, looking over Pam's shoulder.

Gesturing the couple back, though they had shown no desire to enter the bedroom, Pam tiptoed silently forward, as though afraid to wake the bed's occupant. One arm hung out at the side of the bed, a striped shirtsleeve covering it. The hand that protruded from the buttoned cuff was obviously male but of a peculiar purple-red with a tinge of green. The pretty comforter almost completely covered the rest of the person. Pam was not tempted to remove it. The hair that she could see was straight and platinum blond against a red pillow, rather a brownish red that clashed with the pink, and . . .

Pam backed up a step, one hand going to her mouth. That pillow was not naturally red—it was covered with dried blood, blood that also showed in spatters on the bedpost and the wall.

She coughed again, uncontrollably, as she backed out of the room and closed the door behind her. "Police," she said faintly, herding the Rossiters ahead of her to the front door. "I'll call dispatch from my cell phone."

"I guess we won't be looking at any more houses today, Mother," Mr. Rossiter said.

Mrs. Rossiter clucked her tongue.

Chapter 12

AT 11:05 ON Friday evening, Nick lay in bed, half-asleep, with one ear cocked for the eleven o'clock news on KING TV. He always tried to stay awake long enough to catch the news, but often slept soon after his head hit the pillow—sign of a clear conscience, his mother always said. Or a nonexistent one, Nick usually added. Just in case, he set the timer on the bedroom TV to shut off at midnight.

His attention was suddenly caught by the very name he'd been thinking about while the TV had been droning along.

He pushed himself upright against his pillows and focused his startled attention on the perky anchorwoman.

On Wednesday, the anchorwoman said, a real estate agent showing a vacant house in Crescent Beach, a popular resort on the Pacific coast, had discovered the body of a man who had been fatally shot in the head. The screen cut to a male reporter who said the police were calling the death a suicide, though no suicide note had been found. An autopsy had been performed and time of death was estimated to be approximately a week ago. The deceased had been identified as Bart Williams of Oak River.

Shocked fully awake, Nick threw his pillow on the floor and recited a string of Italian cuss words he'd learned from his grandmother. They did nothing to relieve his feelings.

He had wanted to find Bart Williams himself. He had wanted to prove that Bart Williams was the Snowman, and then he had wanted to kill him, after making sure the man understood why. This plan had lain dormant for the last twenty-three years, ever since he had stood staring out through that stained glass window in the church basement.

He'd thought he'd buried all thoughts of revenge once he realized how slim the chances were that he'd ever find the Snowman, but they had been resurrected when Arnie passed on his news.

And now, when Nick had been on the brink of finding out if Bart Williams really was the Snowman, Williams was dead. By his own hand.

Swinging his legs over the side of the bed, he reached for his billfold on the nightstand, extracted Maddy's card, then picked up the telephone. It was late, but he was pretty sure she wouldn't be sleeping.

Her "Hello" sounded both weary and wary.

"I hope I didn't wake you," he said.

"Oh, Nick. No. I'm in bed, but I doubt I'll sleep tonight."

He'd seen her bedroom, had admired the Asian-style bedding and other accents, the earthy colors creating a quiet atmosphere. His own bedroom featured the same basic colors, but it just looked stark. Minimalist to the max, his mother called it.

He had a sudden vivid image of Maddy Sloane lying in her queen-size bed, her hair tousled, blue eyes sleepy.

He wished she'd say something. He had no idea what to say to her.

"I was afraid you were another reporter, Nick. Did you—"

"I just heard. TV news. The media bugging you?"

"Can't really blame them. It's great story material—body found in empty house by a real estate agent, been there several days without anyone knowing it. Nice messy, smelly suicide. A lot of blood." Her voice roughened and cracked on the last words.

He hesitated. "I ought to be able to come up with something helpful to say, and you've probably noticed I'm usually fairly glib, but there never are adequate words for such a situation. I'm so sorry, Maddy."

"I can't believe it."

He stiffened. "You don't believe I'm sorry?"

"I can't believe Bart's dead. That he committed suicide." Her sigh was long and full of pain. "I keep seeing him rushing by me saying, 'Rest room.' Scowling at me as if I'd done something he considered stupid. I saw that expression a lot. It made me mad. I've been mad at him for months, more than ever since he disappeared. And now I know he was—" She broke off, started again. "I would have sworn Bart wasn't the kind of man to commit suicide, but then I haven't known for the last six months what kind of man he was. Maybe I never did know."

"What convinced the police that he committed suicide? On the news they said he was found in a vacant house."

"He was lying on a bed, facedown, almost completely covered with a quilt. The gun—the weapon, the lieutenant called it—was lying on the floor, his arm hanging down as if he'd just dropped it. It had been fired, and there was gunshot residue on Bart's hand."

She paused again, and he could hear her breathing. "I had to go to the morgue and identify him."

She stopped again.

He waited.

"He—Bart—was such an awful color, Nick. And he'd . . . he'd been shot in the head. It was partly . . . I couldn't bear it. But I had to."

She hesitated again. "I stayed in a Crescent Beach hotel

last night and talked to the officers this morning. They were very kind. The lieutenant—Lieutenant Saperia—said there wasn't much . . . decomposition because there'd been a cold spell at the coast and the house was unheated."

Her voice, which had sounded almost robotic, caught again, and dropped to a whisper. "This is the darkest place I've ever been to."

There was nothing he could do to help her escape the darkness, so he offered the most prosaic thing that occurred to him. "Was the quilt over his head when the real estate agent found him?"

"According to the lieutenant, the real estate agent said he was almost completely covered except for his arm—his right arm—hanging down." She hesitated. "You're thinking if the quilt was over his head, it's less likely he shot himself?"

"Well, I suppose it would still be possible. If the police say it looks like suicide, then probably—"

"I'll ask the agent first thing tomorrow. Dyson. Her name's Pam Dyson. I wasn't really thinking straight, Nick. It was such a . . . such a shock."

"You should have called me to go with you."

"You think it would have been a good idea to turn up to view my husband's body with another man beside me? How would I explain you? My personal private detective? How would that have looked?"

"You'd engaged me to find your husband. You'd reported him missing. It would have been okay." Yeah, sure it would. Until the police checked up on Nick, hauled him in, and demanded to know what the hell he was up to.

She didn't comment on that. "Lieutenant Saperia called me a little while ago to say that only Bart's fingerprints are on the gun. The detective wanted to check if the weapon belonged to Bart."

"Did it?"

"I didn't know he owned a gun, but it's possible, I guess. They say it wasn't registered. But of course that doesn't mean it wasn't his."

"What kind of weapon was it?"

"They said it was a .357 Magnum. I don't know much about guns. There was an autopsy."

"That's not unusual when it's a . . . violent death."

"I guess." She sounded unutterably weary. "Evidently Bart had been drinking heavily. Way beyond the legal limit. There was an empty whiskey bottle in the room with his fingerprints on it, as if he drank directly out of it. I never knew him to drink. Do you suppose he drank to give himself the courage to . . . shoot himself?"

"Would you like me to come over?" he asked.

"Tonight?" She sounded startled.

Best not to push her. "Or in the morning. We could talk. I've made some inquiries, mostly designed to find out where Bart might have gone, which isn't much use to us now. Have the police turned anything else up?"

"Not that they told me. There was no note. But Lieutenant Saperia seemed convinced it was suicide. And the coroner ruled on it. The lieutenant told me he's an M.D. The coroner. County coroner. Evidently they aren't always doctors, but this one is. I suggested to the lieutenant that it seemed a bit strange that Bart would brush by me in the marketplace saying he was going to the rest room, then drive three hours to Crescent Beach, go into a house that's been standing vacant for two months, drink a bottle of whiskey, and then lie down fully clothed on the bed and shoot himself. No note, no last phone call. Why would he be so desperate? The lieutenant agreed it did seem unusual, but said people do strange things all the time. He also said if it wasn't suicide, it would have to be a homicide. He gave me the strangest look. I think he was hinting that I might be the number one suspect."

"Well, I can vouch for you there."

"How can you? They can't establish the time of death all that precisely."

"Ah."

She was silent for a few seconds, then she sighed very deeply and said, "I feel so damn guilty."

He reached for the remote and hit the power button to

turn off the TV. "What do you have to feel guilty about?" he asked cautiously.

"I was about to leave him. I told you that. I *wanted* to leave him, couldn't wait to leave him. He had taught me to dislike him intensely. I never wanted to see him again. I wanted him out of my life. And now he's dead. Maybe he sensed I was going to leave him. Maybe he did care after all."

"Your wish wasn't father to the deed, Maddy."

She didn't answer.

"Do you want me to come over tomorrow?"

"The funeral's tomorrow. They thought I shouldn't wait—the condition of . . . his body. He's been transported to the Green Meadow Memorial Park. I called Simon Hatfield as soon as the coroner released the . . . remains."

She paused. "Such a horrible, horrible word."

He waited.

"Mr. Hatfield took over all the arrangements—the casket, the graveside ceremony, the minister. I let him. I did make sure the service will be nondenominational. Bart would hate any service at all—he told me once that he'd never wanted anything to do with religion. He didn't believe in hell and damnation, he said. But it seemed to me there ought to be something to mark his passing. Left to myself, I would have arranged something private, but Mr. Hatfield kept reminding me that Mawsom Pharmaceuticals is a family company—and the 'family' would take care of the details for me."

Speaking of family . . . "Did you talk to your parents yet?" Nick asked.

"Oh, yes." She sighed deeply. "I should let you go, Nick. I'm glad you called, though. I needed to talk to someone."

"I'm not going anywhere. You can talk some more if you want to."

She was silent so long, he thought he was going to refuse, but then she said, "Yes, I called my parents. I was afraid Bart's death would show up on the news in Victoria. My father, predictably, figures it's all my fault. 'Only you could misplace a husband,' he said. He kept asking me what I had done to make Bart go off like that. 'No man would just walk past his wife and say, "Rest room," and disappear and then shoot himself,' he insisted. I couldn't argue with that. I was there and it still sounds damn unlikely to me. My mother retreated into her Scottishness. 'Dinna fash yerself,' she kept saying to my father. To me, she just said, 'He was such a bonny lad.' "

He was very lucky to have Bridget Ciacia for a mother, Nick thought, not for the first time.

"Tell me about them," he encouraged her. The feeling of intimacy was growing. In her as well as him, he thought. Her voice was hushed, as his was. And she seemed calmer. It might be a good idea to keep her talking awhile longer. About something other than Bart Williams. "You said your parents live in Victoria. Are they Canadian?"

"No, they're American citizens. My father, Will, was career air force. I was an air force brat—we moved a lot, in the States and overseas. Will met my mother, Isobel, at a party in London, at one of the embassies. She was from Edinburgh, staying with a friend for a couple of weeks." She paused. "I call them by their first names— they prefer it that way."

"I don't know what's with parents anymore," Nick said. "My mother's always after me to call her Bridey. Her name's Bridget. I call her Ma."

"Bridget doesn't sound Italian."

"She's not Italian, she's Irish. She and my father met in Chicago. She tried to become Sicilian for him, but never quite made it. But anyway, Irish or Sicilian, she's Ma to me. Always was, always will be."

"Where does she live?"

"In Seattle, not too far from—" He broke off. Hell, he shouldn't be telling her this. She could get curious, call Ma up, go to see her.

"She winters in Arizona," he substituted smoothly.

Which was true, except she never drove south until after
Thanksgiving.

"What about your father? Oh, you told me he was
dead, didn't you? I'm sorry, I wasn't thinking."

"It's okay, Maddy. It was a long time ago." And as
clear in his mind as if it had happened yesterday.

She sighed deeply. "I love my mom and dad, Nick, but
sometimes it's not easy. Will's never really accepted that
I'm grown up. And he's never accepted my earning more
than he ever did. He doesn't understand how people working for technology companies could make so much
money. When all those dot-coms started failing in 2000,
he began to feel better, but seemed disappointed when
TheHub didn't go belly up."

"Feeling inadequate himself, I guess," Nick put in.

"Probably. Although he was very good at what he did
in the air force and he retired as a colonel."

She sighed again. "I don't spend a lot of time with my
parents. They bicker a lot. Genteelly, but it's still annoy-
ing. They call each other 'Darling' while they argue, but
they say it through clenched teeth and at the same time
as they are complaining."

"How did you end up in Washington State?"

"Will's last posting was to McChord AFB. I went to
U Dub—the University of Washington. At that time, Will
became upset by the way America was going—the crime
and lack of discipline in the young, et cetera. And Isobel
was homesick. Will balked at living in Scotland, so when
he retired seven years ago, they moved to Victoria. I
didn't want to move anymore, and I wanted to live my
own life. Will was furious."

She paused again. He had the feeling she hadn't talked
to anyone about all this in a long time. "The only time
Will ever really approved of anything I did, ironically,
was when I married Bart," she continued. "Bart was a
successful man. Will considered sales a real job—he had
never really caught on to what recruiting for a dot-com
company was all about. And Bart always seemed to have

plenty of money. My father equates money with success, except where I am concerned."

A longer pause. She seemed about to say something a couple of times, but broke off, then finally went on. "Will and Isobel both kept campaigning for me to quit work and settle down and make babies. I'd thought I might just do that when I married Bart, but within a very short time I knew I didn't want to have any children with him. Do you have children, Nick?"

He was taken aback by the sudden question, but answered after only a slight pause. "No kids. No. I do like children—I still remember being one. I had a great childhood and I'd like to pass that kind of unthinking happiness on. But I'm not married, haven't been married."

He smiled briefly, rather grimly. "I have this built-in early warning system. I imagine I'm hearing Mendelssohn's wedding march and I exit stage left. Most of the guys I've known have been married more than once. Some of them get to see their kids on weekends and holidays, some don't. I've had relationships, but nobody live-in, nobody I wanted to do the forever thing with. Wouldn't be fair to bring kids into my kind of life. I'm not sure it would be fair to bring a *wife* into my kind of life. Most of the women I've dated have been scared off by the kind of work I do."

He could hear puzzlement in her silence. "You get into dangerous situations?" she said at last.

I'm supposed to be a private investigator, he reminded himself. "Not too often, but I work long hours sometimes—odd shifts." He laughed shortly. "I get the same kind of pressure from my mother that you get from yours, though she hasn't expressed any desire to be a grandmother yet."

Changing the subject, he asked, "I believe you told me your parents never visit?"

"Oh, that's a recent development. They did come to my wedding. But they couldn't wait to get back home."

"Will they come to be with you now?"

"They won't cross the border, Nick. They are both

afraid of terrorists. My father's convinced the U.S. is swarming with them."

He couldn't think of a suitable response to that. Before he could create one, he heard her yawn. "I really think I might be able to sleep now," she said. "I didn't sleep at all last night. Thank you for letting me vent. I guess I needed that."

"My privilege," he told her. "But before I let you go, I need to know what time you want me to be there in the morning. I'll drive you to the cemetery."

"Kazuko's going to be here. She offered to drive."

"I'll drive you both."

She hesitated, and he was afraid she was going to protest, but then she said, "The funeral's at ten-thirty."

"I'll be there at ten," he said.

Chapter 13

SIMON HATFIELD HAD suggested cremation would be a good idea. Maddy supposed he was thinking of the condition Bart had been found in and wanted to spare her feelings. But Maddy had felt obliged to decide against cremation. "Bart had some kind of hang-up about fire," she told Nick as he drove her and Kazuko to the cemetery. "Remember that really cold spell the first week of October? I went looking all over the house and yard for firewood—I love a wood fire. Bart was on a trip—somewhere in California, I think—so I asked Kazuko and the people at the gardening syndicate that handles the yard work about firewood, but nobody remembered ever seeing any firewood in either of the sheds on the premises."

"*Dannasan* never had a fire all the time I worked for him," Kazuko said from the backseat. "I don't think that fireplace was ever used."

"It sure didn't look as if it had ever been used," Maddy added. "But one of the lawn guys brought some wood over, and Kazuko and I decided the fireplace and chimney looked okay. So we had a fire."

Nick glanced over at her when she paused. She looked very fragile in a tan raincoat, her face pinched, pallid. Her choppily cut hair had lost some of its luster. Shadows haunted her beautiful eyes. "Why do I have this idea Bart wasn't thrilled?" he said gently.

"You have good instincts," she said with some bitterness. "Bart was very perturbed. That was the word he always used when he was mad. 'I'm very perturbed, Madison,' he would say."

"To me too, *okusan*," Kazuko said.

"Bart never did get hot and bothered," Maddy went on. "He was always polite, but his voice could acquire a tone that would chill you to the bone."

"Like he'd been chewing on ice cubes," Kazuko said.

Nick frowned. "He was *afraid* of fire?"

"Well, he didn't say so. He never admitted to fear of anything. Not to me anyway. But he had this look on his face when he saw the fireplace had been used. Kind of a sick look around his mouth and eyes. I interpreted it as fear."

"Some trauma in his childhood?"

Maddy sighed. "I don't think he had a childhood. He would never talk about it, or his family in Germany, or anything else that was personal. He told me once he was a very private man." Her mouth tightened. "I'd use the word *secretive* myself. A secretive and secret man, hidden from everyone, maybe including himself."

She turned as if to look out the car window and drew into herself for the rest of the short journey. She had been talking too much, talking without thought. It seemed as if Nick Ciacia brought stuff out of her without any effort at all. She needed to stop talking, to gather herself for whatever the rest of the day had in store.

It was raining steadily, had rained all night. Rain was still falling when everyone gathered at the graveside for the service. Mr. Hatfield had wanted to have the ceremony in the chapel, but Maddy had persuaded him that Bart would not have appreciated that.

So here they all were in the rain. Which wasn't such

a bad thing, in Maddy's opinion. Raincoats and umbrellas and unremitting drizzle with some sleet in it seemed to belong at a funeral, along with the hushed, plummy voice of the minister and the occasional cough of someone in the group representing Mawsom Pharmaceuticals. Odd how there was always someone who coughed during a solemn occasion, whether it was a play, a dramatic scene in a movie, a wedding, or a funeral.

Lara and Todd were there. So was Sally. Some of Maddy's friends at TheHub probably would have come too, but Maddy hadn't encouraged them to. They hadn't known Bart well, having met him only a couple of times before they were married and again at the wedding. Afterward, Bart had refused to go to any of TheHub's company dinners or parties. And he'd discouraged Maddy from inviting her friends to his house. He'd been so snotty with Sally that she had stayed away after the first and only visit. Another of Maddy's friends, one she worked with on a daily basis, had visited unexpectedly and had been so taken aback by Bart's cold reception that Maddy's friendship with her had suffered.

Bart and Maddy's social life had consisted of Mawsom's annual picnic—soon after their wedding—a company trip on a large sailing vessel on Puget Sound, and something the pharmaceutical company's executives called a "dining in," which actually took place in a restaurant overlooking Lake Washington.

Lara had wanted to cater a post-funeral reception at Bart's house, but Maddy hadn't been able to bear the idea of having people hanging around, being sympathetic while maybe wondering, "Why did he do it? Was something wrong in the marriage? What kind of a woman was she? What kind of a wife? Why did he marry her?"

She recognized, of course, that they probably would not think such thoughts and that her own automatically guilty response was a product of her upbringing. Her mother had been able to make Maddy feel guilty for everything, from her mother's frequent migraines to wars and rumors of war in diverse places.

Maddy was surprised that so many of Bart's coworkers showed up. Probably drafted by Simon Hatfield, she thought, remembering again the "family" image of the company Mr. Hatfield was so anxious to project. At their wedding and the three company events she'd attended with Bart, his colleagues had been pleasant to her and to Bart—but hardly overwhelmingly friendly. She'd thought them surprisingly distant until she realized it was Bart who was creating the distance.

The graveside service was mercifully brief. The minister, not knowing Bart or Maddy, did a heroic though fairly generic job of wishing the deceased well, but Maddy sensed there was a feeling of "Thank God *that's* over," throughout the group when he finally stopped. Mr. Hatfield said a few words, calling Bart a reliable, punctual, and efficient employee.

Not much of a eulogy, Maddy thought.

Mr. Hatfield asked if anyone else wanted to say a few words, and nobody volunteered, not even the young Mawsom woman who had rhapsodized about how gorgeous Bart was. The lack of comments was a bit embarrassing, but not terribly surprising.

"You want to come home with us for a couple of days?" Lara said as she and Todd, Kazuko, Sally, Maddy, and Nick all stood awkwardly in the parking lot, Lara her usual dramatic self in a flowing black wool cape, her long black hair rippling down the back, Sally crisply businesslike in a tan wool overcoat and fedora.

Maddy was tempted to accept the invitation, to just surrender herself to Lara's care, let Lara feed her and serve her good wine and talk to her in her dramatic manner, closing out all the guilty voices that kept popping up in Maddy's head, telling her she hadn't tried hard enough to be a loving wife, had certainly done something wrong to make Bart turn away from her right after the wedding and then finally kill himself just when she was about to leave him. Had he guessed? Had he known? Who could have told him? Yes, it would be a relief to have her good friend Lara drown the voices out.

But then she reminded herself she was a grown woman, a strong woman. Her current weakness was temporary, it would pass. She would make it pass. She shook her head. "I have things to do at the house, stuff to take care of."

"If you change your mind, you come at once, okay?" Lara opened her arms as Maddy nodded, and Maddy returned her hug with great affection.

"This has all been very difficult for you," Lara said. "You must not go on worrying about what might have been, or why this dreadful thing happened. You must get on with your life. You are a young woman, beautiful, intelligent, with much to live for."

Maddy hugged her again. "I'm not suicidal, Lara."

"Well, you are too pale," Lara said, as if that were something that would surely lead to disaster. "And you look much too thin. At least come back with me to Buon Gusto and have a good meal now. You and Nick too, and Kazuko, Sally—all of you."

"Please do," Todd added.

Maddy hugged him too. He was a big, kindly man with a great deal of warmth about him. He didn't talk much, but then Lara talked enough for both of them—mostly it was difficult to get a word in.

"I'm sorry you're going through such a bad time," he said now. "I guess it was no secret I didn't like Bart, and I'm pretty sure he didn't like me, but I wish I'd known he was contemplating ending his life. Maybe I could have talked to him, helped him in some way."

"I don't think any of us could have prevented Bart from doing anything he wanted to," Lara said.

Maddy kissed Todd's cheek as he released her. "Thank you for inviting me," she said to Lara. "But much as I love your antipasti, I'll take a raincheck, okay?"

Maddy and Sally hugged, then Maddy stiffened her spine and managed a smile, hoping to reassure her friends she was okay. "I have to thank Mr. Hatfield," she said, with a slight gesture toward where Simon Hatfield stood beside his Lincoln Continental. "He said he wants to talk to me."

"We'll get together soon?" Sally asked.

One of the things Maddy really appreciated about both Sally and Lara was that neither of them tried to argue her into any particular course of action, but just accepted whatever she decided.

"Of course we will."

Her three friends shook hands with Nick, but Maddy could tell they were curious about his presence here. She imagined questions would be forthcoming from both Lara and Sally.

Kazuko and Nick waited in his car while she walked over to thank Simon Hatfield.

"My sympathies, Madison," Mr. Hatfield said in his most unctuous voice, taking her proffered gloved hand and holding it captive. Anyone else she would have asked to call her Maddy. Anyone else she might not have eased her hand free from so quickly.

"We don't want to lose you from the Mawsom family," he continued. "Please call me personally if you need anything. Anything at all."

"Thank you for taking care of all the arrangements for me," she said without committing herself to whatever he had in mind. "I do appreciate your help. I'm sure Bart would have appreciated it too."

"I was so very sorry to hear that things weren't going well between you and Bart," he said as she began to turn away.

Shocked speechless, she turned back and stared at him.

"Bart told me a couple of weeks ago he was afraid he was going to lose you."

She hadn't said a word to Bart about leaving. She'd kept him completely in the dark, hadn't so much as hinted of her plans to move. Only Lara and Todd and Sally had known she was going to leave Bart, and none of them would have told him.

"He was quite hurt, you know," Mr. Hatfield continued. "He stood there in my office, looking hangdog, not at all like himself. You told him it was a career decision, he said, but he was a dull stick, he said, and you were so lively, you were most likely just bored with his quiet life-style. I was afraid he was going to cry when he told me you were the love of his life, that he'd waited to find you for many, many years and he knew he could never find another woman like you—he wasn't sure he'd ever re-cover from losing you, but you were absolutely set on leaving."

Hatfield is thinking this was why Bart killed himself. She could read it in his eyes, the false piety of his ex-pression.

"I guess it's moot now," she finally managed.

"Yes indeed."

"Are you okay?" Nick asked as she got into his car.

She nodded, still too stunned to talk.

"You're very pale. What did Hatfield say to you? He was looking totally smug as you walked back here."

She shook her head.

"Did that man upset you, *okusan*?" Kazuko demanded from the rear seat.

Maddy shook her head again.

She saw Nick turn his head and exchange a glance with Kazuko, then to her relief Nick started the car without questioning her further.

Chapter 14

WHEN NICK STOPPED the car beside Kazuko's in the driveway, Maddy got out, still looking frail in her trench coat. She said "Thank you" in a strained voice to each of them, then let herself into the house and closed the door behind her.

Nick looked questioningly at Kazuko in the rearview mirror. "I never saw *okusan* like this before," she said. "I don't know how to help her."

"I don't either, but I'm going to try," Nick said. He turned around, leaning an arm on the seat back. "Are you okay with going on home—letting me handle this?"

She nodded briskly. "I think you are a good friend to *okusan*."

"I want to be," he said, meeting her gaze.

Maddy didn't open the door right away. He rang the bell again. Finally, he heard her footsteps in the entryway.

"I'm not leaving until I'm sure you're okay," he said when she opened the door.

She looked beyond him, watching as Kazuko backed her car out to the street, then opened the door wider.

He yanked his parka over his head and she took it from him and hung it in the entry closet. Then she led the way to the living room.

She sat down on the sofa. She hadn't taken her trench coat off.

He sat on the chair opposite her. "It's tough, isn't it?" was all he could think of to say.

She sighed and looked down at her hands clasped in her lap. "I didn't want to be married to Bart anymore, or even to be with him, so I can't pretend to mourn him as a wife should. But I've got all these mixed emotions running around inside me. I'm terribly sorry that he died, especially given the violent way he died. I do feel responsible. And I mourn the man he was when I first met him. I just hope I can remember him that way, rather than the way he became, so cold and distant, so locked up inside himself, so hateful. I've been so angry and frustrated with the situation and with him. It had been building up in me for six months until I was ready to explode. And now all that anger has nowhere to go. He's dead. How can I go on hating someone who's dead?"

She shook her head. "I'm sorry, Nick. I keep forgetting I hardly know you."

"The circumstances have a lot to do with that, I think," he said carefully. "Problems, adversity, bring strangers closer together, turning them into friends. I do want to be your friend, Maddy. I'm not in this just to find . . . Quentin."

She gave him a tentative smile that had a slight tremor at its edges. "When I was a little kid," she said, "some other little kid punched me in the stomach. Hard. I've no memory of why, or if I deserved it, or if it was a boy or a girl who did it, but I do remember how it felt. I felt that way when Lieutenant Saperia called to tell me Bart had killed himself, and again when Mr. Hatfield talked to me after the funeral."

She hesitated, obviously gathering her thoughts. "Before all of this, I would have thought of myself as being as strong as a rock, but right now my rock must be an

uncut diamond—only strong as long as you don't hit it
in the wrong place and shatter it into worthless dust."

Her eyes were as dark as the sea at midnight.

He had a sudden urge to put his arms around her, to
hold her and comfort her. Do more than comfort her.
Lusting after a woman who had just buried her husband
was one of those things society frowned upon. Especially
when the husband had committed suicide. Especially
when you'd planned all along on killing the man, and now
planned on making use of her to find out if he really had
been the Snowman. And most especially when you were
becoming more and more attracted to her and wanted to
go way, way beyond a sympathetic hug.

"What did Hatfield say?" he asked.

She told him, her voice husky, strained.

"You didn't know Bart suspected you were going to
leave?"

"He *couldn't* have suspected. If it were anyone else,
I'd say he might have sensed it, but I'd swear Bart didn't
have that much sensitivity. If he *had* sensed it, I'm fairly
certain he wouldn't have cared."

"You think Hatfield made it up?"

"I don't know what— Wait a minute."

A thought had jolted her mind—something related to
Hatfield's earlier statement about joshing Bart, telling him
he needed a wife to be part of the Mawsom family. She
examined it, laying it mentally alongside Hatfield's recent
shocking disclosure.

Nick waited patiently. He really was a good listener.
Few people would wait without interrupting for your
thoughts to catch up with you.

"I doubt Hatfield would go so far as to lie about something like that," she said at last. "Which means I have to
accept that Bart actually said all that to him. I may have
an inkling . . ."

She swallowed. "This is going to sound really dumb,
but when I went to see Hatfield the day you and I had
lunch at the Space Needle, he told me he'd spoken to Bart
some time ago about being single at his age. He 'joshed'

him, was the way he put it. I've an idea he might have suspected Bart was gay. Hatfield's the type who would find that offensive. Anyway, he gave Bart the company line—he thinks of the staff as family, they should all hold family values dear, et cetera. So then the next thing he knew Bart showed up with a suitable wife. Me."

Nick frowned. "You're thinking that's why Bart married you? To make Hatfield happy, so he could keep his job?"

His tone was unbelieving, for which she could hardly blame him. "I told you it was going to sound dumb. But I've been trying for the last six months to figure out why Bart did marry me. He tried really hard to get me, but once he got me, he didn't do a single thing to keep me. It was as if he'd just decided he'd better get married, so he did. And that was as far as his effort was ever going to go."

"But all that about you being the love of his life. That doesn't fit with your scenario at all."

"It does if you turn it around. Maybe he was getting ready to dump me. If he married me to keep his job— which he was sure was the perfect job for him—but he didn't really want to be married, then maybe he was preparing Mr. Hatfield for the likelihood of us separating. Maybe he thought if he could convince Hatfield I was the only woman in the world for him, then once he'd dumped me and I was out of the picture, he wouldn't have to worry about getting married again."

"Devious," Nick acknowledged.

"But possible?"

"To someone with a warped mind, maybe."

"I think he *was* warped. I think he was not quite . . . whole." She realized her hands were clasped together so tightly her circulation was in danger. She relaxed them deliberately, stood up, and took off her trench coat, tossing it over the back of a nearby chair.

Sitting down again, she said, "On the other hand, I may be making up excuses so that I can avoid any responsibility for Bart's suicide."

"Do you honestly think you could be responsible for his suicide?"

"No." She spoke without hesitation, then laughed shortly. "On the other hand . . ."

He got up and moved over to sit beside her. Taking both her hands lightly in his, he said, "One, Hatfield is a jackass. A cruel jackass, given that he'd say such things to you. Two, why would he want to make you feel guilty? Maybe he has some reason to feel guilty himself? Three, if that is the case, then it's highly likely he did lie to you about what Bart said to him. And four, no matter who said what to whom, as long as you know you did nothing to drive Bart to suicide, then what the hell are you worrying about?"

She laughed a little more genuinely. "You make it sound simple."

"Most things are." He was still holding her hands. She hadn't made any attempt to remove them. He liked holding her hands. A lot. He wanted to hold a lot more than her hands. *Slow down, Ciacia*, he instructed himself. You're still not certain this woman is completely innocent of knowing anything her husband might have been involved in. She just buried him; no matter how little she cared for him in the end, that has to be tough.

He told her the results of his visits with Hatfield and Powell. "Not much to go on," he admitted.

She frowned over the description of Bart hopscotching up and down I-5. "Why would he *do* it that way? I'd have thought it would make more sense to—" She broke off. "I don't suppose it's important now."

He let go of her hands, and she realized she'd had no feeling of entrapment such as she'd felt when Hatfield held on to her. Only an encompassing warmth that was comforting and disturbing at the same time.

"Thank you for going to see Hatfield and Dr. Powell," she said, with some warmth of her own. "I do appreciate it very much. Don't forget to keep—"

"A record of my expenses."

They both laughed. Gently.

"So what else can I do for you?" he asked.

She shook her head. "I don't think—" She stopped, then started again. "There is one thing."

"Name it."

"You probably don't have time for it."

"You're paying me, remember?"

"I think I've discovered something," she said, standing up. "I noticed it early this morning."

Halfway up the stairs to show him what she'd found, she stopped abruptly. "You must be hungry. I didn't even think about that. Would you like something to eat first?"

"Are you kidding? My curiosity turns on, my appetite turns off. We can eat later."

He was elated that she was trusting him with something, didn't want to give her time for second thoughts.

Her find was at the top of the wood-paneled staircase. "Here, see," she said, indicating a small keyhole in one of the wall panels.

After going into Bart's office, she handed him a ring of small keys similar to those used to open luggage.

"It's a secret room?" Nick asked.

"I haven't looked. I'd never noticed the keyhole before. Normally, I just come up the stairs looking upward, not sideways. But around five o'clock this morning, I had the idea I should look carefully at every wall and ceiling and behind every picture. Bart kept his safe behind a picture in his study, remember?"

He remembered. An exceptionally demented picture. Little nude people standing around in water or riding on horses. Fantastic constructions of some kind in the upper regions. A tremendously talented artist. But that kind of art was not one of his things. He was a practical guy. He liked pictures you could understand, people you could recognize as human.

"It seemed to me Bart might have other secret places around, but . . ." She paused.

"You didn't want to look at it alone."

She nodded. "There may be nothing in there, but the fact that it's locked . . . Anyway, just in case, I wanted to have a witness. I was going to ask Kazuko, but I don't feel I should burden her—she's already keeping—" She broke off.

Keeping what? he wondered. Keeping quiet? Keeping other secrets?

He took the keys from her, his fingers brushing against hers, causing an electricity that wasn't static. He was becoming more and more aware of her. Not something he could follow through on. Once again, he felt a twinge of regret for what might have been if they'd met under other circumstances. "Okay, let's see what it looks like," he said in a voice that was much too cheery.

The panel slid open easily once he found the right key. Behind it was a fair-size crawlspace. Roofing nails bristled through the slanted roof like a fakir's bed.

"The utility room is underneath," Maddy explained, as she leaned forward beside him, close enough so he could feel her warm breath on his face. Sweet clean breath. "Washing machine, dryer, shower stall, and toilet—sort of a mud room—accessible from the back hallway."

"I'll go first," he said, and promptly banged his head into the top of the opening. Blinking to disperse the subsequent stars, he hauled himself the rest of the way in.

Maddy followed, scrambling easily over the opening's sill. The air was dusty, the floor littered with wood shavings that had fallen when the cedar shake roof was nailed on. "Keep your head down," he warned, and immediately went facefirst through a large spiderweb. He spent several seconds wiping it off.

A light flicked on. She'd found a switch on the other side of the opening. "Nothing here." She sounded disappointed. "I was hoping for another safe."

He nodded ahead. "There's something at the other end."

A long strip of Berber carpet, a couple of feet wide, had been nailed down over the floorboards. It made it easier to crawl. And made him think it would only have been laid if there was something important to crawl to.

The something was a three-drawer filing cabinet. The drawers were locked. "Shit," he muttered.

Maddy moved away from him, back to the opening, then crawled back, holding the ring of keys he'd left in the keyhole. None of them opened the drawers.

"Hang on," she said, and took off again, returning in a few minutes with several more small keys for him to try. In the meantime he'd eased himself into a sitting position because his knees were protesting. He needed to put in more time at the gym—with jobs like this cropping up, he couldn't afford to get out of shape.

The second key worked. The drawers were full of files. In the bottom drawer were several small ledgers, apparently records of expenditures. A five-year diary yielded information on business trips—names, addresses, doctors, surgeons, hospitals, type of drugs.

"Didn't you say Bart's records were in the safe that was emptied the day he disappeared?"

"That's what he told me was in there."

"Well, if all his records are here, we might start wondering what was really in the safe. For now, we need to get this stuff out into a better light." Crouching, he tested the heft of the file cabinet, ducking his head to avoid the nails above him. "Damn thing must be made of iron," he grumbled.

"I'll get some boxes," Maddy said, and crawled back to the opening.

They loaded all the files into the three large plastic containers she returned with, then exited the crawlspace, Nick managing to avoid a concussion this time.

"Lunch," Maddy decreed after they'd carried the boxes out. Nick was not opposed. She put out roast beef sandwich makings and a bag of salad, and they stood side by side at the island counter, putting the meal together in companionable silence, alone with their own thoughts.

"I'm not sure I want to look in those boxes," Maddy said as they settled on the high bar stools. "I'm afraid they might be like Pandora's."

Hands and mouth full of sandwich, Nick could only

look his question at her. The remnants of his spiderweb had caught in her hair and he reached out a hand to brush it free. Her eyes widened. "Cobwebs," he said tersely.

"Oh. Okay." Her cheeks had gone a little pink.

"Pandora," he prompted.

"It's a Greek myth. Pandora's box. The woman, Pandora, was created by Hephaestus, the god of fire and metal working, endowed with great beauty and skills, and given a box containing a whole bunch of evil stuff."

"Why?"

"The old gods did stuff like that. Old gods do something, you aren't supposed to question." She relented. "Something to do with Zeus being angry with mankind, I think. Anyway, Pandora wasn't supposed to open the box, but she was curious, so she pried it open and released all the evils that have since plagued the world. No way to lock them up again once they were loose."

"You think Bart's boxes might be full of evil?"

"I don't know. It's the part about not being able to put back and forget whatever's in the boxes once they are open that worries me."

She put down the half of a sandwich she'd nibbled at and fixed him with the clear and steady gaze of her blue eyes. "Can I trust you, Nick?"

The least he could do was hesitate before saying, "Yes. Sure. Of course you can."

She kept her gaze on him for a couple of seconds, then nodded as though she'd just settled an argument with herself. Then she started talking about the books in the bookcases in the living room. She and Kazuko had actually found money in them. Probably close to a couple of million dollars, she said.

He'd *known* there was something suspicious about those books. "What did you do with the money?" he asked.

"Kazuko and I hid it." She didn't say anything more.

Okay, so Bart wasn't the only one who kept things secret. Evidently she still didn't trust him completely. Smart lady.

He remembered her saying earlier that Kazuko was already keeping something. Ah, Kazuko was keeping the money. "Somewhere safe, I hope," he said.

"Do you think I ought to tell the police?"

"What do you think?"

"I don't want to tell them."

"Why not?"

"I don't know. Gut instinct. Maybe something to do with me not wanting to help them find out too much about Bart until I find it out myself."

Interesting. And encouraging, implying she really didn't know what Bart had done or might be doing now.

"What do you think knowing about the money might tell them?"

She spread her hands in an endearing gesture of helplessness. "I don't know. They might think he stole it, I guess. I wonder that myself. When you said you were a private investigator and you'd already told me you were a CPA, I thought maybe Bart had robbed a bank and that's why you were after him."

She shook her head. "Maybe the police would think *I* stole that money. Bart's not around. It might be easier to stick me with the blame."

He thought for a minute. If he told her to give him the money, she'd suspect the worst. If he told her to put it in a bank for safekeeping, the bank manager would think the worst. The Japanese woman had impressed him with her straight from the shoulder attitude. He had an idea Kazuko might be the safest guardian of that money for now.

"Okay," he said. "We won't tell the police. Not yet anyway."

Maddy looked relieved.

After lunch they took the boxes into Bart's office and went through them. Bart had been a meticulous record keeper. They found his work itineraries, expense sheets, credit card receipts. Looking at these records, an investigator could follow his every step for years back. A bonanza, Nick thought, though the records didn't go far enough back for his purposes.

At first glance, everything looked completely innocent. What had he expected, something with a red flag that shouted, *Here I am—this is Bart Williams's real identity!*

After they reached the bottom of the first box, Nick sat back and shook his head, then saw that Maddy was frowning over a document she'd taken from a file in her pile. She handed it over when he looked inquiringly at her. It was a copy of an application for a Social Security number that had been filled out twenty-six years earlier. Twenty-six years ago, when Bart had arrived in the U.S.

Bart had given his father's name as Emmerich Franz, his mother's as Gerda Franz, his own as Bartel Wilhelm Franz, with a Chicago address.

"Is this supposed to be Bart?" Maddy wondered aloud. "Why would his name be on there as Bartel Wilhelm Franz when he told me it was formerly just Bart Wilhelm?"

"Look at the date of birth," Nick pointed out. "This has to be your husband. A lot of immigrants changed their names or had them changed for them by some wiseass in the INS. Maybe the person who checked him in just left his last name off."

She shook her head. "But he told *me* it was Wilhelm, and I—" She broke off and gave a bitter little laugh that went straight to his gut. "Why am I surprised that he lied?"

"I believe you said he'd become an American citizen?"

"So he told me. I'm beginning to wonder if anything he told me was true."

"Did you have a chance to look for his naturalization papers yet?"

She nodded. "Yes, I looked in his office. No, I didn't find them. Maybe they're among these papers somewhere. Or a copy at least."

"They aren't supposed to be copied. You might find a note of the naturalization number though."

She didn't respond—she was thumbing through the rest of the papers in the file. Then she gave an exclamation. "Look at this!"

"This" was a Visa bill.

He looked a question at her, not sure why she thought it significant.

"He had a MasterCard credit card," she pointed out. "All of these work-related expenses were charged to MasterCard. This is Visa."

Nick shrugged. "So he had more than one credit card. Many people do."

"But the statements on this MasterCard bill show hotel and meal charges." She pulled more documents from the file. "So do these Visa bills. But they are at different hotels."

She started comparing the two lots of accounts. It took a while. "Apparently, Bart usually stayed at small hotels or bed-and-breakfasts," she said at last. "But every once in a while he'd leave the small hotel and spend one or two nights in a Travelers' Haven. Those are the ones he charged on the Visa card."

"Maybe he kept work accounts separate from personal accounts."

"But his only trips were work-related." She hesitated, staring at Nick. "At least that's what he said. Maybe he *was* having an affair, or hiring a prostitute."

"Or he just added a day or two for vacation?"

"I suppose that's possible." She frowned. "I really didn't know this man I married, did I? My only excuse is that when he changed, I lost interest in what he was doing or how long he was gone. I lost heart, I guess."

An image popped up unexpectedly in her mind. Herself in her wedding gown, walking down the aisle toward Bart and his best man. The people in the church. A much bigger wedding than she'd wanted. Bart's choice. To impress his boss with the fact that he really was getting married?

She sighed and started putting the papers and journals back in the box. "I think I've had enough for one day, but—"

She broke off and stared into space.

"What?" Nick said.

"The best man. It just occurred to me. I never saw him

again. But he had to have been a friend of Bart's. The best man's usually a friend, isn't he?"

"I would think so. Who *was* best man? Someone he worked with? None of the people I talked to mentioned—"

"Someone he met at his gym, he said. Bart worked out regularly at a gym near here."

Nick remembered following Bart to the gym the day before he disappeared, waiting outside in his car until Bart emerged. He stood up. "Let's go."

"I don't remember the guy's name—wait a minute, it would be on the marriage certificate. He and Sally, my matron of honor, had to sign as witnesses."

The certificate was in the secretary in her office. She found it and pulled it out of its envelope. "Walt Chambers," she said.

She put on her trench coat, and Nick picked up his parka from the front entry closet.

The gym was in Jordan, a private enclave that was part of, but fenced off from, Oak River. Bart had held a membership in Jordan's country club, which had entitled him to use the gym.

A young, sinewy, dark-haired woman wearing bicycle shorts and a sports bra with "Kat" embroidered over the right breast was guarding the desk in the entry to the Jordan gym. She nodded when Maddy presented Bart's card. "You can use the gym," she told Maddy, "but your friend would need to be sponsored by a different resident and would have to pay the annual fee, which might—"

Maddy interrupted. "We don't want to use the gym. We're interested in talking to one of your members—Walt Chambers. May I leave a message asking him to call me?"

"Why don't you talk to him yourself?" the young woman said.

"He's here?"

"Always," the woman said. "He works here. He's one of our trainers."

"I don't . . ." Maddy began, puzzled, but then she saw that the young woman was gesturing to a man in sweats at the back of the gym. He was supervising a teenage boy doing circuit training.

As the man approached, she saw that he was around forty, very buff, and indeed the man who had stood up for Bart.

He recognized her instantly. "Mrs. Williams. I wouldn't have expected to . . . that is, I sure am sorry about Mr. Williams. I heard on TV that he'd . . . that he . . . Well, I'm really sorry." He looked at Nick and frowned, then looked back at Maddy.

"*Mr.* Williams?" Maddy echoed, wondering why he'd be so formal.

"It wasn't him? I mean, it wasn't *your* Mr. Williams? I thought they said Bart."

"We understood you were a friend of his," Nick said. "Mrs. Williams is surprised that you called him Mister."

"Me, a friend? Gosh no." He laughed in a nervous way. "I knew him, of course—he was one of our regulars— but that was all."

He seemed embarrassed, Maddy thought. But why?

"You were best man at our wedding," she reminded him.

"Yes, I know, well, sure, but that didn't mean . . ."

"If you weren't a friend, how come you were his best man?" Nick asked, cutting to the chase.

The trainer looked around as if for an escape route, then shrugged and met Maddy's gaze straight on.

"He paid me," he said.

"To be his best man?" She was astonished. Watching the man approach, she had begun to wonder if Bart had been gay after all. She was pretty sure the trainer was— his mannerisms seemed to indicate it, though she hadn't noticed that at the wedding. For one wild moment she wondered if Bart and Walt had been involved in some kind of relationship. Had Bart married her not only to hang on to his job but to cover up his own sexual persuasion? Had he paid Walt to ensure his cooperation?

"Why would he *pay* you?" she asked.

"Well, I had to take a day off from here, lose a day's

pay. But he made it up to me and then some."

"I think Mrs. Williams wants to know why he'd *need* to pay someone to be his best man," Nick put in.

"Oh. Yeah, well, I wondered about that myself. But he made a good offer, and I can always use a little more of the ready, you know what I mean."

"Bart worked out here," Maddy said.

Walt nodded.

"And out of the blue, he asked you to be his best man at our wedding."

"Said his friends were all going to be out of town. Offered to provide the tux and I could keep it, plus paying five times what I'd make here in a day. Offer I couldn't refuse. I was wanting a tux, as it happened, and he bought me a really nice Pierre Cardin, with a ruffled shirt, studs, a tie, the works."

"Have you seen him since?" Nick asked.

"Well, sure. Mr. Williams comes in regular as any clock. Came. Monday, Wednesday, Friday when he was in town. Kept up with his workouts when he was on the road too. He was in really good shape."

"When did you last see him?" Maddy asked.

"About ten days ago, a week last Wednesday."

The day before Bart disappeared.

"Did you talk to him?"

"Heck, no. Mr. Williams didn't want any conversation when he was working out. Very concentrated he was, always. Never was one to chat, frowned on people who did, asked them to keep it down. Made a few people mad. He wasn't all that friendly to anyone. That's what surprised me when he asked me to . . ."

He looked at Maddy. "He didn't *tell* you I was his trainer?"

"No."

Maddy became aware that both he and Nick were looking at her with sympathy. Pathetic, she thought. What had she been thinking to stay with that strange cold man for all those months?

"I think you could use a drink," Nick suggested as they

left the gym. She nodded without really thinking about what he was saying and was surprised when he parked the car in front of a local Irish pub.

"My mother and I like a Guinness once in a while," Nick said. "She swears it's good for whatever ails you."

She nodded again. She felt robotic, unable to think for herself. Whatever he suggested was okay with her. She'd stopped wondering or even thinking about Bart. Her mind felt as if everything had emptied out and someone had switched the light off.

They hurried through the rain into the pub. There was a log fire burning in the fireplace. Nick and Maddy chose a table near the fire and started unzipping and removing their damp outer clothing.

The froth on top of the Guinness had a shamrock stamped on it. Maddy lifted the tall cool glass hesitantly. The first sip surprised her. The beer was rich, creamy, full-bodied—a far cry from the ale that was all she'd ever sampled until now.

"It's good," she said.

"Would my mother lie?"

He was trying to pull her out of her stunned state, she recognized. And as she sipped the rich stout and felt her muscles relax in the warmth of the crackling fire, she could feel life returning.

She took a deep breath and looked at him. Raindrops glinted in his black hair. Her hand moved slightly as though it wanted to brush them away. Judging by past history, her mind was not always in control of her body. She needed to remedy that, put her brain in charge. What she mainly needed was to get away from Nick Ciacia before she gave in to any hormonal urges.

"Are you hungry?" he asked.

Had he read her mind? Maybe she *was* hungry, she thought. Hungry for a love that would wipe out the memory of Bart and her own idiocy in staying married to him past that first failed so-called love-making episode. Why had she thought it only fair to give the marriage time to jell, to maybe even catch fire?

"No," she said firmly. "I'm not at all hungry. I'm sorry I got you into all this," she added. "I'll be able to manage okay from now on."

"You're dispensing with my services? I'm fired?"

"I wouldn't put it that way. I'm sure you can find better things to do than trail around with me."

He seemed about to retort, but changed his mind.

"You must think I've been incredibly stupid," Maddy said. "I can't believe I was dumb enough to marry a man who had to pay someone to be his best man."

He shook his head. "You didn't know that. And I'd never call you stupid. Hey, I've been taken in by a woman or two in my time. People aren't always who you think they are."

He held her gaze and she felt a different, internal warmth that had nothing to do with the blazing hearth. For the life of her she couldn't look away. How serious this man always looked, in spite of the humor that popped up regularly. How intense was the expression in his dark, almost black eyes.

He was the first to blink. He also moved a little in his chair, making her aware of the size and strength of his body. So much for putting her brain in charge of her body.

"What do you want to do next?" he asked.

Don't answer that, she instructed herself, almost, but not quite, making herself smile.

"I think I've done enough sleuthing for one day," she said after a pause. "It seems to me it might be a good idea to go through Bart's papers and journals and then follow in his footsteps, starting with that last trip that he was so perturbed about when I questioned him. I might just do that, see where it leads me."

She took another sip of the life-giving Guinness. "It may seem ridiculous to you under the circumstances, but I feel a need to know exactly what happened to Bart to change him from the man I married. Whether he'd want me to or not, I feel it's my duty to find out what happened to make him do something so drastic."

"I don't think it's ridiculous at all. I'm impressed. Not many people talk about duty."

"I imagine you feel strongly about duty yourself."

He nodded. "That I do." He hesitated. "Can you get the time off work?"

"I've already asked for a month away from the office. As I mentioned earlier, virtually all dot-com companies have been losing market value recently. TheHub is still holding on, but the company has tightened its corporate belt and is doing very little hiring. So I won't be missed for a while at least. I can take along my laptop. I'll need to check in to my office by email or voice mail, return calls to candidates, and check with a staffing coordinator to make sure my candidates are being taken care of—moving through the process, interviews scheduled, and so on."

"I'd like to come with you, continue helping you," Nick said.

Her gaze turned measuring. "Why?"

Creative thinking coming up. "Quentin, remember? Bart's the only link I've found to Quentin."

Lame, Ciacia. But he certainly couldn't tell her that it would be much easier for him to question people, and to get answers, if he was accompanying the "grieving widow."

"I see." She didn't look as if she did see, and she looked as if it wouldn't take much to color her thoughts with suspicion. Which was a shame, considering she'd been bestowing softer than usual glances on him.

She had narrowed her eyes in thought. Never a good sign. But after a minute or so, she shrugged. "Bart's last trip ended in Portland," she told him.

Was she saying yes to his accompanying her? He leaned forward, arms folded on the table. "We ought to be able to follow the paper trail from there, retrace Bart's steps on his last journey, visit the places he visited, stay in the hotels or motels he stayed in. Maybe we'll get lucky."

"You have time for all this?"

"I have no other commitments right now." It made a nice change to tell the truth.

"Okay then," she said. "Same business arrangement as before, though."

She'd put a lot of stress on "business."

"I'll pay you for your time and I pay the expenses."

No way, he thought, then stuck his figurative tongue in his figurative cheek. "It's a deal."

Chapter 15

IN THE END, they decided that before they launched themselves on an odyssey down I-5, they should start at the finish line—Bart's final destination, Crescent Beach—and show Bart's photo to people in stores and hotels, asking if they'd seen him or known him.

The weather grew more and more blustery the closer they drove to the coast. On the final winding curves leading to Crescent Beach, the wind rocked Nick's Chevy every time there was a gap between the tall evergreens. Rain kept the windshield wipers fanning constantly.

They stopped at a grocery store, picked up a shopping and hotel guide to the area, then bought a couple of lattes at the store's espresso bar, sitting on high stools, looking out at the rain and a huge American flag snapping back and forth in the wind.

Nick suggested it might be a good idea for Maddy to check in at the local police department first, let them know she was in town before they heard it from anyone else. "I'll go in with you if you want me to," he offered, but the offer didn't sound wholehearted.

"Best I go alone," Maddy said, and he didn't argue, just agreed to wait for her in the car.

Lieutenant Saperia didn't seem all that pleased to see her, but he greeted her amiably enough. "What can I do for you, Mrs. Williams?" he asked after gesturing her to a chair.

She folded her gloved hands in her lap. "I just wanted to know if you'd found out anything else about my husband's . . . death."

He studied her before answering. He had a kind face, she thought. He was not a young man, a little too heavy for his uniform, but healthy-looking, with a ruddy complexion and alert, youthful brown eyes. "Doesn't seem to be anything more to find out, ma'am. As you know, the coroner ruled Mr. Williams's death a suicide. His fingerprints—the only fingerprints—on the weapon. Gunshot residue on his right hand. We checked with you that he was right-handed, correct?"

She nodded.

"Seemed open and shut to us, ma'am. Nothing to indicate anyone else was with him or involved in any way."

"You said you didn't find a key to the house he was discovered in, but there was no evidence of a break-in."

"That's correct."

"How do you suppose he got in then?"

"Maybe the front or back door was open. Or a window. We have a volunteer property watch here—you'd be surprised how often people go off and leave doors or windows unlocked. Property watch people close them up. This particular house wasn't on the list for the volunteers to check on. It had been unoccupied a long time."

"When I talked to you before you hadn't tracked down the owners of the house."

"We discovered that the original owners went to southern California for the winter. The husband died there—heart attack in the middle of September. They had relatives down there, the widow decided to stay, and she authorized Ms. Dyson to sell the house for her, lock, stock, and whatever."

He hesitated. "Once he was inside the house, your husband could have opened the garage with the button near the inside door, driven his car in, and closed up the place. There's no way of knowing."

He leaned forward, his nice brown eyes showing sympathy.

"I don't believe there's anything more I can tell you, Mrs. Williams. I know it's difficult to accept that your husband committed suicide, but that's the way of it. As I told you at the time, the alcohol level in his blood was off the charts. I know you told us he wasn't a drinker, but it isn't easy for anyone to shoot themselves cold sober. If anyone's ever going to get drunk, that's the time to do it. I haven't seen anything to indicate any other person was involved."

It was Maddy's turn to do some face studying. The lieutenant's face was an open book, no guile in sight. No matter how strong her feeling that Bart's death needed more examining, more explanation, he was telling her the truth as he saw it, and she'd be stupid to keep banging her head against this particular wall.

"Do you have any objection to my asking some questions around town?" she asked. "I'd still like to know if my husband was seen with anyone else, or if anyone possibly noticed anything unusual. I'd feel better if I could get some glimmer of understanding as to why he killed himself."

"No law against asking questions, ma'am. But I doubt . . . well, that's entirely up to you. This is a friendly town. People will talk to you."

He stood up.

"Thank you for your time," she said, standing herself.

He shook her hand. "You take care, now."

"Yes, of course. Thank you."

ONLY A COUPLE of store owners recognized Bart from the photo—and they'd seen it previously in the local newspaper. They appeared excited, even titillated, by the

story of the decomposing body in the vacant house, but
no real information was forthcoming.

At the last of the resort town's many restaurant-bar
combinations, this one with a country-western theme, the
bartender, a handsome young black man wearing a name
tag that identified him as Tyler, nodded as he studied the
photograph Maddy handed him.

"That's the dude Pam Dyson found, right? Scared her
out of a year's growth, she said."

"Did you ever see him in Crescent Beach?" Maddy
asked.

Tyler inclined his head to one side. "What's it to you?"

"He was my husband," Maddy said.

"Wow. Hey. That's tough."

"Did he ever come in here?" Maddy persisted.

The bartender wiped the bar with a cloth as carefully
as if it were the most important task anyone could ever
have.

"He might have been in Crescent Beach on Halloween,
or during the next day or two," Nick said.

"Halloween," Tyler echoed. "Lot of people in here that
night. We had a live band. Line dancing."

"Here?" Maddy asked, looking around the crowded
bar. "You have a dance floor in here?"

He gestured over his shoulder. "Back room. Popular
event. No idea if this guy showed up in here. I just pour
the drinks. Mind my own business. Sorry I can't help."

He had folded his cloth into a perfect square. He didn't
make eye contact.

"Can't help with what?" a female voice queried.

A waitress with a tray loaded with empty glasses had
shown up next to Maddy at the end of the horseshoe-
shaped bar. "You trying to get information out of Tyler?"
she asked cheerfully. "You'd have better luck getting
blood out of a rutabaga."

"Lena!" There was a warning in Tyler's voice as he
took the tray from her.

The waitress made a face at him. "Same again for these
guys," she said, indicating the tray.

She was fair and pretty, young, dressed in a tee and high-cut suede shorts. "Tyler here thinks a bartender's akin to a priest," she said to Maddy. "Anything anyone tells him is sacred. What do they call that, Tyler? Bartender-lush privilege?"

She laughed raucously, causing several heads to turn.

"I never saw that dude in here," Tyler said firmly, setting the photo back down in front of Maddy.

"Eew, that's the man shot himself," Lena said. "He was in here all right. The week before Pam Dyson found him in that bed. Halloween. I already told the police about it. He was in only the once. Lousy tightwad. Sure, all he drank was mineral water, but it comes in a bottle, bottle has to be opened, stuff has to be poured. You'd think someone could fork over a dime or ten for that kind of service. Sheesh."

Tyler, Nick, and Maddy were all staring at her, Tyler with dour disapproval.

"He was this lady's husband," Tyler said.

Lena grimaced. "Oops!"

"You're sure it was him?" Maddy said.

"Sure I'm sure, honey. I got one a those pornographic memories!" She laughed at her own joke.

"He didn't drink at all?" Nick queried. "You're sure?"

"The guy at his table kept trying to get him to have something, asked me if I'd ever heard of this rare breed of German that didn't drink beer. The guy you're talking about"—she tapped the photograph—"*this* guy, shot him a look would freeze the . . . tail . . . off a monkey."

"The guy at his table?" Maddy queried.

"Isn't it time you took care of our customers?" Tyler snapped, handing Lena her tray, now filled with brimming glasses.

She rolled her eyes sideways at him and took off, the tray expertly balanced on one upraised hand, but she was back in no time. Tyler had meanwhile moved across the horseshoe to serve another customer.

After depositing her tray, Lena studied Bart's photo again. Maddy held her breath.

"Don't see many men with hair that light," Lena said. "Didn't look bleached either. Women now, yeah, we got a black gal comes in here Friday nights regular has real light blond hair about a quarter inch long. Guess she just rubs bleach all over her head. Can't be good for your brain, that. And plenty of old people have hair looks sorta like this, but this guy wasn't old. Forties maybe? Great-looking guy, your husband. Not a happy camper though."

"What makes you say that?" Maddy asked.

Lena shrugged. "The way he looked. Everybody else in here was having a great time, but he was mad at the world. Fit to be tied. Vibrating with it. Teeth clenched, fists clenched. The other guy told him it was going to be okay."

"What was?" Nick asked.

Lena raised impatient eyebrows. "How should I know? I may be more observant than old Tyler there, but I don't hang around eavesdropping."

"Sorry," Nick said at once. "I didn't mean to imply anything. I was just hoping you might have overheard something."

She shook her head.

"Do you know who the other man was?" Maddy asked. "The man who was with my husband?"

"Some guy in a cowboy hat."

"Everybody in here was wearing a cowboy hat that night." Tyler was back and listening in. "*You* were wearing a cowboy hat," he reminded Lena. "Looked weird with your fishnet panty hose."

"Guys *like* fishnet panty hose," Lena said. "I get way more in tips when I wear them, cowboy hat or no cowboy hat. It wasn't *my* hat anyways, some guy from BC put it on me. Took it back later, more's the pity. It was a great hat. Black with silver gizmos around the band."

All this cowboy talk was striking a chord in Maddy's memory. She set the thought aside to be examined later.

"What's the deal here?" the bartender asked her. "Your husband run out on you before he came down here and killed himself?"

"Something like that," Maddy said.

"Did the two men stay long?" Nick asked Lena. "Did they come in together, leave together? Did either of them appear to have been drinking before they got here?"

She shrugged. "Nah, they were both sober, though the cowboy did have a beer. But this place was packed solid to the walls. Even more than tonight. Jumping. I didn't notice if they came in together or left together or when they got together. They might just have met—people sit down anywhere they can when it's that busy."

"But you said the cowboy—the man in the cowboy hat—told my husband it was going to be okay," Maddy said. "Doesn't that sound as if they knew each other?"

Lena shrugged. "Coulda been talking about the weather."

Maddy supposed she could be right, but she doubted it.

"You said you talked to the police?" Nick said.

"Sure did. Said in the paper they wanted any information anyone could come up with. I was hoping there was a reward, but they said not."

She looked hopefully at Nick, then at Maddy. "I'd be willing to pay for information," Maddy said.

Lena brightened again, then sagged. "You already got everything I know, honey. Like I told the police. The guy was in here, drank a whole bottle of mineral water—Pellegrino, the tall bottle. Don't often get people who ask for it by name. Mostly they just say water. The few who even ask for water. Not too many people come in a bar and drink water. Anyhow, all I know is, he and the guy in the cowboy hat talked some. The German guy, he was very serious, never cracked a smile, looked mad at the world, like I said. I guess he at least told the cowboy he was German. Was he German?"

"Yes," Maddy said. "And he preferred Pellegrino water to others."

"You didn't hear a name?" Nick asked. "Do you remember anything at all about the cowboy? Was he tall, short, dark-haired, old, young?"

Lena frowned. "Saw him sitting down. Not so short you'd notice. Hard to tell though. Dark hair, I think. Maybe middle-aged. Shirt with a red pattern on it—you know, like flames or something. Like maybe what Garth Brooks would wear when he does one of his spectaculars." She spread her palms. "That's it, end of story."

"People over there waving for you, Lena," Tyler said.

Lena stuck her tongue out at him, then patted Maddy on her arm as she turned away. "Sorry for your grieving, honey," she said kindly.

Nick and Maddy stopped at a few stores and one bed-and-breakfast a couple of streets back from the oceanfront, but they had apparently exhausted every bit of evidence Crescent Beach had to offer. There seemed to be no way to find out where Bart had bought the whiskey he'd drunk, if he'd bought it, or where he'd drunk it.

"Maybe right there in that bedroom," Nick suggested.

Even Pam Dyson, the real estate agent who had discovered Bart's body, couldn't add anything to what the police had already told Maddy, though she did describe the entire experience in vivid detail. "No, the quilt wasn't completely over his head," she said in answer to Nick's question. "I could see that he'd been—I could see the blood all over his hair and the pillow—part of his head was completely gone and—"

She broke off. "I'm never going to forget that," she finished, her face paling, her eyes conveying the horror of the discovery.

Maddy shuddered deep inside. No matter how Bart had changed toward her, no matter that he'd become someone other than the man she'd married, there had been a time when she had touched him, had kissed him, had thought she loved him, had lain with him in bed. More than ever, she was determined to find out what had led to his lonely, violent death.

On the way back to Oak River, she sat silently beside Nick, who was also silent. Watching the windshield wipers go back and forth, she remembered going to a friend's house for a housewarming party several years ago, before she met Bart, back when her life had been simple and straightforward—work, home, dating, shopping, cleaning her apartment, smiling. In retrospect, it seemed to her she'd done a lot of smiling then.

Entering her friend's house, she'd been given the end of a red string and instructed to follow it as it wound around the legs of chairs and tables and desks and standing lamps, in and out of various rooms. Other people followed other strings, blue, green, yellow, brown, purple, occasionally colliding with one another, all laughing, exclaiming over the cleverness of a game that led the guests on a tour of the new house and ended at a bar in a recreation room in the basement.

Maddy was convinced that there had to be strings that led to whatever had caused Bart to change so drastically and to finally end his life. She would sort them out, she vowed, follow them one by one until her questions were answered.

Chapter 16

MADDY SPENT THE next morning, a Monday, packing up Bart's clothing, with Kazuko's help, and filling a wheeled tote with casual clothing for herself. She settled her laptop into her briefcase, which she'd already crammed with Bart's papers.

Kazuko would deliver Bart's clothing to the thrift shop her church sponsored, and would check on the house and water plants when necessary. Maddy and Nick would start down I-5 the following day.

In the afternoon, Maddy made arrangements for the newspapers and mail, and typed up a list of the places Bart had visited over the last year. After wheeling her tote into the entryway, she went through her bedroom clothes closet and selected her outfit for tomorrow: a royal blue fleece jacket that zipped up the front into a high rolled collar, a white sweater, black-and-white striped wool pants, a pair of stretchy black winter gloves, and lined black ankle boots. The forecast called for freezing temperatures in Seattle and close to that on the road.

She had mixed emotions about the proposed journey.

Though she felt relieved to be actually doing something that might provide answers, she was also extremely nervous about spending so much time with Nick Ciacia.

According to Bart's journals, most of his medical contacts practiced in large hospitals fairly close to the I-5 corridor. The last surgeon Bart had seen was a Dr. Brenda Milligan, in Portland, Oregon.

The city of Portland was one of Maddy's favorites—located at the confluence of the Columbia and Willamette Rivers, which divided Oregon from Washington. It was not only a tourist's city, it was a livable and walking city, with fabulous waterfront promenades, rose gardens, attractive buildings, parks, statues and fountains, and interesting and diverse neighborhoods, not to mention a great zoo. It was also rich in bookstores, art galleries and museums, shops, microbreweries, and restaurants of all kinds, with wine country nearby, and the Pacific Ocean not too many miles away. All of this and the Portland opera and Oregon symphony too.

Traffic was heavy in both north and south directions on Tuesday morning, the weather cold and damp and socked in, none of the mountains showing.

The hospital parking lot was already full when they arrived at eleven-thirty a.m. Nick had to wait for someone to come along and vacate a slot for his Chevy to slide into.

Maddy noted that he waited patiently, unlike Bart, who would have simmered silently, taking the lack of a space personally. He'd been known to give up on an errand rather than search farther afield for a spot to park in.

Dr. Milligan, a slight, red-haired, freckle-faced woman, had just completed a successful brain tumor surgery and was obviously feeling buoyant. She'd be happy to join them for coffee, she assured them.

In the half-filled cafeteria, they took their mugs to a window table that overlooked wintry but appealing gardens that were brightened by big clumps of late-blooming yellow daisies.

Getting down to business right away, Maddy said, "We're here to ask about Bart Williams."

The doctor frowned, showing lines around her eyes and across her forehead that made her look older than Maddy had estimated. "Mawsom's sales rep? I'm not sure I—"

"Bart is—was—my husband," Maddy said.

Dr. Milligan's face made the adjustment from puzzlement to sympathy. "I saw a report on Northwest Cable News. I'm sorry. Suicide, they said. I'm not sure how I can help."

Maddy nodded. "I don't expect you to have any information regarding Bart's death, Doctor. I'm just—Nick and I are just tracking Bart's territory, getting an idea of where he was recently, who he saw, hoping we might come up with some clues to his . . . state of mind."

The doctor nodded in a cautious way, not committing herself, then she glanced questioningly at Nick.

"I'm a friend of Mrs. Williams," Nick said, smiling over the rim of his coffee mug. "I'm just here to support and help."

Maddy tried not to show surprise, but couldn't help glancing questioningly at him. Why hadn't he said he was a PI? That would surely lend some authority to this inquiry.

He twitched one dark eyebrow. She wasn't sure what message he intended to convey, but decided to go along with him for the moment. But she gave him a level look that was meant to tell him there would be questions later. The glint in his eyes told her that *her* message had been received and understood.

She looked back at Dr. Milligan, who was busily stirring sugar substitute into her coffee and had evidently missed the exchange. "According to Bart's records, you were the last surgeon he visited. It would have been the twenty-fifth of October."

"Sounds about right. I can consult my appointment book if you think— No, come to think of it, we didn't have an appointment. He was just dropping in on some of his accounts on his way back from San Francisco. I remember that he didn't have anything new to discuss, he was just checking on any results I'd noted, any questions I might have. He was always very thorough."

Maddy nodded. "I don't think the exact time would make any difference."

Nick put his coffee mug down on the table and shifted in his chair. Did that mean he *wanted* the doctor to be exact?

"He seemed about the same as usual," Dr. Milligan said. "He was never one for small talk, you know. I mean, he never suggested we meet in the cafeteria like this. He was a very . . . formal man, you know what I mean?"

"Yes," Maddy said shortly.

"I'm not being critical. He was damn good at his job. No wasted time. He was always prepared, always one step ahead of my questions. Could always back up his statements about whatever treatment we were discussing."

She leaned back, squinting thoughtfully. "I have to tell you, Mrs. Williams, your husband was not the friendliest of men. Some of the other reps, well, we'd talk a little about the state of the world, or how Tiger Woods was doing—I'm a big admirer of that young man—or movies or the weather, politics."

She leaned forward. "I'm a people person. I enjoy chit-chat. My work is stressful, and small talk relaxes me. Bart obviously didn't enjoy that kind of thing. He was always very much to the point. Came into my office, did his presentation, answered questions, packed up, and left."

She frowned worriedly. "I hope I'm not giving you the impression I disliked your husband. We got along fine. It was just all business, every time. I got used to him, I guess."

"He was a very businesslike person," Maddy said.

"He never said anything personal?" Nick queried. "This last time, did he maybe mention any problems he might be having? Did he seem nervous, worried?"

"Anything but. As I recall he seemed quite relaxed, not in as much of a hurry to leave as he sometimes was. Not that he got all pally or anything, he was just a little looser.

I remember thinking his trip to California must have been a successful one. Anyone else I'd have asked, but he never seemed to want to talk about himself."

She hesitated. "But he was really good at his job," she said again. "Some reps, you can almost see their sales training showing through. You know, the stimulus-response approach, concentrating on saying things in a way that is expected to produce a favorable response, laboring away to demonstrate that I have needs they could fill. That might work well selling vacuum cleaners, but it doesn't work in this environment. Bart would just stick to the facts, ma'am, if you know what I mean. The rest was up to me."

A middle-aged woman with tightly curled salt and pepper hair approached, giving Dr. Milligan a meaningful glance. "I guess I'm wanted in the office," she said. Finishing the last of her coffee, she stood up and shook hands with both of them. "Sorry I wasn't much help," she said, then gave Maddy a compassionate look, holding her hand a moment longer. "I really am sorry for your loss."

Maddy nodded. "Thank you."

"I thought it was better not to bring an investigative air into the proceedings," Nick said as soon as the doctor was out of earshot and before Maddy could ask. "When people know I'm on the job, it sometimes makes them uneasy, unwilling to talk. Better if I just play it out as your helpful friend. If that's okay with you."

She supposed there was something to that. "What did you think?" she asked.

He let out a long breath. "It's becoming pretty clear your husband was okay on the job, but didn't socialize for even a minute with anyone. Either he wanted to appear businesslike, or he didn't believe in wasting time, or he just wasn't that interested in people."

"The last," Maddy said.

His eyes showed sympathy. "What did *you* think?"

"Well, Dr. Milligan indirectly confirmed one thing I'd noticed. As I think I told you, a couple of times since we've been married, Bart was nervous when he started out on a trip, but much more relaxed when it was over. I suppose sometimes his job was more stressful than others."

She shook her head. "I'm making guesses. I could never, ever get Bart to talk about his work or how he felt about it."

She drank some of her coffee. It was cold. "I'm not even sure 'nervous' is the right way to describe how he was those times. Intense, concentrated, almost as though he'd hypnotized himself into a trance. I'd speak to him, he wouldn't hear me."

"He wasn't out to win any Mr. Congeniality awards, it seems." His expression was sympathetic. "You want something to eat?"

"Not here. I'm not picky, but eating in a hospital . . ."

"A little farther down the road then."

"I'm not sure we're going to get anywhere on this trip," she said gloomily. "I'm probably wasting your time. And mine."

"Hey," he said softly, putting a hand on her shoulder. "We've only just begun. Sometimes you can do a half dozen interviews without any usable results, then all of a sudden you get a break. You can't give up this early."

The weight of his hand was comforting, warm. Maddy felt a sudden urge to lean her cheek onto it. The idea sent a surge of heat through her. Her breath seemed to be trapped somewhere deep in her throat.

She picked up her coffee cup again and gulped the contents. "I guess we'd better get going," she said.

His hand was still on her shoulder. He was looking at her in a questioning way, and there was a certain glint in his eyes that made her wonder. . . .

Feeling flustered, she stood up. His hand dropped away.

He stood too, his gaze on her face. "So it's okay with you for me to say I'm just a friend of the family, so to speak?"

"Sure," she said briskly. "Whatever works."

Chapter 17

THEY STOPPED FOR avocado and turkey sandwiches and more coffee at a Togo's eatery in Tualatin. The restaurant overlooked a pleasant small lake where a man was playing with a radio-controlled model submarine. He was wearing a quilted parka and a knitted cap. The weather had turned extremely cold.

This side of the window a small girl was playing with some *Toy Story* action figures. As she ate, Maddy watched the girl set the figures on the table and move them around. Hamm, the piggy bank, reminded her of Rachel in the market, and she replayed the scene when Bart had charged straight by her. Why had he done that? What demons had been chasing him, and were they demons of his own making, or someone else's?

The little girl was making Buzz Lightyear fly around above the table. Another memory. Her old boyfriend Buzz Ellison. What a terrific lover he had been. He had taught her a lot. She could smile at the memories now. At the time his inability to make any kind of commitment or even admit that he loved her had gradually killed her affection for him. The Peter Pan syndrome, she'd decided; the boy who didn't want to grow up. She should have known—anyone who hung on to an old school nickname that long after graduation . . . "Wouldn't you, if your real name was Norman?" he'd demanded when she teased him.

"Share the joke?" Nick asked.

She smiled ruefully. "I was just remembering an old boyfriend. Buzz. I told you about my failed relationships, remember? The little girl's toy—the one in the space suit—is Buzz Lightyear."

He looked blank, and she moved her head slightly to indicate the child.

"Oh yeah, the kiddie movie. I guess I saw the posters."

"*Toy Story*," she told him. "It's a very good movie, though I didn't care for this one character, a really nasty little boy who dismembers toys and puts them back together in weird combinations. My friend Sally's kids—I baby-sit them sometimes—absolutely love *Toy Story*. They cheer and jeer all the way through. Buzz Lightyear, the space ranger, arrives on the scene and puts Woody's nose out of joint. All the other toys are agog over Buzz. But eventually Woody and Buzz get over their rivalry and work together."

"Which one's Woody?"

"The cowboy."

She frowned and set her sandwich down.

"What?" Nick asked.

"Woody. I'm wondering where I . . . Oh my God, I've got it. I've been trying to figure out what it was about the cowboy."

Nick was waiting patiently, working on his sandwich.

"The day Bart disappeared. I guess that's why it made an impression. We saw all those trick-or-treaters when we drove into Oak River, remember? There was a whole gang of kids in *Toy Story* outfits. There was even a Mr. Potato Head."

He nodded. "I remember."

"There was a man with the kids. Because he was with

them, I thought he was dressed like Woody. But he was wearing a white cowboy hat. Woody wears a brown hat—see?"

He glanced at the little girl and her toys, then looked back at her.

"The man in the street was actually just dressed up like a cowboy."

"Maybe that was the closest outfit he could find."

"I guess. But I wonder . . ."

She paused again and again he waited. It pleased her that he always let her finish her thoughts. "That same day in the market, I saw a man wearing a white cowboy hat. I remember thinking he had to be a good guy. In old Western movies, bad guys always wore black hats."

Now Nick was getting interested, leaning forward. "Where did you see this cowboy?"

"I've no idea. I just vaguely remember seeing a cowboy. I don't think I even saw his face; I just registered cowboy—white hat." She shrugged. "It didn't seem significant. But Lena, the waitress in the Crescent Beach tavern, said the man with Bart was wearing a cowboy hat. And that was just before Bart died."

"Tyler said everyone was wearing a cowboy hat."

"Everyone wasn't sitting with Bart."

"True."

"All in the same day, there was a cowboy at the market, a cowboy in the street near the house, a cowboy sitting with Bart in Crescent Beach."

"It was Halloween—people were dressed up. The last one was in a country-western bar. It could be a coincidence." He paused. "Or not."

"You think it might not be."

"I try to keep an open mind."

Maddy tried to see the first cowboy in her mind, but couldn't. Lena the waitress hadn't mentioned the color of Bart's cowboy friend's hat. Maybe she should call her.

"I guess all we can do is keep an eye out for a cowboy," she said at last.

Nick nodded.

They sat in silence for a while, then Nick suggested it was time to move on, and they went out to the car.

Nick didn't start the car immediately. When Maddy looked at him questioningly, she saw that his dark eyes were glinting again. "Where are we staying tonight?" he asked.

Maddy swallowed. Somehow the question sounded less innocent than he probably intended. Reaching to the backseat, she picked up the briefcase containing Bart's records. She pulled out the list of stops he'd made and laid it on top of the briefcase.

"Usually Bart stayed at the Sitka Inn in Eugene. In October—last month—he stopped there before going on to Portland. After his appointments, he went a little south of Eugene to a Travelers' Haven for two nights. It's apparently just off I-5."

She shook her head. "I can't imagine why he'd switch to a Travelers' Haven some trips and not others. Unless the smaller hotels were full. But he was traveling during the week, and if he *were* having an affair, you'd think he'd pick something intimate."

"Perhaps he thought a chain hotel would be more anonymous."

"But the Visa card is in his name, same as the MasterCard."

"True, but would anyone remember or even notice if he met someone in a Travelers' Haven and took her to his room? In a small hotel or motel or B-and-B where there are less people, any actions on his part might be noted."

"Oh." She managed a shadow of a smile. "I guess I've a lot to learn about being a PI." She hesitated. "Which hotel should we stay at tonight then, the Sitka Inn or the chain hotel?"

"The occasional extra nights that apparently aren't a Mawsom business expense seem most intriguing to me," Nick said. "Let's try the Travelers' Haven."

On the way, they stopped in a hospital in Eugene to interview Dr. Paul Avery, a charming black man whom

Bart had paid a brief visit to on his last trip. He showed
no more personal knowledge of Bart than Dr. Milligan
had. Nick asked a few more questions this time, but didn't
elicit any more information than Maddy had.

The huge motel seemed overheated to Maddy as she
and Nick waited to register behind an elderly couple who
had a lot of questions about the hotel facilities. There was
definitely something suggestive in standing next to a
man—an undeniably attractive man—while waiting to
book into a hotel room. Especially when, over the course
of the past several days, she had felt a definite reaction to
him. An entirely inappropriate reaction.

Perhaps her sudden nervousness was because she was
concerned with what she might find out about Bart. If they
discovered he'd been having affairs, or even importing
local prostitutes into his room from time to time, it would
mean he'd ignored her since their wedding because she
hadn't turned him on.

Not that she cared anymore what Bart had thought of
her, but still, that would be a bit insulting.

"Separate rooms," she heard Nick say, and felt an un-
expected sense of relief. Surely she hadn't thought he'd
expect her to share a room with him?

She became aware that Nick and the desk clerk were
both looking at her with an expectant air. "Your credit
card?" Nick suggested.

"Oh, of course." She fished it out, feeling flustered,
which wasn't at all like her. "Charge both rooms to this
card," she told the clerk firmly.

"But I've already . . ." The clerk glanced at Nick.

"We'll settle up later," he said to Maddy.

"But—" She broke off. The clerk, who looked about
nineteen years old, was regarding them both with barely
suppressed amusement. It was obvious what she was
thinking. "Fine," Maddy said.

The rooms were adjoining. Maddy used the bathroom
facilities, washed her hands and tidied her hair, then studied the connecting door. It was locked. Of course it was
locked.

A few minutes later they were seated in the manager's office. Frederick Liu listened attentively and in a kindly manner to their questions and explanations about Bart, then personally checked the hotel's computer system for information.

Unfortunately, all he came up with was confirmation that Bart Williams had stayed there for two nights in October, the 23rd and 24th.

Maddy questioned Bart in her mind. Why switch from the Sitka Inn to this hotel? He liked to work out—the chain hotels had facilities. Was that a possible answer?

Or was it as Nick had suggested, that in chain hotels nobody was likely to watch too closely or to care if you brought in a woman for a night or two?

When Nick pressed for more information, Mr. Liu called in the young desk clerk who'd checked them in and asked her if she had any memory of a guest named Bart Williams. Maddy showed her the photograph. She shook her head, then offered to show it to the other clerks. Nobody remembered Bart, but then, Mr. Liu said solemnly, unless Mr. Williams had done or worn or said something unusual, it would be unlikely that he would remain in hotel employees' memories. "So many people traveling on I-5 . . ." he said, spreading his open palms wide.

Maddy thought it might be a good idea to test her theory by checking the fitness room.

Nick showed up in sweatpants and a tank top, revealing a very presentable set of muscles. Maddy wore her usual sweat shorts, plus a sleeveless top that showed she had biceps and triceps too.

The buff young man in charge gave them a towel apiece and answered questions reluctantly. No, he didn't remember the man in the photograph. No, he hadn't worked at the hotel last month. The guy who had worked there before him had left to join the navy. No, they didn't have guests sign in. If they had a room key, they were welcome.

Maddy took out her frustration by loping along on the treadmill, working up a good sweat, while Nick worked

out with weights and a couple of the machines. He moved
very smoothly, she noticed. No macho clanging of the
weights as he pulled or pushed, no groaning or heavy
breathing to show how hard he was working.

As she headed for the women's shower room, he called
after her: "How does a hot tub sound? There's one down
by the pool in the atrium."

It sounded good and she'd brought along a suit, thinking a morning swim might get each day on the road off
to a good start. It didn't even occur to her that a hot tub
was an intimate kind of place to be in until she entered
the area and saw Nick leaning back against one of the
jets, arms spread along the tub's rim. He looked fully
relaxed, very fit, and dangerously macho. She could hardly back out now.

He watched her appreciatively as she stepped down
into the tub and settled herself into the comfortingly hot
water.

"We're not moving too far forward, are we?" she said.

"In regard to what?" he asked, then frowned. "Sorry,
I have this built-in wisecrack machine—operates without
any intention on my part."

"I've noticed."

He held her gaze for a long moment, then said, "I take
it you meant we weren't getting far in our investigation."

She pretended to be puzzled. "What else would I
mean?"

She watched him almost respond to that, rethink it,
then decide to say something anyway.

"You could have meant we aren't moving forward on
whatever it is that's happening between us."

She swallowed. There it was, out in the open. About
to deny knowing what he meant, she chose a more dis-
creet path. "I was talking about our investigation."

"Uh-huh." His gaze met hers, one eyebrow raised, but
he answered readily enough. "Detecting is not the action-
packed affair it's portrayed as on television and in the
movies, Maddy. Mostly it's slow, boring slogging along,

trying to uncover the facts. We've barely cracked the surface. We'll get there, never fear."

There was a look in his eyes that made her wonder if he were referring to their relationship with that last statement. He had a way of narrowing his eyes that was very suggestive.

She leaned back against the pulse of water and willed herself to let go of the tension that had shown up between them the minute she got into the water.

Ten minutes, she thought. As long as she didn't look at him, she'd be safe for ten minutes. She shouldn't stay in the hot water longer than ten minutes anyway—she'd shrivel up or go to sleep.

Sleep would feel good. A nap. A power nap.

Let go, she told herself, just let go. She concentrated on relaxing her face, emptying her mind of thought, picking up each thought that tried to enter her mind and pushing it back and back. Eventually, she felt the tension seep out of her muscles, felt herself going limp, boneless, dark.

She looked fragile around the eyes, Nick thought. Shadowed. He liked the bronze color she smudged around her eyes, the matching mascara that tipped her lashes with gold. At least he guessed it was mascara—maybe it was natural. She had good skin, flushed right now from the heat. Damp. He wanted to touch it. Touch *her*. Anywhere. Her other attributes weren't bad either. Understatement of the year. The one-piece black swimsuit, cut high in the thigh and low between her breasts, showed off her shapely figure to perfection. Thoughtful of her to close her eyes so he could study her. The way he was feeling, if she caught him looking, she was liable to slap his face. Did women slap faces nowadays? He'd never done anything to cause a woman to slap his face anyway. He was a patient kind of guy. He knew to wait until what would seem like a threat too early on became a desirable situation.

Women probably didn't slap faces anymore—most women nowadays were more likely to kick a guy's shins or other parts. Maddy Sloane seemed like a pretty strong woman.

He'd better quit looking at her, he decided. Adrenaline was coiling through him, causing a reaction in certain areas. Adrenaline, hell—testosterone was the guilty hormone here.

He reminded himself that people of all kinds and natures and apparent innocence could be extremely devious. This woman had been married to the man who might have—almost certainly had—killed his father.

Arnie had said the Snowman had shifted his "operations." Nick still had no way of knowing if Maddy Sloane was involved in those operations, whatever they might be. Sure, she'd *said* she was about to leave Bart Williams, she'd *said* she didn't really know him, she'd *said* she disliked him. But he'd seen angelically innocent eyes before and heard their owners lie through their teeth. He'd known women as lithe, as graceful, as classy, and far more beautiful than Madison Sloane Williams, who had hearts as black as the dark side of the moon. Katharine, Vicky, Merry, Olivia . . . No, Olivia's heart had been in the right place—she just couldn't live with his work schedule. If he'd taken some vacation time while they were still together, maybe . . .

Last he'd heard, Olivia was involved with a guy who taught history at the university. Now that was someone who was solid and dependable . . . and *there*.

Of course, where Maddy was concerned, there was that other minor detail—that he was being fairly devious himself. If she ever found him out, she was going to be furious as hell.

It was just too damn bad he hadn't met this woman under other circumstances, circumstances in which he could have explored the possibility of . . .

What the hell was he thinking? This was a *case* he was investigating. A personal case. A case in which he had no standing, but one he wasn't about to let testosterone jeopardize. *Remember your own rules,* he instructed himself. *Keep it light. Keep it surface. Play it the way you've been*

*playing it all along. Friendly flirtation, so she doesn't
suspect any serious motives.*

The trouble was, in spite of all his wise instructions to
himself, he wanted her. Now. Right now.

SHE COULD HEAR him breathing.

But that was crazy. He was across from her, not beside
her. The bubbling jets were noisy—no way could she
hear . . .

She opened her eyes. He was looking at her. "I was
afraid you were going to slide right down under the water," he said. "I was getting ready to grab you by your
hair to hold you above water."

"I wasn't sleeping," she protested.

"No? You sure were giving a good imitation, snoring
like that."

"I don't snore." She looked at him uncertainly. "Do
I?"

His grin told her he was teasing. Finally, a grin. She'd
been waiting for one, she realized, had decided he was
just one of those guys who delighted in appearing solemn
even while they were joking. The grin made him look
younger, more carefree than she had ever seen him.

She lifted a foot and splashed water at him. He grabbed
her ankle and held it. His fingers were strong, but gentle.

She stopped breathing. Her gaze met his for a split
second, startled, aware, then she pulled her foot free and
shook her head at him. "I guess it's time to eat again,"
she said briskly, sitting up straight.

"Do I make you nervous, Maddy?" he asked.

"Good God, no. Of course not. Why would I be nervous?"

He raised an eyebrow. "Me male, you female."

"Ha!" It was meant to be a mocking sound, but it came
out on the weak side, and she shifted her gaze.

He felt a sudden urge to tell her the truth about himself—who he was, why he was on this journey with her,
why he really wanted to find Bart Williams.

Not in the hot tub, he decided. Not anywhere else. Yet.

"We should get on the road fairly early tomorrow," she said.

"We can ask for a wake-up call. It's not late yet. Are you really that hungry?"

"Bart might have eaten here. One of the restaurants is Mexican and he liked Mexican food."

His grin appeared again, showing teeth; did he recognize that she was avoiding his more personal remarks? Was he laughing at her? "Okay, Maddy," he said, then stood up, giving her a close-up view of rock-hard abs and killer pecs before he stepped out of the tub.

The water suddenly felt hotter than before.

They ate delicious enchiladas in the hotel's Mexican restaurant, awareness stretching like an invisible cord between them.

The tired-looking middle-aged waitress who took their order introduced herself as Cleo. She seemed ill-at-ease in her flamenco costume. She thought she might have served the good-looking man in Maddy's photograph. There was no way she could remember when, she added.

"He spent a couple of nights here in October," Maddy told her. "October twenty-third and twenty-fourth."

Cleo shrugged, then brightened. "Columbus Day weekend." She shook her head. "Nope, that was last year. This year it was earlier. Maybe I saw him. Can't be sure. He does look sort of familiar."

"Can you associate anyone else with him?" Nick asked. "Do you remember if he was alone?"

She sighed. "I want to say he wasn't, but I don't really know."

"Could he have been with a woman?" Maddy asked.

The waitress looked at her sharply. "What is this about, a cheating husband?"

"It's possible," Maddy said.

"Men are disgusting," the waitress said.

Nick smiled at her. She glowered back, and looked at Maddy. "Don't even bother to check up on the guy, honey. If you think he's cheating on you, just up and tell him to take a hike. Save yourself a ton of grief. Trust me on this."

"He's dead," Nick told her.

The news didn't faze her. "In that case," she said, still looking only at Maddy, "you're probably better off without the bastard. Don't give him another thought."

"*Do* you remember seeing him with a woman, or anyone else?" Nick persisted.

She shrugged.

"You don't remember?"

She sighed. "What I said before. What the hey difference does it make if he's already dead?"

"There's some mystery about his death."

She shrugged again.

"Thank you," Maddy said, realizing the futility of questioning the woman further.

Nick suggested they should take a look at Maddy's notes and maps before hitting the sack. "I need to make sure I know where each hospital is. We'll be crossing into California some time tomorrow."

He paused, that devilish glint invading his eyes again. "How about I meet you in your room in ten minutes?"

"Bad idea," Maddy retorted.

"You don't trust yourself around me? We could open up the doors between our rooms so I can beat a hasty retreat if I need to."

She shook her head at him. "The lounge will do fine. We can spread the stuff out on a table."

"So we can," he agreed with a dramatic sigh.

It didn't take long to work out a plan for the next day over a Guinness for each of them. The tables in the lounge were small, but she managed to avoid physical contact. But not awareness. She kept remembering his teasing, "How about I meet you in your room in ten minutes?" To her dismay, she found herself wishing she had said yes.

He insisted on escorting her to her door, where she made a hurried entrance.

"Sleep well," he said softly as she closed the door,

practically in his face. She thought she heard him chuckle as she clicked the dead bolt on.

As she pulled off her sweater and slacks, she made up her mind that she was going to sleep as soon as her head hit the pillow. Which she did.

She also dreamed.

There he was, walking into her room as if he belonged there. She must have forgotten to set the security lock. He sat on the side of her bed, one hand reaching out to touch her hair.

It was the kind of dream where you know you have to move and you want to move and you want to say something like "What the hell are you doing in here, Ciacia?" but you seem to be paralyzed and unable to speak.

Certainly if she hadn't been dreaming, she would never have allowed him to ease his big body in under the covers with her, smiling confidently all the time as if he had an absolute right to be there. Nor would she have just lain there as he gathered her into his arms and began kissing her in a way that was new to her—softly, tenderly, silently, his mouth moving patiently over hers as though he had all the time in the world.

And then she was responding, brushing his lips with her own, touching his face, his crisp clean dark hair, gazing into his brown eyes, losing herself in their warmth, feeling desire wash through her in waves that mounted steadily in strength. There was such gentleness in his face and in his touch and in his mouth on hers.

Quite suddenly she was awake and feeling bereft, gazing wide-eyed at the ceiling, clutching the covers to her aching breasts.

Chapter 18

IN THE MORNING, they had breakfast in the hotel's coffee shop—Nick ate a couple of bagels and cream cheese while she toyed with a small fruit plate.

Maddy had felt mildly embarrassed when she first saw him, but recovered quickly. He'd done nothing to activate the dream her long neglected libido had conjured up, and he certainly had no knowledge of it.

But she was still under the spell of the dream, and she couldn't seem to react normally to anything Nick said. Sensual images and feelings kept floating languorously through her memory.

The people working in the coffee shop didn't recognize Bart's photograph. But at least talking to them, questioning them, restored Maddy's sense of balance and reality.

Back in her room, she gave herself an internal pep talk as she cleaned her teeth, took her still-damp swimsuit off the shower rail and wrapped it in the shower cap from the hotel's bathroom offerings, packed her things in her wheeled tote bag, and put her makeup in her shoulder bag. Dreams came from subconscious worries. When standing in line at the hotel desk and relaxing last night in the hot tub, she'd probably been afraid that Nick might have plans of his own where she was concerned. "Do I make you nervous, Maddy?" he'd asked. "Me male, you female."

He'd been teasing, of course. He would never have expected her to take him seriously. But obviously her subconscious had picked up on the whole idea and transferred it into the dream.

Pleased that she'd managed to explain the experience away, she was able to greet Nick in a more normal fashion when she met him again in the hotel lobby.

Apparently Bart hadn't made any other side trips on his last trip through Oregon. At least none that showed up in his journal entries or accounts.

Bart's name and photo were immediately recognized at the hospital in Medford and the medical center in Redding, which they reached after a hairy drive through a blizzard that made the steep and winding roads of the mountain pass into California fairly hazardous.

They managed to catch the nurses and admin people in the oncology departments of both hospitals just before and after shift changes, and the doctors and surgeons between rounds and surgical procedures.

But none of Maddy and Nick's questions brought out any information other than the fact that yes, Bart Williams usually stopped there either on his way south or when heading north. No, there was nothing unusual about his last visit or any other visit. No, they didn't really know him personally. But he was okay, they guessed. He did his job.

That was the most-used phrase. *He did his job.*

Oh, gosh, they said—it was too bad he was dead.

In San Francisco he had spent four days in a small hotel not far from Union Square, visiting several hospitals in the Bay Area.

The last time he'd checked into the Travelers' Haven, which was not far from the Cliff House, overlooking the Pacific Ocean, was February 14. He'd left there on February 16. According to his journal, he'd had an appoint-

ment with a Dr. Applewhite at four p.m. on the afternoon
of the 14th.

It was getting late as they reached the outskirts of San
Francisco. Traffic was heavy, almost at gridlock in spots.
They stopped for gas, and Maddy went into the minimart
to pay while Nick got ready to pump.

When she came out, she stood for a while, lifting and
then dropping her heels to relieve the stiffness in her legs,
idly looking at the car next to Nick's. A long-haired, huge
Hispanic man in a dark suit was just removing the nozzle
from his gas tank, hanging it up. Another equally large
man, also dressed in a dark suit, got out of the car, and
they said something to each other, then each opened a
back door of the car and bent inside.

She was curious now, and a little nervous. What the
hell were they doing in there for so long. Was there any
danger to Nick?

About the time she was ready to yell at Nick to look
out, one of the men emerged carrying an infant car seat,
while the man on the other side came out holding a pretty
little girl with dark curly hair.

The first man wiped out the car seat with a rag, and
inserted himself back into the car to lock the seat in place.
The other man took the baby into the minimart, carrying
a diaper bag in his free hand. The first man got back into
the car and drove it to the side of the lot.

Maddy let out a breath she hadn't realized she was
holding. "Maybe we're making too much out of all this
stuff," she said to Nick when they were on the way again.

"I don't think so," he said.

She told him what she'd seen and how she'd perceived
it as being dangerous.

He grunted. "If this journey of ours turns out to be a
search for a paper tiger, I'll be delighted," he said, adding
in the next breath, "And very surprised."

They decided to check in at the Travelers' Haven and
follow Bart's hospital route the next day. If nothing turned
up, they'd check out the other hotel.

Nobody remembered Bart in the Travelers' Haven. "I guess Bart must have blended with the wallpaper every time," Maddy said with a sigh, as they ate dinner in the hotel restaurant. It was an Italian menu this time, so Nick was happy. "It occurred to me about the time we got here that he had this hat he wore often, a flat cap, very European. It covered his hair. He wasn't nearly as noticeable when his hair didn't show."

Nick nodded, but she had the feeling he wasn't listening to her. He seemed deep in thought and didn't really rouse himself until they were eating their gelato dessert.

"I'm not sure this approach is working too well," he said. "I've a feeling we're not going to get anywhere with any of these doctors. There's a missing piece, something that would give us a direction or at least a place to start."

"What kind of piece?"

"I've no idea, but I'm doing some heavy-duty thinking."

"I can tell."

He seemed about to smile, but the smile faded before it quite reached his lips. He hadn't flirted with her once today, she realized. Maybe he'd sensed somehow that she'd had some sensual thoughts where he was concerned and, manlike, he was getting ready to run.

He hadn't even suggested the fitness room or hot tub this time, and after dinner, he decided to take some of Bart's papers to his room and do some browsing. Maybe she could look through the journals she'd brought along, he said.

In the morning, he told her the only thing he'd turned up was the fact that there was no regularity to the times Bart tacked on extra days or nights to his trips. They were evidently random choices. "Maybe he just got tired sometimes," he said. "Maybe he found a poker game, or he just decided that he wanted to hang loose."

Random wasn't a word Maddy would have connected with Bart Williams, nor was the phrase *hang loose*, but she hadn't found anything earthshaking either. Just records of Bart moving up and down I-5 at fairly regular intervals, with no mention of the bumps of time that he used up in Travelers' Havens. As far back as she'd read, the journals dealt only with his doctor and hospital appointments. The extra days and nights were still shrouded in mystery.

Nick had called and made an appointment for ten-thirty a.m. with Dr. Vernon Applewhite, a lanky, middle-aged man with a ruddy face who looked more like a rancher than a surgeon. He remembered Bart well and gave them the usual tale of efficient meetings, no wasted time, prompt appointments. "I've always required an appointment of any sales rep," he said. "Not that I'm so all-fired important—but my time *is* tightly scheduled. Bart Williams, now, he seemed to understand that, always came in right on time—said he was a stickler for punctuality himself."

He paused. "Don't know as there's much more I can tell you folks. Not as if we ever socialized. Sorry to hear about your trouble, Mrs. Williams."

He lapsed into silence, his forehead furrowing.

Just after Nick and Maddy had glanced at each other and started to rise from their chairs, he suddenly spoke up again. "Though I should maybe tell you about last February. There was something different about him last February."

Nick and Maddy exchanged another glance. "What?" Nick asked, sounding hopeful.

The doctor nodded several times, rocking a little on his swivel chair on the other side of his desk. "Yes, February fourteenth, it was. He had an appointment with me for eleven a.m. But he didn't show. I was scheduled to fly out of San Francisco airport down to San Diego to give a lecture that night, so I wasn't about to wait around. Figured he had to be sick, because he never missed an appointment before."

He laughed shortly. "You know how airports are these days. You've got to get to them a couple of hours in advance so you can get through security in time to make your plane."

He held up a hand, palm out. "Not that I object to that. Hey, I'd sooner miss my plane than have someone get on board who has mischief in mind." He frowned. "Though I must say I don't know why I always get picked on to be wanded and searched. Take my hat off, take my shoes off, empty my pockets. I ask you, do I look like a terrorist?"

Both Nick and Maddy were sitting on the edge of their seats, willing him to get back to the subject at hand.

"But this time I'm lucky. I get through in double-quick time and I have a snack at the restaurant across from my gate. It's getting close to time to board my plane, so I get up and pay my bill and I'm coming out of there when who do I see but Bart Williams, walking along among a crowd of people who look like they're heading for baggage claim or ground transport.

"Bart looked real surprised when he saw me. And not too happy about it."

"Did you talk to him?" Maddy asked. Her throat was so dry she was surprised the words even came out. Why did she have this strong feeling that this story, this long-winded story, was leading to something awful?

The doctor's gaze met hers. "Sure did, ma'am. Asked him why the heck he hadn't shown up at the proper time. He said he'd had car trouble, so he'd left his car at a Seattle garage and flown down instead. Then he swore our appointment was for the afternoon, not the morning. Well, that wasn't the case at all, and I knew it and I had the feeling he knew it—heck, if he was just starting to drive down that morning, he wouldn't have made it by the afternoon anyway—but I wasn't going to get my Jockeys in a knot about it, so I just told him to call my office and set up another time. He said he would, and I walked on over to the gate."

"Are you sure of the date and time?" Nick asked.

"As a matter of fact, I am." Applewhite waved a hand in the air. "Oh, I'll check on it to convince you, but I really don't need . . ." He was flipping pages on his desk calendar as he spoke, then turned it around to show them.

"See there, February fourteenth. There's the appointment, eleven a.m., and there's the time of my plane, 4:02 p.m. Never can understand why the airlines give such precise times. Hardly ever get there right on the money. Don't think I don't check!"

"I guess Bart must have made a mistake," Maddy said.

"Yes, that's what he told me. Certainly, I never would have made an appointment and my secretary never would have made an appointment for four p.m. when I had a four o'clock flight. I was booked for that talk months ahead."

He brought the calendar back around and adjusted it to the day's date. "Reason that date stuck in my mind so clearly was that right after I'd bumped into Bart and he finally got through apologizing for messing up and went on his way, I found out my flight was delayed, some problem with the wiring. So I'm sitting in the waiting area, watching CNN and getting impatient, and this story comes on about Rafael, known as Rafe, Donati—that fella who blew the whistle on that big racketeering scheme at some international hotel chain—Castleberry or something like that . . ."

"Castonberry," Nick said. He was leaning forward, looking tense. He seemed to realize it, and sat back.

"Whatever," Dr. Applewhite said. He went silent again.

"So what did that have to do with Bart?" Maddy asked.

The doctor smiled at her. "Sorry, ma'am, I lose track sometimes. Didn't have anything to do with Bart—didn't mean to mislead you. Let's see, where was I . . . Oh, yeah. CNN said Rafe Donati had gotten himself drowned sometime during the morning."

He frowned. "Don't remember the details, but at the time I remembered reading off and on about the man in the newspapers. Quite a party guy, as I recall."

He shrugged again. "Well, Rafe Donati's neither here nor there as far as your concern about Bart goes. It's just that the anchor person, whoever she was, not Paula Zahn—I really like Paula; she's good at the job, a smart lady—but somebody else, some other female who was

kind of cynical, said it seemed altogether fitting that he'd
die on Valentine's Day. I guessed she was referring to the
famous St. Valentine's Day Massacre that took place in
Chicago in 1929. That was February fourteen, you see,
and so was this. That's why it stuck in my mind."

"Where did Donati drown?" Nick asked.

"Well, seems like it was Portland, Oregon, but I
couldn't swear to it. Couldn't hear all of it too well. Lot
of people around, you know, waiting. Some fool next to
me with a cell phone, bellowing out orders to someone
on the other end about cleaning the bilge out of a barge
or some darn thing."

"Have you seen Bart Williams since then?" Nick
asked.

"Oh, sure." The doctor flipped pages on his desk calendar. "Bart came back on March fourth, May sixth, and
September sixteenth. Then again on October twenty-
fourth. I'm very interested in a new drug Mawsom's coming up with, one of the epidermal growth factor receptor
blockers. They attach to receptors on cells and—"

"Did he seem okay each time?" Nick interrupted.

"Sure. As okay as he ever was. Wasn't exactly Mr.
Personality, but hey, I don't care as long as they aren't
perky. Can't stand perky."

They thanked him and left, then sat in Nick's car for
a while, thinking things over.

"It doesn't seem like Bart's usual MO to fly down for
an appointment or to get the time mixed up," Maddy said.
"What are you thinking?"

"I'm just following a hunch."

"To do with Bart?"

Nick didn't answer. He just sat there for several
minutes, drumming his fingers lightly on the steering
wheel, obviously in deep thought. Maddy imagined she
could see the circuits lighting up in his brain, sending
messages back and forth, collating, decoding.

"I'd like to talk to a few people who might know something about Donati drowning," he said at last. "I remember hearing about his being a whistle-blower and thinking

he was taking a hell of a chance going up against a big organization like Castonberry. I just wonder . . . I don't remember the details. It wasn't in my—"

He broke off again.

Why was he going off on this other case Dr. Applewhite had mentioned? The Donati thing didn't have anything to do with Bart—it was just something that had made the doctor remember the date! Still, Nick had helped her so much already. Surely she could spare some time to help him.

"I have my laptop with me, remember?" Maddy said. "We can probably find the Donati story through TheHub's search engine. I can check on it for you."

He gave her an approving look. "Great! Thanks, Maddy. Depending on what we find out, I can make some calls. After that, maybe we can take another look at Bart's papers—the ones I went through last night. If we tackle them together, maybe you'll find something I missed, some anomaly besides the odd couple of days spent at Travelers' Havens and Bart flying instead of driving. Then we can decide whether to go back to Washington or to drive on down to Los Angeles and San Diego as we had intended and see a few more doctors who may or may not have information."

Well, at least he wasn't giving up on Bart.

Without waiting for any comments, he turned the key in the ignition and started the car. "I have this gut feeling there's something here I should look into," he muttered, almost to himself. "Operations, Arnie said. Operations. How would you define operations, Maddy?"

"Some kind of activity? Projects? Enterprises?"

"Undertakings," he added. "Ventures. Exactly."

Chapter 19

NICK ABSOLUTELY REFUSED to talk any more about his "hunch" on the way back to the Travelers' Haven. He didn't seem to want to talk much at all.

Maddy was hungry—the fruit hadn't stayed with her—so when they got to her room, she rang room service and ordered a couple of sandwiches, then brewed a carafe of coffee in the bathroom.

When they were through eating, she pulled out her laptop and plugged into the data port on the desk, typed TheHub's URL in Internet explorer, then entered "Rafael Donati," hoping she'd spelled the name correctly.

She had. TheHub came up with 1,251 references. Stories and articles from all over the country.

Nick brought his chair alongside hers and watched as she opened up the various files. Together they read that Rafael Donati had owned the Portland branch of the hotels in the Castonberry chain and had made allegations of racketeering against Castonberry. Few details were given, but kickbacks, embezzlement, money laundering, and, surprisingly, something to do with procurement of naturalization papers were mentioned here and there.

Castonberry, as might be expected, had replied on several occasions through its attorneys that it had no comment on the case.

Reading between the lines, it was obvious that Rafael Donati was to be the chief witness for the prosecution if the case came to trial.

Maddy came up with a Television Online heading:

RAFE DONATI FOUND DEAD

Shortly before noon today, Rafael (Rafe) Donati, flamboyant former heavyweight boxer and gambler, now owner of the famous Castonberry Las Vegas and Castonberry Portland, was found dead in Portland's Columbia River, alongside a hiking/biking trail. Death by drowning, probably sometime between seven and eight a.m., was the verdict of the medical examiner. Police officials said that the death appears to be accidental but is under investigation, and that all possible leads are being followed. It was well known that Donati often ran a couple of miles along the Columbia River early in the morning before breakfasting and going to work in his world-class hotel.

Rafe Donati recently charged Castonberry International with racketeering. The case is pending.

"Hmm," Maddy said. "Nobody actually came out and said Castonberry had a number one first-class motive here, but that sure is a far from subtle hint."

She scrolled back through some of the stories, skimming over them as she went. "Why do you suppose they'd say it 'appeared' to be an accident?" she asked.

Nick shrugged. "Reporters like to dramatize."

He'd been sitting slumped in his chair, leaning to look at the laptop screen. Now he straightened up.

"Just for kicks," he said, "put in 'Organized Crime.'"

TheHub reacted rapidly.

"Wow," Maddy said. "It gave us 750,000 entries. We honest people don't stand a chance."

"Scroll down slowly."

"It's all I can do with this silly track point. I usually carry a mouse but I didn't . . ."

For once he wasn't listening. She kept scrolling.

"Stop," he said.

Mafia, Yakuza, Triads, Terminus.

Criminal groups that were Italian, Japanese, Chinese, and . . . "What's Terminus?" she asked.

He didn't answer. He was staring at the screen, looking horrified.

There wasn't a link. She called up TheHub and typed in "Terminus." There were four thousand references. Games, a hotel, something to do with *Star Wars*, a band. She kept scrolling. Finally: *Terminus—a criminal organization formed in 1960, loosely based on the old Murder Inc. operation.*

She sat back. "I think I've heard of Murder Inc. Maybe a television documentary or something. It was around a long time ago, I seem to remember. Thirties, forties? Some organization to do with the Mafia. Any one of the Mafia people in the U.S. could ask for a hit man to take care of someone they wanted to get rid of."

Nick was still distracted. It took him a minute to respond. "It was the press who dubbed it Murder Inc."

"So is Terminus part of the Mafia?"

She could sense him trying to pay attention.

"As I understand it," he said slowly, "it's a whole different organization, strictly guns for hire, headquartered in Chicago—where else? But not connected. With the Mafia, I mean. It's divided into regions. . . ."

His voice trailed off. He was somewhere else again.

"What?" Maddy asked.

He shook his head. "Tell you what. I'm going to go make a few calls. How about we meet for dinner, say around seven o'clock."

"You can call from here, Nick, charge it to my room."

"That's okay. No sense in me disturbing you. I'm sure you can find something to do."

"Well, I could check with . . . the office, I guess."

He stood up, still frowning, still intense. "Yeah, me too."

He had an office? That was the first she'd heard about him having an office. It wasn't just *his* office, obviously. Who would he check with?

"I take it we're spending another night here?" she called after him just before he got through the door.

"Absolutely," he said.

She frowned, then shrugged. No knowing what he was thinking but obviously the comments about Terminus had struck a chord with him. It could have nothing to do with Bart—and Nick obviously wasn't going to share whatever it was.

After checking her email and sending a couple of emails to the office in answer to some queries, she called in to TheHub and was glad she had. Her assistant had been trying to get hold of her to conference in on a meeting due to begin in ten minutes. She talked to Angie for a few minutes, checking to make sure one of her candidates had signed and faxed in the offer she'd made him. She'd given him a week to think about it. He had accepted, so she could forget about him for a while.

She hung up, then called back in on the conference call and spent the next hour getting updates on company information.

Deciding she needed physical exercise, she changed and went up to the floor the fitness room was on. She had it to herself except for a teenage boy whose gaze was fixed on one of the five TV sets. She picked up a headset and tuned in to CNN while she jogged on the treadmill. It felt good to get her circulation going. Without Nick there she could concentrate on some interval training.

Showered and refreshed, she met Nick in the lounge for a predinner glass of wine for her, a beer for him. Depression hung over him like a storm cloud. No eye contact, no banter.

"What's wrong?" Maddy asked.

He drank a hefty swallow of beer before answering. "I made some calls about Donati. Didn't get far, though I was able to put out some feelers. But along the way, I found out that this guy I know—Arnie Arnold, a cabdriver in Seattle—had turned up dead."

She leaned forward and put her hand on his arm. "I'm so sorry, Nick. Was he a friend?"

He sighed deeply. "Not exactly. He . . . helped me out on a case or two."

"What did he die of?"

"Apparently he drank too much and went to sleep in an abandoned building and died. Hypothermia. That cold snap a few days ago. He had some kind of heart problem too, he'd told me. That possibly contributed."

"How awful." She hesitated. "Apparently? Do you like to dramatize too?"

He finally met her gaze and attempted a smile. "You're a bright woman, Maddy Sloane. I'm thinking it wasn't an accident."

"You think somebody killed him?"

"I think somebody persuaded him to drink, knowing he was a recovering alcoholic and it was dangerous, and then left him there to die."

"Why?"

"He gave me some information recently. Knowing Arnie, it's entirely possible he told someone he'd given me the information. He always needed money—always. Or maybe he told his wife, also a drunk. She could have passed it on."

"What kind of information?"

His mouth twitched and he didn't answer.

Another secret, she supposed. He sure had bunches of them.

"Are you going back to Seattle?" she asked.

"Not right away. There's nothing I can do for Arnie. Other people are checking into his death. I gave them my input."

She was silent for a moment, then asked, "Did you get any information at all about Rafe Donati?"

"Just that the area where he was found was clean."

"What does that mean?"

"You ever hear of Locard's exchange principle? No? Dr. Locard, a French criminologist, conceived this principle more than half a century ago. It's still regarded as one of the important tenets of forensic science. 'Either the perpetrator leaves marks on his intervention on the scene, or by an inverse action, he takes his actions on his body or clothes.' In other words, any person passing through a place will unknowingly leave something there—hair, clothing fibers, DNA, whatever—and take something away—grass, carpet fibers, and so on."

"So in the Donati case, there wasn't any of that stuff?"

"Nope. It was raining that morning. It looked as if he tripped or slipped, hit his head on the path, suffered a severe concussion. Might have tried to get to his feet and tripped or slipped into the river. Evidently he went in right where he was found. The only odd note—and in my experience, if there's an odd note, there's usually a reason for it—was that he went into the river at all. There's a wide strip of grass at that point between the path and the river. How bad a concussion would it take? Besides which, it's somewhat suspicious for a whistle-blower to meet an untimely end."

He made an obvious effort to throw off his depression, put his hand over her hand still on his arm, and to her amazement produced a smile that was like the sun bursting through clouds. It made her bones melt.

"You think you could stand to go over Bart's papers one more time after dinner?" he asked. "I have a feeling we've missed something somewhere that might open up a new line of questioning."

Maddy was pleased to see that he was still gung ho on Bart's disappearance. She'd been afraid these other cases were going to take precedence.

"I can stand it," she said.

This time, they tried to cross-reference the Visa and

MasterCard bills and other receipts with the journals and Bart's desk calendar, plotting out Bart's trips and expenses for the whole year.

That's how they finally came up with a usable clue, or rather clues. Two of them.

In February, when Bart told Dr. Applewhite his appointment had been at four p.m., he'd had it on his calendar for eleven a.m. So either he'd been completely befuddled, which was not like him, or he'd lied to Dr. Applewhite.

Why?

He'd said his car had problems and he'd left it at a garage. But the only car-related receipt for that time was for a garage in Portland, Oregon. His flight to San Francisco had originated in Seattle, stopping briefly in Portland. So he had driven to Portland, then flown on to San Francisco and tried to convince Dr. Applewhite he wasn't due until later.

Why?

Maddy wasn't sure she could see the significance of any of it, but Nick seemed excited by it.

The second clue was a note on Bart's calendar of an appointment that wasn't recorded in his journal. A July 11 appointment with a Dr. Paula Joseph in Eugene, Oregon. According to his MasterCard accounts he'd stayed at the Sitka hotel on the 10th and 11th. No side trips to the Travelers' Haven, but they decided to check it out.

"Okay, let's go back to Eugene tomorrow," Nick suggested. "But this time we'll stay at the Sitka Inn. There's no mention of any other hotel in the records for that trip."

Chapter 20

DR. PAULA JOSEPH was a beautiful woman around forty, dark-haired and olive-skinned, and with some Indian genes, judging by her high cheekbones and beautiful brown eyes. Her office was in the oncology department of a different hospital from that of Dr. Powell but the same one as Dr. Avery's.

After Maddy and Nick explained their mission, it took them a while to settle on the date of Bart's appointment. Dr. Joseph insisted it was three p.m. on July 10 when Bart visited. She was off-duty on July 11, her twin daughters' fifth birthday.

"Guess Bart made a mistake," Nick said.

Another mistake, Maddy filled in. Bart had never seemed the type to make mistakes, especially in his work schedule. Reliable, punctual, Simon Hatfield had said. *Everyone* had said.

"Seemed a mite stressed," Dr. Joseph offered.

"In what way?" Maddy asked.

Dr. Joseph leaned back in her office chair and narrowed her eyes for a minute, then nodded. "You know the way some men will tap one foot fairly rapidly? You don't see it often in women. It's like the man can't keep his leg still. That's a sign of stress, nervousness, impatience. He had a twitch around his eyes too. And he was in an awful hurry. I had some questions, but he just brushed them aside, said the literature would explain everything. It didn't. Annoyed me that I'd set aside time to talk to him about this one new drug and he didn't want to take the time to talk to me."

"Was he always that impatient?" Maddy asked.

"No. He didn't waste any time, ever, but he was usually just businesslike and to the point. But this time he seemed to be in a big hurry."

"What time did he leave?" Nick asked.

"I can't say I made a note of it, but within a half hour." She straightened her chair. "You might check with the floor nurses. Maybe they can shed some light."

They did check, but none of the nurses could actually remember seeing Bart in July. They saw him fairly often, they pointed out. They promised to check with the nurses on the next morning's shift and let Maddy know if they came up with anything new.

When Nick and Maddy left the hospital, it was getting dark. They decided to check into the Sitka Inn before hunting up some dinner.

The desk clerk at the small hotel remembered Bart staying there from time to time but said the earlier records weren't available. "No, I can't say I noticed anything remarkable," he said in an offhand way.

"Did he have any visitors? Was anyone with him?"

"Not that I noticed," the clerk said, still sounding bored.

The hotel had a pool that was closed for the winter, but didn't have a hot tub or even a restaurant, though it provided a continental breakfast in the lobby.

The concierge recommended a restaurant a few blocks away. "Gets a lot of the university students," she told them. "They serve wonderful pasta and salads."

Nick suggested they walk to the restaurant—he was feeling kinked up after driving so much.

The concierge had told the truth. The chicken fettuccini was great, and the salad had an olive oil–based dressing that was touched with lime and garlic. Nick was delighted. As they weren't driving, they shared a carafe of wine.

By the time they finished eating and left, the restaurant was emptying out, and traffic was fairly light. They were feeling relaxed by the good food and wine, but still tired.

They approached the last crosswalk, passing a corner convenience store. As they slowed their pace to wait for the light to change, a car suddenly made a turn against the light and angled in their direction, its headlights pointing directly at them, blinding Maddy.

Nick was looking up at the stoplight. Maddy grabbed his arm and yanked him sideways, causing both of them to fall over the low rock wall that edged the convenience store's parking lot.

The car zoomed past, two wheels on the sidewalk, almost clipping the wall.

"What the hell!" Nick exclaimed.

Maddy picked herself up and examined her knees. Both of her pant legs were scuffed and dusty. When she brushed at them, she felt tenderness underneath. Her palms were slightly scraped, but she'd escaped serious injury. Her purse had flown from her shoulder and burst open, scattering keys and her billfold and some coins on the ground. She retrieved them as Nick was similarly dusting himself off and taking stock.

"I didn't even see the stupid idiot," he said.

Maddy put her hand on his arm. "The driver wasn't stupid, Nick. It was deliberate. The light was still red. He aimed the car right at us."

"Are you sure?" he asked, looking worriedly at her.

Suddenly she wasn't quite. The lights had blinded her. Maybe that had disoriented her. "It seemed that way, but I suppose I could have just panicked unnecessarily. In which case, you can sue me."

"Are you okay?"

"I'm fine. Shaky."

"Yeah, me too. That was close. I don't suppose you had time to get a license number? I sure didn't."

"I don't even know what kind of car it was. Happened too fast. Just a dark car. I don't know if it was a man or woman driving. Somehow I think maybe a man."

"He didn't happen to be wearing a cowboy hat, did he?"

"I didn't see him that clearly. It happened too fast. Too unexpectedly. If he did usually wear a hat, he'd take it off while driving, wouldn't he?"

"I've heard tell real cowboys don't take their hats off except when they go to bed."

She squinted at him.

"Sorry," he said, without looking sorry. Always the joker. "You're not sure now that the driver was out to get us?"

"Well, he or she did drive through the red light, but I guess the car might have skidded. I don't know why that would happen, though. The ground's perfectly dry."

There was nobody nearby. No cars had stopped. Obviously nobody had noticed anything untoward.

"I suggest we get across the street and into the hotel before that driver decides to come back," Maddy said.

Nick nodded, took her arm, and stepped into the street as the walk signal came up.

She felt him hesitate and looked up at his face in time to see him grimace. "What?" she asked.

He shrugged and kept walking, urging her along with him. Not walking. *Limping*.

"You're hurt!"

"It's nothing. I guess my foot twisted as you dragged me over the wall." His voice was light, but she could see he was definitely in pain. "I noticed you have muscles, but I didn't realize how strong you are. Remind me to stay on your good side."

As they entered the hotel's parking lot, Maddy suggested he come to her room so she could take a look at his foot.

"I've been waiting for you to invite me," he joked. "Too bad I had to get wounded before it happened."

"Should we report this to the police?" Maddy asked as she pointed him to the bed. The rooms in the Sitka hotel were sparsely furnished. The only chair was a straight one at the desk.

Nick shook his head, then shrugged out of his leather jacket, sat down heavily, and began removing his left shoe and sock. "Damn," he said.

The ankle was already swollen, puffing like rising dough over the bone.

Tossing her own jacket aside, Maddy knelt and gently lifted his foot in her hands.

"God, your hands are cold," he complained, then added, "What would we report? We don't have a description worth beans, nobody witnessed it, and there's nothing to go on."

"True," she agreed. "Maybe the driver was old or drunk or on something. Or maybe I drank too much wine. But that car did come straight at us. I'm absolutely sure of that. Can you wiggle your toes?"

He obliged, then grunted.

"We should go get it x-rayed," she suggested.

"I've had enough hospitals for now. It'll be fine."

She looked up at his determined chin and decided it would be a waste of time to argue. She was reasonably sure nothing was broken. "Okay, Mr. Macho, but if it's still swollen in the morning, we'll go see a chiropractor. In the meantime we'll use the RICE method. Rest, ice, compression, and elevation."

Standing up, she pulled out from under the covers a pillow for him to lay his head on, helped him swivel carefully flat, then put the other pillow and an extra from the closet under his foot.

She looked down at him, hands on hips. "I'm going for ice. I'll make you a temporary ice pack, then I'm going to the nearest drugstore for a proper ice bag and an Ace bandage."

As he opened his mouth to argue with her, she put her

fingers over his lips. His hand immediately came up to hold her hand there, and he kissed her fingers lightly, then held on to her while he recited: "O woman! in our hours of ease / uncertain, coy, and hard to please, / when pain and anguish wring the brow, / a ministering angel thou!"

Her breath came out in a rush. "Mr. Macho quotes poetry yet," she teased, frowning playfully to cover up the wave of heat that had surged through her at his touch. "I think you left out a couple of lines."

"Sir Walter Scott didn't really need all that stuff about a quivering aspen."

"And you even know the poet! I'm impressed. But I'm still going for supplies."

He had yet to release her hand. "You thought I was all brawn and no brains, did you?"

"Brawn *and* brains," she said.

He was looking at her hand. He reached for the other one. "You're hurt."

"Just scraped a little. I'll put some lotion on when I'm through with you."

He kissed the inside of her wrist. It was one of the most seductive things Maddy had ever experienced. He looked slyly up at her as another heat wave washed over her. "Maybe we do need Scott's line about the quivering aspen after all."

She pulled her hands free, went into the bathroom and washed them, then reached for the ice bucket on top of the television set. "I'll be right back. Don't you dare move."

"What if I need to go to the bathroom?"

"You'll have to wait."

He was laughing as she left the room. He was right— she was definitely shaky. She wished she could say it was because of the accident.

Accident? No matter how much she tried to rationalize, that was no accident.

Nick was still lying on the bed when she came back with ice wrapped in the bucket liner, but the pillows were not in the same position. "You weren't supposed to move."

"I had to go. Wine makes me pee. I mostly hopped, honest."

"Uh-huh." Wrapping the ice pack in a washcloth, she straightened the pillows and laid the ice against his ankle. "I have directions to a drugstore," she told him. "It's only a block away."

"The car keys are in my jacket pocket."

"But it's only . . ."

His gaze met hers steadily. "Take the car."

"You don't believe it was an accident either, do you?"

"I think it's safer to assume it wasn't."

She picked the keys out of his jacket pocket, grabbed her jacket, and gestured to him to pass her purse, which was on the bed next to him. He swung it over to her, grunting as if it were a huge weight, which wasn't far off the mark. She made a face at him.

"Be careful, Maddy," he called after her.

She nodded.

She had no problem finding the drugstore or the supplies she wanted, and no problem with traffic. She was back in fifteen minutes. Nick looked relieved to see her.

"Who would try to run us down?" she asked as she pulled the chair up to the bed near his foot and sat down.

He didn't answer right away but seemed to be thinking as she carefully bandaged his ankle and settled the ice bag she'd bought and filled against his foot. She wished she had a gel pack—it would be more supple—but she had no way to freeze one even if she'd bought one.

"Someone who thinks we are getting too close to the truth," he suggested.

"Truth about what?"

"Bart Williams."

He looked very solemn. "But who would want us not to find out what happened to Bart?"

"I don't know, Maddy."

For a moment, she was too stunned by the suggestion to speak, then she managed, "You're saying someone killed Bart and whoever it was might have been driving that car?"

"I'm not sure yet, Maddy. I'm getting a few glimmerings, but not enough to talk about yet. I'm just looking around for ideas. Don't worry about it, okay? I could be totally wrong on all counts."

"How can I not worry?"

He lifted his head off the pillow and studied her face. "Could you possibly shuffle up here a little closer?"

She wasn't sure that was a good idea. . . . Oh, what the hell. She got up and moved the chair so she was sitting sideways next to his upper half instead of his lower half.

He took her hand and looked at her solemnly. "Maddy, I think you should go home."

"Me? Just me? Why?"

"I think this running around, asking questions, is putting you in danger. If that driver did intend to hit us, then it would have to be a hell of a coincidence for it to be anyone who wasn't connected in some way with your Bart, so I think—"

"Please don't call him *my* Bart."

"Sorry. What I was going to say is that we may know something we shouldn't, and whoever drove that car wants to make sure we can't talk about it. Either that, or we've been followed and we seem to be getting close to something we shouldn't know about."

"You're serious, aren't you?"

"Very."

Maddy took a deep breath. "Okay. In that case, it's time you told me what it is you are putting together."

"I am?"

She pulled her hand free. "Don't fool with me, Nick. I'm not made of cotton candy. Whatever it is you're thinking, I can take it. It's not just the car coming at us that's got you worried, is it?"

He shook his head. "I keep forgetting how smart you are."

"I've noticed." She took a deep breath. "I'm guessing you're connecting the Donati case with your friend the cabdriver. The cabdriver who gave you some information. Information about Bart? Are you also connecting the other deaths to Bart's?"

"I don't know for sure that there's a link, Maddy."

"But you are considering it as a possibility?"

"What are you, psychic?" He gave her a palms-up signal of defeat. "Okay, yes, I'm considering it."

"So tell me about it so I can consider it too."

"Not yet. I'm not quite sure enough of some elements."

"When then?"

"As soon as I am sure. I swear. But in the meantime I think you should go home and let me see what I can find out alone. Maybe not home, meaning Bart's house, but perhaps you could stay with Kazuko again, or Lara."

"You think I'm a hindrance to you?"

"Not at all. I just don't want you to get hurt."

"Why not? Why should you care?"

"I do care, Maddy. I care a lot."

She was speechless. "You . . . you . . ."

He laughed. "I don't kiss the wrists of women I don't care for, Maddy."

She got her breath back. "Well, I guess you were right about something going on between us," she said, smiling.

"So then you'll be a good girl and go on home?"

She stopped smiling. "Your wording leaves a lot to be desired, Ciacia. I'm not a girl, I'm a woman."

"I've noticed."

She didn't let herself be distracted. "Danger's not something I'd willingly get into, Nick. I'm no damsel in distress roaming around the castle courtyard at midnight, inviting a bop on the head. But I'm not going to be terrorized by some imbecile who tries to run me down. I'll be more cautious from now on, as I'm sure you will be. But I'm not going to run away."

There was fire in those vivid blue eyes. She had never looked so beautiful to him. He would still prefer to pack her in foam pellets and tuck her away somewhere safe, but he couldn't help admiring her attitude.

"Could you possibly lean over here?" he asked.

She shook her head. "I want to look at your foot again."

Scooting the chair back, she put her hands on each side of the bandage, then touched the flesh above it. "It doesn't feel so warm now."

"It shouldn't. You're freezing me to death with that ice pack."

"You're not a very grateful patient."

"*Au contraire.* If you were to shuffle back up here, I'd show you gratitude you wouldn't forget."

She smiled at him.

His answering smile flickered and vanished. "You can treat sprained ankles. Can you treat what's ailing other parts of me?" he asked softly.

She met his gaze. No more games. "I may be suffering from the same malady myself," she admitted. "Maybe . . ." She stood up and took a deep breath; she felt like she was on the verge of hyperventilating. "Maybe we could treat each other."

He reached for her hands, then with a quick movement pulled her over on top of him. "Your foot!" she protested.

"What foot?" he asked.

And then he kissed her softly, gently on the lips, in just the way she had imagined in her dream, his mouth moving slowly over hers, covering it, savoring it, not insisting, not taking, just suggesting, asking, persuading.

A sweetness washed through her and found its center in her groin. As she answered his kiss with her own mouth, her hands went to the buttons on his shirt.

He laughed against her lips, his mouth taking breath from hers and giving it back. Taking hold of her cotton sweater, he pulled it up and up, until she had to break away from him and get off the bed so she could help him get the sweater over her head.

Gesturing with his hand for her to step back, he swung his legs off the bed and gazed at her with that familiar wicked glint in his eyes. "Go ahead," he said. She caught his meaning at once and started stripping for him, slowly, teasingly, while he hastily peeled off his own clothes. She had to help him get his chinos over the bandaged foot and worried that she might be hurting him, though he certainly didn't look as if he was in pain.

They made love as if they had known each other's bodies for months, hands and mouths charged with energy, touching and kissing whatever part of their bodies was in easy reach as they moved together and apart. And as they kissed and breathed and touched, they watched each other, until the pressures inside them rose and became unbearable and finally broke in a release that left them clinging together closer than ever.

It was a long time before either of them moved. Maddy felt exhilarated but exhausted.

"Am I hurting you?" she asked at last.

He brushed a kiss across the shoulder nearest his mouth. "How could you? You don't weigh anything at all."

"I do too. And I meant your foot."

"What foot?" he said again, then laughed and rolled with her just enough so they were side by side. "There now. That's just fine."

"You want to go to sleep?"

"Not yet. I'm not planning on moving again in the near future though." He tilted his head so he could see her face and stroked her cheek with the back of his fingers. Her skin was even softer than he'd expected it to be. It looked . . . incandescent. Now, there was a word! Since he'd met her his vocabulary had expanded—incandescent, melodic . . .

"Amazing what a near-death experience can do for the libido," he said.

"You think that's what turned us on?"

"No, it was your fingers brushing my leg that got to me. A formerly undiscovered erotic zone that I hope you will explore again in the very near future. What got to you?"

"Your stunning male beauty."

"Ah, I thought so."

It had been a long time since she had laughed following sex. It had been a long time since she'd had any sex. And when she had, with Bart, it had been far from enjoyable—sex by the numbers, she'd thought of it. Her old boyfriend Buzz had been her best lover. He'd always been able to make her laugh, and between them they had used up every idea either one had ever thought of where love-making was concerned, and usually, every piece of furniture in a room. Such athleticism hadn't seemed necessary with Nick. It had seemed natural to just make love, without any discussion of how and where and what do you like and this is what I like.

"Your brain is seething with thoughts," Nick said next to her ear, his warm breath stirring her hair.

"I'm thinking about the way we made love."

"It was the right way."

"It sure was."

He had been astonished at the way her body had responded to his. He was beginning to sense that he'd been waiting a long time for a sensual, responsive, intelligent, beautiful woman like this one. No, not *like* this one. He'd been waiting for her, Maddy.

"Of all the men's rooms in all the markets in all the world, she had to walk into mine," he said.

She came right back at him. "We'll always have Pike Place."

He produced one of his rare sun-bursting-through-clouds smiles.

"*Casablanca* is such a wonderful movie," Maddy murmured. "Except Ingrid should have gone off with Humphrey and let Paul Henreid save the world by himself."

Nick was suddenly looking much more wakeful. "You want to do it again?" he asked.

She raised her head and looked at him. "You're not serious."

"I'm not serious. But next time it will last longer, I promise."

She relaxed against him again. "There's going to be a next time?"

"You thought this was a one-hour stand?"

"I haven't decided what to think." She frowned. "I can't commit to anything, you know."

"Isn't that supposed to be the guy's line? My line?"

"Well, my motivation is probably different from yours. The next time I commit, it's going to be to someone who really loves me. Someone I really love."

He grimaced. "Aargh, you said the bad L word."

She laughed. "I'm sorry, I didn't mean to scare you. I guess what I'm really saying is that if I ever commit again, it will be to someone with a steady job who is home all the time and wants to make babies. And I'm guessing that's not exactly your goal in life."

"You guess good. Although come to think of it, we might have made a baby right here. For once in my life, I didn't even think of protection."

"I'm safe enough. It's the wrong time of the month for me to be ovulating."

"Too much information," he said, and she laughed.

"In case you're worried, I'm also perfectly healthy," he assured her. "It's been a long time for me."

"Me too. I mean, you don't need to worry." She hesitated. "So we can just enjoy what we have while we have it, right?"

"Works for me," he said sleepily.

He *was* going to sleep. They'd had a fairly busy day and he'd done all the driving. And she knew enough about male chemistry to know it was perfectly natural for a man to get sleepy after sex. She was content to watch him as his face relaxed and his body went limp. When she was sure he was sleeping soundly, she raised herself carefully away from him and slipped out of bed. He didn't stir.

Still moving carefully, she took care of bathroom needs, then packed the ice bag with fresh ice from the bucket and put it back against his foot, first making sure the foot was not twisted in any way.

Then she pulled her robe out of the closet, carried her laptop to the desk, and connected to the data port on the telephone. Her chemistry didn't seem to require her to go to sleep, so she'd just take the different elements of this puzzle Nick was working on and see what she could figure out for herself.

Chapter 21

NICK WOKE UP with a start, feeling a throbbing in his left ankle. It took him a moment to remember, then he felt a satisfied, maybe even smug grin spread across his face.

"You're awake," Maddy said.

He opened his eyes and squinted at her. She was sitting at the desk, the chair turned to face him as though she'd been waiting for him to wake up.

"How long did I sleep?"

"Just a couple of hours."

"You haven't slept?"

"I've been working on the laptop, researching."

He sat up and raked his hair with one hand, then followed an urgent need out of the bed toward the bathroom. "Yow!" he hollered as his foot hit the floor. He hopped the next two steps and managed to get clear of the bathroom door and close it.

When he was through, he ran water and sluiced it over his face and head, hopped out again, found his Jockey shorts on the floor, put them on, and lay back, propping his foot on the pillows again.

"The foot hurts," he commented.

"It will for a day or two. You need to try to stay off it. I'll do the driving for a while." .

There was little warmth in her voice. Something robotic about it. He turned his head and looked at her and realized belatedly that she was tense and pale.

He sat bolt upright. "What happened?"

She took in a deep breath, let it all the way out. "I found out you could be right. There may be a connection."

"I don't . . . I'm not following, Maddy."

"I've bookmarked the Web pages. If you can sit on the side of the bed, I think I can pull the desk over to you. I'll get online again and show you what I found."

"Let me help."

"Stay!" she said.

He pulled the blanket up over his shoulders.

The desk was not large, but it was awkward to move over the carpet. She managed it, though—she was a strong woman. He remembered her hauling him over that wall when the car had come at them. Making love to her, he'd appreciated the firmness of her body as much as the softness of her skin and hair.

When she sat down beside him, he wanted to kiss her, but she was obviously not in the mood.

After booting up the computer, she started him on a tour of the sites she'd been browsing.

"Okay," she said as the first page was loading, "we've determined that Bart was in Portland on the day when Rafe Donati drowned."

"Looks like," he agreed.

The newspaper page that opened was dated September 11. "Dr. Joseph said Bart visited her July 10," Maddy said. "The day *before* Bart's calendar said he visited her. This newspaper only archives lead stories for ninety days, but there was a reference to a July incident."

She angled the laptop so he could read the headline easier. REMEMBERING JONATHAN WINSTON, A PHOTO ES-

SAY. In smaller print below was the note: *Readers will remember that reporter Jonathan Winston took his own life on July 11, shooting himself in the head in his car. Photographer Leila Ramos, who often worked with Winston, collected the photos and headlines that illustrate Winston's work over the past year.*

Jonathan Winston had been an investigative reporter who concentrated on crime stories, mainly those that dealt with developers who made kickbacks, bribed officials to look the other way when pollution was likely, or otherwise tried to run the world for their own profit and hang the environment. He had received prizes for his work, including one Pulitzer.

"I found the original story," Maddy said, and clicked on the bookmark.

The date on the story was July 12.

Jonathan Winston, a reporter for our "rival" newspaper, was found shot to death in his car today, the victim of an apparent suicide. He was thirty-three years old.

"There's that dramatic word *apparent* again," Maddy pointed out.

Nick grunted and kept reading.

No suicide note was found, police said. Winston had been drinking. An empty vodka bottle was found on the seat beside him. It appears to be a clear case of suicide.

"We are all saddened by the loss of our friend and colleague Jonathan Winston," editor Sean O'Connor said. "Jon was a reliable, dedicated, and prize-winning reporter and a loyal friend. Our hearts go out to his family, along with our prayers." Winston's body was discovered at noon today by a police officer checking on a car parked at the edge of a wooded area not far from the newspaper offices. Colleagues said Winston often brought a sandwich from home and ate his lunch in that area. "It gives my mind an airing," Winston had said.

Judging by Nick's morose expression, Maddy knew he understood immediately why she was showing him this report, which confirmed her guess that she had discovered the connection he'd suspected.

"I guess we could look into it, but it seems fairly cut-and-dried," he said. "If there was even a hint that he didn't commit suicide—"

"There's a hint in the next story," Maddy said. "The death took place on June second, in Las Vegas."

His head came around immediately. "Vegas wasn't on Bart's route."

"No, but I found an Orbitz receipt for a plane reservation to Vegas in the folder with the Visa receipts. He flew into Las Vegas on June 1 and flew out June 2. That was one week before our wedding. He never mentioned Las Vegas to me."

The page was again from a local paper. "This paper had archives going quite a way back," she said. "I was able to come up with the original story right away."

" 'Notorious dancer Ruby Red Rawlings victim of hit-and-run accident,' " Nick read aloud, then glanced at Maddy.

"Keep reading," she said.

The scantily clad body of dancer Ruby Red Rawlings was found sprawled in the parking lot of the Skyline Hotel early this morning by a security officer doing rounds. She had been hit by an automobile and left to die. Police theorize that a late-night reveler may have hit her without even realizing it and gone happily on his drunken way. A member of the Gem Femmes dancers, Ruby had performed in two evening shows with her usual enthusiasm, nightclub manager Ambrose Marley stated. She had then gone into the kitchen to pick up some food to eat in her dressing room. After that she would normally shower and change into street clothes and drive home to her apartment, but on this night she inexplicably went directly to the parking lot and was struck by the car.

Marley suggested that as Ruby was black and the brief costume she wore for her act was also black, it might have been difficult for anyone to see her if he didn't have his brights on. She was found near the back of the parking lot, where a streetlight had gone out.

Ruby is the girlfriend of Emmett Everard, who is presently in jail awaiting trial for the strangling murder of dancer Pearl White, another member of the Gem Femmes troupe. Seems something of a coincidence that Ruby would also die by violence.

Anyone who might have seen anything or have any information about Ruby's death is asked to call the Las Vegas Police Department.

Maddy showed Nick two more stories from a couple of years back—one from Los Angeles, and one from Bellingham, north of Seattle. One featured a *probable suicide*, the other an *unfortunate accident*.

"All of these coincide with Bart's trips," she said woodenly.

Nick put an arm around her shoulders. She was unresponsive. "And your conclusion is?"

"They are all reported as either accidents or suicides, but they sound fishy. Like Donati's drowning. And every one of them has some connection to a crime." She hesitated, looking at him, her eyes huge. "I think you've already made a connection between Bart and Donati's drowning."

He nodded. "A tenuous one, based on a hunch."

"You think Bart killed Donati."

"I'm not far enough along to say that with any certainty," he hedged.

He closed the files she'd shown him and shut down the computer.

"We'll talk in the morning," he said. "We've had enough excitement for one day."

"But—"

"I can't do it, Maddy. I'm not functioning on all cylinders. I need sleep."

She nodded and helped him ease back on to the bed, then pushed the desk back into place and climbed in bed beside him. He put an arm across her waist and she felt comforted. Relaxing deliberately, emptying her mind, she fell asleep.

When she woke up at seven-fifteen a.m., Nick was gone. His clothes were gone. He'd probably gone back to his own room, she decided as she stumbled into the shower. Her eyes felt gummy. Too much computer and not enough sleep.

When there was no sign of Nick by eight o'clock and she was dressed and ready to go, she decided to inspect the hotel's continental breakfast. But first she looked up a chiropractor's number in the telephone directory.

There were several people eating at a gathering of small tables at one side of the hotel lobby. Maddy was halfway across the room to join them when she noticed Nick talking to the same desk clerk they had interviewed the previous evening. The clerk evidently worked long hours. Maddy hesitated, trying to decide if she should join Nick or wait for him at one of the tables. She decided to join Nick.

But just as she came near, Nick reached under his jacket, pulled a thin wallet from the back pocket of his chinos, and showed it to the desk clerk. Maddy came to a halt. Was he checking out? she wondered.

But then she noticed that there was a badge pinned to the wallet. He lifted the flap to show what looked like an ID card with a photo in the corner.

The clerk began talking quite volubly, though very quietly.

Nick listened intently as he folded the wallet and put it away.

Maddy felt like Wile E. Coyote air-walking off a cliff.

She'd be okay as long as she didn't look down, she thought. Somehow she managed to go over to the buffet table, where she toasted a pair of bagels, gathered up some butter and cream cheese, filled two mugs with coffee, and added a couple of bananas to the tray.

As she turned, Nick appeared before her. "Hey, you're up."

"Let's eat in my room," she suggested.

He grinned and limped after her.

He was still smiling when she set the tray down on the desk in her room and turned to face him. Then his smile faltered. She supposed her face was showing some of the strain she was feeling.

"What?" he asked very quietly.

"I saw you talking to the desk clerk."

He frowned. "Yes, I was questioning him again about Bart's July visit. Actually, he's the hotel manager. I managed to get a little more—"

He broke off as she still stood rigid. "Shit," he said.

She nodded. "My sentiments exactly."

"You saw me show him my creds. My credentials."

"I did. You're a police officer?"

"FBI."

"I see." She sat down on the desk chair and began furiously buttering her bagel.

He leaned over the desk and did the same, only more gently.

"I guess you're not too happy about that." Taking his bagel and plate with him, he sat on the edge of the bed.

"The word of the day is *outraged*," she said stiffly. "You've deceived me all along. Bart deceived me all along. I guess I'm still dumb when it comes to men." She looked at him directly. "Was the sex really a necessary part of the act?"

"Ah, Maddy, no." He put the bagel down and touched her face gently, moving a strand of her hair back behind her ear, stroking her cheek with his thumb.

She stayed stiff.

"That was real, Maddy." He hesitated. "Are you going to let me explain?"

"Sure, go ahead, tell me how you used me."

He winced, picked up his mug and gulped some coffee down, returned it to the tray, then took both her hands in his.

She didn't resist; nor did she respond.

"This was not an official investigation," he said. "My supervisor knows about it and is supportive, but I'm not acting as a bona fide agent."

"Why?"

"I was afraid that if Bart suspected an FBI agent was on his tail, he'd take off."

"He did take off."

He nodded. "It's entirely possible he saw me waiting in Pike Place Market. He didn't know me, but he may have suspected I was waiting for him. I guess we'll never know."

"And you couldn't have told me all this at the start?"

"I didn't know you well enough, Maddy."

"You thought I might be in cahoots?"

"I thought it was a possibility. At first—and not for long. I also figured I'd get more information from people—doctors and so on—about Bart's business trips if I stayed incognito."

"Using the poor grieving widow as an excuse to interrogate people."

"I prefer the term *interview*, Maddy. And I wasn't really only using you for my own purposes. It was more like I was helping you at the same time I was helping myself."

"So you could find Quentin?"

There was a jeering note in her voice now. Nick swallowed. "Quentin was a stand-in, yes. I wanted to find Bart all along. I've been looking for him for years."

"Because you suspected him of what?"

"I was looking for a man who was nicknamed the Snowman because of his platinum blond hair. Three weeks ago, my informant Arnie, the taxi driver who died,

told me he'd heard a couple of guys talking in prison
about the Snowman. They said his real name was Bartel
Franz—well, actually Arnie heard the name as Bart L.
Fritz, but my research indicated it was possibly Bartel
Wilhelm Franz. The two convicts had also said the Snowman was born in Germany. I found out through some
contacts that Bart arrived in Chicago from Stuttgart, Germany, when he was eighteen, became a citizen when he
was twenty-one, changed his name to Bart Williams, and
moved to the Seattle area."

"So you started following Bart, and then me."

"Yes."

She withdrew her hands from his, and she was still so
pale and rigid, he was afraid to risk trying to get them
back.

"You still haven't explained what you suspected Bart
of."

He looked away. "I'm afraid that's classified information."

"You said you weren't acting officially."

She was so sharp. He wondered how he'd been able
to deceive her at all.

"The information is still classified," he said firmly.

"But you think Bart is mixed up in these different accidents and suicides. You think he's a killer? Do you have
any proof?"

"Nothing yet that would hold up in court. He just appears to have been in the right places at the right time."

"The wrong time for other people."

He nodded. "Maddy, the manager told me Bart stayed
here for two nights in July. July 10 and 11. While he was
here he was visited by a man wearing a white cowboy
hat."

Once again she felt as if someone had punched her in
the stomach. "I was right then—about the cowboy," she
said when she got her breath back. "He *is* important."

"The manager thinks Bart might have been carrying a
weapon when he stayed here. Evidently his shoe slipped
on the floor in the lobby. When he stumbled his jacket

pulled open a little and the manager saw what looked like a shoulder holster on Bart's left side. The manager said he was quick to look away. But he'd felt Bart's gaze on him for a few seconds, and it had made him shiver. That's why he didn't want to talk about Bart—he was afraid. Until I showed him my creds."

"What else did you find out?" she asked.

"That's it. I've got someone checking records in Stuttgart to find something on his family. I already knew that he worked in a pharmacy after he immigrated to Chicago. I talked to the pharmacist on the phone. He said Bart was a good worker, but not sociable."

"Even then."

She folded her arms across her chest, gripping her upper arms and swaying a little as though she were cold.

"Maddy?" He put out a tentative hand to touch her shoulder.

She didn't appear to notice. "I was married to a killer. He touched me. Not recently, but early on. He touched me. I thought he'd changed after we were married, but it looks as if he was already a killer when I met him, when he was so charming. They say Ted Bundy could be charming. He persuaded women to help him, then killed them. Bart killed again a month after our wedding. I slept in his bed. For a while. Not long. But I did sleep in his bed."

Her eyes were wide, staring but not seeing.

Nick took a chance and gathered her into his arms. She was stiff for a few moments, then she collapsed against him, shaking.

"We may be completely wrong, Maddy," he told her.

She shook her head slightly against his chest. "No. It . . . feels right. He was such a cold, cold man. It doesn't take much stretch of the imagination for me to believe—"

She broke off, shivered again, then eased herself out of his arms.

"Am I forgiven?" he asked.

She put a hand on each side of his face and looked solemnly at him for what seemed a long time before she spoke. "I don't know if *forgive* is the right word. I guess I understand why you didn't want to tell me right off that you were an FBI agent and even why you didn't want to go officially into the hospitals, at least until you had enough evidence against Bart. But you still deceived me, and I believed in you, even though I did suspect you had an agenda of your own. So I'm not sure I can believe anything you tell me in the future."

She dropped her hands but kept her gaze on his face. "And I'm not sure I can . . . make love with you again."

"Maddy . . ."

He reached for her, but she drew away. "Let it go, Nick. Right now I'm still angry. I don't know if my anger is for Bart or for you or for my own stupidity. Probably all of the above. Whatever the cause, it's a hell of a lot of anger. Right now would not be a good time to let it all out. So don't push it, okay?"

He took a deep breath, then released it on a sigh that held both longing and regret. "Okay."

Standing, she told him in a clinical voice to lie down— she wanted to look at his ankle.

"I think the bandage probably needs redoing," he said, as he obeyed. "I took it off to shower and didn't do a very good job of putting it back."

"You've got that right," she muttered as she unwound it, then deftly bound his ankle again. "It's still swollen," she commented.

It felt a lot better to Nick. Sitting up, he pulled his shoe on, leaving his sock off. "What do you want to do before we go see a chiropractor?" she asked.

This was no time for a wiseass answer, even if it was the one he wanted to make. "I'd like to get back on the computer and see what else we can find about Terminus," he said instead.

She shot him a look, but didn't ask why.

It took only a few minutes to find the listing they'd discovered earlier: *Terminus—a criminal organization* . . .

Maddy stopped reading and looked at Nick. "You said

something about Terminus being divided into regions, but
then you quit talking. Why?"

She saw him debate with himself whether to tell her.

"If this has something to do with Bart, I have a right
to know," she insisted.

He nodded but still hesitated. She waited him out. Finally, he said, "Arnie, my informant who overheard the
guys in prison talking about the Snowman, told me that
one other thing they said was that the Snowman was the
West Coast rep."

"As Bart was, for Mawsom."

"It occurred to me when we read about the regional
divisions—"

She was already there. "You think those guys might
have meant some other kind of West Coast rep? For Terminus?" She closed her eyes and shuddered. "I was married to a *professional* killer, a *hired* killer."

"It's still conjecture at this point, Maddy."

It was an effort, but she pulled herself together and
looked back at the screen. There was a link she hadn't
noticed before to something called *Terminus in Our
Town?* She clicked on it, though she thought it was probably something to do with one of the computer games.

Instead it was an article, written by one Jude Rodriguez, a Portland columnist, about the death of Rafe Donati. It was too much of a coincidence, Jude Rodriguez
reckoned, for Donati to die "accidentally," right after he'd
blown the whistle on the Castonberry group. The situation
reminded her of the Terminus modus operandi, which involved calling in a hit man from somewhere handy and
arranging a suicide or accident for whomever had been
found offensive. She'd been researching accidents and suicides across the United States for months, she said, and
there were too many similarities for them to be coinci-
dences.

She ended the column with a warning to Terminus that
if she was to have any kind of accident, or was found
dead of an apparent suicide, all law enforcement person-

nel in the Pacific Northwest would know who was responsible.

"Brave lady," Nick commented. He glanced at his watch. "It's still early enough for us to check out."

"I take it we're going back to Portland?"

"Portland it is. Jude Rodriguez sounds like someone who might be inclined to be helpful. We can keep running around checking out each case, but she just might provide a shortcut."

He stood up, and winced. "Let's go," he said.

"After you see a chiropractor."

"That's not—"

"Nick, I know men hate to admit they may have a problem with any part of their miraculous, testosterone-marinated bodies, but if you have that ankle adjusted by a chiropractor it will get better faster, which will make you far more efficient. Your efficiency just might be important right now, wouldn't you say? Doesn't your insurance cover chiropractic?"

"It does." He sighed. "I suppose you've already made an appointment?"

"You know me so well." She glanced at her watch. "I haven't actually made an appointment, but I have the number to call."

She called, and the chiropractor's office manager agreed to fit Nick in since they were just passing through.

Maddy drove. The chiropractor was a charming, middle-aged man with big hands. He took an X ray, agreed with Maddy's diagnosis that nothing was broken, and adjusted Nick's ankle with deft, efficient movements. Then he strapped it up again and complimented Maddy's bandaging skills. Nick arranged for the office manager to bill his insurance.

"Was that so terrible?" Maddy asked when they were headed north again.

"Probably unnecessary," he grumbled. But he did manage a smile.

Maddy didn't smile back. She didn't think she had a smile left in her.

Chapter 22

A HELPFUL WOMAN at the newspaper office told them Jude Rodriguez worked from home. She wouldn't give them the address, but when Nick introduced himself as an FBI agent, she did call Ms. Rodriguez and ask her if she'd talk to them.

The upshot of that was that within half an hour they were greeting Jude Rodriguez in her very untidy home office.

Seating herself behind a rickety-looking metal desk, she gestured at a couple of straight chairs opposite. Nick turned his around and straddled it. Maddy never understood why men did that. It looked very uncomfortable and even hazardous to their health.

"What happened to your leg?" Jude asked Nick, peering over the desk at his bandaged ankle.

"It's just a sprained ankle," he told her.

"You want some ice? A footstool?"

He shook his head.

Women were so nurturing, Maddy thought. Would a man have offered such amenities?

They'd stopped on the way to Portland for a quick lunch, but accepted the coffee Jude gave them in big mugs with pictures of cats on them. Judging by the enormous coffeemaker that sat on a shelf at the back of the room, Jude was a caffeine addict, not an uncommon ailment in the Pacific Northwest.

"My doctor said it wasn't a good idea to take coffee intravenously," she said when she caught Maddy looking.

"So," Jude added to Nick, getting down to business, "the FBI is interested in Terminus."

"We've always been interested. Proving everything we suspect is something else."

She eyed him suspiciously for a moment, then looked questioningly at Maddy. Jude was a tough-looking woman, with strong features and thick dark hair cut in a no-nonsense Dutch bob, straight across and straight down.

Maddy took a breath. "My husband died recently. The coroner ruled his death a suicide. We think—"

"We think Terminus is involved," Nick interrupted.

"You let this guy speak for you?" Jude asked Maddy.

"He has a tendency to do that. So far I haven't objected. Though I reserve the right to."

Jude gave her a broad smile that evidently meant she approved of the answer, or of the attitude.

A small calico cat appeared beside Maddy's chair and sprang up without invitation into her lap. She stroked the cat's head, which brought her another approving smile from Jude. "One of my girls," she said. "There are four of them around here somewhere."

The cat settled in, purring. Maddy felt comforted. She'd never owned a cat. Her mother thought they were too much trouble, and pets had always been banned in apartments Maddy had lived in. She wondered if she'd be allowed to have one in her new condo.

"What can I do for the feds?" Jude asked Nick.

"We read your article about Donati. We've had our suspicions about Donati's death ourselves."

"We being the FBI?"

"We being Maddy and me. I'm not engaged in an official investigation. This one's personal."

Maddy looked at him sharply, but he kept his gaze on Jude. Personal? she wondered. He'd told her it was unofficial, but he hadn't said anything about it being *personal*.

"You got some ID?" Jude asked.

Nick produced the wallet Maddy had seen him show the manager of the Sitka hotel. Jude reached out to take it from him, but he held on to it. She leaned over her desk to look at it closely, squinting at it, maybe even sniffing it. Did she think it was a fake?

She finally sat back, and Nick replaced the wallet in his pocket. "Terminus killings are either fixed to look like accidents or suicides or dressed up as happening during the commission of a burglary," she said.

She glanced at Maddy, her dark eyes showing sympathy. "Which makes your husband's death open to question, especially if there was anything odd about it."

"There was," Maddy said. "His blood alcohol count was very high, but he didn't ever drink. He called alcohol the 'number one destroyer.' He worked out, was careful about what he ate, didn't smoke. He was an ascetic, without the religion."

"And you lived with this paragon how long?"

"Six months. Six months too long."

Again Jude nodded approval. "Glad you recognized your mistake."

She turned back to Nick. "You know what Terminus is then?"

"I do. We do—we being the Bureau. Murder Inc. reincarnated, without the Friends, as they call them where my family is from."

Jude nodded. "You look Italian."

"Not Italian, Sicilian."

She raised an eyebrow. "You're too tall to be Sicilian."

"My mother's Irish."

She was almost flirting with Nick, Maddy thought. She discovered she was stroking the cat a little too intensely.

Surely she wasn't jealous? She despised a tendency to possessiveness in anyone, including herself.

"One big difference," Jude said, turning businesslike again. "The Mob decreed that hit men would only be dispatched to dispatch those who were involved with the Mob. You couldn't order up the killing of an innocent bystander, a police officer, a politician, or a reporter. Not out of any righteousness on their part, but because such crimes pulled down too much official attention."

Taking their coffee mugs and her own, she refilled all three, then sat down again. "Terminus, on the other hand, stops at nothing. Their only rule is that there should be no obvious killings, none of the old Murder Inc. methods of weighing a body down with a pinball machine or sinking a cleaver in someone's skull. Terminus does still follow the rule of silence—the old Mafia *omerta*. But it's an equal opportunity service—anyone can ask for a killer to be provided. There's probably a secret website around that you can go to if you can find out the URL. Probably has a FAQ page in it. You could probably charge the bill on your Visa. One-stop shopping. Put in your zip code, we'll send the local rep."

Maddy winced, and Jude gave her a long look. "You wanted to get back at Nick here, you could call on Terminus. As long as you have enough money, no problem. Got a business rival, a cheating wife or husband—Bob's your uncle, as the Brits say."

"What bothered us about Donati's killing," Nick said, "was that there's a wide strip of grass between the trail and the water. We thought it would take quite a blow to make someone so disoriented that he'd stagger that far."

Jude nodded. "What bothered *me* was the lump on Donati's forehead. One, how many people fall straight forward like a tree on a flat path? And two, the soft surface of that particular trail wouldn't do that much damage."

"You think someone hit him with something," Maddy said.

Jude nodded.

"Do you know about the hit-and-run in Las Vegas?" Maddy asked. "Ruby Red Rawlings?"

"Sure do. How did you come by it?"

"We did some research on the Web," Nick said.

"Ain't that Web fab!" Jude said. "I wrote an article about Ruby Red too," she added. "She was Emmett Everard's girl."

Standing, she rooted through a tall filing cabinet and came up with a manila folder which she tactfully placed on the desk between them.

Maddy opened it. Jude told her the sentence in the Las Vegas report that had caught her attention was "Seems something of a coincidence that Ruby should also die of violence." "Also," Jude added, "I don't believe in that light being out so fortuitously, right where she was run down."

She sighed. "I read that article, I knew the case was one for my files on Terminus. Called up the reporter, and sure enough, he was being sarcastic—didn't know about Terminus but was damn sure it wasn't an accident. Said the local police figured it was probably a revenge killing. Everard killed Pearl, and Pearl's boyfriend probably killed Ruby. Only thing was Pearl's boyfriend had a cast-iron alibi. He was in one of the restaurants, having a late-dinner with several of his cronies. Plenty of witnesses besides his own people—waiters, other guests, even one of the local police officers."

She shook her head. "You ever been to the Treasure Island resort in Las Vegas?"

They both shook their heads.

"They enact a big gunfight several times a day between a British naval frigate and a pirate vessel. Cannons, gunfire, masts being felled. Finally the British ship sinks, captain standing bravely at attention, going down with it. Someone once said, 'The pirates always win in Las Vegas.'"

They were all silent for a minute, then Maddy asked, "Have you ever heard of a cowboy being involved in any of this?"

Nick gave her a nod of approval, but Jude shook her head.

Nick asked, "How about the Snowman?"

Maddy cringed.

Jude wasn't looking at her—her attention was mostly on Nick. She pulled her chin in when he asked the question. "Whoa! Now you're talking. What do you know about that guy?"

"I asked first," Nick said, and Jude blew him a playful raspberry.

"Couple of my sources have mentioned him," she said. "Said he got the nickname because of his white or blond hair. Supposedly between forty and fifty now, but he always had this noticeable hair." She tapped her forehead with a long index finger, as if to stir up her memory. "Born in Germany. Stuttgart. Longtime member of the Terminus staff. He's one of those guys people whisper about. They're afraid to talk out loud, in case he hears about it and comes around to deal with them. Cool customer, I understand, in more ways than one. Lethal."

"He's still in business?"

"Last I heard."

"Did you ever see a photograph of him?"

"Hell, no, a guy like that doesn't let himself be photographed. All I have is hearsay."

"You don't know his real name?"

"Nope. I just know I wouldn't want to run into the creep on a dark and stormy night."

Nick looked at Maddy. She'd lost all of her color. For a moment he thought she was going to either faint or throw up. But she was made of strong stuff. She took her hands off Jude's cat, gripped the arms of her chair for a minute or two, and swallowed hard. Then her color returned as though she'd willed it to, and she began petting the cat again. He admired her self-control and could only guess how much it had cost her.

Fortunately, Jude had been thumbing through the papers on her desk as she spoke and hadn't noticed Maddy's reaction.

* * *

"I DON'T WANT to talk about it or even think about it," Maddy said. They had left Jude's house and were driving toward the freeway. "Not yet."

"We can do one of two things," Nick said. "We can spend the night in Portland, or you can drive to your house. I'll leave you there. I'm sure I can drive on without any problem."

"You're ending our investigation? But we haven't—"

"Not ending, no. I'm going to drive to SeaTac airport and fly to Las Vegas."

"You're planning on going without me?"

He turned to look at her. "I got the impression you didn't want to be with me anymore."

"I said I didn't want to talk about what Jude said, and I said I couldn't make love. I didn't say I was ready to quit." She avoided the question of whether she wanted to be with him.

"I've no idea what I might get into in Las Vegas, Maddy. And I don't think . . . I think this is very hard on you."

"Are you going officially or unofficially?"

He hesitated. "I've got enough now to interest the Bureau, but as Jude said, all she told us is hearsay. I'd like to follow this track first to see if I can get some actual proof and maybe even tie up a few loose ends before I turn it over."

"Like what?"

"Like what Bart was doing in Las Vegas. You said you'd found a receipt for an electronic plane ticket among Bart's documents."

"Then I'm definitely coming with you. I want to know the truth even more than you do. Anyway, I couldn't possibly just hang around waiting to see what you might come up with."

He seemed about to say something more, maybe to argue, but he stopped himself.

"Okay." He pulled out his cell phone. "No point going all the way to SeaTac then. I'll get the number for the

Portland airport and find out flight times for tomorrow morning. We can leave the car at the airport."

As he punched numbers, he added, "Better yet, I'll see what's available tonight. The flight is only a couple of hours."

There was a plane at eight p.m. through America West.

MADDY HADN'T THOUGHT about Nick being armed. As an FBI agent, he had to be, she supposed. He also had to show his credentials at the ticket counter and fill out a form to report that he was armed.

This caused a bit of a delay, and then someone had to escort them through security and inform the airline personnel at the gate.

"You go through this every time?" Maddy asked.

Nick nodded. "It's okay as long as they don't decide to announce they are boarding all passengers traveling with small children, or needing assistance, or carrying weapons. They're not so likely to do that nowadays, but it's been known to happen."

The best part of all of this was that they were bumped up to first class.

Maddy spent much of the flight looking out the window, seeing lights below from time to time, wondering as always about the lives of the people they were flying over and would never know, wondering if the people wondered about the lives of those who flew over them in planes.

Oddly enough—or maybe because if she wanted to retain her sanity, she couldn't possibly let her mind dwell on thoughts of Bart and what they had learned from Jude Rodriguez—she spent the rest of the time thinking about her father.

She and Will didn't have anything in common and rarely saw each other, but all of a sudden, probably because she was on the way to Las Vegas, he showed up in her mind.

"Years ago, Will—my father—was stationed at Nellis Air Force Base, in Las Vegas," she told Nick.

She did some arithmetic. She hadn't thought about her

father's age for a long time. He was sixty-four now. He could live another thirty years. More and more people lived into their nineties, and he was a tough guy. But then again, sometimes people did die in their sixties or seventies, and he did have high blood pressure. . . .

She frowned, feeling suddenly sad, wishing they had a better relationship.

"Will told me a couple of stories about Las Vegas when I was in my teens. Before he was quite so . . . I don't know what the word is. Congealed? Set in his ways, not about to budge on any opinion? Boy, does he have opinions. Is there a word for all that?"

"Rigid?" Nick suggested.

"Will's that, all right. But he told me one time that he and a friend were hitching a ride into downtown Las Vegas, and a man and woman picked them up and asked them to be witnesses at their wedding. Will and his friend tossed a coin to see which one would be best man and which the bridesmaid. Will lost, so he had to carry the flowers."

She laughed at the image. It felt good to laugh. Cleansing. "Another time someone bet him he couldn't swim across Lake Mead. He got halfway and realized it was a hell of a lot wider than it had looked from shore. But there was no way he was going to quit. When he made it to the other side, he tottered out on shore and fell on his face, breathing and laughing, thrilled to be alive, he said."

She sighed. "It's hard for me to imagine him being so lighthearted. He never was that way with me. What is it that happens to people, Nick?"

"Life," he said, looking somber. "Or death," he added, and she realized they had both been fatherless, though in different ways.

They arrived in Las Vegas at ten p.m. and rented a car at the airport, which Nick insisted on driving. Riding down the Strip, Maddy looked out at all the lights and the traffic and the people and marveled at a place where Egypt, New York, Rome, Greece, and Hollywood could exist side by side.

"Hard to imagine this was a valley filled with wild grass when the Spaniards passed through on their way to Los Angeles," Nick said, then added, "Las Vegas is Spanish for 'the Meadows.' "

"Sounds peaceful," Maddy said wistfully.

Nick took her hand and held it. "You'll find peace again soon, Maddy, I promise."

She felt a jump in her blood pressure. Evidently her body still wasn't paying attention to her mind, which had decided there could be no more lovemaking until she cleansed herself somehow of Bart and could be sure she could trust Nick.

Impossible goals, perhaps. All the same, this time she didn't want to remove her hand from his.

They headed to the Elizabethan Village, which was a direct copy of cottages in Shakespeare's Stratford-upon-Avon but included a ten-story central building decked out in fake plaster and timbers.

The temperature at ten p.m. was as warm as Portland at midday, around fifty degrees. "It'll be seventy tomorrow," the desk clerk promised them. Then he told them they had only one "cottage" vacant.

The biggest movie cliché there ever was, Maddy thought. The couple forced to room together. Everyone in the audience knew what was going to happen next. "We'll take it," Nick said, after determining there was a sofa bed in the sitting room portion.

As Maddy discovered when they entered the cottage, there was also a huge black hot tub. Heart-shaped.

"I don't know about you, but that would feel really good on my foot," he said with a glance that challenged her. "We can't do anything until tomorrow anyway."

The tensions of the day had been so strong that she was aching all the way down her back. She resisted the hot tub idea for all of ten seconds, then succumbed.

"Here we are again," Nick said, as they sat opposite each other, both in swimsuits, even though they had all the privacy anyone could want. "Not quite the same though." His mood seemed as somber as hers. After a minute or two, he leaned back and closed his eyes.

Her face, sad, pale, and resigned, stayed in his mind. He wanted to put his arms around her, to hold her, to comfort her. Most of all he wanted to make love to her. But she had retreated to a place where he couldn't reach her. Perhaps to that place of darkness she'd talked about after Bart's body was found.

Knowing that did nothing to ease the urgent prompting of his body whenever he looked at her. He couldn't remember the last time he'd actually been conscious of blood pulsing through his veins. He had an idea it had nothing to do with his injured foot, which he had to admit was feeling a whole lot better than before.

Maddy studied Nick's face. There were shadows under his eyes, as there were under hers. She couldn't really continue to blame him for covering up his identity. She understood that it had been necessary.

But still, she could no longer trust him to be honest with her. And she couldn't imagine letting him, or any man, ever touch her again. She couldn't even let her mind play around the edges of what Bart had done.

She put her hand over her mouth to hold back the nausea that kept coming over her. When she felt stronger, she removed her hand and caught sight of her wedding ring. She hadn't felt it would be a wise move to take it off as soon as she heard Bart was dead. Though she'd wanted to. But if Detective Bradford had noticed, he might have wondered. . . .

"I think I'll go shower now," she said loudly.

Nick opened his eyes and nodded.

"Let me know when you're ready for me to bandage your ankle again," she said.

He nodded again. He looked almost as miserable as she felt. Walking wounded, she thought. Both of them.

After her shower, she stood by the sink, soaped her finger and pulled off the plain gold ring. She had no idea of its value. She should probably give it to a thrift shop or the Salvation Army. But Bart had touched it—it might pass on the evil.

Even though she recognized the idiocy of such a superstitious thought, she knew she just wanted the ring to disappear. Now. If she'd been near dirt, she'd have dug a hole and buried it. Maybe with a stake through its heart, she thought with a touch of black humor.

Instead, she wrapped it up and flushed it down the toilet, feeling marginally better as the bundle whirled and vanished. Pulling on the terry-cloth robe the hotel had supplied, she tied the sash tightly around her middle. Then she stared at herself in the mirror. No doubt about it, she was a mess. She wasn't going to be able to close off her mind, to stay silent. If she continued to keep it all inside, she was going to explode.

She shut her eyes, then opened them again and lifted her chin. She was not going to fall apart. Not yet.

As she exited the bathroom, one huge question was uppermost in her mind, repeating and repeating, drowning out every other thought.

How could I not have known?

Chapter 23

"THAT FELT GOOD," Nick said when she came out of the bathroom.

He'd dried himself in her absence, drained the tub, and put on his own robe. He was sitting on the sofa, barefoot, holding his rolled bandage in one hand.

She repositioned the armchair, pushing the ottoman toward him for his foot to rest on. Then she leaned over and wrapped the bandage around his ankle and foot, taking care not to let her hands linger.

"You took your wedding ring off," he said.

She nodded. "I flushed it down the toilet."

His smile flickered, then vanished. "I've heard of flushing a goldfish, but a gold ring . . ."

"I wanted to get rid of it."

His fingers gently touched her cheek. "It was a good thing to do."

She nodded, then looked back at his foot. "Your ankle's really much better," she said.

"I suppose you're going to take all the credit for that?" He was trying to lighten things up, she realized.

When she clipped the end of the bandage in place, he thanked her, then said, "I was worried about you when Jude described the Snowman. You blanched."

"I almost blacked out," she admitted. "I know we'd pretty well established that Bart was your Snowman, but to hear another person confirm it with that description was hard to take."

She went silent for a minute. "I don't know what to do, Nick," she said, her voice almost, but not quite, breaking. "I don't know how to get used to the idea that I was married for six months to a monster. I keep thinking of how good-looking Bart was—especially when I first met him and he was so charming. He had this way about him. What a fool I was not to suspect that he was so . . . evil. Especially as I know, I absolutely *know* from reading newspapers or watching the news on television, that evil can live in the heart of an innocent-looking schoolboy— he was so quiet, such a good boy, people say—or behind the face of a beautiful woman or a drop-dead gorgeous guy like Bart. But I still subconsciously expected evil to wear an evil face. I expected madmen to act like madmen, to rend their hair and clothes in public, blood dripping from their fangs."

She was staring straight ahead, but the pupils of her eyes were abnormally large and Nick was quite sure she wasn't seeing him; she had her gaze fixed on some grisly internal image. He wanted to interrupt her, to sympathize, empathize, something, but he sensed it was better for her to get out what she wanted to say.

"Bart evidently had another persona that he hid from me and the rest of the world. Maybe his victims were the only ones to see it."

She blinked and appeared to see him again. "It's such a paradox to me that on the one hand he was promoting life-saving drugs, and on the other killing for payment. Think of all the honest and honorable pharmaceutical reps there must be, and I had to pick one who was evil."

She shivered, her face pale and drawn. "It may sound melodramatic to say this, but I feel as if I've been tainted by his evil. As if I'll never be clean again."

He leaned forward, wanting to touch her but afraid to. "It may sound like a cliché to say *this*, but it *will* pass. The experience will leave you feeling a little harder, a little more cynical, but you'll be yourself again soon. If you're not, then you can always consider getting help, talking it out."

"Therapy, you mean."

"If that's what it takes. Counseling might be a better term. Then again, you might do better on your own, letting time go by. Sometimes the best thing to do is just to hold on."

"Are you holding on?"

"Sure. Not by the skin of my teeth or the tips of my fingers, but just doing it. It's called living."

She studied his face for a minute, then smiled briefly. "I guess you've run into evil fairly often."

"You could say that. It goes with the territory, part of the job."

"You told Jude the thing with the Snowman was personal."

His bandaged foot required all of his attention for the next few minutes. But at last he looked up. "Well, it's *become* personal because of my feelings for you."

"You still have feelings for me?"

"I still have feelings for you. Strong feelings." He looked at her directly, his eyes so dark she couldn't tell where the pupils ended and the irises began.

They were both silent for a while. She thought if she tried to speak she might cry. "What are we going to do tomorrow?" she asked at last.

His gaze held hers for what seemed a very long time. Then he looked away. "I want to talk to the reporter who wrote that article about Ruby Red Rawlings. Then I want to go to the hotel she was dancing in, see what I can discover there. If I could find one person who actually saw Bart Williams in Las Vegas, I'd be closer to proving he was involved."

"I want to come with you."

"I'd rather you didn't come when I talk to the reporter. He might speak more freely if it seems more official."

As she opened her mouth to protest, he added, "You can certainly come with me to the hotel."

She decided not to argue. "You'll tell me whatever the reporter says, even if you think it might upset me?"

"It's a promise."

His gaze met hers again and she wondered how she could possibly doubt him, and then remembered how often he'd looked at her just as frankly when he was pretending to be a CPA or a private investigator.

In the morning, she was surprised by how well she had slept. Exhaustion had a way of overcoming will. She had slept alone. A maid had opened the sofa bed and Nick had immediately laid claim to it.

While she blow-dried her hair, Nick dressed, strapped on his gun and holster, and put on a lightweight jacket he'd pulled out of his duffle bag. "What do you do when it's really hot?" Maddy asked. "To hide your gun, I mean."

He gave her the fleeting grin that seemed to be all he could manage recently. "I sweat," he said. "Or else I wear a loose shirt over a holster that hooks over my belt and sits inside my pants. Another option is an ankle holster, but that works only for a smaller pistol and it makes you a little lopsided."

He went out to scout out breakfast possibilities.

The knock on the door came about the time she was beginning to expect him back. She opened the door at once, thinking he had his hands full. Maybe he'd found something at a buffet. She hoped so—neither of them had eaten enough the previous day and she was starving. . . .

The young man who had knocked was a stranger. A big blond man wearing a truly god-awful Hawaiian shirt and a mud-colored fanny pack.

Before she could react, he barreled into her, knocking all the breath out of her, lifted her off her feet, and flung her onto the sofa bed that Nick had slept in.

"What, who?" was all she could manage as he

slammed the door of the cottage shut and drew a mean-looking little handgun out of the fanny pack.

She was sure he meant to rape her. But then he said, "Where is he?"

He wanted Nick. He was after Nick. Well, he wasn't going to get him! The protective impulse that shot through her was new to her, but very strong. "Who?" she asked, playing for time.

"Don't give me no dumb bitch act."

"He's gone—didn't want to hang around. I don't know where—"

"You got one more try," he said.

"I don't know where he is—I really don't. He went out, maybe to get some breakfast. I didn't see him go. He's probably gone to the airport."

She needed to distract him. Sitting up on the sofa bed she asked, "What do you want? I don't have any money or jewelry that amounts to anything."

He glanced down with a tight grin at her leather shoulder bag, which was right at her feet. "We'll check into that later. Right now, I want him here. He comes to the door, you tell him to come right in. You tell him I'm here, you'll get a crack in the face and then some."

He wasn't a bad-looking man—blond and tanned, big and bluff and hearty, like a soccer coach with a lousy dress sense. How many men would wear a fanny pack with a Hawaiian shirt? The tough talk didn't even sound natural to him. More proof that evil didn't always wear an evil face.

Maddy tried out various scenarios in her mind. The lamp next to the bed was fairly sturdy. Was that a marble base? If she could get in the right position . . .

The gun was the only thing holding her back. She seemed to remember hearing once, maybe in a movie, that a gun looked much bigger from this side than the other. Whoever said it was right. That gun had seemed small when he drew it out. Now that it was pointing right at her, it had become a hell of a lot bigger. And he was acting fidgety. Any move she made, he was liable to shoot. Which wouldn't help the situation. It certainly wouldn't help her.

"Don't even think it, lady," he said, sounding nervous enough to shoot without even waiting for her to move.

"Who *are* you?" she asked.

"You can call me the exterminator," he said with another unsuccessful try at sounding tough.

Maybe some conversation would calm him down, or at least get him off guard. Mainly she didn't want to sound scared. She *was* scared, but she wasn't about to let this lowlife know it. Act tough, she told herself. "Really?" she said. "Is that what your employer calls you?"

"I don't have an employer."

"This is all *your* idea? What do you want?"

"I want both of you. We're going for a ride."

"People really do that? I thought that was only in the movies. If this is a movie, it has to be a B movie."

He was not amused. The gun moved slightly to point at her face.

"Were you the one driving that car in Eugene?" she asked, still hoping to distract him.

He didn't even change expression.

The phone rang. He gestured for her to answer it. "If it's him, tell him what I told you."

She picked up the phone. "Looks like a pretty good breakfast buffet," Nick said in her ear. "You want to come on over?"

"Sweetheart," she gushed in a little-girl breathless voice, "I do hope you are on your way back to me. I can't wait one more minute to see you."

"Trouble," Nick said. A statement, not a question.

The gun moved a fraction closer to her.

"I'm here on the bed waiting," she said.

The gun indicated she should hang up. She did, then stood up. "Sit down," he said.

She called up her most innocent expression. "You put the security lock on, remember? He won't be able to get in. I was just going to unlock it for him."

"I didn't lock it. Who do you think you're fooling?"

he said with a bit of bluster, but he turned his head to look all the same.

In that one second of inattention, Maddy grabbed her shoulder bag and swung it up from the floor, connecting with his gun hand. The pistol flew out of his grasp, and she lunged after it and kicked it under the sofa bed. The man dived after the gun, and Maddy turned her bag upside down, grabbed her keys as they fell, and only then remembered she'd left her pepper spray canister in the car at the Portland airport because it wasn't allowed on airplanes. The first time she'd ever really needed to use the damn thing and it was a thousand miles away!

Just as the intruder was getting ready to push himself to his feet, she remembered her instructor in the self-defense course saying, "Use your hands, feet, knees, fingers—whatever comes to mind," and she gave him a hefty push in the rear end with her right foot. With an audible clang, his head connected with the metal bar that was part of the sofa bed's folding mechanism. Cussing mightily, he started backing out. Maddy poised herself, ready to kick again, just as Nick charged into the room and stopped short.

"His gun's under the bed," Maddy said.

"Good place for it," Nick said.

Grabbing the intruder by the collar of his loud shirt, Nick yanked him upright, pulled his arms behind him, and took a pair of handcuffs out of his own jacket pocket. Nick was always prepared for anything, obviously.

"He was waiting for you. I was afraid he was going to shoot you," she told Nick as he was cuffing the man. "I thought I'd better do something."

"You did good. Damn good."

He had his own weapon out now. The intruder was groaning and shaking his head from side to side.

It took a minute for Maddy to realize the other sound was Nick laughing. "What's so damn funny?" she demanded.

He sobered at once. "I'm sorry, Maddy. I realized I sounded like 007. Here *I* was afraid something terrible was happening to you, so I came barreling in here like gangbusters to rescue the dame in distress only to find you'd already beaten the bad guy to a pulp. Figuratively speaking," he added when she opened her mouth to protest.

"It's supposed to be a damsel in distress," she told him.

"You're more of a dame than a damsel."

She laughed. How could she not?

"Do you want me to get his gun?" she asked as he forced the intruder, none too gently, to sit on one of the dining chairs.

"Nope. Let it be for now. You can put out the do-not-disturb sign and set the security lock, though. I saw the maid's cart not too far away." He glanced at her face when she came back. "Are you okay? Did he . . ."

"Nothing happened," she said hastily. "It was my own stupid fault he got in. I thought it was you at the door and opened it, and he sort of threw me onto the sofa bed. He said if you came to the door I was to tell you to come right in. We were going for a ride, he said."

"He did?"

Nick's face was tight with anger now, and the younger man looked worried. And frightened.

When Nick identified himself as an FBI agent, the man groaned some more and muttered something under his breath. It was obvious that this was news to him.

"I asked him if he was the guy driving the car in Eugene, but he wouldn't answer," Maddy said.

She was surprised to discover, as Nick told the man to stand up and then started going through his pants pockets, that she was no longer afraid of the situation. She'd knocked the gun out of the man's hand. She'd kicked it under the bed. She'd kicked *him*. By rights, she ought to feel shaky, but she didn't, not a bit. She felt powerful. *Man, I feel like a woman.* She giggled.

"You sure you're okay?" Nick asked.

Probably he thought she was on the verge of hysteria. Maybe she was. She bent down to scoop her belongings back into her shoulder bag. "How did his weapon come to be under the bed?" Nick asked.

"I knocked it out of his hand with my bag, then kicked it under."

"Remind me never to make rude comments about your bag again."

While he talked, he was going through the contents of the intruder's billfold. The intruder sat looking sullen, his mouth clamped shut.

"Dennis Preston, CPA," Nick read aloud from the man's business card. He laughed. "How about that! See, Maddy, I told you accountants didn't have to wear suits."

"What are we going to do with him?" she asked.

As answer, he looked sternly at Dennis. "I'm going to have to turn you over to LVPD, but first I'm going to ask you a few questions. I want you to understand you are not under arrest. You don't have to answer the questions. This is just a friendly interview."

"Yeah, right!" Dennis said.

Nick ignored him. "What do you know about Terminus? Have you ever heard of a man known as the Snowman? How did you know where we were?" When he didn't get any answers, he had Maddy show Dennis the photograph of Bart. "Do you recognize this man?"

She thought she saw Dennis's eyelashes flicker after each of the questions.

After half an hour of Dennis's tight-lipped silence, Nick shook his head at Maddy. "Our pal Dennis is obviously scared to death," he commented. "Seems to me if he's afraid to talk, he must have been hired by someone and knows what would happen to him if he talks."

"You said I didn't have to answer the questions," Dennis pointed out.

Nick smiled at Dennis. It wasn't a pleasant smile, more feral than friendly. "You don't. But what do you suppose will happen when whoever it was who hired you finds out you've been in here with us for this long? Especially if we make sure he hears how you failed to kidnap us, but how cooperative you've been ever since. I could call CNN maybe. Does your boss watch CNN?"

Dennis studied Nick's face for a few tense minutes. "I tell you what I know, you gonna cut me a deal?"

"Depends on how much you know."

"A lot," he said, looking smug.

"It won't be up to me," Nick said.

"But you could put in a good word, right?"

"I can tell the local officers you cooperated—that usually helps."

Dennis thought it over. "That photograph," he blurted out. "That's the Snowman all right."

"You've actually seen him?"

"I met him. He recruited me."

"For what?"

Dennis looked over each of his shoulders. He acted so shifty that Maddy wouldn't have been surprised to see him get on his knees and look under the bed, and he wouldn't be looking for his gun. "Terminus," he said at last.

Maddy saw Nick let out a long breath. She was doing the same. Though this was nothing new, it *was* confirmation.

I will not throw up, she instructed herself.

"When did you meet Bart Williams?" Nick asked.

"May."

"You're that new in Terminus?"

Dennis nodded, hesitated, then said, "That guy in the photograph, Bart Williams, he told me I'd make a lot of money, I'd only have to whack maybe two, maybe at most four people a year. He didn't say nothing about whacking a woman."

"He ran down Ruby Red Rawlings."

"Yeah." A streak of scarlet appeared on each of his cheekbones.

Maddy saw Nick note that.

"You were in the car the night Rawlings was killed." It was a flat statement, not a question.

"How'd you know that?"

Nick didn't answer. "Who ordered the killing?"

Dennis shrugged. "Nobody told me. That was my first time out. It was a kind of test, I guess."

"You must have some idea of how it works." Nick was very intense, very focused.

"All's I know is if someone in your region needs to be offed, you get a phone call from the bosses with the assignment. After it's done, you get paid. Cash. No paperwork, ever. You talk, you die."

Maddy thought about all the hundred-dollar bills in Bart's "collectible" books and Kazuko saying, "Some kind petty cash."

"Bart Williams is dead," Nick said.

Maddy swallowed.

So did Dennis. Visibly. "I know. The guy told me."

"What guy?"

"The guy who told me to off you and her."

"You don't know who he was?"

"Nope. No names, remember. Just a voice on the phone."

"Do you know who was in the car that tried to run us down in Eugene?"

Dennis blew through his lips. "Way it works, nobody knows nothing they don't have to know."

"Is that a no?"

"That's a no. I don't know nothing about Eugene. Is that a place, or a person?"

Nick's gaze sharpened. Had Dennis sounded a little too breezy?

"But you do know something about us," Nick said, indicating himself and Maddy.

"The guy told me I should kill you both, make it look like an accident. Said to take you for a ride, like in the movies. Said you'd rented a car. I should maybe push it over a cliff or whatever was possible. Walk back. He told me to be creative."

"So what did you come up with?"

"Nothing. I was hoping something would come to me, some way to do it, like in the lake or something. But I didn't know if I could walk that far back." He glanced at Maddy. "Mostly I was hoping I could get out of killing the woman. I didn't want to kill no woman. Especially not no pretty woman."

"Everyone has his standards," Nick murmured.

"Exactly," Dennis said. "That Ruby Red Rawlings was a looker, and now this lady here. That's not what I thought it was all about."

He looked at Maddy. "Guess you got me out of it. I ought to thank you for kicking me in the butt."

Was she supposed to say "You're welcome"?

"Anybody tell you why we had to be killed?" Nick asked.

He was very calm. He was obviously able to distance himself from the situation. His attitude was relaxing Dennis, who had obviously decided his best bet was to tell everything he knew. He was probably right, Maddy thought.

"Nope. The guy just said you had to be killed. Nobody gives reasons, Bart told me. Like I said, you just get a phone call. Voice tells you who. Nothing else."

"I don't believe you," Nick said.

Maddy was surprised—it had sounded workable to her. Very simple. You don't like someone, someone does you wrong, call up the nearest hit man, tell him to whack the wrongdoer. He does it, you pay him, end of story. One-stop shopping, just as Jude Rodriguez had said.

She remembered phone calls coming for Bart. She remembered that he hadn't wanted caller ID. She was beginning to see why he'd thought his job was so perfect for him. He'd get a call, come up with a reason to visit one of his customers in the area, combine that visit with his Terminus duty. Nothing to it.

She couldn't let herself think too long about Bart being a professional killer. A hit man. Not now. Maybe not ever. She'd do like Scarlett O'Hara and leave it until tomorrow.

Dennis was still thinking over Nick's statement.

"You don't tell me the truth, I call CNN," Nick said.

She sensed that Dennis was going to cave a second

before he did. "Somebody followed *her* after the Snowman got—after the Snowman offed himself," he said, indicating Maddy. "Then they reported some guy was with her, figured he might be somebody she hired. Said the two of them were traveling the Snowman's territory. His work route. His day job. They figured the Snowman might have told her about Terminus. He'd done something they didn't like, cheated them some way, so they didn't trust him no more."

"If this safety of yours you're so concerned about is going to work, you have to tell the whole truth," Nick said.

"I don't know what the Snowman did. Honest." There was a whining note in his voice now.

"You know he didn't kill himself."

"The guy said he did. I didn't believe him. But I don't *know*."

A thought occurred to Maddy. She nudged Nick. "Ask him about the cowboy," she whispered.

He did.

Dennis shrugged, then shook his head, but his eyes narrowed and he rubbed his nose. Nick prodded. "You're sure?"

Dennis nodded.

Nick stood up. "You did good, Dennis," he said.

Dennis looked hopeful.

"Like I said, we have to turn you over to the local PD. I'll see what I can do for you. Be a good idea you tell the officers every detail you can think about Ruby Red's killing. I've an idea somebody will be coming to help you remember all about Terminus."

Dennis's face had gloom written all over it. "There's gonna be a leak, I know it. I'm dead meat."

Nick called 911 and talked to dispatch. Police officers responded very quickly. They immediately recognized Dennis as being a local and minor crook who was wanted already and informed him of his rights. They then took Dennis and his gun into custody, leaving an officer behind to get a report from Nick and Maddy.

They ended up accompanying the officer to the police station, where after introductions and a few brief questions, the lieutenant in charge asked Maddy to take a seat in the waiting room. It was a good hour before Nick came out to join her.

The same officer drove them back to the Elizabethan Village. Maddy felt weary to the bone. Her earlier high had completely dissipated.

Back in the cottage, she brewed some coffee. Nick went out once again in search of food and came back with sandwiches and containers of salad. She was as hungry as a rabbit for greens and ate greedily.

"Okay," she said. "What's the story? What took you an hour?"

"Well, after Lieutenant Lightbourne and I discussed Dennis and his actions, I got in touch with the local FBI guys."

He frowned. "There are certain turf issues between FBI divisions, Maddy. The local guys would have been a little cranky if they'd found out I was working in Vegas without their knowledge. Fortunately, I have an old buddy here. I've done a few favors for him in the past. He introduced me around and vouched for me. Also fortunately for me, though not for anyone else, there's a major bust going down at one of the casinos, so everyone was industriously engaged and weren't bothered that I hadn't checked in with them first thing."

He paused to take a bite of his sandwich. "I talked to Lieutenant Lightbourne about the Ruby Red Rawlings case. He's very cooperative, secure enough not to be worried that I was trying to trespass in his jurisdiction. Enough of a maverick to accept that I'm working on my own. Says they have a good spirit of cooperation between the various departments here."

He took another bite and chewed thoughtfully. "It's pretty well established that Ruby—that's her real name by the way—was killed in revenge for the slaying of Pearl White, the other dancer. That's also a real name, but she changed it in court. Her original name was Mabel. Just as

Jude said, Lightbourne was pretty sure it was probably Pearl's boyfriend who killed Ruby, because he believed Ruby's boyfriend, Emmett Everard, killed Pearl."

"Why did Everard kill Pearl?"

"The story is that Pearl dissed Ruby the previous day, she and Ruby had a big knock-down-drag-out fight, and Ruby ended up with a swollen eye and mouth, which was going to put her out of work for a while."

He hesitated. "I asked Lightbourne if he'd heard of Terminus and he said he had but not in this area. He was very interested in the idea Terminus might have been operating in the neighborhood."

"Terminus meaning Bart in this instance," Maddy said woodenly.

"And Dennis, the reluctant hit man. I've an idea we'd have been perfectly safe in his hands."

"Safer than anyone would have been in Bart's hands." Her voice sounded harsh, even to her own ears.

Looking at her with great sympathy and something more, Nick reached out a hand to touch her face. "Maddy . . ."

She let her cheek linger against his fingers for a moment, then moved her head aside. "No, Nick. I can't."

He dropped his hand and sighed. "Well, as long as we've got whatever information is available, we don't need to talk to the reporter. I've probably got enough now to take to my supervisor. So I guess we might as well head back to Washington and regroup."

Chapter 24

"DID YOU MEAN that about protecting Dennis?" Maddy asked Nick when they were on the airplane going back to Portland.

He nodded, looking surprised. "Sure I did. Soon as I can, I'll be talking to my supervisor. Once I let him know what Dennis has told us about—"

He broke off, glanced around, and continued very quietly. "What Dennis has told us, he'll make damn sure he gets stashed away somewhere. We've been trying to get closure on . . . this group for a long long time."

Maddy wondered if he suspected they were still being followed. Someone behind them on the airplane, listening in? Would she ever feel safe again? she wondered.

Looking down at the mountains, the ruined top of Mount Saint Helens, Mount Rainier soon afterward, she tried to empty her mind, to relax. She actually did achieve a measure of calm, until the cowboy wandered back into her memory.

"I think Dennis did know about the cowboy," she blurted out.

Nick nodded. "I agree. But he wasn't going to budge on that one."

"Perhaps because the cowboy is an important player?"

"Could be. Or too unimportant to buy any concessions with."

"Good God!" Maddy exclaimed suddenly.

"What is it?"

"I am so stupid. So damn, damn stupid!"

"No, you're not. What's the problem?"

"My camera. Where's my camera? I had it with me that day, the day Bart disappeared. Maybe there's something on it."

Nick frowned. "You took it into the house with you."

"Yes. Yes, I did. I went into the living room and . . . no, I dropped it in the hall with my shoulder bag. I don't know that I ever picked it up again. Maybe Kazuko did. Or the lab people who came with the detective."

"What do you think you might have photographed?"

"The cowboy. I thought I might have seen him in the market, remember? I mentioned the possibility when we saw the little girl in Tualatin, with her action figures— Woody from *Toy Story*."

Nick nodded. "We could drive directly to the house from Portland."

Maddy shuddered. "I don't know that I can bear to go back in that house."

"You don't have to go farther than the front entry. I'll be right there with you."

She shook her head. "No, that's stupid too. Not you," she hastened to add. "I mean me—being afraid of a house. I can pick up fresh clothing while I'm there. I need to do that anyway. I should probably just stay the night, drive into Seattle in the morning."

"I don't want you staying in Oak River, Maddy."

"Well, I definitely do not want to stay in Bart's house," Maddy agreed. "But I could stay with Kazuko. She'd be delighted—"

"How about staying with me?" he asked, then shook his head. "Don't look so stricken, Maddy. It was just a suggestion. Could we both stay with Lara and Todd to-night, do you think? Or in a Seattle hotel? I don't want you out of my sight until I'm sure there isn't another Dennis on the loose. We still don't know who was after us in Eugene. I was thinking we'd pick up my car in Portland, drive to Seattle. Now that Terminus has entered the picture, I'm going to have to report in to my super-visor and tell him about Dennis and let him know every-thing we've been up to. But first . . ."

He hesitated. "But first I want to go back to Pike Place Market one more time without it being official. I'd like to have one more go at Ellie from the children's clothing shop. Also, she mentioned the owner and I'm thinking it might not be a bad idea to talk to him. I'm still pretty sure Bart drove into the market that day, the day we met."

"The day you tailed me, you mean."

"The day I tailed you," he agreed. "Let's think about it. Bart had some kind of meeting, he told you. According to Simon Hatfield, it wasn't a business meeting. So what was it? A meeting of . . . that group? If so, then where would they meet? Somewhere in Seattle?"

"Well, he did say he was going to Seattle. He didn't say it was *at* Mawsom. I just assumed that, and asked him for a ride."

"So let's say the meeting *was* in Seattle. So then he's going to pick you up at the market. He's unexpectedly late, but he does show up, which would seem to indicate he's expecting to pick you up. But then he sees me, or someone else—maybe the cowboy, who knows?—and he tells you he's going to the rest room. But he didn't go to the rest room. Or if he did, it was a hell of a fast trip. So then where did he go? Did he actually *leave* the market at that time? Or did he stay there until a later time?"

"Whoa!" Maddy said softly.

Nick nodded.

Maddy thought it might be a good idea to stay with Lara and Todd. She hadn't seen them since Bart's funeral. She hadn't thought to call Lara before leaving town. Lara would be wondering. And it would be a lot less . . . awkward . . . to stay with Nick there than in a hotel.

"We can take the camera with us to Seattle," Nick said. "How do you view the photos?"

"It's a Sony Mavica. It records on a floppy disk. An ordinary floppy."

"Okay, we'll take it along, bring the photos up on a computer after we get to Seattle. Unless you want to look at them on your own computer at the house?"

She shook her head immediately. "No, I don't want to spend any more time there than I have to. I feel . . . contaminated enough. I have Photoshop on my laptop. We can view the photos in that."

"Great, we're all set then."

SHE PULLED HER suede jacket from her tote bag after they landed in Portland, but still felt chilled. In contrast to the temperature in Las Vegas, Oregon seemed colder than when they'd left. She insisted on driving again so Nick could rest his foot. He finally quit arguing.

The house smelled damp and musty. Maybe it was her imagination, Maddy allowed, as she switched on the lights.

The smell was overlaid by the lemon-scented polish Kazuko always used on the furniture. Obviously she'd been taking good care of the place in Maddy's absence.

While Nick waited on the bench in the entry hall, she emptied clothing from her tote bag into the hamper in the laundry room, then went up to her bedroom and put a couple of fresh outfits and underwear into her tote.

The camera bag wasn't where she'd left it, next to the archway into the living room. It was in her office, on her desk, where Kazuko must have placed it for safety. She picked it up and headed back to tell Nick she was ready to go, noting as she did so that Nick was looking into the living room at the bookcases.

The bookcases. Sometime soon she had to get the money back from Kazuko. Sometime. Not now. She couldn't deal with anything else right now.

As they left the house, Nick held out his hand for his

car keys and she gave them to him. She was too tired to argue, possibly too tired to drive.

"Best we go directly to the restaurant," she said when they were back on I-5. "Lara and Todd will both be there by the time we get to Seattle."

Nick nodded. He'd turned the heater on, and she tilted her seat back and closed her eyes, suddenly exhausted. She was safe for the moment, she realized. She'd gone into Bart's house and she'd survived. Even as she thought this, she felt herself sliding slowly into warm and comfortable darkness.

The next thing she knew they were heading into Seattle's University district, where Buon Gusto Ristorante was located. "Thank you," she said to Nick. "I needed that nap. You must need sleep too. You look worn out."

"I'll catch up later," he said. "Glad you could rest."

There was a police car parked outside the restaurant. Maddy's stomach tied itself into a knot. What now?

Several other parked cars indicated dinner was already under way. Inside the lobby, Lara, magnificently draped in bronze satin, was talking volubly, with accompanying gestures, to a police officer and a tall, balding, elegantly dressed man.

"Maddy!" Lara exclaimed.

The police officer turned to see whom she was talking to. Lara hurried over and enveloped Maddy in one of her huge warm hugs. "I've been worrying about you, *cara*. You disappeared from my radar screen. Explain yourself!"

About to respond, Maddy realized Nick had turned around and was leaving the restaurant. "Nick?" she called.

"I'll be back," he said over his shoulder.

So much for not letting her out of his sight. "I'll explain later," she said to Lara. "How about you explain the cop?"

Lara threw up her arms. "Imagine! Mr. Alexander here," she said, indicating the tall man, "one of our regular patrons, parked outside the restaurant, in our very own parking lot, and came in for dinner. Ate spinach and garlic ravioli and a large green salad, with a good chianti. Tiramisu for dessert. And espresso—of course the espresso, a double shot."

Maddy waited for Lara to get through with the menu. It was no use interrupting her when she was talking about food.

"So then he pays," Lara said. "He compliments everyone and walks out through the door and . . . poof, no car."

"Someone stole his car?"

"Yes indeed. A Porsche, no less. Nobody saw anything. Mr. Alexander is very upset. Mr. Alexander," she called, "this is my friend Maddy Sloane. Maddy—"

The man interrupted, speaking to the officer, ignoring Lara and Maddy, for which she didn't blame him. "This is supposed to be a safe neighborhood."

"It *is* a good neighborhood," the police officer said, then added soothingly, "We have an excellent recovery rate. We'll probably have your car back to you in a day or two."

"Yeah, sure, but in what condition?"

"If it was kids joyriding, it could be fine, except for maybe some damage to the locks and ignition."

"And if it's not kids?"

"Well, we'll have to wait and see," the officer said, but Maddy could only imagine that the thieves would tear the car apart for parts, or change the license plates and move it out of state.

Why had Nick left so abruptly? What was he up to now?

"Be sure to call your insurance company," the officer said, handing Mr. Alexander a slip of paper. "Here's the case number and my name and badge number. You need a ride home?"

The man muttered that he lived nearby and would flag down a cab or walk. He started to leave, but then he stopped and looked hard at Maddy. "That guy you came in with, wasn't that Nick Ciacia, the FBI agent? Is he a friend of yours?"

Sensing information, Maddy nodded.

"Did he ever find the guy he was looking for? The Snowman?"

Maddy was in shock for a moment, then was almost about to blurt out that the Snowman was dead, but forced herself to wait. "I don't think so. Do you know anything that would help?" she said at last.

Mr. Alexander shrugged. "I own one of the local cable stations. Ciacia's checked with me from time to time over the years. I promised him I'd keep my ear to the ground for this Snowman he was looking for—the guy who shot his father." He shook his head. "Never did hear a murmur. Sad story, that. Sorry I didn't get to talk to him. Nice guy. Tell him hello, will you?"

While Maddy was still speechless with shock, he turned to Lara to say good-bye, and she sympathized with him about the theft of his car. Then he left.

The officer had also left, Maddy realized.

"Maddy? *Cara?* What is it? You are so pale. Are you sick? Come and sit down. What's wrong? What is all this about Nick being an FBI agent? Speak to me."

She took hold of Maddy's arm, trying to ease her into the hall that led to her private office, but Maddy stood rigid, resisting.

"I have to go . . . somewhere," she managed at last.

"But where *is* Nick? Why did he leave so suddenly? Was Mr. Alexander right? Nick is with the FBI? Where are you going? Do you have your car?"

"I've . . . I'm . . . it's okay . . . I'll call Nick," she said, not intending to.

Without being quite sure how she finally got away from Lara's well-meaning clutches, she found herself outside. As she stood there, unable to decide what to do next, unable to even think, Nick drove into the lot and pulled up in front of her. "Sorry about that. My foot was hurting," he said. "Are we going to Lara's house?"

She shook her head. "I don't want to. I didn't even ask."

He hung out of the open window, studying her face. "He said something. Miles Alexander."

"A mouthful."

"Get in the car, Maddy, please. I'll explain."

She didn't know what else to do, so she walked around the car and got in.

He drove to a parking lot behind a nearby mall and parked in an empty area at the back. "He told you about my father." It was a statement, not a question.

Maddy nodded.

"What exactly did he say?"

"He asked if you'd ever found the Snowman—the man who shot your father."

"Shit." Nick took in a deep breath, let it out audibly.

"I thought everything was out in the open now," Maddy said. "I thought you were being honest with me now. I accepted you were with the FBI and you had a job to do. I even accepted that you had to use me the way you did."

"Maddy, it's very difficult for me to talk about my father."

"Try."

Pain showed in his eyes and in the tightness of his mouth, but she wanted to know it all right now—had to know it all.

"You told me he died when you were thirteen," she prompted.

He turned to look out the windshield, at the trees facing them. They were swaying in a light breeze, bare of leaves. It was dark out, of course, but the parking lot lights shimmered along the branches as they moved.

"We lived in Chicago," he began, his voice sounding wooden, even to his own ears. "My father was off-duty, coming home from a meeting of the Italian-American Police Officers Association. There was a neighborhood store called Figlioli's. It was late, but a light was showing from inside the store. My father checked the door, and it was unlocked, looked as if it had been busted open, so he went inside."

He paused, then went doggedly on. "Somebody shot him. Hit him in the chest. As he . . . went down, he saw a man dressed all in black going past him out the door. Slender. Black knit hat pulled low, but some white hair poking out one side. He thought it was odd that the man had white hair. He was such a very young man, very good-looking."

Maddy swallowed. "How do you know all this? Was someone else there? A witness?"

Nick shook his head. "My dad didn't ... die right away. He managed to get himself to the store's telephone, called for help, told the responding officer what had happened, then died on the way to the hospital."

"Was the killer, the Snowman, burglarizing the store?"

"That was the general conclusion."

"There was an investigation, surely?"

"I was told there was. All anyone could tell me was that my dad was apparently in the wrong place at the wrong time."

"Apparently? There's that word again."

He nodded, leaned back as if exhausted, and closed his eyes. "I was never sure. I'm remembering that his boss, a Captain Riley, didn't like him, didn't like Italians."

"You think his boss had him killed? Because he didn't *like* him?"

"I was told at my dad's funeral by a man whose name I don't know to this day—I was too stunned to ask—that my dad was killed by the Snowman. We now know the Snowman was a hired gun, a professional. When a hired gun shoots someone, it's usual to suspect someone hired him. So far I haven't found out who that might have been."

Maddy sat back. She kept thinking there couldn't be any more shocks coming where Bart was concerned, and she kept finding out she was wrong.

"My husband killed your father," she said flatly.

"Seems like."

"I don't suppose the fact that Bart's dead makes you too unhappy?"

His voice sounded almost robotic when he spoke, as if the words were coming out without him planning to say

them. "I had always planned to kill the Snowman myself.
If I ever found him."

Yes, it was still possible to discover new shocks.

She turned to look at him. He had opened his eyes.
There was enough light coming into the car for her to see
that he looked every bit as miserable as she felt. "*Did* you
kill Bart?"

"No."

"*Could* you have killed Bart?"

"Yes."

There was silence between them for a while. Then
Maddy asked, "Is that everything? Have you told me
everything?"

"Yes. I'm sorry, Maddy. I couldn't . . ."

She made a dismissing gesture. "I don't need apolo-
gies. I just want this . . . *all* of this to be over. I still want
to know who killed Bart. Obviously, he deserved it, but
I'm stubborn enough to want to know who. Then I want
to clean it all out of my mind and try to go on with my
life."

"Maddy." He turned toward her, his eyes intense, and
she was afraid he was going to reach for her, to touch
her. She didn't want to be touched. Not by anyone.

"What do I do to find out?" she asked. "Bart is dead.
You've achieved your goal. I don't suppose you want to
help me achieve mine."

"I'm not giving up, Maddy. I'm going to talk to my
supervisor, bring him up to date. I have a new goal."

"Terminus."

"Yes. Terminus, and finding out who hired the hired
gun. Tomorrow we'll stick to the original plan. We'll go
back to Pike Place Market. That's where it began. I'll
have one more try with Ellie."

He hesitated. "You want me to drive back to the restaurant so we can spend the night with Lara and Todd?"

She shook her head immediately. "Lara has too many
questions."

"My place?"

"No. Listen, there doesn't seem to have been anyone

following us, right? Just drop me at a hotel. You can pick me up tomorrow morning. I'll stay in Seattle until we find out something."

"I'm not parking you in any hotel, Maddy. I told you I'd stick with you and I will."

He was silent for a minute or two, then he said, "I could take you to my mother's place. She'll ask questions too, but I'd be the one in the hot seat."

She looked at him sharply. "You told me your mother was in Arizona."

"Um." His mouth twitched into a slight grimace. "Not exactly, Maddy. I said she winters in Arizona. She doesn't go south until after Thanksgiving."

She made a sound that was between a sigh and a hiss of exasperation.

"You haven't told me the truth about much, have you?" Before he could answer, she asked, "Does your mother know that the Snowman killed your father? Does she know about Bart? And me? She won't want me around if she knows about my association with Bart."

"She knows the Snowman killed my father, yes. She's known that as long as I have. But she doesn't know anything else. She doesn't know I've kept on looking for him, or that I found him. I've kept it all from her."

"You believe in keeping women in the dark, is that it?" Again she interrupted before he could protest. "Sorry, that was below the belt. Let's just get a solid night's sleep, okay? If you want me to stay with your mother, I'll stay with your mother, as long as you'll promise to stick with me until we get this job done. Then I'll be out of your life, and you can con someone else."

He winced. She'd obviously hurt his feelings badly, but right now she was too tired, too *weary* to care.

Chapter 25

NICK CALLED HIS mother on his cell phone to warn her—and, remembering the comment she'd made a while back about her love life, to make sure she was alone.

Bridget greeted them warmly at the door to her condo apartment, but glanced from one to the other to their luggage, her green eyes extra bright.

"Maddy needs a safe place to spend the night," Nick told her after he'd introduced the two women and Bridget had shepherded them into her living room. As usual there was evidence of her many interests on view. Her piano. Sketch books and a pencil box, bird books and an astronomy map, the telescope in front of the glass door to the balcony, bookcases full of mystery and science fiction novels and cookbooks from around the world.

"You're very welcome to stay," Bridget said with a smile for Maddy. "Put Maddy's things in the guest room," she added to Nick. "Will you be minding sleeping on the davenport yourself?"

She always became more Irish with him when her curiosity was aroused.

"That'll suit me fine, Ma," Nick said with no change of expression.

She stopped him as he started to pull Maddy's tote bag toward the guest room. "You're limping."

"It's a mild sprain, Ma. It's strapped up and a bit uncomfortable. It'll be fine. Maddy's taken care of it."

"Has she now?" She looked extremely pleased. "Well, have you both had your dinner?"

Maddy started to say she didn't need anything, but Nick spoke over her. "We're half-starved. We flew into Portland from Vegas and drove up to Seattle, expecting to get a meal in town, but we didn't have a chance to. All we've had since breakfast was a bag of pretzels on the plane."

His mother still looked as if she were about to burst with curiosity, but was also delighted.

"Cooking is one of Ma's many passions," Nick explained to Maddy as Bridget disappeared into the kitchen. He looked at her wan face with concern. "How would you like to take a shower or something while she's fixing the meal? I think I've been keeping her in the dark long enough. It's not going to be easy, telling her all this. I think it would be easier on her if we . . ."

"If you were alone." Maddy nodded. "Could we make it a bath?"

"We could indeed." He showed her where the bathroom was, then escorted her to the guest room, pulling her tote bag along. She thanked him and started to close the door. "Maddy," he tried again, but stopped when her expression closed him out.

His mother placed a glass of red wine down in front of him as he sat on one of the high stools at the kitchen counter. She was settling one of the Baggies of pesto that she made up every summer and stored in the freezer into a small bowl of hot water.

"You going to tell me what's going on, me boyo?" she asked.

He took a sip of the wine. Merlot. A very good merlot.

"It's a tough story to tell, Ma," he said, and took a deep breath. "It has to do with Dad."

She straightened up and met his gaze steadily.

"You remember a while back you said you were glad I'd given up looking for the Snowman?"

She nodded tensely.

"I let you believe that, Ma, but it wasn't true. I never stopped looking for him. I talked you and Nonna into coming to Seattle because the man who told me about the Snowman in the first place also told me he'd gone to Seattle. I had the idea that all I had to do was come here, and he'd fall into my clutches. But it wasn't that easy. I began to think the little man had lied to me. At the very least, it seemed as if the Snowman had fallen off the face of the earth. But I'm stubborn enough, I've kept asking around, especially since I've been with the Bureau. A week or so before Halloween an old informant of mine showed up in town. He'd been in prison. While he was there he heard a couple of inmates talking about the Snowman."

He saw no need to tell her he'd paid Arnie for the information or that Arnie had died, possibly—probably—because of talking to him.

She worked on putting antipasti together while he talked about taking his annual leave to track down Bart Williams, how he'd followed him, then lost him, and then met up with Maddy.

"Maddy was married to the Snowman," she repeated, putting down the ricotta cheese. "That young woman in my bathroom was married to the Snowman?"

"And about to leave him," he said, and told her why and how short a time they'd been married. He then explained about Bart Williams being found dead in an empty house at Crescent Beach.

"Why, I heard about that," she exclaimed. "I didn't see it on the TV myself but one of the Loose Women did and told us all about it. Her son has a place in Crescent Beach. Weekends and holidays, she often goes there herself."

She stopped talking abruptly, staring at Nick. "That

was the Snowman? Jackie said the reporter said the man
had shot himself." She paled. "Nick, you didn't . . ."

"No, Ma, I didn't." He looked away from her suddenly
frightened eyes, afraid she'd read in his own eyes that he
would have shot the man, given half a chance. "I did go
with Maddy to his funeral. I didn't know for sure then
that he was the Snowman, but I wanted to be sure he was
buried, just in case."

"Did she know he'd killed someone?"

"She had no idea, Ma. She was taken in by him—he
could be charming. But she was disenchanted very early.
He was a hollow man, she said. A cold man."

"A block of ice for a heart. That's what the man told
you at your dad's funeral."

He nodded. "Maddy's horrified that she was living
with a man like that. A monster, she called him, when
she found out all he'd done."

"He'd done more?"

"He was a professional hit man, Ma."

"La Cosa Nostra?"

"No, Ma. Something else. I can't tell you more about
the organization because we're investigating it."

"There's a lot more to it, isn't there?" Bridget said.

He nodded and told her about Maddy tracking Bart's
trips on the computer, finding out about the killings in the
places he'd been. Then about Bart recruiting Dennis,
though without telling her Dennis had come after them
armed—just that they'd found him and questioned him
and he was being held in Las Vegas. And that he'd confirmed that Bart Williams was the Snowman.

"And did you find out why he killed your father? I
never did believe it was a burglary the man was engaged
in."

"I don't know yet, Ma. I'm still trying to find out."

It was then that Maddy emerged from the bathroom.
She'd changed into beige slacks and a thin black sweater
with long sleeves. Her hair was damp and tousled, her
face pale and drawn.

Bridget went to her at once and put her arms around

her. "Nick's told me," she said. "I'm so sorry that man cast his dark shadow over your life as well as mine."

There were tears in Bridget's eyes and they brought tears to Maddy's. Nick thought it would be good for them to cry, but they were both working at fighting the tears back. His own eyes were burning.

"Have I time for a shower?" he asked his mother.

She hugged Maddy again before releasing her, then laughed shortly. "Goodness sake, I've barely started on the dinner. I haven't even got the water on for the fettuccine. Be off with you. I'll pour wine for Maddy and me and wait until you're done."

He surrendered himself to water as hot as he could stand it and just stood there limply for some time before soaping up and rinsing off.

When he came out of the bathroom, wearing clean clothes but barefoot and carrying his bandage, the two women were standing side by side in the hall, looking at the photos of Alfeo. They were both red-eyed, he noted, as they turned to look at him. He was glad they'd managed to let go. On an impulse he put his arms around both of them, and they all huddled together in silence for a while. He was able to let his own guard down at last.

"Well, now, that's the first time I've seen tears in your eyes since you were a lad," his mother said, when they separated.

Nick went off to find tissues in the bathroom and mopped himself up. He brought the box back to Bridget and Maddy, and they each helped themselves, both still sniffling a little.

"You know, Nick," Maddy said, when she recovered her poise, "when I asked if Bart might have seen you watching me that day in the market, you said he wouldn't have known you. But looking at the photographs in the hall, I realized that you look so much like your father you could be a clone. Maybe Bart *did* know you. Maybe he remembered?" She swallowed hard. "Do you think he'd remember all the people he killed?"

"I don't know, Maddy."

"Maybe he did at the end. Maybe that's why . . . maybe he really did kill himself."

"Maybe." He didn't believe it, but if it made her feel better . . .

But she was already shaking her head. "That sounds more like a Hollywood scenario," she said. "Sin, suffer, and repent."

She looked at him directly. "I'm sorry about your father, Nick. I was so shocked before, I don't think I even told you how sorry I am."

"Thank you, Maddy."

He realized his mother was watching them looking at each other, but he didn't want to be the one to break away. Instead he tried to put all the affection he felt for Maddy into his gaze. No, not affection—that was too weak a word. Love.

As if she'd recognized his sudden insight, her eyes widened, then she looked down, her eyelids hiding whatever expression had come into them, perhaps hiding the fact that she rejected whatever he had to offer.

"Find a seat and I'll put the bandage on again," she said.

"I think it probably doesn't need bandaging anymore," he told her.

She looked at him. He recognized the look. It was one all women, including his mother and countless former girlfriends, had perfected. It was a waste of time arguing with a look like that.

When the pasta was ready, they sat down and started eating as though they hadn't eaten in a week. A release, Nick supposed.

Watching Bridget glance from him to Maddy, Nick sensed that she hadn't quite satisfied her curiosity. There'd be more questions later, that was for sure, but for now, she seemed content to make sure they were both fed and comfortable.

Content was hardly the right word, he discovered, when she spoke again. "I have to admit I'm damn glad that man is dead," she said flatly. "It's a release for Alfeo, and for me." She looked lovingly at Nick. "And for you, I think."

"Me too," Maddy said, and Bridget exchanged a glance fraught with meaning and an affection that was new but nonetheless warm.

As for Nick, he was still resentful that he hadn't been able to have a face-off with Bart at the end. He'd never know now if he would have killed him or not. He hoped he might have been satisfied to see him finally brought to justice. Though how could any justice be done when who knew how many deaths were involved?

"Should we look at my photographs?" Maddy asked after they'd helped Bridget clear the table and she'd shooed them out of the kitchen.

Nick nodded and went to fetch the laptop and camera bag from the guest bedroom, then helped Maddy set up the computer. Taking a floppy disk from the camera bag, she slid it into the laptop disk drive, then opened the pictures in a gallery that showed the photos in thumbnail size. She clicked on each one in turn, enlarging it, taking him on a tour of the market stalls he'd followed her to that first day.

The second-to-last picture on the disk was of the market clock. Nick remembered very clearly how she'd turned to look at the big market-clock above the entrance and had taken a photo of it. He'd stepped back beside the pillar, hoping she wouldn't see him. A second later, she'd taken a shot in his direction.

"Can you make that last picture bigger?" he asked, crouching to look over her shoulder.

She enlarged it to fill the screen, which blurred the picture a little, then resized it so it was clear. It was a good shot, looking much more vibrant and alive on screen than photos looked in print. If he hadn't known he was by that pillar, he might not have noticed himself, but there he was, just a slice of him showing at the edge. There were the fish laid out in rows, one fish just being thrown, people with their hands up to clap.

And there was a man in a white cowboy hat just disappearing out of the left edge of the photo, behind Nick.

"That's why I wasn't sure where I saw him," Maddy said softly. "I saw him through the viewfinder, didn't really even notice him at the time, but he registered in my mind."

There was no way to get a clearer look at the cowboy's face. If she enlarged it any further it became a mass of colored pixels, only just recognizable as someone's profile.

"He may not even be the same cowboy," she said, shaking her head. "We had a glimpse of the man I thought was dressed as Woody not far from my house, and Lena, the woman in the bar in Crescent Beach, said she thought he had dark hair."

"The manager at the Sitka Inn in Eugene swore he couldn't remember what the cowboy looked like," Nick put in.

"And now this," Maddy added. "The only common denominator is the cowboy hat. I want to ask Lena if that cowboy had a white hat, but I don't even know if that would prove anything. There seem to be a lot of white cowboy hats around."

"Too many to be a coincidence," Nick said.

Maddy suddenly ejected the floppy from the drive and set it aside. Picking up the camera bag, she took out the camera and removed a similar floppy from the side of it.

"What?" Nick asked.

"I took the floppy out and put another one in that day. I don't like to put too many shots on one floppy, in case I want to copy any back and run out of space."

She pushed the disk into the laptop's drive and opened the single file. "I think I might have caught Bart in this last one," she said.

She had—from the waist up. He was scowling, but still looked good enough to make a living as a model. The children had been too short to show in the photo. Behind him were a couple of Asian men, cameras raised as if they were taking photographs of the market entrance. Nothing suspicious about them that Nick could see.

"That's him?" Bridget's voice said behind them.

Nick straightened and put an arm around her. "Yes. Maddy caught him in a photo just a minute before he disappeared. He saw her—she was waiting for him to pick her up and drive her home, as I told you. He said he had to go to the rest room and then he disappeared. We thought maybe there might be someone with him or near him, but it doesn't look like it."

"Looks can be deceiving, can they not?" Bridget said, staring at the screen. "That's a very handsome man. But what is it they say? Handsome is as handsome does."

She turned abruptly on her heel and left the room.

Chapter 26

MADDY DIDN'T SLEEP for the longest time, though the queen-size bed was cozy with an Irish green down comforter and pillows, the room attractively decorated with green velvet tab drapes over muslin and framed watercolors—Seattle scenes signed by Bridget Ciacia—grouped on one wall.

She tried to imagine her own mother making someone as welcome as Bridget had made her, and couldn't. Cooking was only one of Bridget's many passions, according to Nick. *Passion* was not a word Maddy could associate with Isobel Sloane.

She tried not to think about Bart, but images and words kept fighting to take over her mind. The things he had done. The people he had killed.

The only way she could quiet the mental turmoil was to count backward from a thousand. That soon got tiresome, so she resurrected a device she'd used as a wakeful child: she imagined herself flying gently over a beautiful landscape of green grass and bright flowers—not flying with beating wings, but gently floating, like a bird caught in a thermal.

She woke to the sound of someone moving around in the bathroom next to the bedroom she was in and saw that she had slept after all. It was eight o'clock in the morning.

"You'll come back to see me?" Bridget asked as Maddy and Nick prepared to leave after eating a delicious breakfast of omelettes with cheese baked right into the batter and the best bread Maddy had ever tasted.

"I'd like that," Maddy said, though she knew she could never return while she still felt so poisoned by Bart, in spite of—or maybe because of—her feelings for Nick. Feelings she wasn't yet prepared to analyze.

Nick looked as if he hadn't slept well either, she thought as they drove toward the market. But he insisted his ankle was cured and needed no more treatment.

"Let me do the talking," he suggested when they arrived.

She shrugged, not committing herself. She'd butt in if she deemed it necessary.

Ellie did not look delighted to see them. It took her at least ten seconds to put on her perky face. "Back again," she said cheerily. "You still looking for that good-looking guy?"

Nick decided on a direct approach. "Not this time." He noticed a door standing ajar in the side wall of the store. "This time I want to talk to the owner. Is he here?"

Ellie's eyes widened. "Gus? What do you want *him* for?"

"I just want to ask him a few questions," Nick said politely. "Do you expect him in any time soon?"

"No, I don't—he doesn't come here, he doesn't do any of the work. I do."

"It's very important that I talk to him," Nick insisted. "Where can I get in touch with him?"

Maddy, standing a couple of feet back from Nick and Ellie, sniffed the air, and sniffed again. "Old Spice," she said, and turned. "Nick?" she added.

There was a note in her voice that caused him to whirl around.

The man standing in the doorway was as tall as Nick, but heavier, a considerable belly hanging over and straining his large silver belt buckle. He was smiling genially, showing nicotine-stained teeth, wearing jeans and a heavy cotton shirt with long sleeves and silver buttons. A white cowboy hat was set at an angle that might have looked sexy on some other man.

"I'm Gus," he said, approaching Nick with his right hand held out. "Gus Noonan. The owner. What can I do for you?"

"This is the guy who asked about Bart," Ellie warned, and the cowboy did a sudden about-face and headed rapidly for the exit, almost bowling Maddy over on the way.

He didn't make it out the door. For a big man, Nick could move very fast. It seemed he'd told the truth about his ankle. "Let's all just stay put for a while, okay?" he suggested calmly, blocking the doorway. "I'm an FBI agent, and I would appreciate a few minutes of your time."

His eyes were narrowed, showing only a dangerous slash of glinting dark brown.

"Well, hey," the cowboy said genially, "why the hell didn't you say so? I thought you were one of the bad guys."

"Which bad guys?"

"The ones got Bart Williams. Don't know any names." He laughed shortly. "Don't *want* to know any names."

"Is there somewhere we can talk privately?" Nick asked, as a couple of mothers with babies in strollers stopped to look in the store window.

"There's a back room," the cowboy offered, smiling, eager to please. "We have coffee back there."

Instructed by Gus, Ellie placed a closed sign in the store window and locked the door, to the obvious disappointment of the two mothers.

The back room was small. The solid-looking oak table almost filled the available space. Ellie poured coffee, then sat back a little from the table, as if she didn't really want any part of this discussion.

Everything seemed perfectly normal—a little meeting between friends. But there was an edge of danger in the air. Trouble was, Maddy couldn't decide where the danger was coming from.

"Okay," Nick said to the cowboy. "This is Maddy Sloane, Bart Williams's wife. A few weeks ago, she was waiting for Bart to pick her up at the front of the market. When he showed up, he said he had to go to the rest room. Then he disappeared. Next time he showed up, he was dead. Would you like to explain your connection?"

The cowboy didn't hesitate. "I was a friend of Bart's," he said. "He came here that day, said he was in trouble with his bosses."

"At Mawsom?" Maddy asked.

Gus shook his head. "Nah, not Hatfield. Hatfield wasn't . . ." He pushed his cowboy hat back. "Guess it doesn't hurt Bart any to say now that he was mixed up in something illegal. Never did tell me what he did, but he was in deep, he said. Somehow he'd managed to upset the bosses of whatever organization he was mixed up in and they wanted a reckoning."

"Mafia bosses?" Nick asked.

"Maybe yes, maybe no. Don't know what they call themselves."

"What kind of reckoning did they want?" Nick asked.

"Money, what else?"

"He'd stolen money?" Maddy asked, looking alarmed.

She was thinking of the money Bart had stashed in those books, Nick realized.

"A ton of money," Gus said.

"Thousands?" Maddy persisted. "Millions?"

Nick shook his head at her. Bart had done a lot worse than steal money; they didn't need to worry about that now.

"I don't know how much," Gus said, looking rattled. "He said he'd blackmailed people his bosses were after, protection money, I guess. His bosses found out, called him in for a meeting that morning. They were hopping mad they didn't get their cut. Said he had to pay up, or else . . ." He made a slashing movement across his throat with the side of his right hand.

"Go on," Nick said.

"He said he was planning on picking up his wife, getting the money from his house. He was gonna give it all to the bosses, hope they'd let it drop. Said he reckoned he was valuable to them, they'd let it go if he gave them the money. But then he saw someone else waiting besides his old lady."

He looked at Nick.

"Go on," Nick said again.

"Said it was a ghost of some guy called Alfeo."

Nick swallowed. Maddy had been right. Bart had recognized the resemblance.

Nick had been right too. Bartel Wilhelm Franz, aka Bart Williams, aka the Snowman, had killed his father. Somehow the confirmation wasn't as satisfying as he had hoped it would be. His father was just as dead.

"Seeing you—I guess it was you—"

Nick nodded.

"Bart came here to the store," Gus went on. "He told me the story, asked *me* to get the money for him."

Nick looked at Ellie. "You were here too."

She shook her head. "I didn't know any of this. I don't know what Gus is talking about. This dude, Bart Williams, came in, he'd been here before. A friend of Gus's. He and Gus came into this room to talk, Gus came out after a while and told me to lock up the store and go home."

It all sounded very facile, but Nick's gut told him she was not telling the truth. He nodded at Gus to continue, but kept Ellie in his peripheral vision.

"We figured I'd get the money from his house," Gus said. "Then I'd take him to a safe house. He'd see that the money got to his bosses and make sure there wasn't going to be any retribution, then he'd come back. The bosses had made it clear at the meeting that if he didn't give it back, he'd be killed. What he didn't know was what they'd do if he *did* give it back. He wanted a place to hide until he could find out. So after I fetched the money, we went to Crescent Beach. That's all I know."

Nick shook his head. "Details," he said. "How did he get away from here?"

Gus sighed. "He'd left his car on one of the side streets up the hill. I drove him to it. Then we drove separately to his house, left our cars down the road in the park. He stayed there while I put gloves on—he had these doctor gloves he kept in the car—and then I went in the house and got the money."

"From where?" Maddy asked before Nick could.

"He had a safe upstairs in his office. Didn't he ever tell you?" He laughed. "It was just like in the movies. Tucked away behind a big picture. Hell of a deep safe, stuffed with money, hundred-dollar bills. In the attic or whatever you call it, he'd stashed another box full of money. Took me three trips between the house and the park. Place was crawling with kids in Halloween costumes." He resettled his hat at its former angle and laughed. "I fit right in."

He sobered immediately. "We packed the money in the trunk of Bart's car, then he followed me to Crescent Beach. I knew about a house there that was standing empty a long time. A window wasn't locked. Got me a friend who lives nearby—told me about it. Bart went in and opened the door, we parked his car in the garage, and that was it. I left and came home. Next thing I knew, TV said Bart had killed himself. I don't know what the hell happened to the money."

"That's it?" Nick said. "You didn't happen to go anywhere else in Crescent Beach?"

Gus met his gaze, then his own gaze faltered and he groaned. "I guess you know about the bar?"

Nick nodded.

"So okay, we went for a drink first. Carrying all that money, smuggling him out of here, I needed a beer. Or two. Bart never drank. He didn't want nothing to do with no bar—he was almost peeing himself worried about his bosses showing up any minute. But I couldn't remember where the street was, the street the empty house was on. Had to ask someone, so I asked in the bar. Hey, maybe that's how the bosses knew where to find him!"

Nick kept looking at him.

Gus shook his head. "I don't know if he really killed himself or his bosses found out where he was and killed him. I heard the story on TV, I thought maybe he called his bosses and told them where he and the money was, and they came and got it and finished him off. But maybe someone was following him all along. Who knows? I been worried ever since the bad guys'd find out I had something to do with his going off to the coast, might come after me. That's why I was freaked when Ellie told me a guy and a woman had been around asking questions, and again when you showed up today."

He turned to look at Maddy. "I've been right curious about you too, ma'am. Didn't have any idea you were such a looker. According to Bart it was—what did he call it?—a marriage of convenience. Said the only important thing was that he couldn't marry or even touch a woman who didn't have blue eyes and blond hair. Said he had to make it look real so you couldn't get it annulled. Said his boss at Mawsom was making noises about family values."

"Who else knew where Bart was?" Nick asked to get Gus's attention away from Maddy, whose face had blanched. His move didn't work.

"Sorry, ma'am," Gus said, looking at her with apparent sympathy, though it had an edge of spite in it, Nick thought. "Your husband was a cold son of a bitch, if you pardon the expression. Probably would have sold me out to his bosses to save his hide. That's what's been worrying me."

"So why were you his friend?"

He shrugged. "Hell, he got me out of trouble a couple of times. Long time ago. Gambling. Some losses I couldn't make up."

Nick persevered. "If Bart was with you when you went

to his house, how come you jimmied the back door?"

"Bart's idea, to make it look like someone broke in and stole the money." He looked at Nick and Maddy in turn with a self-righteous expression on his broad face. "I've an idea maybe he wasn't altogether happy with the idea of giving all that money back to his bosses. I think maybe it was possible he was planning on splitting."

Gus seemed a very unlikely sort to own a children's clothing and equipment store, Nick thought, as Ellie got up to refill the coffee cups. His pale blue eyes, though wide and as ingenuous as his constant smile, had a way of narrowing in a cunning way every once in a while.

"Why did you visit him in Eugene?" Nick asked abruptly.

The smile vanished, then reappeared. "I just happened to be in the area. He'd told me he was going down there. I called him on his cell, found out he was in the neighborhood."

"You visit Eugene often?" Nick asked in a deceptively mild voice.

Gus shrugged. "Once in a while."

Nick seemed to debate with himself for a moment, then evidently decided to let the question of Eugene go. "Do the names Rafael or Rafe Donati, Ruby Red Rawlings, and Jonathan Winston ring any bells with you?" Nick asked.

The cowboy shook his head quickly. Too quickly. Evidently noticing Nick's suspicious expression, he produced his broad smile again. "Let's see now, Jonathan Winters, did you say? The comedian?"

"He's not buying it, Gus," Ellie said, and quite suddenly she was standing up behind Nick and there was a gun in her right hand.

Nick moved so fast, Maddy wasn't sure afterward quite what he did first, but it had something to do with his chair going over backward and knocking Ellie sideways while at the same time Nick's hand closed over her wrist and the gun was suddenly pointing upward. A moment later,

Ellie was down on the floor and Nick was standing over her with the gun.

The cowboy had his mouth open. He hadn't otherwise moved. Nor had Maddy. It had all happened too fast for her brain to process it.

"What the hell did you do that for?" Gus yelled at Ellie as Nick yanked her up and plonked her into her chair. "We had it made—we had them going."

"No, Gus," Nick said, sounding only slightly out of breath. "No, you didn't. Hands on the table," he commanded.

Gus obliged promptly, Ellie reluctantly.

"Well now, people," Nick added after he'd patted both Gus and Ellie down thoroughly. "I think it's time we made this show official."

"No way," Gus said. "Look at me—you can't say I haven't been cooperating. You want more cooperation, I talk to you here and now. I'm offering you my services. Free of charge. You know damn well if Terminus hears I've been picked up, my life is worth zilch. They kill me, I can't tell you a damn thing."

Nick looked at Ellie. She batted her eyelashes at him, still playing the innocent. Not too believable at any time, not at all since the gun incident.

"She's okay," Gus said, following Nick's gaze. "She got carried away, is all. Young folks do that. You just let me tell you all about it, okay?"

It was Nick's turn to think it over. Taking this investigation further without official sanction was not only putting him way out on a limb, the limb was hanging over the Grand Canyon. By a thread.

His mind produced a flashing series of images of his father in the photos on his mother's wall. This was maybe his one chance to find out exactly what had happened to Alfeo. He just hoped Toss would step up to the plate for him if need be.

"Okay," he said. "Because I have foreknowledge of this case and a special interest in it, I'm going to ask you some questions in the interest of clearing some things up.

Based on your answers, we'll decide who gets to do what and where each of you is going. But at this moment you are not under arrest. This is a voluntary interview. Nobody is forcing you to speak."

"I'm not speaking," Ellie said flatly.

"That's your right," Nick said.

She smirked at him.

"Have at it," Gus said to Nick. "Better you than them."

"Them being Terminus?"

Gus nodded.

"You're willing to help us out a bit here, cut some of our corners? Find out how grateful we might be? Before you start, you might like to know we've got another guy already aiding our investigation into Bart Williams and the Terminus organization. Somebody Bart recruited fairly recently. Is he likely to know anything about you?"

Gus winced, but didn't answer.

"Suppose we agree that you're going to tell the truth, okay?" Nick suggested. "You and Ellie are both members of Terminus, right?"

"No way," Ellie said, but Gus had already nodded. All the bluster had gone right out of him.

Nick glanced at Maddy. She was pale, and her usually beautiful eyes looked drained of light. But she was holding up okay, leaning a little forward, obviously as anxious as he was to get at some truths.

"You and Ellie here were Bart's . . . handlers?" Nick asked.

"Managers," Gus said.

"What's in a name?" Nick quipped, then banished all humor from his expression.

"Let's look at that question about Eugene again," he suggested. "You happen to be driving the car that attempted to run us down there?"

Gus shook his head. "Nah, if I'd attempted it you wouldn't be sitting here now."

"Not a good time to be bragging about your superiority in using deadly force," Nick said.

Gus shrugged. "That would have been Chip Sadler, the

Salem guy—he's the closest. Getting old, time he retired."
He sighed. "Time I retired."

"I may be able to facilitate that." Nick took a breath
and fixed his gaze on Gus's face. "You were Bart's 'manager' from the start? From when he got here from Chicago? You told me earlier that Bart thought he'd seen a
ghost when he saw me. A ghost named Alfeo."

Gus moved uneasily on his seat.

"You can tell me anything about Alfeo's killing, it
would make me feel much more cordial toward you."

Gus thought for a while, then glanced at Ellie, who
was sitting as still as a statue, mouth firmly closed, hands
on the table. "Ellie doesn't know anything about this
part," he said. "She's too young. She came into the organization way after Bart got here."

Nick nodded, then held his breath.

"We talked about it not too long ago. Bart and me.
Talked about how we both got into the organization. Bart
was just twenty-one. Working in a pharmacy. But he
wanted money, real money. It's usually about money," he
added with a philosophical air and a flyaway gesture of
his left hand. "He was just a kid. Some Terminus manager
heard he was looking for something on the side, gave him
the contract. Alfeo was a cop. Don't know his last name.
This was in Chicago. First guy Bart ever whacked. It was
a setup."

"Who set the cop—Alfeo—up?" Nick asked, strug-
gling to keep his voice level. "He happen to tell you that?"

Gus thought some more, then laughed suddenly. Nick
wanted to hit him, but restrained himself. "Another cop,"
Gus said. "Alfeo's boss? Some Irish name."

Nick made himself wait, not wanting to plant any
names in the man's mind.

"Riley," Gus said. "Captain Riley. But after Bart did
the job, he heard Riley was looking for him, threatening
to kill him. All self-righteous-like. Wanted to leave himself in the clear, Bart figured. That's when Bart left town,
double quick."

Nick got up and drew himself a paper cup of water

from the corner cooler, giving himself time to adjust to finally knowing the details of what had happened to his father.

Ellie made a move to get out of her seat, but he hadn't taken his gaze off her. Putting a hand on her shoulder, he pressed her back down.

Maddy was watching him, he saw as he returned to his seat. Concern and compassion were written all over her face. But she didn't speak.

"Did Bart know *why* the cop was set up?" he asked when he trusted his voice.

Gus squinted as if he were trying to see inside his brain for the memory of the conversation. "Riley was accepting payoffs. From drug dealers maybe? Some kind of lowlife. Alfeo found out. Riley was pretty sure Alfeo wasn't going to keep it a secret. He was a Dudley Do-Right type. Straight arrow."

Nick nodded, took another swallow of water, and crushed the cup. "Let's say I believe everything you've told me about Bart, except for the part about being Bart's friend. As I understand it, Bart Williams didn't have any friends."

Once again, he could almost hear the wheels running in Gus's brain as he tried to decide how to answer. Finally, his mouth twitched and he started talking again. "Okay, we weren't exactly best friends. But we did talk from time to time. Everybody needs somebody to talk to sometimes. I was that somebody for Bart. But mostly I was just his manager. I got the word, passed it on to him, he did the job. He was reliable. Efficient."

Maddy winced, her eyes darkening.

Nick gave her a sympathetic glance. He loathed the irony of it himself—Gus using the same description Hatfield, Bart's colleagues, and the doctors had used.

"You never killed anybody yourself?" he asked Gus.

"Not directly."

A regular decent citizen. How many had he killed indirectly? Nick wondered.

"Bart said one time it wasn't the money he got off

on—it was a pleasure," Gus said. "He *liked* killing. Said it made him feel powerful. Immortal."

He gave a mirthless laugh. "Guess he wasn't immortal, after all though, huh?"

"He knew all along you and Ellie were members of Terminus?"

"Well, sure."

"You were *pretending* to help him when you drove him to the beach?"

Gus nodded. "That's how come I suggested we go to the bar. That made him easier in his mind, so he was okay with it, even though he didn't drink. My plan was to get him drunk, but it was the old case of leading a horse to water."

"You want to amend the story about how you got the money from Bart's house?"

"Nah. That's the way it was. Except after he was dead we turned it all over to Terminus."

"Terminus instructed you to kill him?"

"*I* didn't kill him," Gus said, then jerked his head toward Ellie.

Ellie started to stand up, her hands out, fingers curling as if she was going to reach across the table and throttle Gus. Nick pushed her back down in her seat again, then offered Gus a cynical expression.

Gus caved. "Oh, okay, both of us." He sighed. "We thought about drowning him in the ocean—but there's a hell of a riptide at Crescent Beach, and Ellie was afraid we'd get caught in it. She's not much of a swimmer."

Ellie was looking at Gus as if she wished there were a riptide handy right now.

"So all *I* did," Gus went on cheerily and virtuously, "was get him to drink the whiskey. At the house in Crescent Beach. At gunpoint."

"Is that how you did the taxi driver?"

Gus's eyes twitched. "You know about that, huh?"

"I guessed."

Gus smiled grimly. "Didn't need a gun with old Arnie.

He was happy to share a bottle with me. Guess he forgot to go home after, huh?"

He shrugged. "Bart now, he got the message right away. Didn't make a fuss. Knew it was inevitable. We thought for a minute or two he was going to throw the whiskey up. Wasn't used to it. But he passed out instead. We got him onto the bed, facedown. Then Ellie took his gun—it was one he'd gotten from them for the last job he did."

"You fool," Ellie said.

Gus ignored her.

" 'Them' meaning Terminus?" Nick queried.

Gus nodded. "They supply a different gun every time. Ellie put on gloves, put the gun in his hand, put her hand over his, put the gun to his head. She was happy to do it—had a fancy for Bart, she did, but he never gave her so much as a nod. Woman scorned." Cocking his fingers to the side of his head, he added, "Pow," loudly.

Ellie jumped, glared at him.

"You said he'd been blackmailing the people he killed?" Nick said.

"Don't know as you'd call it blackmail," Gus said, looking thoughtful. "Blood money, maybe. Except he shed the blood anyway."

As Nick frowned, Gus explained that if Bart suspected the target—the person Terminus had agreed to kill—had money, he'd tell the target his days were numbered and offer to cover up the disappearance if the target wanted to pay him off and take off.

"Where did they go?" Nick wanted to know.

"Hell, that was the beauty of the scheme," Gus said. "They didn't go anywhere. Soon as they paid up, he killed them the way he was supposed to."

He shook his head, though whether in awe or disapproval was not clear. "Told you he was a cold-blooded son of a bitch."

"You aren't?" Nick asked.

Gus looked offended.

Satisfied Gus had told him everything he personally

wanted to know, Nick pulled his cell phone out of its belt holster and punched familiar numbers.

A short time later a couple of men in suits came along and took Gus and Ellie into custody. Ellie was still snarling as she was taken away.

Nick followed the agents to the FBI building on 3rd Avenue, Maddy riding along with him. Once inside, he disappeared into one of the offices for a fairly long time, then came out, looking grim, to tell Maddy she could leave, as long as she was willing to make herself available when needed. Or if she wanted to wait, he'd drive her wherever she wanted to go.

"I'd like to go now," she said.

"Lara and Todd?" he suggested.

"I'll call Kazuko," she said. "Not so many questions."

He checked that he still had Kazuko's address and phone number.

"Okay," he said.

Chapter 27

A BUSY COUPLE of weeks later, Nick telephoned Maddy at Kazuko's house.

"Maybe I could meet you in Seattle," she said. "Kazuko's been wonderful but she tends to mother me. She might get defensive around you."

He suggested a walk through Freeway Park, the innovative preserve that straddled I-5 between First Hill and downtown. It was a cold and damp day, but the sun shone fitfully through light overcast.

It was always surprising to Nick how trees and shrubs and flowers could thrive so close to ten lanes of traffic. He liked this city a lot, had liked it ever since he and his mother and his father's mother had moved here all those years ago. He especially enjoyed the *idea* of a city that could conceive and build such a park.

Maddy was wearing a red raincoat that brightened the scene considerably. He didn't own a raincoat, but his parka was water repellant.

As they walked up steps and terraced paths, he could almost see Maddy's hair curling in the damp air. She smelled wonderful—not strongly perfumed, just of something clean that made him think of sunshine and sea breezes. He felt the familiar lift of spirits that occurred whenever he was around her.

He brought her up to date on what was happening with the investigation into Terminus. She'd already been interviewed extensively and intensely, and would be required to testify when the various people involved came to trial.

Nick had reported to the other agents everything he and Maddy had found out about Bart and his actions in the last few months. Bart's body had been exhumed so that DNA could be extracted and processed. A task force had been appointed and, with the eager help of Gus Noonan and Dennis Preston, was hard at work closing previous unsolved cases and reinvestigating suspicious accidental or suicidal deaths. So far, very little had been reported on the local news, or any other news, but it was bound to start breaking soon.

"When everyone is through with the house," Maddy said, when he was done, "my friend Sally is going to sell it for me. I'll find a charity to donate the proceeds to."

She had already turned over the money she and Kazuko had found in Bart's books to the FBI, as well as all of Bart's paperwork and complete access to his house. She had removed only her clothing from the house, leaving even the furniture and paintings she had bought. Bart had sat in those chairs, looked at those paintings.

"Are you going to move into the condo you bought?" Nick asked.

With all that had happened, Maddy had forgotten to pass on the news she'd received from Sally. "Someone from back east came up with a much higher offer than the one I made," she said. "I was given the chance to make a counteroffer, but I decided I couldn't handle the hassle right now."

"So you're going to stay on with Kazuko?"

She stopped walking, put a gloved hand on his arm. "Unless the FBI needs me right now, I thought I'd go up to Vancouver Island," she said. "I'll stay with my parents in Victoria for a while. I've already arranged with TheHub for a couple of months of sick days. Luckily, they think enough of me to want me back."

"Me too," he said.

Her eyes were sad as she looked at him.

He put his hand over hers and held it against his arm. He could feel the warmth of it clear through his parka to his skin. "I thought you didn't care that much for your parents."

"I care. They drive me crazy, but I care." Her smile was wistful. "Maybe I'm trying to return to the safety of the womb."

"I'd rather you stay in this country," he said.

"Is that an official request?"

"A personal one. You and me."

She took her hand away and started walking again. "I can't think about that yet, Nick. I'm sorry. I just can't."

"Because I deceived you?"

"No. I understand why you had to. I understand how you felt about your father, finding the man who murdered him, finding out why he was murdered. I had the same goal where Bart was concerned, and I had come to hate him. You loved your father."

They walked on in silence for a little while, then Maddy said, "I'm not sure why I can't think about you and me right now, Nick. I'm still in shock, maybe. I feel . . ." She hesitated. "I feel as if I've been poisoned and I haven't yet found the antidote. I don't even know where to look. I guess that's why I want to get completely away for a while."

He nodded. "I understand." He remembered his mother telling him years ago, in connection with some girl who had broken up with him—broken his heart, he had thought—"The only way to love is with open hands. Sometimes you can't do anything but let go."

He made a supreme effort to sound casual. "You'll stay in touch?"

Her gaze met his. Her eyes were very blue, sad, and shadowed. "I don't know, Nick. I'll give you my parents' address, of course. I imagine you'll need that officially. Personally—I don't know." She laughed shortly. "I keep saying that. But it's true. I really don't know. I got to thinking of Bart as a hollow man, and now I'm the one who's hollow. But I do care about you, Nick. That much is true."

It wasn't much to hold on to, but it would have to do.

MADDY'S PARENTS LIVED in a roomy condominium apartment in a high-rise building overlooking Victoria's inner harbor.

It had a small balcony outside the living room, and Maddy would sit there with her morning tea—her mother loathed the smell of coffee—bundled up in a parka, breathing in the crisp salt-scrubbed air. At first she felt like a tubercular patient in one of the old movies she watched on television—someone pale and weary, languishing on a chaise longue on a sanatorium verandah, perhaps having fallen in love with a male patient who had already died, coughing gently, afraid to cough too much in case the telltale blood appeared on a snow-white handkerchief.

After a while, she felt more like a small quiet animal in hibernation or some once winged creature that had forgotten how to fly and was now resting in the protective covering of a cocoon.

Time passed. Nick wrote her weekly, keeping her informed on the more public ramifications of the Terminus investigation. She wrote him back. She hadn't brought her laptop with her. Her parents didn't own a computer. Once in a while, she called the office to see if anything had come up that needed her attention. Once in a while, someone at the office called her.

Having heard the whole story of where exactly Bart Williams's apparent wealth had come from, Maddy's parents seemed to have shrunk into themselves and become quite chastened, not as sure anymore that their opinions were the only ones that mattered and that hers were automatically worthless. Since Maddy had last seen her

mother when Maddy had married Bart, Isobel's shoulders
had rounded and she was thinner than she'd ever been.
She'd let her hair go gray. Will seemed less military, not
quite as rigid in posture. They both looked smaller to
Maddy, which made them seem more human, even lovable.

They still argued incessantly, but with pleasure rather
than with bitterness. Mostly they didn't know what to do
with Maddy, so they fed her and offered her plenty of tea
and left her to her own devices.

The television set was a great comfort to her. The
condo building had a satellite dish on its roof and excellent reception. When Maddy wasn't watching old movies,
she was getting all wound up in reruns of American pro-
grams. For some reason she enjoyed police-type dramas
more than any other—maybe because justice usually tri-
umphed in them. *Law & Order. NYPD Blue. Nash
Bridges.* She especially liked *Nash Bridges* for the star's
bantering humor, which reminded her of Nick's.

Watching *Nash Bridges* one Tuesday afternoon, she
was suddenly granted some insight into Bart's behavior
where she was concerned. The story was about a young
armed robber who supposedly suffered from multiple personality disorder. A psychologist demonstrated how the
various personalities who lived inside the man could surface without the others knowing anything about each
other.

Idly, Maddy wondered if maybe Bart had been affected
by a similar disorder. It would explain the big change in
him from when he courted her to the way he was after
their marriage, to the things he had done, the people he
had killed.

But then, in the TV drama, Nash Bridges proved that
the armed robber had been *coached* by the psychiatrist—
he was merely *acting* as the various personalities he presented.

Had it been as simple as that? Maddy wondered. Had
Bart just been a good actor? He had decided he needed
to get a wife in order to keep the job that was so perfect

for his real life's death-dealing work. Rather than changing into someone else after the wedding, had he been that same monster all along? Had he just *acted* the part of the perfect suitor, then dropped the act as soon as he and Maddy married? Had his behavior not had anything to do with her personally at all?

Could it really have been as simple as that?

It seemed possible.

She thought later that it was at that moment she had begun to heal. But that was quite a while later. In the meantime, sometimes, if the weather was kind, as it often was that December, she would take walks around the inner harbor and find herself smiling over the way her parents were constantly involved in one or another of their incessant and silly arguments. . . .

"You were supposed to pay the hydro bill, darling."

"No, darling, remember, we decided you would pay all the bills all the time."

"Well, then, darling, you should have left it on my desk and not in the fish tank area."

"Why do you insist on calling it the fish tank area when we haven't had a fish tank for five years?"

"We'd still have live fish if you had remembered to feed them, darling."

"You were the one who mended the filter with hot glue and killed them all off."

Maddy had gradually come to realize that Will and Isobel enjoyed bickering. It was part of the way they related to each other, perfectly choreographed and equally balanced.

After a while, instead of irritating her, their arguments amused her.

There was, for example, the egg discussion.

"You don't want the water to be boiling so hard—it will crack the eggs."

"No, it won't, dearest, trust me."

"You should turn it off and put the lid on the pan, let it sit."

"The eggs will turn green if I do that, darling."

"No, they won't. Why are you putting them in ice water, dear?"

"I always put them in ice water after they boil for fifteen minutes. It makes them easier to peel."

The familiar arguments became as soothing as background music, or the constant gentle flow of water.

Victoria's inner harbor was dominated by the regal and magnificent Empress Hotel that had recently been restored to turn of the century grandeur. There was always something going on in the picturesque harbor. Seaplanes took off and landed; tour boats took visitors out sightseeing or looking for whales and brought them back again; ferry boats came in and disgorged passengers, filled up again, and left; and seabirds flew by or perched on railings or pilings.

There was a serenity and an order about these comings and goings that soothed Maddy's wounded spirit.

At Christmas, Isobel insisted on a tour of the famous Butchart Gardens. Maddy bundled up and obediently exclaimed over the lighted displays of the Twelve Days of Christmas set at intervals on the winding paths.

"Wait till the spring when the flowers bloom," her mother said as they drank hot tea by the fireplace in the coffee shop afterward. "The gardens are unbelievable then. Incredible."

It began to seem unbelievable to Maddy that she would still be in Victoria when that time came. Though her relationship with both parents had improved considerably, she certainly didn't want to spend much more time underfoot. Isobel might have lost some of the sharper side of her nature—she had definitely mellowed—but she was not by any means a nurturing kind of mother.

Will hadn't mellowed a bit—he still couldn't watch television without going off into a tirade—but he was at least being pleasant and cordial, treating Maddy like the invalid she felt herself to be, often taking her out in the evening to the Sticky Wicket for a pint of Guinness, which he insisted would thicken her blood. What it did was remind her of Nick.

On one such evening, she told Will about remembering his stories as she was flying into Las Vegas. He smiled so widely, she could suddenly see the young attractive man he had been.

"I've become very dependent upon your mother," Will said to her abruptly on another of those evenings.

Maddy smiled at him. "I never thought I'd hear you say that."

"I never thought I'd say it," he admitted, laughing a little, then he added almost as an afterthought, in the most casual voice imaginable, "I'd like it if you'd call me Dad."

For a moment, she thought she was going to cry, but she managed to say, "I'd love to, Dad."

Mostly, her visit was calming and gentle. And yet there began a stirring inside her that suggested maybe she was getting tired of living in a cocoon. Tired of being alone.

But she wasn't completely alone.

So what did she really mean?

She was tired of being without Nick. Some vital part of her body was not operating, would not operate until she was once again with Nick.

Soon, she thought, she'd be ready to go back to Seattle. There was no doubt in her mind that Nick would be happy to see her. But she wasn't quite sure what he would want to do with her.

New Year's Eve came. Isobel waxed nostalgic about the Scottish custom of first footing—the first person to enter a house after midnight would decide the luck of all who lived there. Heaven help the family if a redheaded person was the first one in. It was even worse luck if the redhead was female.

Nobody entered the condo, and the three of them retired to bed after a token glass of wine apiece.

It was a surprise when the doorbell rang around noon on New Year's Day. Not that Isobel and Will didn't have friends, but since Maddy had been there, they'd been cautioned to stay away, told that she was convalescing, grieving over the death of her husband. Maddy hadn't objected to the excuse; it was certainly preferable to the truth.

Isobel answered the doorbell. Maddy heard her voice bidding someone welcome. She sounded excited. Maddy wondered if she could escape to her bedroom before the visitor was admitted.

And then Nick entered the living room. It was not a large room. He seemed to fill it with his presence and the warmth of that smile of his that appeared so rarely.

Isobel's excitement was easily explained. "A tall, dark, handsome man is the verra best first foot to have," she was telling Nick as she followed him in. He might have been bewildered by that statement if he'd been listening, but it was obvious to Maddy that he was not.

She stood up and took hold of his outstretched hands and felt as if he'd thrown her a lifeline. Heat and energy shot through every part of her so abruptly that she realized how totally dormant she had been.

"I got to missing you too much," he said simply. "I couldn't wait any longer."

She nodded. "I missed you too. I think I was about to come back to Seattle."

Isobel had disappeared from Maddy's peripheral vision, but Maddy could sense her mother staring at them. Will had gone out for what Isobel called his postprandial constitutional.

"Nick's a friend," Maddy told her mother.

Nick and Isobel shook hands, then stood around awkwardly.

"Maybe we could go out for a walk," Maddy suggested.

"It's cold out," Nick said. "But it's a beautiful day."

"Yes, it is. Very beautiful."

"The harbor looks interesting."

"It is."

Not much of a conversation. But the real dialogue was going on in every glance and body movement.

Afterward, Maddy couldn't remember if she'd even excused herself to her mother or had just walked out—or rather, floated out.

In the elevator she wanted to fling herself into Nick's

arms, but restrained herself. He reached out and took hold of her hand, quite naturally and easily.

Still hand in hand, they walked around the inner harbor to the blue Johnson Street bridge and along the water, talking. Nick brought her up to date on the investigation and how far the tentacles of Terminus had reached. Maddy told him about the *Nash Bridges* program that had opened her eyes to Bart's prewedding behavior.

"How's your mom?" she asked.

"Good. She was shook up for a while, having Dad's death brought up all over again, but she's a tough cookie."

"What about you?"

"I'm okay. Better."

He told her he'd heard back from his contacts in Germany. "I know why Bart was afraid of fire. His parents died in a blaze that consumed their home when he was seventeen. He was lucky to escape. Friends of his parents brought him to the United States when they emigrated from Germany, but he didn't stay with them long."

Maddy stopped walking. "Is there a possibility he started the fire?"

He turned her toward him, took her hands in his, and held them against his chest. She could feel the warmth of his hands dissolving her bones. "I don't know, Maddy. Evidently there was some suspicion, but no proof."

"You think he was always . . . a freak of nature?"

Nick looked at her solemnly. "According to my source, he was always a little *different*, even as a small child."

Maddy nodded, unsurprised. "I remember reading a novel by John Steinbeck, *East of Eden*, where the narrator talked about the strong possibility of a monster being born to human parents. Sometimes a physical monster, sometimes a mental monster with a malformed soul."

She shook herself a little. "I guess I had a narrow escape," she said, with a slightly nervous laugh.

"The point is—you did escape."

"I did, didn't I?"

She was suddenly filled with a feeling of lightness such as she hadn't experienced in many months. She had been a happy person once, she reminded herself. In college and after, until she married Bart, she'd had a great time. She could be happy again. Looking at Nick, holding on to his hands, she thought that she could even be joyful.

Something of what she was feeling must have shown on her face. Nick touched her cheek and said, "What about you and me, Maddy? Are you ready to talk yet about you and me?"

She smiled at him, letting all her joy show. "Do we really need to talk?"

"You need to be sure it's real this time."

"I know it is. I knew it the minute you walked into my parents' apartment." Her arms reached up around his neck and his arms went around her waist. He pulled her close. They were near some trees, and no one else was there to see them.

"I want to kiss you," he said.

"I want to kiss you too, but I'm afraid if I start I won't be able to stop."

"And the problem with that is?"

Before she could form an answer, his mouth brushed hers, tentatively at first. Then, as her own mouth responded, his lips closed over hers, and heat rose from somewhere deep inside her body and came up to meet his heat. Familiar stirrings awakened as his hands moved over her back and cupped her bottom. "I've been wanting you a hell of a lot," he murmured against her mouth.

"Likewise," she murmured back.

He lifted his head. "There's something I have to tell you."

Her spirits sank like a rock in a deep pool.

"It's about my job."

"You have to go somewhere? You're being transferred?"

"No, nothing like that. Not right now, anyway. But the thing I want you to understand is that something like that can happen anytime. I could be assigned anywhere—from San Diego to New York City to Phoenix, Arizona. Quite often things happen that I can't talk about. Ever. During my time with you, I was actually on annual leave. I was there for you all the time. That's rare. When I'm on the job, I work long hours. On a big case I could be sent off to the other side of the world. Sometimes people hate me, hate all of us—to them we represent repressive government, Big Brother, what have you. That attitude is sometimes hard for people around me to live with."

"Why are you telling me all this?" she asked with a teasing smile.

"You know why."

Her smile changed from teasing to loving. "Yes. I do understand what you are saying." She touched his face. "I do love you, you know."

He nodded. "I know that. I knew that when I saw your face, when I got here."

"Does my loving you scare you?"

"It terrifies me. I think you'll change my life in ways I can't begin to imagine. Because what we're talking about here is permanent, isn't it? The church, the ring, the flowers, my mother smiling triumphantly, organ music, the whole life sentence, kids even?"

She nodded. "As I told you before, I'm not getting involved again unless it *is* permanent. And real. And mutual. And forever."

He pulled her even closer, hesitating when his mouth was a breath away from hers, then brushed her lips with a warm, gentle, featherlight kiss that deepened into something so demanding, she felt it clear down to her toes.

A heartbeat later, he lifted his head. "Did that feel real?" he asked.

She nodded, breathless.

"Did it seem mutual?"

"Oh, yes."

"Then I guess I'm ready to tough it out forever." He produced the sun-bursting-through-clouds smile that always melted her. "I'm even feeling tough enough to say the bad L word."

"What if I start reorganizing your life?"

"I'll kiss you into submission," he said, demonstrating.

"Okay," she said, when they finally surfaced. "Say it."

He took a deep exaggerated breath, let it out slowly, and said with great sincerity and emphasis, "I love you, Maddy Sloane, and I want to marry you." He looked suddenly solemn again. "Will you marry me, Maddy?"

She looked at him with all the love that had been building up in her since she met him. "I'll marry you, Nick Ciacia."

She realized he had something else he wanted to say. "What?" she asked.

"The Bureau requires a background check of a prospective spouse. I've told them absolutely everything about your relationship with Bart Williams, and they were impressed by you in your interviews. But they'll still do a thorough check."

"I've never even had a parking ticket," she assured him. "Bart was my only mistake."

"There's also the fact that a few people are peeved with me," he added. "I didn't play according to Robert's Rules of Order, so to speak. I'm hoping it's going to smooth out okay with my supervisor's help, but I can't be completely sure yet. There may be repercussions. On the other hand, between us we gave them Terminus, and that's got to be worth something."

He turned mischievous again. "I can always get a job as an accountant. I have the business cards."

"Or you could be a stevedore as I suggested once before. You have the body."

They both laughed, then sobered abruptly and simply gazed at each other.

The wind had blown his hair into spikes. She reached up to smooth it down, and he turned his head and kissed the inside of her wrist in the same delicate way he had when she had bandaged his ankle.

Then he quoted *Casablanca* again. " 'Kiss me as though it was the last time.' "

She shook her head. "As though it was the first time," she amended.

And so he did.

They stood there by the screen of trees for the longest time. Holding each other. Holding on. "I'm hearing Mendelssohn's 'Wedding March,'" she said at last. "How about you?"

His smile warmed her all the way through. "Loud and clear."

"But you're not exiting stage left?"

For answer, he kissed her again, lingeringly, and held her close.

Berkley Books proudly introduces

Berkley Sensation

a **brand-new** romance line
featuring today's **best-loved** authors—
and tomorrow's **hottest** up-and-comers!

Every month…
Four sensational writers

Every month…
Four sensational new romances from
historical to contemporary,
suspense to cozy.

Now that Berkley Sensation is around…

**This summer is going to
be a scorcher!**